I0582933

# RESISTANCE

## THE JACK RANDALL THRILLERS
### BOOK 6

## RANDALL WOOD

TENSION BOOKWORKS

RESISTANCE. Copyright © 2017 by Randall Wood.

For information contact:

Tension Bookworks

248 Nokomis Ave. Venice, FL 34285

www.tensionbookworks.com

Tension Bookworks and the portrayal of the screw are registered trademarks of Tension Bookworks.

Jacket and Cover design by Derek Murphy

Book design by Matty Dalrymple

Cataloging-in-Publication Data is on file at the Library of Congress

Wood, Randall, 1968-

Resistance / Randall Wood – 1st ed.

ISBN-13: 978-1-938825-91-0 (Ebook)

ISBN-13: 978-1-938825-45-3 (Paperback)

ISBN-13: 978-1-938825-46-0 (Large Print)

ISBN-13: 978-1-938825-47-7 (Hardcover)

ISBN-13: 978-1-938825-48-4 (Audio)

2024122701

# WARNING!

This book ends in a cliffhanger!

The story of The Twelve Shepherds was originally released as a serial novel and was published in several separate episodes. Due to the readers' requests, it has now been re-published in novel form. The resulting manuscript was too large to fit into one novel and as a result the Shepherds saga will now encompass six novels.

This book, *RESISTANCE*, is part two of The Twelve Shepherds saga, and also book six of the Jack Randall series.

The author and the publisher apologize for any confusion.

## re•sis•tance

the refusal to accept or comply with something;
the attempt to prevent something by action or
argument

armed or violent opposition

a secret organization resisting authority, especially
in an occupied country

the underground movement formed in France
during World War II to fight the German
occupying forces and the Vichy government

the ability not to be affected by something,
especially adversely

# 1

*"Fighting corruption is not just good governance. It's self-defense. It's patriotism."*

—*Joe Biden*

Anna watched as the smoke billowed out of the boat. She had heard nothing after pushing the button, but her target obviously had. She'd seen his head jerk around for a few seconds before smoke appeared through the open hatch. The man had waved at it, and then had tried to duck under it before she had lost sight of him. She had expected it to come out of the cockpit post, but it obviously had found an easier path downward and into the interior of the boat. Maybe the open hatch created a wind tunnel of some kind? She dismissed the thought as a shout went up from another boat. She looked around her and saw several people pointing and staring as others ran down the dock. One of the other captains stopped at his own boat long enough to grab a fire extinguisher. She returned her gaze to the boat in time to see the lawyer stumble off the stern and land on the dock. The smoke was thick and white, more prevalent than she remembered from her army days, and it just kept coming. The cloud now reached from the boat all the way to the other side of the canal. The man with the extinguisher disappeared into it as others pulled the lawyer to his feet. She lost sight of him again when the breeze shifted.

With a start, she realized it was past time to go. She backed away from the railing and into the gathering crowd, her spot immediately filled by a fellow bar patron. With everyone's eyes on the docks, she managed to cross the bar and leave without drawing attention. She found her way to the concrete wall of the canal and walked along it toward the park. Her hand snaked inside the bag, and she palmed both phones, keeping them hidden until she reached the end where the wall took a jog, and the marina ended. As she turned the corner, she let the phones fall from her hand and into the water. Their splash was covered by the sound of an approaching siren. Another joined it from her left and she looked that way as casually as she could. A police car was coming right at her from a side street, and she turned her head away just as it took the corner. A young couple approached, pointing in the direction of the smoke, and she used the opportunity to turn and see what was happening.

The smoke was a thick cloud that covered most of the marina and reached well out into the canal, the wind slowly pushing it out towards the sea. A fire truck was approaching from the other side; she could hear its air horn clearly as it pushed through the traffic. The path behind her was clear. No one seemed to be following her. Still, she needed to leave the area. She turned and headed for the parking lot.

She spotted the strange car in her spot long

before she reached it. Her car was gone! Her eyes frantically searched the lot for it, and she forced herself to keep her breathing and pace normal. What had happened? Had somebody tried the door and found it unlocked? What about the key? She had hidden it in a place where only she or Dayton would have known to look for it. Did it get towed? There was no reason for it to be. A million thoughts went through her head. Was someone watching her? Was she being set up?

"Don't panic. Think it through," she told herself.

She passed the spot where her car had been without breaking stride and continued on down through the parking lot. She had two choices. Keep moving or hide in place and move when it was safer. But where to hide? It was too far to walk; it would take her hours, and nobody walked over the causeway. She could go shopping for a few hours on Ocean Drive, but that meant appearing on multiple store cameras, and it was not something she wished to do. Besides, she had less than twenty dollars, not even enough cash for a cab. If she didn't buy something, it would look odd. She could play tourist, wander around and gawk at the locals, but that wouldn't work either as she looked more like a local than most. She passed a hotel and considered lounging in one of their beach chairs, but that would draw the attention of a waiter, who would ask her for her room number. Negative. She traveled on and the beach grew more crowded. Perhaps the beach? Hide in plain sight. Miami style.

Without breaking stride, she snatched a towel off a vacant chair and tucked it under her arm. Leaving the sidewalk, she angled toward the water and was soon weaving around the tan and tight bodies of the South Beach crowd. She looked for a spot and soon found a perfect one. Two men of her age were oiling up their already tan and muscled torsos. She dropped her bag next to them and spread out her towel. Without hesitation, she pulled the sundress up over her head and tossed it aside. Her bra followed a moment later, and she adjusted her thong to fit her existing tan lines. A glance at the two men confirmed her first impression. They were oiling each other and paying no attention to her. She made a show of digging in her empty bag and pouting.

"Boys? Could I maybe get some of that oil? I seem to have forgotten mine."

"Sure, us locals take care of our girls." One of them handed her the bottle without an offer to help her apply it.

"Thank you," she cooed.

Anna applied a thick coat as quickly as she could, before handing it back with a smile and settling down on the towel where she could turn her head to see toward the marina. The smoke had dissipated, and she could see the flashing lights of the police and emergency services vehicles in the distance.

"What's going on over there?" one of the men asked.

"I dunno. Maybe a boat fire?"

"Great, that'll tie up the tourist traffic for a few hours. We won't get out of here until after four."

"Fine by me. I've got nowhere I need to be."

"Yeah, me neither."

The man rolled over and adjusted his sunglasses. Anna watched him out of the corner of her eye as he got comfortable. She was close enough to him that a casual observer might think they were together, even if his boyfriend was just as close on the other side. The beach was crowded, but Miami people didn't mind being close together. She always thought of pictures of Rio when she came here: nothing but tan and half-naked bodies for over a mile. She was naturally camouflaged.

She decided to stay where she was, at least for

now. If the boys weren't leaving until four, maybe that would be her way out. She'd sunbathe for a while, then see if she could make some friends. She still had to get off the island. That, and she needed some time to think.

What had happened to the car? And where the hell was Dayton?

---

HIS NAME WAS HARPER. It was his fifth or sixth name—he had lost count—but this one had stuck for the last ten years, so he kept it. Not that he needed it today as there wouldn't be any introductions being made.

He had started out like most in his field. First the military, then work with contractors, then a ride on the revolving door with other branches before being tapped by the Secret Service and rising to the Vice President's detail. There, his skills had been noticed, and he'd quickly become the VP's go-to man when things needed to be done quietly. He wasn't even sure if he was a government employee or not anymore. Like the others on the man's detail, he had blurred those lines a long time ago. His LLC, which existed on paper only at a PO box in Delaware, received paychecks for consulting fees on a regular basis, and he had long ago stopped wondering where they came from.

Today he was moving pieces in place. Like a game of chess, he would position people and equipment in various locations, and when the time was right, they would strike with a lethal punch. Since this war was not the declared type, the pieces would then fade away, usually propelled by a large paycheck, some to be saved for later use and others discarded. Or eliminated. That was always an option. One of the pieces he was meeting today was new, and he hoped there would not be a need for that.

A hotel lobby used to be safe for such meetings. Now they were crowded with cameras, so as he left, he kept his head down and his eyes under the brim of his baseball cap. It got an adjustment as soon as he left the double-wide doors. The valet brought his car up and he slipped the man a tip before sliding in. The seat had been moved but the mirrors were still in place, and he added sunglasses after making the adjustment. Between the hat, the sunglasses, and the tinted windows, he was confident his face would be hidden from any cameras he encountered on the way.

It was a Thursday night, and that meant football. He had picked a sports bar near the airport for the meet, counting on it being full and loud, and pulled in around the corner from the main entrance. The bar had outside seating under a metal roof. It vibrated with the passing planes, and the TVs on the wall shook along with them, but he didn't care. The noise was a positive in his book. He entered the bar and slipped to one side before scanning the tables. He saw them seated outside at a corner table, both of them staring up at the screen over their heads. Amateurs, they should have been watching for him. He circled around and was in front of them before they noticed, but he dismissed the error; they were simply not trained as he was. They did however have other skills, ones that Harper's employer needed.

The short haircuts and the sunglasses sitting on the table identified them as aviators. Unlike the commercial pilots around them, they were military and far from their base. The taller one eyeballed him nervously and picked at the label on his sweating beer, while the other just nodded a greeting. It was his third time working with the older one, a first for the new guy.

He ordered a beer and watched a bit of the game for appearances sake before dropping his coaster on the floor. When he retrieved it, he swapped it for one he had borrowed a few weeks ago. On it were written coordinates, times, a few details, and a dollar amount. The senior man examined the numbers, and his eyes bulged a little when he recognized their corresponding location. A nod of acknowledgement was all that he gave before slipping the coaster in his pocket.

"Questions?"

"Will this be soon?"

"Sometime in the next thirty days."

"Then I think we're good."

Harper rose without another word and walked away, taking his beer with him. He placed it on the bar, where it was quickly grabbed and disposed of, before leaving out the side door. He had already checked out of the hotel. The flight back to DC would leave in forty minutes. The baseball hat went into the first trashcan he saw; he hated the things. After finding another bar inside the terminal he ordered himself another beer. He burned the time nursing it and replaying the meeting in his head. The older pilot had proven to be reliable; he hoped the younger one was smart enough to follow his lead. The man had a young wife and a new baby; the money was sorely needed. If that wasn't enough to keep him on track, well, they had other options.

Finishing his beer, he pulled the cell phone

from his pocket and waited for the security software to link and then scramble his text message.

"Transport in line" was all it said. The former Vice President would know what it meant.

"Good" was the reply.

They called his flight, so he powered the phone off before boarding. A pair of headphones kept any chatty seatmates at bay, and he feigned sleep for the two-hour journey to avoid them altogether.

---

THE BOYS WERE LEAVING. She had to make a decision. She had talked them up a bit on two opportunities, but she had ended it before it got too far. Mostly to make jokes about passing tourists or to comment on the cruise ships leaving the docks.

"Are you heading anywhere toward downtown by chance?"

The bigger one cocked an eyebrow at the question. "What happened, girl? How'd you get here?"

Anna made a show of being embarrassed to tell. "I got in a fight with him on the way here and, well, I ditched him at a stoplight. Problem is, I grabbed my beach bag and left my purse behind.

Asshole's got my money and my keys. I've got no way to get home."

"We can drop you downtown; that's no problem. What about him? Is it your place or his?"

"Oh, it's my place. Security can let me in. Wouldn't be the first time I've lost my keys. I'll be all right."

"What about him?"

"It was something stupid, and he's not the type to get physical. We'll fight for a minute, then get naked."

The men laughed. "Good for you."

They packed up and she followed them to their car. A pair of officers in uniform were on the sidewalk examining the crowd, and she adjusted her path to put her new friends between them and her. Looking for her? She couldn't tell. The car was a BMW convertible, and the top came down to let the heat escape. She would have preferred if it'd stayed up, but she really couldn't say anything. They pulled out and headed south: right toward the marina. A pair of police cruisers sat in the parking lot with their lights still on, and she saw a very plain van parked next to them. An evidence unit? She had hoped her "bomb" would be written off as a prank. Evidently not. She spotted the lawyer's car still in the lot as well. Were they still questioning him or was he just waiting for them to leave?

The boys were chatting away over the sound of the radio and the breeze as they headed toward the causeway. To her horror, she saw another cruiser parked on the side of the road with an officer standing outside it examining the passing traffic. Was he stopping people? The traffic was slowing for no reason other than him being there, and she felt the car she was in do the same as they got closer.

She saw it a second too late. The officer had a camera set up on a tripod and was recording the passing cars. She ducked behind her new friends and swept her hair across her face to hide her features. It blew around as they passed, so she couldn't be sure if she'd been successful. The boys dismissed the cop as soon as they were past him and sped up to weave through slower traffic. She gave up trying to hear them over the roar of the wind and sat back in the seat with a frown.

Facial Recognition Software. Dayton had warned her about it. It was a growing concern as more and more departments got the training and access to the database. They would gather video from every source they could and compare it to people they had on file. She knew how it worked.

It was basic math really. The software would pin the distance between her eyes, nose, mouth, and other features to come up with a facial fingerprint. Then it would run it through the database until it had a match. It could be defeated with glasses and makeup to a point. She'd had sunglasses on and had used her hair to disrupt the shape of her face, but had it been in time? Hopefully she would never find out.

The car made it to the mainland without another camera appearing and was quickly swallowed up by downtown traffic. Anna made small talk until they got within a few blocks of her condo. At the next light, she gave them each a hug and a peck on the cheek, and they left her on the sidewalk. She waved and walked in the opposite direction of her condo until they were out of sight, then circled the block. Pausing at the corner, she shielded her eyes and gazed up at her floor. The balcony appeared as she had left it, but then she could only see a fraction of it. She circled the block again checking out the parking entrance and the front. Nothing looked out of place. She could see the security guy behind the counter through the glass entrance. Brian something; she forgot. A bodybuilder who liked to show off his arms in a uniform shirt a size too small. But he was polite, and thorough, and just a bit intimidating—evidently, it was what the owners wanted him to be. She took a deep breath and walked in.

"Hello, Ms. Olson."

"Hey, Brian. You won't believe this, but I lost my key. Can you get me in?"

"Sure, hold on one second."

She watched as Brian activated the video timer, then placed a sign on the desk. "Back in five minutes," it read. She had only seen it twice, and it usually meant he was either in the bathroom or making a delivery. The surveillance cameras would now record the lobby and other entrances continuously until he returned and reset it. All of this information had come to her via William, and as usual he had been right. Brian punched his access code into the cipher lock on the key vault and found the one to her condo before standing and joining her.

"You got some sun," he observed.

"A little. The tourists are mostly gone now, not as crowded."

"I still use the tanning beds. You lost the keys at the beach?"

"Not sure, but most likely. I have a spare set."

"Okay then. Let's go."

The elevator ride was quick, and they stepped

out on her floor to see it just as she had left it. Brian used another key to hold the elevator before he stepped to her door. She stood to one side as he worked the key into the lock before pushing it open a foot and turning around. She eyeballed the gap nervously while managing a fake smile.

"Thanks, Brian."

"No problem. You have a nice night."

She was tempted to ask him to wait but didn't, instead she stepped in and shut the door behind her. She examined the interior and listened, but she heard nothing. Stepping to the nearest chair, she pulled a loaded Glock 9mm from a holster attached with Velcro to its bottom. Taking comfort in the weight of the weapon and keeping it in front of her, she cleared the kitchen, dining room, laundry, and balcony before working her way down the hallway to the bedroom. Some motion caught her eye, and she realized it was the shadow of the bedroom curtain blowing in the wind. Had she left the slider to the second balcony open? She couldn't remember. Keeping the gun in front of her, she edged around the corner.

A pair of feet dressed in casual shoes and khakis were resting on a table. The man attached to them was out of sight, sitting in a chair around the corner. With a glance behind her, she edged farther into the room. Slowly, the man's legs appeared, then a hand holding a beer. It was one of hers, from her own refrigerator! Two more steps, and she saw his profile looking out over the ocean.

"About time," Dayton said. "Where the hell you been?"

# 2

---

*"The accomplice to the crime of corruption is frequently our own indifference."*

—*Bess Myerson*

White House Chief of Staff James Cook settled back in his chair and tossed the report on the table in front of the man who had brought it. It was thin and he said so.

"I know," the Attorney General replied. "But it's all we have right now. Agent Randall is reporting daily, but they have little to go on."

"What about Texas? The judge's case is offering nothing?"

"In Texas, they basically have half a crime scene, the other half drove away with the shooter. The Moretti case has more. I think concentrating his assets there is the right call. At least until we have something new to add."

Cook tapped a finger and gazed out the window for a moment before thinking out loud. "It'll be Sunday soon, and I don't know what we're going to say yet."

The AG nodded but offered nothing. The Chief of Staff was referring to the Sunday morning talk shows. The Twelve Shepherds had been the main topic for the last few weeks, and every producer and talking head were requesting guests from the West Wing. Cook had sent Parker twice into the fray, and he had so far done well, but that wouldn't last—he was simply running out of ways to say, "the FBI is investigating." The people wanted results, and the government didn't have any yet.

"A description and some really lousy video footage. I need more than that. You're sure Agent Randall is getting everything he needs?"

"We've granted every request, and they all get flagged for my attention. So far, he hasn't asked for much, but then he doesn't have much to go on. He's plugging away at what he has, and sometimes that's all you can do. Deacon thinks it's best to let him run with it. I agree."

"*Hummph*," Cook answered. He had to agree as well, even though it wasn't his style. Cook was known for applying pressure until he got what he needed, but he also understood when that was counter-productive, and this was unfortunately one of those times.

"Where is this going, Carl?"

When the Chief of Staff used your first name, it meant that the meeting had just gone off the record. He settled back on the man's couch and sighed.

"I'm not sure yet. But I can tell you one thing, the public is divided, and I don't mean by a small margin. Half of them are calling the Shepherds traitors, the other half are sharpening their pitchforks and asking where they can sign up to join them. You should see the mail we're getting. Half of it is calling us incompetent, and the other half is telling us to get out of the way. Some of it is listing names and pointing fingers at who they think should be next. We've had to call the Capitol Police and Secret Service a few times."

"Anything concrete?"

"No, mostly hotheads spouting off and too dumb to realize they're committing a federal offence when they do so. They get a visit from someone, and they get the message. If it gets worse though, we may have to make an example of somebody."

Cooks head came around at that. "Not without calling me first. That's all we need is some loudmouth on TV claiming we trampled on his first amendment rights to threaten government officials."

"Threatening a judge, or a member of congress, *is* a class C felony."

"Not without calling me first!" Cook repeated.

"All right, James, but it's going to happen, and we just can't ignore it when it does."

Cook sighed and acknowledged the man's statement. "I know, but until we can't, we keep these lessons quiet."

Carl nodded and wisely changed the subject. "You've spoken with the President about this?"

Cook glanced at his watch. "I'll brief him this

afternoon. He's doing some photo ops right now; some Boy Scouts from Michigan, the Stanley Cup winners, stuff like that. It's his form of a nap."

"Want me to stick around?"

"No, I'll do it. Just keep me informed if something new happens. You'll have somebody brief Mr. Parker before Sunday?"

"I'll have Deacon give him a call."

"That'll work. Thanks, Carl."

"Anytime."

The AG rose and gathered his paperwork before departing, and Cook walked him to the door. As soon as he was gone, Cook's smile faded, and he gave some short instructions to his secretary.

"Tell Mr. Parker I need him."

"Right now?"

"Right now."

Cook turned and retreated back into his office. Crossing to the opposite wall, he opened the door to the President's private study and walked the two meters to the door of the Oval Office. He listened first and heard the man himself talking to people who were obviously on their way out. Cook opened the door to see a group of large men leaving through the opposite door. He waved and smiled to the stragglers as the President grinned, slapped backs, and shook hands. As soon as they were gone, his secretary shut the door. The President scooped up a jersey off the couch and tossed it to Cook, who barely managed to catch it.

"Signed by the whole team. This is an awesome job!"

Cook held the jersey up and gave it a good look before replying. "Impressive, sir. Are any of these guys from America?"

"Don't you ruin this for me. The teams from Detroit, the Motor City! That's American enough for me. You're just jealous they didn't bring you one."

Cook had never seen a live hockey game in his life, but he knew better than to go against the President's fandom. "That's true, sir. I am," he deadpanned.

The President took his jersey back with a scowl and rounded the desk. "I have some Boy Scouts and then the Secretary of the Interior. What's on your mind?"

Before he could answer, there was a tap on the door he had entered from.

"You called?" Parker asked.

"Yeah, get in here for a minute," Cook replied. He turned to the President, who had painted a frown on his face. "Sir, I just talked with Carl, and we've nothing new on the Shepherds issue. Some weak leads on the Moretti shooting, but little else. I'm concerned about what we're going to say come Sunday."

The President turned to Parker. "You're doing the shows?"

Parker exchanged a look with Cook. "I ... don't know yet. Am I?"

"You are. You can expect a call from Deacon, but he's not going to tell you much. We need to say something to show the public we're taking action."

"What action? We're investigating, but beyond that we can't comment on the investigation without tipping off who we're after."

"Not that kind of action. It doesn't have to be concrete, just something to appease the public."

The President sank into his chair with a sigh. "If I react to the Shepherds now, it'll say that they are right, and we can't do that. They'll say we did nothing until a banker and a judge got killed. It'll be spun that we didn't care until one of the rich white people got taken out."

"So travel in time," Parker said.

"I'm sorry?"

Parker paced a bit before replying, forming the idea as he did so. "Announce the findings of an investigation, or better yet, the creation of a special team of some kind. One that was formed months ago to address the Shepherds issue. Just make everything retrograde, and it'll show you've been on the problem for months. All it needs is a catchy name."

The President twirled a pen while he considered the idea. He looked up at his Chief of Staff. "Will it work?"

Cook looked at his deputy. "What kind of findings can we announce?"

"It doesn't matter. That won't be the story. The story will be the existence of the ... Corruption Task Force. We'll pull people from every department and make it work."

"Better make it the Anti-Corruption Task Force; we don't want to send the wrong message."

Before they could continue, there was a knock on the door and the Presidents secretary stuck her head in. "Sir, your one o'clock is here."

"I need a moment."

"It's two o'clock now," she scolded.

"I know." He waved her away. Parker and Cook exchanged an amused look. Mrs. Lancaster had been with the President since he was a mayor and was not intimidated by his current title in any way.

The President waved them toward Cook's office. "Draw up your plan for this task force, or committee, or whatever, and get it back to me. I want to see a rough draft tonight." He paused and Parker took the cue and left.

"What's our exposure here?" the President quietly asked when he was gone.

Cook checked the door before replying.

"You mean from the Shepherds? Will they target us? Is that what you're asking?"

"My predecessor is, by every definition out there, a war criminal. When I took office, I basically absolved him of his crimes. So I'm asking, yes, will they target us?"

Cook frowned. "I don't know, but I'll give it some thought."

"Please do."

———

ANNA STARED AT HIM OPEN-MOUTHED. The gun did not waver. All he offered was a disarming smile.

"You ass! You took my car and left me there! On purpose!"

"Okay, calm down. Can we point that thing somewhere else first?"

She looked at the gun in her hand and back at him. She kept it where it was.

"First tell me why."

Dayton dropped his hands and gave her a look. "You know why."

"Am I done? What? I didn't pass one of your stupid tests, so you're cutting me loose? Just let the cops scoop me up and lock me away?"

"Think it through. If that was true, would I be sitting here right now?"

"How do I know you're not just waiting for the clean-up crew to come and take everything away? Erase me again?"

"You've been gone for hours." He sipped his beer. "They'd have left some time ago."

"So this is another test, see if I can get away clean with no help? Seriously?" The gun dropped to her waist, and she fought the urge to throw it at him.

"I needed to know if you could keep your head and make a proper exit, one which wouldn't draw attention or lead back to you in the future."

Anna stewed silently for a moment. She was still pissed, but now curious as to how she had done.

"And?"

He smiled as he pulled out his phone. He punched a few buttons before showing her the screen. It was a profile shot of her on the beach, ninety-nine percent naked and covered in oil.

"I'd say you failed at the drawing attention part, but I have to say I approve of your camouflage techniques." His grin was back.

"Fuck you." She spun to leave.

"Where are you going?"

She yelled over her shoulder as she stormed out. "I have sand everywhere, salt in my eyes! My hair is a rat's nest, and I'm still covered in oil! On top of that, I'm pissed!"

Dayton heard the sound of the refrigerator slamming shut, and the rant continued as she walked back. "Never mind that I haven't eaten in hours, and there's an asshole sitting on my deck, drinking my beer! What the ..."

She rounded the corner to find herself yelling at an empty chair. She spun in the doorway to find him right in front of her. He took a step toward her, and she was suddenly against the wall, his face inches from hers. The rant died in her throat, and she sucked in a breath before meeting his eyes. He was looking at her like he hadn't before. His hand traveled down her arm, and she bit her lip when it quivered. His hand found hers.

Taking the beer from it he stepped back. Their eyes stayed locked before he broke away and walked to the door. He took a pull on the beer before opening it and stepping through. Before it closed, he spoke.

"By the way, you passed."

She let the breath escape and stared at the closed door. What was going on with him? Something was stopping him, something deeply rooted.

Her legs cramped, and she sank down the wall to a crouch. She was exhausted: both mentally and physically. Emotionally, she was a mess. She could solve the first two easy enough; it was the third that would take some work.

Pulling herself up, she walked to the bathroom. Tonight called for the Jacuzzi tub. It would be the first time she used it.

But first, another beer—if there were any left.

---

JACK FOUGHT his way through the crowd, weaving around those both standing and sitting, all of them ignoring the fresh bodies on the floor. The dead varied in countless ways. Some wore suits and still clutched briefcases in their hands, their faces ripped away by passing bullets. Others were covered with tattoos and blood, their bare heads marking them as skinheads. One of them sat in the corner and screamed as blood poured from both ears. The people around him seemed to not even hear. They smiled at each other and ignored Jack as he pushed his way through.

The train lurched and Jack lost his footing, landing on the sticky red floor. He looked up to see an old woman smiling at him, her feet resting comfortably on the bloody body of a Klansman still wearing his white robe. She wasn't frightened by the blood pooling around her feet, nor by the gun in Jack's hand. They stared at each other in wonder for a moment before Jack threw himself up and pushed on. More gunshots rang out from the car ahead, but the people didn't even flinch. Jack squeezed around a man reading a paper and clawed at the door.

The next car was even more crowded. A teenager held an overhead rail and calmly scanned his phone while he stood on the body of a dead gangbanger, his body shredded by an explosion. Another tapped his foot to the tune on his earphones against the arm of a dead prisoner clad in an orange jumpsuit. The blood on his shoe rasped against the floor with each beat. Jack shoved the sight aside and fought the crowd toward the front of the car. More shots rang out, and this time the crowd gave a slight cheer before returning to their individual distractions.

"Get out of the way!" Jack screamed. Nobody moved. It was as if they couldn't hear him. He struggled on, none of them even acknowledging his presence as he pushed and shoved. They seemed to grow in number the farther he got, and Jack was gasping for breath when he finally reached the last door.

More shots. Laughter.

He shoved the door open and charged inside.

A man and a woman stood with their backs to him. Smoking pistols were clutched in their hands, and they laughed as they pointed at the two fresh bodies on the floor in front of them. A man dressed in a blue suit with a red tie cowered in the corner. The couple leveled their guns at him.

"No! Please! I'm a senator!" the man pleaded.

The man laughed and raised his gun.

"FBI! Drop the gun!" Jack screamed.

The man slowly lowered the gun and turned.

"Sam?"

The smiling face of Sam Shepherd met Jack's wide eyes.

"About time, Jack. We were waiting."

"We ...?"

The woman stepped out from behind Sam and smiled at him.

"Where have you been?"

"Debra? What are you ...?"

"Come on, honey. There's one left."

They both turned and leveled their guns again.

"No! Sam! No! Don't!"

Jack raised his gun and fired just as the two of them did. The senator's head exploded across the Plexiglas windows. An old couple sitting nearby softly clapped, the faded tattoos on their wrists plainly visible.

"No!"

Jack jerked awake and rolled out of bed. The Hi-Power was somehow in his fist, and he pushed it out in front of him as he leaped up and cleared the room. His heart threatened to explode out of his chest as he raced across the room and kicked in the bathroom door. He was about to repeat the process on the hallway door when he realized where he was.

His breathing slowed. The gun came down.

"You're in a hotel. You're in LA." He talked himself down.

Jack tossed the gun onto the nearby bed and walked to the window. He parted the curtains and let the late afternoon sun flood the room before sinking to a seat on the bed. The air conditioning forced a shiver as it evaporated the sweat from his torso. Jack stared at the smog-shrouded skyline and mumbled a memorized paragraph to himself. After a few renditions, he was breathing normally. He checked the clock.

One hour. He'd intended to take only twenty minutes—just a little sleep. A combat nap, they used to call it. Normally it was all he needed to recharge.

Jack forced himself to his feet and walked on shaky legs to the bathroom, ignoring the pistol on the bed as he passed. Shedding his underwear, he stepped into the shower. First hot until his skin threatened to blister, then cold until he couldn't take it anymore. He made a half-hearted attempt to dry off but dropped the towel as soon as he reached the bed. He listened to the sounds of the air conditioner running until it automatically shut off and was replaced by the sounds of traffic from outside.

"God damn you, Sam," he voiced aloud to no one.

Eventually the white noise drove his thoughts away. He rose to get dressed. The hotel had a bar.

**3**

---

*"If you look at great human civilizations, from the Roman Empire to the Soviet Union, you will see that most do not fail simply due to external threats but because of internal weakness, corruption, or a failure to manifest the values and ideals they espouse."*

—Cory Booker

Deacon sipped his Scotch and thumbed through the channels before rattling the ice and setting it back down. His wife glanced up from her book long enough to shake her head, but wisely said nothing. Her husband's views on the media where a touchy subject and she was not in the mood to listen to another rant. Eventually, he found a station that had something other than "reality TV bullshit." A news channel had exhausted their supply of political entertainment and was now finishing up the broadcast with a juicy story that had some shocking visuals.

"A popular marina in South Beach Miami today had a scare when an unknown person set off a smoke device on a sailboat. The smoke covered the entire facility and delayed the departure of several cruise ships at the nearby port. After a thorough search, authorities found no other devices nearby. While the episode appears to be nothing more than an elaborate prank, the local police promise to investigate in order to rule out all other possibilities."

The words were accompanied by video showing a thick cloud of white smoke travelling on the wind with several cruise ships in the background. People streamed out of the marina at a hurried pace, many stopping to take pictures before fleeing again. It was what a producer would call good television.

Something in the video caused Deacon to pause the feed. He set his Scotch down and examined the picture closely before rewinding it twice and watching it again. His wife watched and waited. Eventually, he let the feed run again, only to change it when it switched to celebrity dirt.

"See something interesting?"

"I'm not sure."

She waited for more, but it was all he had to offer. She shrugged it off and returned to her book with a sigh. Deacon frowned at that. His wife had called the office and dropped a subtle inquiry as to when he might be home with Margaret, who had wisely advised him to get his butt in the car. They had shared a rare dinner alone and she was now indirectly forcing him to relax. Since he was here, he decided to make the most of it, otherwise he'd have to repeat it sooner than he'd like. He thumbed a few buttons and broke the silence with a question.

"There's a new episode of *Chopped* on."

"Okay, if you'll make me a drink first?"

Deacon paused the show before jumping up

and moving to the kitchen. She watched his reflection in the window and saw him scribble a quick note and stuff it in his pocket before pulling bottles and a glass from the cabinets. She turned and looked at the now frozen picture on the TV.

What had he seen?

THE CONCRETE WAS COLDER; he couldn't come up with a reason why, but he was pretty sure it was colder. The cardboard scrap he had used before was still there, but it wasn't getting the job done. His ass was cold and sore. Fresh cardboard next time for sure, if there was a next time.

So far it looked like it was going to plan. The game tonight was baseball; he could faintly hear the announcer but had yet to figure out the names of the teams playing. Graham was in his deckchair again and hitting the bottle at regular intervals. The woman was in the house in front of another TV, this one a large flat screen he could easily see from his position across the canal. It was a Henry Fonda movie. The one where he and his wife have a kid stay with them at their lake house. He'd been racking his brain for the title for the last hour with no luck.

Graham glanced toward the house, even though the lighting from inside cancelled out any chance of her seeing what he was doing through her window. From the angle of the tip, the bottle appeared to be half-empty, and Marcus was starting to wonder if the man would even make it out of the boat. Should he have used more, or maybe less? He shrugged it off; nothing he could do about it now.

A half hour later, the movie was over. She waddled to the slider and yelled a goodnight into the dark. Graham rallied himself long enough to return something slurred and inaudible. Marcus decided that if she didn't know he was drinking, she was either a fool, or just didn't wish to admit it. The impression he was getting was that she was not thrilled with his early return from prison. He followed her progress through the house as she put her own glass in the sink and turned out the lights. She visited the bathroom, and the last he saw of her was her silhouette in the bathroom door before she turned off the light there, too. A few minutes later, he heard the sound of the machine. It was called a CPAP machine, and he had already forgotten what the letters stood for. He had Googled it the night before out of curiosity while he waited to see if the vodka bottle leaked.

The only information he had found helpful was the line which said it allowed its users to sleep more soundly. So, between that and the noise it made, Marcus considered it a plus for his mission. Now if Graham would just join her, he could get on with it.

It took another thirty minutes, but he finally did. This time the climb out of the boat resulted in a fall to the deck. Graham's head bounced off the stained wood with a sickening thwack, and Marcus involuntarily flinched at the impact. He watched the man struggle to his feet and rub his head. The bottle in his hand was without its paper bag this time, and Marcus could see it was a little more than half gone. If the dosage was right, he would be out for hours. Marcus silently cheered him on as he stumbled to the door and somehow made it into the house. A visit to the bathroom was followed by a slow journey across the great room. Graham traveled down the wall, one hand always in contact as he navigated. Eventually, he reached the dark room, and Marcus could only assume he had made it to the bed. He checked his watch and decided to give him twenty minutes.

While he waited, he tried again to wrap his head around the actions of the man he was here to kill. He had yet to figure out to what end the man had done what he had done. Marcus had ruled out the pursuit of justice. That had been easy; the man had never really investigated the crimes as he was required to. Some of his victims could be loosely tied to the crime in some way, but most were just picked up due to their location and record. The usual suspects. Some had no record at all; they had simply been in the wrong place at the wrong time and fit the bill of what Graham had needed. The confessions were arrived at in truly sick ways; mental and physical torture now only spoken of with words like Iraq and terrorism alongside them. True, it helped bolster Graham's arrest record, but it did nothing to pull the actual criminals off the street. So what was it?

Marcus could only conclude that the man enjoyed it. He reveled in the power he had over those men. Whether it had started in Vietnam, or perhaps even earlier, Graham was a man who enjoyed the infliction of pain on others. The job he held gave him an outlet, and his actions attracted more of his kind until he had corrupted the very essence of what they were there for. Protect and Serve. Graham had only protected his own secrets and served his own sick desires, only to go on and manipulate the system to his advantage when the whole mess was shoved out into the light. If the man sitting on the boat across from the canal had any regrets, Marcus was sure that getting caught was the only one.

Marcus chopped his wait to fifteen minutes when the sound of the man's snoring reached him. He was obviously out cold. Marcus got to his feet on stiff legs and massaged his cold ass before setting off on the route he had chosen last night. He paused only once when he got close but continued on when he again heard the snoring. A look through the window confirmed his suspicions. Graham was on his back, still fully clothed and with one shoe off, snoring along with the woman next to him.

Perfect.

Marcus let himself in by way of the slider as he had before, and this time went straight for the guest bathroom. On inventory of its contents, he found four syringes still in their packaging, and one more sitting out next to an open vial. He gathered them up and traveled to the kitchen. In the refrigerator, he found the rest of the medication stored in the door's butter shelf. He grabbed it all and set up a small assembly line on the granite countertop. Five minutes later, he had all the syringes full. He decided to leave the row of empty vials where they were but made sure he pocketed the trash before moving to the bedroom door.

The light coming from the bathroom gave him plenty to work by. He skirted around the bed until he was standing over Graham. The man had made it easy for him by passing out on top of the sheets. His shirt had ridden up over his ample gut, and Marcus had an unobstructed view of the skin over his beltline. Some bruising showed on the left side. Graham was a righty, and drug users were better coordinated when shooting to the opposite side. A fact he had picked up from the homeless he worked with. His snoring was loud enough to drown out the machine clamped to his wife's face.

Marcus placed a syringe between each finger of his left hand before selecting the first with his right. He picked a spot between two bruises and after one practiced motion stuck it into the man's belly. As he had hoped, Graham didn't even flinch. Like most diabetics he had grown immune to the intrusion of the tiny needles into his skin. Marcus emptied the syringe and selected another, re-peating the process four more times until they were all empty. After capping the last one he dropped it in a pocket with the others before pulling the envelope from the small of his back.

He opened it and shook the sterile one inside out and onto the man's chest. Standing up, he carefully inventoried every item and examined every inch of the bed. He mentally retraced his steps through the house twice before looking back down at Graham and the woman next to him. He almost felt sorry for her, but then he doubted she'd be very surprised by what she woke up next to. Graham's breathing slowed and deepened. It would continue to do so until it stopped. By then Marcus himself would be back on his boat and sleeping.

He turned to leave but stopped. Reaching down, he grabbed Graham's hands and wrapped them around the envelope. He'd be holding his past in his hands when they found him.

The bats were feasting on the bugs gathered around the streetlights as he made his way out of the community. He found his way to the highway and headed north this time. He would take the long way, skirting the east side of Tampa, then looping around to come in from the north. He already had a disposal site ready for the trash in his pocket, and after that he would visit a car wash and give the van a thorough cleaning before leaving it in its garage to dry. From there, it would be the bar at the marina for a few drinks in order to be seen by those who knew him. After watching

Graham drink for the past few nights, he felt he had earned a few himself. Tomorrow he'd get up early and listen to the recording of the police frequency. He'd hear it there first before it was leaked to the press. Either way, it was done.

He set the cruise control at five under the limit before reaching for his phone. The call was answered on the first ring.

"Ockham."

"Hello, William."

"Marcus, so good to hear from you. You have news?"

"It's done. No issues. I left him holding the envelope in both hands."

"Very well. I'll pass that along in the morning. I have a message for you as well."

"Oh?"

"You'll find a letter in your box—two actually, a donation to the clinic from a friend, with another for the kitchen. All very safe."

Marcus smiled; the General had routed some money though his network to him. The safe comment meant it was untraceable.

"Thank him for me, will you?"

"I will indeed."

"Good night, William."

"And a good evening to you, Number Two."

Marcus terminated the call with a smile. The disposable phone went in the waste bag with the trash from the house. A good night of work ended with a reward which would help even more. There were no other jobs like his.

He cancelled the cruise control and took the next exit. He'd need to hurry if he wanted to get to the bar in time. The trick would be to not get talked into staying too late; he wanted to be back at the kitchen early to help Laura serve breakfast.

---

JACK GROANED and squeezed his eyes shut, but the sunlight slipping through the crack in the curtains and the sound of his phone vibrating off the nightstand forced him to open them. Ducking out of the beam, which of course fell right across his pillow, he groped for the phone in time to save it from a fall to the floor. He thumbed the button without looking to see who it was.

"Y ... Yeah?"

"Jack?"

"Yeah?"

"Can you hear me?"

"Larry?"

"No, it's Deacon. Wake up. I think I got something for you."

Jack rubbed his head and forced himself to sit up. His gaze traveled around the hotel room, and he took in the pile of papers on the small table, the clothes draped over every piece of furniture, the room service tray he had forgotten to place outside. He then saw his own reflection in the mirror. Frowning, he turned away.

"Jack?"

"Yeah?"

"You there?"

"I'm here, boss. What time is it?"

"It's daytime. Get yourself together and call me back."

"What?"

"Call me back in fifteen minutes. I might have a lead on our Shepherds case."

Jack's eyes popped open at that. "Okay."

"Fifteen minutes." The line went dead.

Jack continued to hold the phone to his ear for another minute before waking up enough to put it down. Forcing himself to his feet, he pulled the boxers out of his ass on his way to the bathroom. First hot, then cold water served its purpose, and he was fully awake when he walked back into the room, searching for clean clothes while brushing his teeth. He found pants, which still had somewhat of a crease left in them, and a white shirt still free of stains. The last towel fell into a pile by the door, and he reminded himself again to let the maids in. He was gluing his hair in place when the phone rang again. It was Deacon's number on the ID.

"You said fifteen minutes," he scolded his boss.

"It's been twenty-five. You awake now?"

Jack gave up on his hair. He was way overdue for a haircut, but it would have to wait.

"I'm awake. Christ, its only six, sir."

"Six? I thought it was seven. Sorry, time zone screw-up."

"So, what have you got?"

"Watch the news last night?"

"No."

"Somebody at a marina in Miami set off a smoke grenade on a boat yesterday. I saw the footage on TV, and it was a lot. Enough to cover the whole place and reach the other side of the channel. They issued a security alert and held the ships in port until they straightened it out. The press is calling it a prank."

"Okay ... So?"

"Something about the smoke bothered me. It was white and really thick. So this morning I called the office and had them send me the report. It was an HC-White, a military smoke grenade, and it had been wired to be set off with a cell phone."

"It's just smoke, sir, nothing lethal. I don't see where you're going. Who was the target?"

"A lawyer. A tax guy. He owns the boat with one of his friends."

"Okay, so why him?"

"That's just it; he's a nobody. Just a guy with some rich clients who handles their investments and shelters and what-not. He comes up clean in the database, and the IRS says his stuff is legit. All of his friends are in the same group. He works, he goes home, he plays with his boat on the weekends. That's it. None of his friends are claiming responsibility, and the guy comes across as pretty rattled by it."

"So who then?"

"The man claims to have gotten a call from the marina—some woman he'd never heard of before. She said she was a new employee, and that his boat had been damaged in a storm the night before. She asked him to come look at it. When he got on board, the grenade went off."

"And you think it was the Shepherds? Why?"

"Two things. First, the device. I sent the file to

Bill, and he said it was top notch. The components were traced to an army shipment that got lost, and the phone is a pre-paid bought from a Walmart twenty miles south in Homestead. No prints or fibers. Nothing."

"You said two things. What's the second?"

"My gut. I think this was a training exercise; somebody got a lesson in both bomb making and remote detonation. I think this was a practice run."

"I don't know, sir. That's pretty thin."

"It's anorexic, but I still think I'm right."

"A Shepherd in the making?" Jack mused. "I don't see it. Why not just practice out in the boonies? Why do it in public?"

"Realism. The more real the training is, the better you are prepared for the real thing."

"True. Awful risky."

"Yes and no. And there's a third thing."

"What's that?"

"I had our people do a search for me this morning—just got the results a minute ago. Three other similar instances in the last year. A fake car bomb in Chicago: a dye-pack exploded in a guy's face when he shut his car door. A shooting in Tampa: report of a homeless guy shooting a man with a paint gun in a parking garage before slipping away. The target was a grocery store manager."

"And the third?"

"Guy on a motorcycle tosses a flash-bang into a tow truck at a rural stoplight. Victim says he only got a quick look—never even heard him coming. A mechanic that worked for his father."

Jack squeezed his eyes shut before asking, "Where was that?"

"Los Angeles."

Jack couldn't help but groan.

"What?"

"Greg found a motorcycle buried under some brush up on the mountain. We think it was our guy, but Sydney can't find anything to link it to him. She's still processing it."

"And that's bad news?"

"No, I'm bitching because you just tripled my workload."

"I'm not following you."

"The bike is an electric model; it makes no noise."

"Ahh, I see. I think we have three more cases to add to the file, but it's your call."

"No, no, I have to agree. Which one do you want?"

"Man, if I could, I'd be out there with you. You know that."

"This case is too big, sir. I'm having a hard-enough time just keeping up, let alone trying to work out of a hotel room."

"What are you doing today?"

"Oh, you'll love this. I'm meeting with a group of detectives from LA Robbery-Homicide. I'm going to ask them for help."

"And how are they going to do that?"

"By going to the gym."

It was Deacon's turn to be confused, but before he could answer Jack's phone beeped. He glanced at the screen.

"It's Larry, sir. Can I call you back?"

"Keep me informed. I have to go brief the Deputy Chief of Staff, so he doesn't screw us on the news."

"Yes, sir." Jack thumbed the button, praying that it was the right one.

"Randall."

"Jack, it's Larry. Turn on the television."

"Seriously?" Jack tossed papers aside until he found the remote. He thumbed it on to find a picture of a suburban Florida house surrounded by crime-scene tape. The mute was already on, and he left it there.

"I see it. What do we know?"

"John Graham. The Shepherds took him out last night. I already called the locals, and this one was slick. We'll have to wait for autopsy, but it looks like an insulin overdose. The guy was killed with his own medication! Right next to his sleeping wife. They left him holding the envelope in his own hands."

Jack didn't have to ask who Graham was; he was well known in police circles. "The target makes sense. I doubt there will be many tears shed for him."

"No, the local PD already have a group of protesters cheering at the entrance to the complex where he lived. The press got the Shepherds' letter this morning, too, and evidently tipped them off. Same thing's happening in Milwaukee."

Jack squinted to see the station ID on the screen, but he couldn't make it out. The palm trees in the front yard of the house and the angle of the sun had caught his eye though.

"Where did he live, Larry?"

"Little town called Apollo Beach. It's just south of—"

"Tampa." Jack finished the sentence and let out a sigh.

"You sound like you're not surprised. Something I need to know?"

"It's a theory, but it comes from a good source."

"Well, it's too early for beer, so I guess you'll just have to lay it on me without it."

Jack hadn't even had coffee yet, but it was not the time to mention it. He caught his own reflection in the mirror again. This time he frowned for a different reason before sitting back and informing Larry of Deacon's theory.

# 4

"*Corruption has reached an unacceptable level. It devours resources that could be devoted to the citizens. It impedes the proper carrying out of market rules and penalizes the honest and capable.*"

—*Sergio Mattarella*

The newsroom was still buzzing, but Danny had learned to ignore it years ago.

The arrival of a package from the Shepherds was always a big thing. They still addressed them to him, but he was far from being the first one to open it. The FBI had taken that task for themselves, but he understood why. The paper had protested this and finally a deal had been struck with the *Post* and several other papers. After the FBI lab had processed and cleared them, copies of the papers were handed back to them unedited. Certain information was highlighted, and Danny's boss had been chosen to be the only one privy to it. The FBI would make an alteration to the text so that they could identify any copycats. Only Ed would know what was changed. The edited documents were then distributed to the few reporters who had been allowed access. Fortunately, Danny was still one of them.

It would be a few hours before the FBI was back, so he killed the time dumping his thoughts onto a blank page.

*The Twelve Shepherds claimed yet another victim this week, and the American people were once again shown the level to which the country's judicial system has morphed into one that is two-tiered. While the nation divides itself on the issue, those directly involved are now being forced to acknowl-*

*edge something they have turned a blind eye to for some time.*

*America jails more of its citizens than any other country on earth. In 1970, there were an estimated 190,000 people held in federal, state, and local prisons. Today America holds an estimated 2.4 million of its people behind bars. This out of a population of 300 million. Second place goes to China who jails 1.6 million people. China, however, has a population of 1.3 billion. This means we jail 700,000 more of our people than a country with over four times our population.*

*Despite these appalling numbers, America remains one of the most under policed countries in the world. Historically, most citizens would spend their entire lives having little beyond a casual contact with a police officer. In the last few years this has changed. It is now commonplace to see heavily armed police with military grade weapons patrolling our streets. Our phones and internet communications are now monitored and recorded by government entities, all in the name of national security. Local and state police are now equipped and trained with armored vehicles and military arms. Prisons, once established, maintained, and operated by the state, are now handed over to private enterprises, ones that operate them on a for-profit basis.*

*The fact that these businesses employ lobbyists who push for tougher laws, mandatory minimums, and longer sentences, should not be surprising, nor should the corresponding increase in prison populations. More Americans are now finding themselves behind bars for what were previously minor infractions, and for much longer times. To put this in a global perspective, America has only 5% of the world's population but has managed to hold 25% of the world's prisoners behind its walls. Only in America is prison an industry.*

*Funding for public defenders is at an all-time low. It is estimated that a person charged with a crime, and who lacks the means to hire his or her own lawyer, can expect on average no more than eleven minutes of council. That's 660 seconds to understand the situation and fully consider the options available to them before they make a decision that will affect them for the rest of their lives. The goal of the public defender is often one of keeping his head above water rather than defense of the accused. As a result, the plea-bargain or guilty plea is often suggested as they attempt to keep their caseloads at a manageable level. Many of the accused find themselves sentenced before they fully understand what has happened to them.*

*Unless they are rich.*

*Only a person with little power, either in the form of wealth or position, is likely to be subject to the lower tier of the system. If one has the means to break the eleven-minute barrier and mount some form of resistance, the chances of ever seeing the inside of a prison cell drop dramatically. The richer one is, the less likely they are to be held accountable, regardless of the severity of the crime they are accused of. Wall Street firms have committed large-scale crimes, police engage in illegal practices, wealthy sports figures commit rape and assault, and politicians engage in war crimes; all without a single prosecution. The only reason Bernie Madoff is in prison is that he stole from the rich.*

*This has become the definition of the American Justice system today.*

*Sometime soon, the American citizen will see one of its politically elected leaders speaking to the issue of the Twelve Shepherds. They will use harsh language, they will speak about the rule of law, and they will denounce the acts of the Shepherds in their entirety.*

*But they will never admit to being the reason they have come to exist.*

*"Tough on Crime" has been an American political mainstay since the years of Reagan. It has since proven to be a bipartisan talking point in every*

*election since with each candidate vowing to be tougher than his opponent. As a result, we have seen more aggressive policing, longer prison sentences, tougher rules regarding parole and probation, and the abolishment of any practical leniency. Disasters like three-strikes and mandatory minimums grow each year, despite evidence that they are grossly counter-productive in reducing crime. Instead, the public is pointed to carefully packaged issues, that when stripped of their veils become little more than attacks on the poor—the common excuse being that poverty is the root of crime. Politicians run with this ball in order to avoid any risk of being labeled "Soft on crime," this despite the overwhelming evidence provided by Wall St. to the contrary.*

*This has led to the two-tiered system we have now, the one that the Shepherds are pushing into the faces of both the public and the elected leaders. The change they are demanding may be—*

"Is this for a book you're writing, or the paper?"

Danny stopped and looked up to see Steve looking over his shoulder. Normally he would be pissed at the intrusion, but he and Steve had become good friends and often bounced story ideas back and forth.

"The paper. Why? Too much?" He sat back and chewed a nail.

Steve snorted at the question. "A bit. Ed will never consider it."

Danny looked over what he had wrote and frowned. "What if I dumb it down a bit?"

"You won't."

"I think he might like it."

"Oh, I didn't say he wouldn't like it; he'll just never run with it. You're practically calling the Shepherds a balancing force, and then blaming their existence on the government."

Danny spun and faced him. "What's this? Coming from one of their biggest fans?"

"Just because I may agree with them at some level, it doesn't mean I'm ready to say it out loud."

"Ahhh, I see now." Danny smiled and shook an accusing finger at him. "You're a pussy. I've always suspected."

"Fuck you very much, and you know better." He turned to leave.

"So what's your solution?"

Steve stopped and walked back into the cubicle. He put his hands in his pockets and rocked on his feet the way he did when heavy thinking was called for.

"Ask yourself this, Danny. Is there anything the

Shepherds are doing with bullets, that the average Joe can't accomplish with his vote?"

Danny had no answer. Steve left him with that and returned to his own cube across the hall. Danny found himself reading the many bumper stickers Steve had tacked up on the wall over the years. "Elephants and Asses controlling the Masses." "Thinking is not illegal, yet." "At least the war on the middle class is going well!" And his favorite: "The Government: Protecting and Serving you to death!"

Ed's secretary Ginny appeared in front of him with a large envelope. Like two nerdy high schoolers, they had been checking each other out from afar for months, each of them afraid to make the first move. To cover this, they pretended to despise each other.

"What do *you* want?"

"The Shepherd file. Next time come get it yourself." She tossed it in his lap and spun to leave.

"You'd like that, wouldn't you?" he called after her.

All he got was a manicured middle finger thrown over her shoulder. Still, Danny caught her smile as he watched her leave, which he did until she was out of sight.

With a smile of his own, he returned to his desk. Like all the previous communiqués, this one was several inches thick. He settled in to read.

---

"So what does it look like?"

"So far, my guys got nothing, Jack. No forced entry—the wife says he left the doors unlocked all the time. Tox screen will take a while, but the vials are all laying right here and empty. If it wasn't for the envelope in his hands, I'd be thinking suicide."

Jack paced the room behind everyone sitting at the conference table. The Special Agent in Charge of the Tampa office was on speakerphone along with Deacon in DC. They were trying to determine whether to leave for Tampa or stay here in LA.

Larry asked, "How did this guy sleep through this? I mean, if someone was jabbing me with a syringe, I'd be awake pretty quick!"

"The wife says he's a serious drinker. Since he couldn't really leave, she said he spent his time watching sports on his boat and drinking. We found a bottle under the wheel and several empties in the trash. His BA came back at over 400. In other words, he wasn't asleep; he'd passed out.

Also, the wife wears a mask at night to help her breathe, which makes a lot of noise. She didn't hear a thing."

"Amazing."

"Diabetics become desensitized to the needles after a while. They just plain stop feeling them. I'm not surprised," Sydney added.

"How did our guy know all this?" Deacon asked.

"Unknown, sir. Graham's been diabetic for only a few years. Diagnosed in prison. Anybody who he served time with knew. His doctors there. The infirmary staff. Even his parole officer. We'll be asking around. I've already sent a man to the prison."

"Cameras? Neighbors?"

"Still canvassing. It's a small community, but it's not gated. No cameras yet. So far, the neighbors have turned up nothing. They're all retirees—they go to bed at nine. He only had one neighbor next door; the rest of the area is empty lots or under construction. We're going through those homes and talking to the crews, but nothing so far."

"Any homeless in the area?"

"Homeless? Uh, no—not that I saw anyway. It's pretty upscale; not the kind of area I'd expect to see them in. Why? You have a theory?"

"No. Just asking. Any credible threats from locals? I see some protests going on."

"Plenty. Most of them are from a distance—online and what-not. The protestors are more the militant-mom type. A lot of noise, but not much else. Have the Shepherds ever announced a target beforehand?"

"No, I'm just covering the bases. Anything else?"

"Not yet, but I'll keep you informed."

"Thanks, Carl. I'll touch base with you tonight." Jack punched the button ending the connection.

"Well, what do you think? Stay or go?" he asked the group.

Sydney spoke. "Stay. We have more than they do. We should stay and see where it goes."

"Larry?"

"My experience says go—the fresher the scene the better—but I'm not too confident that it's the best option right now, based on what I just heard."

"Greg?"

"Stay until they find something better in Tampa, otherwise we might be right back here in a couple days."

"It's a seven-hour flight. I just got here," Larry added.

"Noted." Jack smiled. "Sir? Your thoughts?"

"I'm inclined to agree with Greg. There's three hundred million people in this country. Any one of them could be a Shepherd. If you stay, you might be able to narrow that down to three hundred. Until you have something better to go on, I say stick with the plan." Deacon replied through the tiny speaker.

"All right then, we stay. What's next?"

"The chief says I can give my speech at two," Larry said.

Jack checked his watch. "Then we better get going."

---

LARRY LOOKED to his right and found Sydney and Greg standing against the wall. He got a couple of nods for moral support, but little else. The room was hostile, despite the deputy chief giving him an intro for those who didn't know him from years ago. He understood their attitude. Yes, Larry may have been one of them once, but he had left. On top of that, he had joined the FBI, a federal agency that had put its boot down hard on the LAPD several times in the past. While most would admit they had done it to themselves, there was still a lot of animosity to be overcome. He'd find out soon enough if that could be done.

The chief finished his intro and gave Larry the nod. He walked to the podium, gripping the edges, forcing himself not to muss his hair.

He said nothing at first. He just looked across the room and examined a few faces.

"Yeah, I wouldn't want me here either."

That drew a few smiles, but little else.

"I had a speech all ready, but let's just shit-can that. Yes, I need some help. They didn't send me because I was once one of you. I had this shitty job before Moretti, and, if you saw the news this morning, John Graham, got their brass jury verdicts, so don't think I'm here because I once shared a car or a few beers with some of you. I'm here because I was dumb enough to say yes. So, I'm just going to lay it out here and tell you what we're up against, and you can take it or leave it."

Larry left the podium and walked to a plastic chair sitting behind him. He kicked it across the floor until it was in front of them all and took a seat.

"Look, we're not just looking for one guy. We're looking for a domestic terrorist group, and while the public may be rooting for them, you and I know where it's all headed. Nobody elected the

Shepherds. Nobody got a vote or sat on a jury. While some people might say they're doing the work we can't, you and I know better. Sooner or later it's going to get political, or racial, or religious, or some other thing. Then the people dying won't be so black and white. People will start picking sides, and we'll have ourselves a nice little civil war. All it takes is one wrong move. You know that better than most. Chicago is learning that right now, but you guys already know it. If we don't stop this, it's going to get ugly. Ugly like only you guys know, on a national scale."

Larry paused and rubbed both hands threw his mop of hair. He started to say something else twice but ended up just throwing up his hands.

"That's all I got. What do you say?"

The officers squirmed in their seats and exchanged looks with one another. Many of them had lived through or heard enough stories about the LA riots after the Rodney King verdict to know that Larry was speaking the truth. Finally, one of them, an old salt from robbery/homicide, spoke up from the back row.

"We'll hear you out, Larry. Tell us what you need."

Larry leaned forward and squinted to see the man. "Joe?"

"Yeah."

"Gawd, you're old."

"You're fat, what's your point?"

The room had a good laugh at his expense.

"True, true. Maybe I can work on that while we do this. What do I need? I need to find a guy." He stood up and motioned to Sydney and Greg. They left the wall and joined him with Sydney getting a few long looks. Larry made introductions.

"Sydney Lewis, she leads one of our evidence recovery teams. You may have seen her on television during the terrorism scare we had awhile back in New York. And this is Greg Whitcomb, formally of the Hostage Rescue team and on loan to me because he was dumb enough to get shot, again, while handling the problem in Niagara Falls."

The cops in the room unconsciously sat straighter in their chairs on hearing that. An involuntary sign of respect. Some had recognized the pair against the wall but could not remember from where. This news refreshed their memories of what the two had done.

"You the one who shot Mukhtar al-a what's-his-name?" one of them asked Sydney.

She nodded. "Right in the head."

The man smiled at the blunt answer. "Well, okay then."

Sydney pulled a remote from her pocket and turned on the large monitor behind her. The picture from the street camera sat next to one from the highway. Both were a bit blurry, but you could make out the basic shape and skin color of the man behind the wheel.

"This is our guy. This footage is from a dash cam on a POV found on the route we think the shooter took when leaving the scene. This is another shot we found on a traffic camera, which shows the van heading south on the Highway 101 out of Santa Barbara. It's the same van. The signs on the side of it are fake. The plate is registered to a dummy corporation with a fake address. It was found abandoned in Oxnard. The van was clean. No prints. No fibers. They rubbed it down with bleach. But it gave us a little information.

"Between the pictures, seat, and mirror positions we have some numbers to work with. Our guy is 6'2", African American, and based on the pictures we think he's a bodybuilder. If you note the forearm and neck in both pictures, and the shoulder width and size in the frontal shot, you'll see he's a big man."

She flicked the image, and they saw a few shots

of the van before they returned to the first two and stayed.

"That all you have?" one of them asked.

"I'm afraid so. I know it's thin, but we have an idea that might work. It's based on some assumptions, but they're educated ones."

Greg stepped forward, and the picture switched to one from the scene up on the mountain. The crowd leaned forward and scanned it as only detectives do.

"This is from the scene of the Moretti shooting. The shooter is well trained. He's most likely ex-military or even ex-law enforcement. He chose his position wisely and extracted himself in a manner that ensured he would not be seen. He used tactics taught in sniper schools to hide his tracks, and he was off the mountain and through the roadblocks before state and local could respond. His cleaning of the van also speaks to his training. We think this guy is operating out of the LA area, specifically north Hollywood, or Burbank. He most likely has a phony job that requires occasional travel and a few different residences that he maintains. He'll be a loner. Since he's a bodybuilder, he may have a few gym friends, but he won't hang out with them outside of it. He has a garage or similar facility for the vehicles and tools he needs to operate nearby.

He'll be single with no steady companions. He may frequent a shooting facility and be skilled with all manner of weapons. We think he's been an LA resident for at least a year."

"How do you know that?"

"We think he may be tied to another case here. One that happened on Mulholland Drive."

"What? I don't remember the Shepherds claiming a body here."

"That's because they didn't kill anyone. That time."

A new picture went up on the screen. This one showed a tow truck parked in the middle of Mulholland. The windshield was cracked, but otherwise they saw no damage.

"Twelve months ago, a mechanic named Jimmy Fields was driving on Mulholland at eleven p.m., looking for a disabled car that had called in needing a tow. When he stopped at Cornell, a man on a motorcycle came up behind him and tossed a flash-bang grenade inside his truck. Jimmy caught sight of him for only a second before he was rendered deaf and blind. A report was filed, but since there were no lasting injuries, and no real damage to the truck he was in, it was quickly forgotten. Now we have reason to think this may have been a training exercise for our shooter."

"Why is that?"

"He reported that the man he saw," Greg read straight from the report in his hands, "'was a really big guy, maybe black, I don't know, on a motorcycle. Except I never heard it come up behind me.' We suspect the two men are one and the same."

"I still don't see the connection."

"Two days ago, we found a motorcycle buried on the side of the mountain. It had been cleaned. All of the serial numbers had been removed, so we're running with the theory that it's the one our shooter used to get off of the mountain so quick. What connects the two cases is that it was an electric motorcycle—they run virtually silent. With the lights off and some dark clothing, a rider would be practically invisible on Mulholland at that hour."

"This mechanic, he had no enemies?"

"We're checking again, but so far he looks like an ordinary Joe with an ordinary job."

Some whispered conversations started, and they let them happen. The men and woman in the room couldn't help it. They were hooked. It was their nature. Once you showed them a puzzle like this, they could not help but start working it.

"So what's the next step?"

Larry stood back up.

"We need you guys to go to the gym—as many as possible and at all hours. Even you, Joe. If you don't go to one already, here's your chance to join one on the Bureau's dime. Most of these places have picture ID of their members, but getting a warrant for this, even under the Homeland Security rules, is too much of a stretch. That and not all of the gyms are that high-tech. We need to find guys who fit the description and check them out. If you see a guy who might be what we're looking for, get his picture and a plate number. We'll start there."

Larry saw many of them shaking their heads and he couldn't blame them. It was a long shot. But he didn't have any other options at this point. Deacon had dispatched a crew from the Tampa office to work the Graham case, and if they found a better lead in Florida than what he had here, they would be on the jet within the hour.

Until then, it was off to the gym.

# 5

_"The inherent corruption of man can often bring down the best system."_

—_Alexis Denisof_

H aney waited until the howl of the scrambling device faded before answering the call.

"What do you have?"

"The Kurds have been informed of the airdrop time and location. We also leaked it to the ISIS sympathizers in the area. They'll no doubt have some people there when the time comes."

"Good. We'll proceed on schedule. You'll inform Mr. Harper of any changes."

"Yes, sir."

Haney hung up without another word. He drummed his fingers for a moment before addressing his number two man.

"What else?"

"You have the media ready?"

"In place by tomorrow. You have what you need in Istanbul?"

"On its way as we speak. I sent the orders out this morning."

"What else?" Haney repeated.

Harper cleaned his nails with a pocketknife and ran through the list in his head.

"What's the fear level here, in the States? Is it time to ratchet it back up a bit?"

Haney considered the question. Keeping the public afraid was a maintenance issue, one that was unfortunate but necessary. The last CIA estimate numbered ISIS at about thirty-five thousand members. They had no airplanes, no missiles, and no navy. They accounted for a small fraction of the yearly deaths in the West. Lighting, toddlers with handguns, and vending machines, all killed more people every year than terrorist did. So, in order for the public to fear them to the point that they endorsed military intervention, they resorted to excessive media coverage to feed it. To do so, it required attacks that were close to home. But even those were few and far between. Not enough to rile the public to the point they were willing to go to war. On occasion Haney had been forced to help them. Marketing, he called it. Their last effort had been a husband-and-wife team in San Diego. The pair had conveniently died at the hands of a few select police officers. The press had done the rest.

"No, I think we're good for some time. Istanbul should be enough if handled properly. When do you leave?"

"Tonight. I'll be in place early tomorrow local time."

"Very well. Wait for my order."

WILLIAM SAT BACK and scanned the multiple
screens. His bots were monitoring communications on a broad number of pathways. He had narrowed their focus to Turkey and had noticed the
NSA doing the same. Now he followed their
progress as well as that of a few other agencies.
Traffic appeared and morphed into readable messages as the bots automatically decoded the
stream of numbers and letters. None of this would
be possible without the roomful of hardware in
the next room. The installation had taken him
months, and security dictated that he had little
help. Dayton and Charlie had provided the necessary muscle, and he'd had the boy crawling under
the subfloor for days to get it all connected. The
power draw was immense and had resulted in the
building of a generator farm, a trio of windmills
on a distant ridgeline and a solar farm in the adja-
cent valley. A small turbine pulled juice from the
dam as well. Together, they made more than
enough power to run the entire facility. The computers called for low temperatures and the air con-
ditioners ran nonstop.

His eyes narrowed when he saw the latest
numbers. Traffic at a military subcontractor had
risen by a factor of four. He clicked the mouse and
pulled up the messages for a closer look.

It was a CIA unit—or at least it used to be. Now a former group that had once been a part of Blackwater. He scanned the message and stopped at the third paragraph. A package was traveling to Turkey from Iraq. A part of another package that would arrive in Istanbul. The item was code-worded, so he could only speculate as to what it was.

"Istanbul, odd," he said out loud.

Istanbul was off limits to most. The Russians avoided causing trouble there as it was their only access to their warm-water ports on the Black Sea. The city was very westernized, a cradle of Turkish business interest, and it sat on a global commerce route. The people in charge didn't like their money to be in danger, thus the city was left alone by both sides. Whatever the package was, William doubted it was for sinister purposes. But then one never knew. He examined the address and, on a whim, decided to trace it back.

He soon had access to the account, but a review of the code kept him from reading it. It was not something the computers were familiar with. Something new? He wasn't sure. It looked ... old? A new puzzle. He loaded a sample into another program and set it to work.

While he waited, he checked on the Shepherds. They had all checked in on time today, so he saw no problems. He scrolled through the cameras and checked a few GPS locators. Two of their number were still out of the country—he did not expect them back for a few more weeks. The remaining ten were in their assigned areas. He clicked on their latest recruit and found her car at the library.

"Doing your homework, Anna? Good girl." He smiled.

A beep from another screen drew his attention, and he clicked on the icon. The computer had found the code. It was Russian. A one-time pad from the 1950s; it had stopped being used in 1958. Odd. He checked the dates and found it had only been cracked in the last ten years. The saved messages had all been decoded and reviewed. Most of them were Cold War traffic, which was soon deemed antiquated. A few documents had some relevance today, but the file had been closed eight months later. Someone had hijacked the code for his own personal use, no doubt hoping that its age would keep anyone from taking interest. Clever, but not something an expert would do. He clicked a message at random and waited for the computer to unscramble it.

An email. From a codenamed source to the owner of the mailbox. Troop movements in Iraq, dated August of 1990. He clicked another. Supplies being leaked to an Iraqi warlord. This was someone on the inside; someone with access to classified orders. He scrolled down and clicked another at random. The sender's name was code-named Angler. The message ordered arms and ammunition to be left unsecured at a remote location. He punched the coordinates in on another screen. Northern Iraq. Kurdish territory. The dates were shortly before the battle of Fallujah. Right when he and the General were there. Who was this?

Angler? Where had he heard that codename before?

He settled in to read further.

SYDNEY SIGHED as she adjusted the tension on the stationary bike. It was her second workout of the day, and she was already tired. Not that she could call it a real workout. Today she had dressed the part of the women she secretly despised. The ones who wore full makeup and designer work-out clothing to the gym. Her plan was to sit on the bike and peddle for an hour or so—just enough to sweat, but not enough to really burn any calories, nor raise her heart rate much. It was an exercise in vanity, and she played the role among a few others doing the same. A couple of them had openly frowned at her, the new girl here to compete with them for the attention of the men in the gym. She felt like she was back in high school.

She ignored them after returning their plastic smiles, and let her eyes wander around the room. She spotted the usual patrons: the muscle-bound men who stared at themselves in the mirror more than anything else; the elderly wearing sweat suits doing their best to keep their ageing bodies working; the young ones who used the gym as a social gathering; a few awkward loners still trying to fulfill their New Year's resolutions to lose weight. It was like any other gym she had been at.

She was about to leave and head for the third gym on her list when he walked in. A tower of muscle wrapped in ebony skin. He chatted briefly with the girl at the desk before crossing the room to the squat rack. A quick warm-up that stirred some chatter among her neighbors was soon followed by plate after plate banging its way onto the bar. She followed his progress in the mirror. He was the right height and the profile was close. Maybe.

Forty minutes later she saw him begin stripping the bar. Her chatty neighbors had left some time ago, off to replace whatever calories they had burned with a latte of some kind. Sydney needed time and an excuse to get closer. She wiped the bike down quickly before moving to the juice bar. Knowing it would take a while, she ordered a peanut-butter chocolate smoothie and leaned on the counter while it was being made. Pulling her phone out, she pretended to examine it when she saw him approach. He once again engaged the girl behind the counter in some light banter, and Sydney used the opportunity to examine him close up. His arm caught her eye, and she quickly took a picture before he turned away. Sipping her drink and still gazing at her phone, she followed him out, lingering long enough to grab a photo of his Mercedes as he climbed in. He was soon on his way, and she made no move to follow.

Suspect number ten, she found out when she called it in. And the day wasn't even half over. They would run the plate and know more the next day. Until then, she was on her way to the next one.

THE MAN HAD A STANDING RESERVATION, but he would not need it tonight. He arrived on time and made sure he was seen by several of his colleagues in the bar before moving toward the end. There, he saw the man he was to meet.

Haney was surrounded by his people as usual, and they commanded a good portion of the room. The steak house was one of the most popular in DC, frequented by the Washington power elite as evidenced by the number of security men waiting outside. A place where hundred-dollar steaks were served with bottles of wine that cost several times that much without a thought given. Not that Haney ever picked up the check; that was his job. He made eye contact and received a wave that could not be missed by the crowd. Shaking hands and pounding backs, he wormed his way through the sea of tailored wool until he was at the edge of the group.

Eyes followed him and he ignored them as Haney shook his hand. A seat opened up next to him, and he slid in. His usual drink appeared on his elbow, and he took a sip for appearance's sake. The small talk continued—stories of hunting trips and vacations, new boats and the places they intended to sail them. The liquor flowed, and the men got louder. Eventually, they moved off to their tables. His reservation was cancelled when Haney invited him to his table. The witnesses were many, as planned. They would think the meeting was to his benefit, not knowing it was the other way around.

He followed the man through the crowd to the private table in the back. Eyes followed, and he did his best to ignore them, but he'd be lying if he said he didn't relish them. The man in front of him was no longer in office, yet he held more power than most who were. The people in the room knew it; it was the people outside the Beltway who were in the dark. But when one thought about it in that way, it became clear: the country was run by the 1%; the rest were there just to provide funding. It was a line the man in front of him liked to use. Well, today he was part of that. Being the head of a major lobbying organization had him in the Rolodex of several of the power elite, but few had the power to summon him on an hour's notice to a dinner meeting, especially since he had already eaten.

He took his seat and sipped his drink when it again landed in front of him. He didn't wonder what Haney wanted; that would become clear shortly. What he did wonder was what he could possibly order that would not tax his already full stomach. A Caesar and another drink should do it. He could pick away at it while he heard Haney out.

The waiter had barely left when Haney spoke. "What's the word on the Turks?"

"They've been quietly asking for the F-16s we're looking to phase out. The sale is already in the works; they just want it expedited now. Some additions to the ordinance package: more GP and cluster munitions. Some heavy ground weapons. Some of our incoming fire detection gizmos."

"I'm not sure if we should be selling the Boomerang system just yet. What else do they want?"

"Other than that, just the usual stuff."

"Can you move that forward?"

"The whole thing was waiting on the F-35 to be approved. Once that happens and production starts, the switch will start. Maybe in fourteen or sixteen months."

Haney grimaced at the number. Sometimes he got in his own way. The planned cost overruns of the F-35 were turning a nice profit. He hated to give that up, but things had changed. "I think we've milked the F-35 for what we can. Let's re-move the roadblocks there and get that going. I want you to push the F-16 sale to Turkey when the time comes."

"Is the time coming?"

Haney ignored the question. "If you run into any opposition, let me know. I've gotten things started with a few, so you shouldn't have too much trouble. Push the anti-aircraft units as well. What's the total package price?"

"Eighteen aircraft with the E/F configuration? Plus all the bells and whistles, maybe four-point-eight billion dollars. The AA package will push it over five easy. Lockheed-Martin will have a nice day when it happens."

Haney didn't react to the bait, he'd already made arrangements to buy a large chunk of stock, as had several others. If the man wanted to make more than his outrageous fees, he could put two and two together by himself.

"This ISIS mess is coming to Turkey, and it's going to force their hand. They'll be looking to go on offence. Watch for the move and be ready to push this."

"What about the Kurds, or the Greeks for that matter? Neither is going to like this."

"The Kurds aren't your issue. I'll take care of the Kurds. The Greeks are too poor to complain about anything right now."

The man took the rebuke in silence. The food arrived and they cut the conversation short while it was served. Haney smirked at his guest's salad while a bloody steak was set in front of him.

"Gotta lose a few pounds," the man explained.

Haney just grunted for a reply as he carved off a bite. It tasted like money.

---

"PEOPLE FIND THIS FUN?"

Larry asked himself the question as he labored on the rowing machine. He had already embarrassed himself just by sitting down and trying to reach the handle. His gut had stopped him by an inch, and he'd had to get back up and adjust the seat before trying again. He now struggled through another ten reps before collapsing back into the seat. He mopped the sweat from his brow with a scratchy towel, struggling to breathe.

"Doing okay?"

He looked up to see the perky young blonde who had earlier taken his money and then showed him around the place. He'd found her Spandex-clad ass distracting, but he managed to pay enough attention to know how the machines worked. She'd also shown him the free weights, but he'd quickly vetoed that idea. He reasoned that if he passed out, the machine would at least catch him and keep him off the floor. He managed a nod in her direction, and she gave him an encouraging smile before bouncing off. He followed her form all the way to the desk as did several others. Everything was in the right size and proportion and wrapped in an outfit that no doubt encouraged people to sign up. She was a walking commercial. Out of his league, but there was no fault in entertaining the idea.

"Probably kill me," he mused.

While he was catching his breath, he examined the room. The machine he had chosen faced the free weight area, where there were three men who fit the description. Two of them were working out together, and their grunts and shouts of encouragement had some of the others rolling their eyes. The third man was bigger, but he showed no signs of needing help. Larry watched him in the mirror as he locked his eyes on the weights in his hands and slowly curled them one at a time. Larry counted the plates and added up the weight in his head. He doubted he could lift one of them off the rack—let alone curl it. The man's muscles bulged under his black skin and sweat poured off him in rivulets to be soaked up by his thin t-shirt.

With a grunt, the man finished and strode across the mat to park the dumbbells back on the rack. Larry forced himself to look away and reached for the handle again. His new sweat suit was already soaked, and his heart was threatening to explode out of his chest, but he had to keep up appearances.

"This is fun," he reminded himself.

By the time he had done ten more the man he was watching had entered the locker room. Larry quickly wiped down the machine he was on and followed. He found the place sparsely populated, so he wandered until he located the man already in the shower. Spotting his clothes piled on a bench, he walked past to get a look.

Air Jordans. Size 12. The shorts were just shorts. A set of keys lay on top. BMW.

Larry made it to the drinking fountain and took a long one. After that, he threw some cold water on his face before exiting. He waved to the sex kitten behind the desk and managed to walk to his car without falling down. Sitting behind the wheel he blasted the air conditioning until he shivered.

Ten minutes later, the man emerged and walked to his car. Larry got two clean shots with his camera phone before he was gone.

"What now?"

He was supposed to try another gym, but he knew that was out of the question. He was spent. Also a little dizzy. He needed food.

Didn't he pass an In-n-Out Burger on the way here?

He dropped the car in gear to go look for it

---

"Everything is in place?"

"We have all the assets in place. The device is waiting for deployment. The initial claim will go through a known ISIS social media account we penetrated two months ago. Three separate escape routes are in place and checked every two hours. We've arranged two known correspondents to be in the city within the window you outlined."

"Who?"

"The BBC and Al Jazeera. Both are interviewing senior state officials for a refugee story."

"Very good." The man sat and waited while Haney checked items off of a mental list. He consulted a calendar.

"Tomorrow. Noon, local. Inform Mr. Harper."

"Yes, sir."

---

"THIS ISN'T GOING TO WORK."

"Why not?"

"That guy over there with the military haircut."

Laurie adjusted her treadmill's speed and examined the guy in the mirror. They had been at the gym for an hour and had not seen anyone matching the description of their suspect yet. They had decided to give it another hour before changing gyms.

"What about him?"

"I think he recognizes me."

"How do you know he's not looking at me?"

Greg smiled at the remark. The woman had been increasingly flirting with him since they had met on the plane. Greg had not ruled it out, nor discouraged it, but they were working here. The Spandex she was currently wearing didn't help much, and he was wondering if that had been on purpose.

"Maybe they are, but I can't risk it either way."

"Jack said you were no good for undercover work after the bank job."

"He said you were no good for undercover work after the dam attack."

"I didn't think I had risen to his level of fame.

Damn it. Now he's telling his buddy. We've got to go."

"Fine. Nobody here matches up anyway."

The two of them quickly terminated their runs and made a half-hearted effort at wiping down the machines before heading to the door. Laurie followed him out and across the parking lot to the car before the two men could head them off.

"Your advertising doesn't help," she said once they got in the car.

"What do you mean?"

"You need some different pants. Not that I'm complaining about the ones you have on, but you can see your calf right through them. It's a dead give-a-way."

Greg looked down and saw what she was saying. The bullet from the AK he had caught in his right calf had torn away a good chunk of muscle. The divot left behind caused his calf to move in an awkward way when walking. Add that to his face and haircut, and she was right.

"Grow out your beard a little."

"And until then?"

"Let's go find you some baggy sweatpants, I guess." She pouted.

"I have some at the hotel."

She grinned for a quick second but pushed the thought aside.

"Do they say FBI or HRT on them?"

"Both."

"Yeah, maybe not. Let's find a sporting goods store. I think you're about to become a fan of the local team."

# 6

*"We mustn't hesitate to cut corruption at its roots."*

—*Felipe VI of Spain*

Harper sat just inside the balcony of the hotel overlooking the city and chain smoked. The overcast sky kept him in shadow, and the gauze curtains moved in and out of the French doors with the moist breeze hiding his movements. He timed his exhale to carry the smoke away as it retreated. Only three stories up, the sounds of life in Istanbul poured easily into the space, and his mind cataloged them without him needing to look. Passing vehicles identified their size on the cobblestone streets and the yells of merchants working the passing tourists could be heard clearly over them. The noise had built steadily over the last few hours. He could have avoided this, opting for a better room at the Pera Palace, or perhaps the Four Seasons, but the mission called for him to be closer to his target and off the radar of any intelligence operatives. They all watched the better hotels. So he had chosen the second-rate facility he was in now.

The city had chosen itself for what he needed. It was a crossroads. For centuries a chokepoint where east met west. It was also a NATO country, one of the two major militaries in the Middle East. There was war on its southern borders, and the ever-looming hammer of Russia to its north. If one needed to spark a fire, there were few better places.

The sounding of the muezzin disrupted the din, calling the faithful to prayer for the second time today. It was Dhuhr, if his memory served, usually around noon or shortly after, when one was prompted to remember God and seek his guidance.

Whatever. He had only learned the ritual so he could exploit it if needed. As he would today.

He crushed out the remnants of the cigarette, then carried the ashtray to the toilet. The butts were flushed, and he would wipe the room down before leaving it for the last time. Pausing at the mirror he examined his reflection carefully. His hair had been dyed black to match the fake beard he had applied earlier. The mix of local and British clothes were oversized, and he checked their fit after adopting the stooped posture he would be using today. Luckily, the weather was cooperating: the unusually cold day allowed him to wear bulkier clothing without suspicion. It served to hide his physique along with the Makarov 9mm pistol in his belt. Deciding his appearance would pass scrutiny, he checked the gun's chamber, assuring himself it was loaded before returning it to the small of his back. He would have preferred a cross-draw holster for faster access, but the mission and disguise prevented that. Besides, if he ended up needing the pistol he had screwed up.

Despite him being in the room for the last two days, it had changed very little. He had arrived in the city, made one stop at a dead-drop to retrieve the Makarov and a few other items, and then sat by the window and smoked. Other than examining the package and reading books on his phone, it had been another exercise in hurry-up-and-wait. A process familiar to all soldiers. This morning differed in only one way: he had received a message. It was time to act.

He could have left the room some time ago—the mission didn't call for a specific time—but he knew the market would be more crowded if he waited. The bigger the crowd, the easier it would be for him to get in and out undetected. It was the excuse he used to justify his choice. He doubted his employer would care, but he had the excuse ready if needed.

The city was a familiar one, and the location he had chosen was within a ten-minute walk. He had considered several target options. The list was plentiful: Hagia Sophia, the Blue Mosque, Topkapi Palace. None of them provided the right mixture though. He needed a place where east met west, in large numbers.

He hoisted the backpack up onto a shoulder and walked to the door. Pulling the tape he had placed over the peephole, he checked the hallway as best he could before opening it and sliding through. The door slammed shut with the breeze before he could stop it, and he frowned at the noise. Ten strides took him to the stairs, and he was soon three stories down and outside through the fire entrance. A light rain began to fall as he made his way down the street. He changed direction at the corner and followed a small group of tourists as they made their own way toward the Grand Bazaar. He matched pace with them as they slowed and consulted their guidebooks under umbrellas. More of them snapped open, and he found himself stooping more to avoid getting gouged in the face. He pulled his hat lower and weaved his way around the tourists snapping photos of the minarets and towering semi-domes. Cameras were everywhere now, so he had to be careful. It was one of the reasons he carried the backpack inside another. He would switch them when the time came and hopefully foil any images of him caught by a snapping phone.

He passed the mosque as men were still emerging from prayer. More umbrellas appeared as they made their way back to their shops. The tourists followed the line laid out in their guidebooks. He knew the route himself; they would eventually make their way to Sultanahmet, then on to Seraglio Point. He had already ruled them out as possible sites; the population there was too western. The mission called for something more mixed.

He passed Topkapi Palace, making sure he kept his face behind a neighboring umbrella as he did so. The palace held priceless crowns and thrones and jeweled weaponry of the period. There were metal detectors at the entrance along with guards sporting sub-machineguns. Cameras covered every entrance, and he didn't wish to appear on their footage. He kept pace with the crowd and kept heading west. The rain increased, and the people crowded under sagging awnings and rusty escarpments to escape it as best they could. Harper wove around these knots of people at a casual pace, occasionally stopping to check for anyone following while he pretended to examine souvenirs, or carpets, or offered food in the many stalls—whatever presented when he needed it.

He slowed further and cursed the rain. The people were now crowded in tight groups, and he needed them to be more mixed. He examined the sky to the west and saw a lighter shade of gray approaching. Perhaps the rain would let up soon.

Not wanting to stay in place while he waited, he made his way toward the spice bazaar. He moved along Marpuçcular Cad with a small knot of Japanese tourists before leaving them at Tahtakale Cad and heading northwest. The rain began to slow, and he slowed his pace as well, occasionally pausing to examine the wares in the many shops. He answered all enquiries with a British accent and politely broke contact soon after—just a tourist seeing the sights. The rain slowed to a stop and people began to crowd the streets again. He set off east and soon turned the corner onto Hasircilar Cad, the main street of the bazaar.

His senses were immediately assaulted by the overload of colors, smells, and noise. Heaping mounds of spices in impossibly bright hues of yellow, orange and red unwittingly drew his attention. The smell of rich coffee and tobacco smoke permeated the air, along with the body odor of several countries. Peddlers yelled over the gathered voices of the crowds, who jostled for space in the tight quarters. Pushcarts full of every flavor and fragrance imaginable were slowly forced through the crowd by Turkish businessmen. Harper's pace slowed to a crawl. He gripped the straps of the backpack and loosened them, letting it fall down his back to cover the Makarov. He couldn't have someone in the crowd press up against it and recognize it for what it was. Not now; he was too close.

The crowd got even thicker as he approached the Kurukahveci Mehmet Efendi, one of the city's best coffee shops and a popular destination for both tourists and natives alike. He had visited it himself many times before. For appearance's sake, and to buy some time, he got in line.

Ten minutes later, he emerged from the shop, a steaming cup in his hand and his travel guide in the other. He wandered until he found the spot he had located on a previous visit. A narrow gap between two shops, just wide enough for a man to squeeze through the pushcarts and reach the wall. We wedged himself in with the coffee and guidebook, visiting each until he became part of the street itself. People flowed past him without a second look. After a moment, he doffed the backpack and slid down to a squat. Just a shopper resting with a hot drink on a cold and rainy day.

His hand fell behind him and he worked the mechanism inside the pack by touch as he watched the tourists pass. Working the zipper back shut required him to step on the nylon and pull against it, but he soon had it closed. He then pulled the second pack from the first. It was a different color and style, and it weighed much less than they had together. He slid the first pack under a cartful of saffron from Iran and left it.

Checking the time, he rose to his feet before draining his cup and moving on into the crowd, the weight of the Makarov now more prominent and giving him comfort. The new backpack rode higher due to its much lighter weight, and he adjusted the straps as he walked. It now held little more than a change of clothes, a few candy bars, a bottle of water, and his false papers. A bottle of stomach medicine and a pack of British cigarettes would mark him as a tourist if his bag were to be searched.

The rain was gone now, and the breeze had left with it. The wet cold still occasionally made itself felt as the awnings dripped down his neck as he passed. Harper moved with the crowd for another block before ducking down a dark side street. He paused in a dark corner to peel the beard off his face and reverse his coat. The beard and the hat went into a nearby dumpster, and a pair of fake glasses went on his nose. He emerged from the dark alley at a casual pace, dressed and looking completely different than when he had entered, checking in all directions with his tourist map in hand. Satisfied he was still alone, he made his way to Ragip Gümüşpala. There, he hailed a cab to take him over the bridge.

Halfway across, he pulled out his cellphone and made a call.

The sound reached him a second later through the open window, and he turned with the driver to see a cloud of smoke rising over the market. A moment later, the sound of sirens reached them. Harper did his best to look concerned as the driver began babbling and searching the radio. Once they were on the other side, he had the man pull over and drop him on a busy corner. He stood on the curb with a few other tourists gazing across the river at the rising smoke. The smoke was high in the sky now, but it was dissipating.

Harper made no outside reaction. He simply turned on a heel and walked away. Several blocks later, he found a safe house. He would spend the night there before taking a train to Ankara in the morning. From there, it would be a flight to London before moving on to DC. By that time, he would be able to read about his mission in the major papers; he had seen a couple drafts before he had left. They might require a little change here and there, but he had kept the mission within bounds. Once the world knew the details they had provided, the fallout would begin.

His job here was done.

"AND NOW TO our Fox News foreign desk, where we are monitoring the situation in Turkey.

"Sources in Ankara are now telling us that the deadly bombing carried out yesterday in an Istanbul market was the work of ISIS. The bomb was set off at the height of the day's activity killing seven Turks and wounding forty-four others, including four British and three Americans. Turkey's Prime Minister has announced a full investigation focused on the extremist terrorist group. Turkey's semiofficial Anadolu news agency reported that the authorities have begun to collect DNA samples from relatives of those suspected of having joined ISIS to help identify possible suspects in the bombing. A senior military official commented outside the market today:

"'We are investigating ISIS as our priority. There has been good progress toward identifying a suspect. One with connections to the extremists. This attack will only strengthen our resolve to defeat these terrorists,' he said.

"The weekend blast came only days after a lunchtime peace rally calling for an end to the renewed conflict between the Kurdistan Workers Party, or PKK, and the Turkish government, and for a united front against ISIS forces on their southern border.

"Turkish forces have been battling ISIS jihadists across a swath of northern Iraq and Syria, and several members of the Turkish government have recently changed their stance on allowing the United States to launch airstrikes on the militant group's positions from Incirlik Air Base in southern Turkey. A move the Prime Minister has been hesitant to approve.

"Turkey has declared three days of mourning over the bombing. Despite warnings from the police, crowds have gathered to protest, expressing solidarity with the victims.

"'This is an attack on all of Turkey. This is an attack directed at our democracy and at our people as a whole!'

"One group, whose members included opposition lawmakers carrying red flowers to commemorate the dead, tried to reach the scene of the blasts, but were blocked from doing so by police officers. Some scuffles broke out, but there were no reports of injury.

"Those same party members are calling on the Prime Minister to request an emergency meeting of NATO, where they will likely ask for a ramping up of military force against the Islamic State. No word yet if that request has been made.

"In other news—"

Haney thumbed the remote and killed the sound before the perfectly coiffed blonde could smile her way through another report. He spun in his chair to nod approvingly at his underling. He had arrived only minutes ago.

"Any problems?"

Harper shrugged and rubbed his freshly shaven face. "The explosive was Semtex—the chemical footprint will lead to Syria. The DNA on the components came from a prisoner being held in one of our facilities. Some of his family are in the group being tested. As for me, my face was hidden, and I changed clothes on the way out. The documents and clothes were destroyed before I left Ankara." He stretched and yawned. "Sorry, sir, there was no way to sleep on the train, and I don't sleep at all on planes. God, I can still smell that train."

Haney smiled at the man's ease. A cool customer, he was one of his best tools.

"I trust the media people have performed as well?" Harper asked.

"You just saw that." Haney gestured to the now silent screen. "Two more leaks to back up the original, then it will take on a life of its own. Well done."

"Thank you, sir. What's next?"

"We push a few buttons here and there. We'll have our war soon enough. In the meantime, stay close. I may need you soon."

"Yes, sir."

---

"THE GLAMOROUS WORLD OF FORENSICS," Sydney quipped.

She sat with her legs crossed in front of a computer screen beside a young woman from the LAPD archives department. Her name was Mellissa, and she worked the day shift in this basement dungeon while attending school at night. Sydney had learned that the LAPD was holding a position for her when she graduated in a few weeks. It didn't take long to see why—the woman was very good at extracting information from the thousands of files on hand and had jumped at the chance to work with an actual FBI agent. She had already warned Sydney that she was after her job. Sydney had advised her to get a good look at it first. They were doing so right now. Dressed in sweatpants and hoodies, they had been in the chilly basement of the building for several hours now going through files of all the suspects coming in from the gym surveillance. Searching for that needle in the haystack. The haystack kept growing every day.

"Isn't it? I mean, if this were anything like television, you and I would be sitting here wearing Armani suits surrounded by hunky detectives. Instead of my ancient Honda, I'd have a Hummer parked outside. I feel cheated."

Sydney smiled. It was the stereotype she railed against in her classes at the academy. The TV show *CSI*, all four versions—or was it five now, she lost track—had done more damage to her profession than one would think possible. Now every jury expected them to have irrefutable scientific evidence pointing to every criminal. Reasonable doubt was now absolute proof. She'd even been asked once by a juror why they didn't have any video of the crime, as if the FBI had cameras set up everywhere just for her. They now had to not only prove that the suspect did the crime, but they had to provide every detail of how they did it. It was as if the cases were now mystery novels. And if the juror didn't get the "how" answered, then it was an automatic vote for acquittal.

The other problem was that the shows revealed a lot of the ways they did their job, so the criminals would watch to learn what not to do. It also told the lawyers where they should look for questions of doubt. She had wrangled with so many amateur lawyer-detectives she could write a book. Most were easily shot down, but some had really done their homework. On top of that, some of her colleagues had actually gone over to the other side, finding jobs working as expert witnesses and advisors for criminal lawyers who could pay the big bucks. It made her sick. Then there were the citizen detectives who thought the FBI needed their help. She had arrived on one crime scene to find it already taped off and a person walking the scene taking pictures. Turned out to be a rabid *CSI* fan who lived down the street. The cops quickly ran him off, but the pictures appeared the next day on the person's website along with his theory of what happened. They had quickly obtained an order taking the site down, but the damage had already been done.

As if her job wasn't hard enough.

"I once had a writer call me and ask how a guy killed his boss—said he needed it for the book he was writing."

"Fiction or non-fiction?"

"More like science fiction. I basically told him to fuck off. He complained to my boss."

"What did he say?"

"He told him to fuck off as well."

Mellissa laughed. "Wish my boss had the balls for that. He's a bit political."

"Most of them have to be. Comes with the job. But yes, I was happy to have him that day. Who are you checking?"

She picked up the file. "Suspect 48, a Mr. Russo. So far, he appears legit. How about you?"

"I've got number 56. Except for a mistress, he's quite boring as well. He'll be caught soon. He's not very good at hiding her."

Mellissa tapped keys and the computer displayed a slowly growing download bar.

"This will take a few minutes. How late do you want to stay?"

"I'm back in the gyms tomorrow. So maybe another hour?"

"That's going to call for some pizza. What do you like?"

Sydney stretched. "I'm a cheese and pepperoni girl."

Mellissa's face fell. "Oh, I go a little lighter than that."

"Like what?"

"Um, I was thinking maybe a white pizza. Chicken and spinach with some goat cheese?"

"Oh, honey, you'll never make it in the Bureau if you keep eating that healthy."

"One of each then?"

"Okay, and a Mountain Dew if they have it?"

Mellissa picked up the phone and dialed from memory. While it rang, she smiled at her new friend. "I'm amazed you're able to dodge bullets and stuff, eating like that," she joked.

"Many have tried, my dear, many have tried." Sydney recrossed her legs and clicked the mouse.

"Number 59. Who are you?" She scanned the file while her new partner chatted on the phone. While she waited, she saw the master file update. Twenty-four new names were added to the list. She stopped.

"How long have you been working on that file?"

Mellissa was caught off guard. She'd been told to be thorough, so she hadn't worried about the time. There was really no way to go faster anyway; they were limited by the speed of the computers.

"Maybe an hour?"

"And how long until you finish?"

"Maybe another. Why?"

Sydney did the math in her head. If they kept

adding files at the current rate, it would take them ... she got lost in the numbers, but it was a long time.

"This isn't going to work. It'll be weeks before we've even caught up at this rate."

Mellissa scrunched her face at the information. "More people?"

"Who? We're already spread too thin." She tapped her fingernail on the desk. Mellissa waited.

"Maybe ... what time is it in DC? Never mind. He's probably up."

"Who?"

Sydney reached for the phone. "I really can't say. Would you mind going up and ... waiting for the pizza?" She put on a large grin.

"Secret FBI stuff?"

"Something like that."

"No problem." She got up, clearly disappointed. Sydney gave her an apologetic smile before she wandered off toward the stairs. She pulled out her phone and as soon as the door clicked shut behind her poked at it until she had her contacts open. She selected a coded name.

"C'mon, you little nerd, pick up the phone."

# 7

"When leaders are no longer beholden to the people who elected them, corruption results and the recruitment of extremists becomes easier."

—Iqbal Quadir

The buzzing phone drew a muffled curse from him, and he thumbed the remote, pausing his show before reaching for it.

"What part of sick don't you understand? I'm not coming in. Leave me alone!" he yelled at it before suffering a coughing fit. He pulled the blanket tighter around him and squinted at the screen. A coded ID. He searched his drug-fogged brain for its owner, but quickly gave up. Still, he had to answer it. He cleared his voice and thumbed the button.

"Yeah?"

"Eric? You sound horrible."

"I feel horrible. Who's this?"

"It's Sydney, you dork. What's the matter?"

"Syd? Oh, sorry. I'm home sick with the flu, and my ears are all ... Anyway, what's up?"

"If you're sick, don't bother. I just had a question that's kind of up your alley."

Eric pulled the phone away from his head and coughed again. "No, I'm okay. What's your question? Did you get the blue screen again?"

"No. It's a case. I need a way to sort a bunch of files."

"A case? Thought you were teaching?"

"No, I got pulled off and, well ... I need, uh ..."

"Seriously? You forget who you're talking to?"

Sydney had reflexively looked for a way to ask her question without revealing what case she was working on. It was procedure. She'd forgotten Eric was with the NSA most of the time now; his security clearance had become several levels above hers. On top of that, they were good friends. If she couldn't trust him, who could she trust?

"Sorry—habit. It's the Twelve Shepherds case. I'm out in LA and we have a long list of subjects. It's growing every day, and I need a way to sort through the pile faster."

"Cool. Okay, tell me more." He settled back down on the couch and pulled another tissue from the box. He tried to keep from sniffling so he could hear what she was saying, but still had to stop her twice to clarify something. After a few minutes, he had the problem mostly understood.

"Okay, I think I see what you're getting at. I can modify some software I have to do what you need, but you'll need to talk to someone else before I can do it."

"Is this security red tape? If it is, it might not be worth it. I can try to get more eyeballs looking at this stuff instead."

They both paused while Eric blew his nose.

"It's not that. If the names on your list are all actual suspects, we're okay—it's that I don't have any criteria to narrow it down with. You'll need to find someone to tell me what I need to program in. Something that will separate the guy you're looking for from the others. Otherwise, the software doesn't know what it's being tasked to do."

There was a long pause as Sydney thought about it. Eric stared at the frozen figure on his TV screen. Why would anyone choose a crossbow to fight zombies with? It just seemed so stupid. His fogged brain attempted to wrap itself around the question, and he almost dozed off. Sydney's voice jerked him back.

"Like what? I'm not sure what to even ask?"

"I don't know, Syd, but I'll need something."

"Okay, go back to bed. I'll think about it."

"Nah, I've slept all day already."

"So what are you doing now?"

"Nyquil and Netflix."

"Sounds like a plan. I'll call you back. Feel better."

"That's the idea."

"Oh, wait. What if I can't think of anything to separate them?"

"I don't know. Try stuff that you can rule out maybe?"

"All right. I'll call you back. Say hello to Bear for me."

Eric dropped the phone on the coffee table and collapsed back onto the couch. He made an effort to reach the remote. It was just out of range.

He was trying to decide if it was worth the effort to move when his dog came in and cocked his head at Eric's struggle. He gave up on the remote and scratched the dog's head instead.

"Hey, Bear. Sydney says hi. Wake me up at six, okay?" The dog thumped his tail twice on the carpet for a reply. Eric rolled over and buried his head in the pillow while the dog curled up in his spot on the other end of the couch.

"Why don't dogs get the flu?" his owner asked. "What's your secret?"

The dog offered no answer. Eric managed to give the question a few moments of thought before passing out again.

---

HANEY WATCHED the video footage in the dark of his office. The afterburners of Turkish jets glowed in the dark as they raced down the runway and disappeared into the night sky. Within the hour they would be raining death on ISIS positions in Syria. Tomorrow a trusted source would have some Bomb Damage Assessments in his in-box. He switched to another network and was rewarded with a repeat of the footage. He could watch it over and over—for some reason he never got tired of it.

The screen on his cell phone came alive. Reluctantly, he pulled his gaze from the bigger screen and examined the smaller one. Few had his number, and even fewer were on his must-answer list. He thumbed the answer key.

"Yes?"

"Things are progressing I see."

"As planned."

"Adjustments?"

"I would increase both Raytheon and Lockheed. Other than that, go as planned."

"Not Boeing?"

"If they expedite the contract, yes. I'll know if that's going to happen. Lockheed is in front though; they can't make Hellfires fast enough for demand."

"GD?"

"General D has been waiting for the arms package to Turkey to get approved. If that happens, they'll move the F-16s. But they already have them built and waiting in the desert. If the stock goes up, it will be on the sale alone."

"Expected numbers?"

"I estimate eight to nine thousand strikes over the next year. Maybe somewhere in the neighborhood of a thirty percent increase. Total will be around 45 billion."

There was a pause while the man crunched the numbers. Haney could almost hear him smile over the phone.

"Very good. How long do we have to make our moves?"

"I would do so by the end of the week."

"That soon? How ..."

"That's not what you pay me for."

The man took the rebuke without pause. "I'll be in touch."

"Yes." Haney ended the call.

Turning on his computer, he brought up a stock ticker. The numbers seemed to climb with the planes on the other screen.

Just as he had planned.

"WHAT DO YOU THINK OF HIM?"

The General looked up from his reading. William gestured to the screen, showing some file footage of the President speaking while they waited for the press conference. The General was already reading an early draft, but there was always the chance of last-minute changes. There was also something to be learned by the tone in which it was delivered.

"Better than most. Certainly better than the last few. The public may not think so, but they don't know the game like we do. I think he's done the best he can considering the degree that he's been hamstrung. He's caved a few too many times for little to no gain, but I can't say I blame him. The oligarchy is too strong. Unless the younger demographic votes in a Congress he can work with in the midterms, it's going to be more of the same. It's the election after that that I'm worried about."

William nodded and the General went back to his reading. William wanted to ask more—a lot more—but it was a dangerous line of thought, one he did not wish to cross even in a theoretical discussion. If the General thought he was entertaining those thoughts, he might reconsider William's place inside the Shepherds. He searched for a way to ask his question without crossing that line.

"At what point do you think they will perceive us as a direct threat?"

The General's head came up again. "The oligarchy? I would hope they never do—that's not our goal. The defeat of the oligarchy belongs to the people—they can do so with their votes. The Shepherds can only draw attention and hold accountable those whom the system fails to hold accountable. We are not here to defeat the emperor, only to show the people that he wears no clothes. I thought that was clear, William. We are not leading a coup. I won't have it. The people themselves will have to decide."

"I understand, sir, but these men ... they will not go quietly. I expect a disinformation campaign to start soon. One that labels us as extreme terrorists trying to overthrow the current government. They will attempt to define us with terms that suit them best. It will be a war—a war of propaganda. They own the press. I'm not sure what I can do to fight them."

The General set the papers down and laced his fingers across his chest as he had a habit of doing when deep in thought.

"In a way it is a war, but one done indirectly. Are you suggesting we take the battle to them directly?"

"No. No, I would never suggest that. As you know I have given up on such decisions. But I feel the day will come when we will have to make that decision and—"

"If it comes to that, we will disengage."

The abrupt answer caught William off guard. "But ... that would end the mission, would it not?"

"It would lead to an insurgency—right here in the United States—a civil war. The damages and loss of life would be unlike anything we can imagine. Better to break off and try again than to escalate and risk the alternative. We must *never* step over that line. If we do, all we hope to accomplish will be lost. This change must come from within to be long lasting. Coups are never without blood, and always short lived. There's a big difference between a coup and a revolution, we must strive for the latter and avoid the former."

He gestured to the silent screen, and William reluctantly let the conversation end. He turned up the volume to hear the President's statements. After the usual condolences, condemnation of the attacks, and statements of unity to both Turkey and NATO, he got to the point.

"I have ordered an additional carrier group to the eastern Mediterranean to support our NATO allies in the region. We must show the terrorists that we stand together and are ready to take action against any hostilities on their part. I have also ordered additional airstrikes against ISIS command and control, as well as key sites of their infrastructure. In addition to that, I've ordered more special operations forces to join our allies in the area to both train and advise them in their fight against these terrorists. Our commitment to the governments of Turkey, Iraq, and Jordon in regard to refugees and the defense of their borders has not changed. We stand with our allies.

"Through these actions and with the coordinated effort of our NATO allies, we will defeat this cancer. Of that I have every confidence. God bless the men and woman of our armed forces, and God bless the United States of America."

They watched as the President ignored the shouted questions and retreated back down the hallway from which he had come. The network switched to their talking heads, who wasted no time spinning the President's words. William shut them off with a tap of the mouse.

"Notice he said nothing about action *inside* Syria," the General commented.

"Or of arming the allies he spoke of," William added.

"Someone convinced him to take them out of the first draft."

"How ...?"

"This is his handwriting in the margin. He added the names himself, but they didn't make it to the final draft. Interesting."

"You think it was someone else's decision?"

"Hard to say. Arming the enemies of your enemies is a dangerous game, one we seem to never learn. The area is a patchwork of ancient wars. Without ISIS, they would be fighting each other. The Turks versus the Kurds. The Kurds versus the Syrians. The Iraq government forces caught in the middle while they fight the Shia versus Shiite battle from within. All with Iran and Russia looming in the background. Whatever arms are sent may end up pointed back at us someday. It leads to more questions."

"Such as?"

"Is that what someone wants? Someone with enough power to get the arms sent but kept out of the President's speech?"

William's brow knitted. A dangerous game, one he was glad to let others lead. He had barely begun to pick at it when the General unlocked his brakes.

"I have another economy lesson with Charlie. I saw a stack of questions on his desk. This may require some Scotch. Care to join us?"

"As enjoyable as that might be to observe, I think I should do some work here, sir."

"Very well. Your loss." He wheeled himself to the security door and paused.

"William."

"Yes, sir?"

"The question you asked earlier. A coup would be a quick solution. When faced with a complicated problem one is often tempted to simply destroy what they have and start over. The problem is that the ones who scream for the overthrow of the existing government, they rarely think about what happens the next day. Leaders must be chosen by the people, not picked for them."

William met the General's gaze before nodding in agreement. It was something he had to admit he had given little thought to.

"Yes, sir."

The door buzzed and the General wheeled himself through.

William turned back to his screens and thought about the man's words. They would keep him up later than usual.

THOUSANDS OF MILES AWAY, the former VP was also watching the President's performance. Harper watched from a nearby couch, his feet up on the mahogany coffee table and a beer in his hand. Haney frowned at him, but let it slide; there were more important things to discuss.

"The drop is happening soon?"

"Tonight. Everything is in place. The pilots will do the rest."

"And on the receiving end?"

"Our people sent the message and instructions, whether they act on it or not is out of our hands. The information chain is too long in my opinion, but it's what we have. I have an internet contact I can use for redundancy, but we're already past that point."

"Who picked the location?"

"Me." The man sipped his beer and glared.

Haney realized he was asking questions the answers to which he would rather not know. He changed subjects.

"You move your stocks?"

"Not my thing."

It was Haney's turn to grin—he knew better. He held his gaze and Harper relented.

"A few. Is it the right time?"

"A little too soon. You don't want to raise any flags."

Harper tipped his beer in reply. Haney stepped behind his desk and adjusted the screen so his underling could not see it.

"What's our next move?"

Haney continued without looking up. "We slowly escalate things. ISIS is small and they lack the arms to make this a prolonged war. We can't count on them to light this fire themselves. If we're going to make any real money on this one, we need to get the big boys involved, then drag it out. ISIS is amateur hour, but they're the only option we have right now. Africa is too small. Ukraine is a stalemate, but we need it to keep Putin in check. Iran maybe, but that's down the road, and we'll have to be sure the nukes are not an option first." He concentrated on his screen.

Harper prodded him. "So how are we escalating things?"

"With your air drop. You never asked what was in it."

Harper didn't really care. It was a paycheck to him. He humored the man. "So what was in it?"

Harper nodded at his screen before leaning back and presenting the grin that everyone hated.

"A match."

**8**

---

*"There is an interesting interplay between power corrupting and corruption empowering. The causality does not go one way."*

—*Bruce Bueno de Mesquita*

William snored soundly in his chair while the screens in front of him streamed information at a rapid pace.

An empty plate with a few crumbs on it sat next to his ever-present coffee cup, its lid on tight and checked repeatedly. A bottle of pills sat next to it. The food and medication had partnered against him, and he had nodded off.

The computer pinged loudly enough to wake him, and by reflex he immediately groped for the mouse. Scanning the screens through half-opened eyes he searched for the source of the interruption. It was a Google alert of all things. Most were false alarms—a coincidence of name, or some other tag he had used when setting it up.

"Travis?" he asked the screen while his mind searched for the connection. He clicked the link and was shown a mug shot. The man's face immediately registered, and William became fully awake.

"Some movement?" He quickly read the article, then read it again more slowly. Like most news stories in the internet age it was written for those with short attention spans. An update followed by a quick rehash before the required rhetorical question. It was the second to last line that drew a reaction.

"Charges dismissed? Are you kidding me?"

William reached for the pills and swallowed one with the aid of some cold coffee. Frowning at both the screen and the coffee, he rose to replace the latter. The pot was twenty feet out of reach on purpose—a practice he had adopted years ago. It forced him to get up and move around. His injury and work posture made him susceptible to DVTs —Deep Vein Thrombosis, a fancy term for blood clots in the legs. The doctors had told him to get up and get moving regularly, or sooner or later one was going to get him. They had him on a blood thinner too. He took it every evening with a bunch of other pills—he forgot what they were all for. A result of his past life.

He now took a lap around the server room with his refilled cup. The man was a target possibility, one he had flagged when the case first hit the press. His digging had revealed a man worthy of their attention, but they had waited to see if the system did its job or not first. This new information changed that. He checked the time. Perhaps the General was free?

Sitting back down, he swept the dishes aside and blew the crumbs off the desk. A pair of Roombas patrolled the floor twice a day to keep the dust to a minimum. The electrostatic air cleaners and the micron filters over every duct kept the room spotless. William himself was their biggest threat, but after a lifetime of eating at his desk he was certainly not going to change now. He thumbed a button and was rewarded with a dial tone, another produced a ring, but only one.

"This is Charlie."

"Charlie, William. I was wondering if the General had a few minutes available this afternoon?"

"He's just finished lunch and is doing some reading. He has a conference call in a few hours. Should I ask?"

"Please."

"Wait one." The connection broke.

William smiled at Charlie's use of radio procedure. It was something he had taken years to stop doing himself. A military imprint on his behavior. To this day he still wrote the date backwards. Charlie returned after a short wait.

"He says he'll be down shortly."

"Excellent. I won't keep him long. Thank you, Charlie."

"No problem."

He settled in to review the file.

Sean Travis was a forty-eight-year-old engineering contractor from Orlando. Three years ago he had been charged with the sexual assault of a teenager he had coerced into his home with the help of alcohol. He had pled guilty and received some time in prison only to be let out early due to overcrowding. His business survived while he was away, and he was able to resume his life in West Palm Beach, where he was not as well known. Learning from his previous incarceration, Travis had developed a new plan.

Renting an upscale house in a nice neighborhood, he set about collecting strays. He would prowl the internet looking for young boys, mostly runaways in need of shelter. Once they were in his lavish home, he would charge them rent in the form of sex. Many of them were running from a home that had ejected them for their sexual preference, and with nowhere to go but back on the street, the boys had little option but to give in. The boys grew in number and slowly decreased in age until a neighbor got curious and called the landlord, questioning the high traffic and unusual make-up of the renters. The landlord relayed the story he had been told, that the boys were all students and part of a mentoring program the renter was running. It didn't add up, so the neighbor watched closer.

When a car possessing Georgia plates pulled up to the curb late one night, and she saw a young boy being led inside, she decided it was time to act. A call was made to the police, who relayed the information to one of their detectives, a member of the FBI's Innocence Lost Taskforce. He quickly determined who was actually living in the house, and after obtaining a warrant, arrived there with a number of deputies.

Travis was caught trying to sneak out a back window wrapped in nothing but a bed sheet. Inside the home police found eight boys, five of them cowering in various rooms, with the youngest scared and naked in the room where Travis was caught trying to escape from. The detective called in the FBI, who took the boys into protective custody and then searched the home. They found very little. Computers were seized, but little was found other than various chatroom conversations and some travel arrangements. A file was found in a locked drawer. It contained the driver's licenses of the boys present and a few others who had passed through.

But the FBI soon found out that Travis had learned. The computers contained only the records of the last day's activities; the remaining hard drive was wiped clean. The driver's licenses all proved to be forgeries. Some of them were ridiculously apparent and others professionally done. They all claimed the boys to be eighteen or older. Interviews with the boys all had a common theme: while they were all underage, they had been provided with ID showing them to be eighteen or older. Scared and behind bars, the boys stuck to their script. Travis refused to speak without his lawyer present.

The FBI kept at it and eventually the boys turned on one another. Two of them were singled out as Travis's procurers. They would find boys that met his needs and recruit them through social media sites. After promising them money and a place to live, they would arrange to pick them up, hastily have an ID manufactured, then deliver them to Travis, who would use them to satisfy his own sexual needs until he lost interest in them, then throw them back onto the streets. The lawyers argued that the sex was consensual and, as far as Travis knew, the boys were all of legal age. After a three-hour hearing, at which was heard graphic testimony from several of the boys, the judge charged him with twelve counts of sexual trafficking, unlawful sexual contact, and human trafficking. His lawyer repeatedly countered that the boys were all of legal age and free to leave at any time. The case soon became one of technicalities. Travis was released on bond pending the trial.

It was at that point that William had entered his name into his computer.

Now he tapped keys and penetrated the email

traffic of the prosecuting attorney's office. What he found did not make him happy. The printer began to spit out paper.

The elevator doors opened, and William heard the familiar double click of the General's chair as it rolled over the gap in the door. He buzzed the man through the security door and watched his progress on a screen until he was close. He turned to find him navigating the distance with a plate of food balanced in his lap. A cup similar to William's rode in the chair's holder.

"Were you eating, sir? I didn't mean to interrupt."

"No, I was supposed to be but got caught up in what I was reading. Charlie scolded me and made me take it with me. He'll be looking for the empty plate when I get upstairs."

William chuckled. "How would you live without him?"

"Almost didn't once, but he's right, I forget to eat sometimes. He texts me when we're apart to make sure, and his spies are everywhere. He's recruited the entire staff. They all work for him now. I give up." The man locked his wheels before picking up half his sandwich. He pointed it at the man on the screen before taking a bite. "I know that face. Did something change?"

"Yes, sir." He handed the General several papers from the printer. "Evidently, the prosecutor is having doubts about the case. I have a statement vaguely attributed to him from a local reporter and a few emails between him and the judge. It comes down to the IDs, the man doesn't think the jury will get past them. They have no way of proving that Travis knew the boys were underage. The two boys who did the recruiting have lawyered up. The lawyers are being paid by one of the company investors. He has a record too, but we can't tie that to him. The FBI thinks they are both members of a trafficking ring, but so far, they can't connect the two. Either way, the boys won't talk—if they do, they lose their lawyers."

"So we're down to just the IDs? You're kidding me."

"No, I'm afraid not. While the stories are ... graphic, none of the actions are deemed illegal among consenting adults. The boys went willingly and knew to some extent what they were getting into. Most of them admitted to having lied about their age in the initial interviews. Some say that Travis asked them if they had younger friends who wanted to come with them, but it's all hearsay—I doubt the judge can allow it. Some of the boys are reported missing. They've run away again."

"Incredible. What's next?"

"The prosecutor will have to make a decision, but I don't think he has it. He's lost half his witnesses, and the others are keeping quiet. The IDs are a technicality yes, but one that the judge can't overlook. I think it's going to fall apart."

The General stewed while William continued to search through the man's emails. He clicked on another folder and soon found what he was looking for.

"Look at this."

The General donned his glasses and leaned in. The letter was still a draft, but its intention was clear.

"Son of a bitch." William printed the letter without being prompted.

"Where's this bastard at?"

William was ready for that one. A map appeared of southeast Florida, and then zoomed in on a modest home in Jupiter.

"He's at a smaller house up the coast, evidently staying out of sight."

"Who ...?"

"The closest is our newest: number twelve in Miami."

"Put it to a vote. Dayton can decide if she's ready."

The General looked down at the sandwich in his lap. His appetite had suddenly left him. He dumped the remainder in William's trashcan.

"Tell Charlie and I'll break your good leg."

William smiled. "Yes, sir."

---

"You called Eric?"

"Yeah, just once—he's fighting the flu."

"What did he suggest?"

"He said I need some criteria to narrow the field. Something we can use to separate our guy from the crowd. The problem is, I can't think of anything. Other than that, it's ruling them out. I thought they were one and the same, but when you think about it, they aren't."

"So, what have you done so far?"

"I now have several groups. This is my married pile, this is my single pile. I just don't see this guy as having a wife and kids while he's doing these things. The orange Post-its are over age fifty. I figured this is a young man's job."

"Not necessarily, but for now I'll agree. What else?"

"I thought about money, as in price tag of the cars they are driving or address of the houses they live in, but the job doesn't require much money really. And houses here cost a fortune anyway, so that's no help."

"Image is a big deal here. People will have cars they can't afford before they upgrade to a nicer house," Laurie added.

"Okay. Larry?"

"I agree with the marriage thing. This guy is single and a loner. Dr. Wong was pretty adamant on that. The money aspect—not so much. The tools needed are not high-dollar; you could have them in a standard two-car garage and the neighbors would never suspect."

Jack stood up straight. He'd been leaning over Sydney's shoulder for the last fifteen minutes looking at her computer screen. He stretched and paced. While he did so, the computer pinged.

"Two more possibilities out of Hollywood," Sydney read. "We've got to come up with something."

"A two-car garage," Jack muttered.

"What?"

"A two-car garage. He wouldn't have this gear at his home. It's a pile of evidence that directly ties him to the crime. No, he'd have it somewhere else. Another home maybe, or a storage facility. A hangar, or maybe even a boat."

Larry nodded. "Might be the trick. If we run all the single names through the property records, we might get a hit. But what if they own it in another name or even a company name? We'd have to find a way to cross-reference for storage units and what-not too. Boats can be registered somewhere thousands of miles away, then parked in Long Beach. Hell, the storage units themselves could be out-of-state even. Nevada is not that far away. Can we do it with the access we have?"

"I think so. But can we do it fast enough?"

They both looked at her, and she frowned.

"All right. I'll call him back."

# 9

*"No science is immune to the infection of politics and the corruption of power."*

—*Jacob Bronowski*

Jupiter was not a large town by Miami standards, but Anna soon found herself wishing it was. It was going to be that much harder to blend in—especially when the population was mostly made up of retirees. After reading as much as she could about the beachside town, she had used one of her IDs to reserve a room at a hotel in the tourist area. She hoped it would allow her to come and go without attracting unwanted attention. So now she drove north, in the center lane and just over the speed limit, while she reviewed the information she had gathered after the call.

She had read the file and voted soon after, before sitting by the phone and trying to ignore it. The anticipation about killed her, but eventually the call came. Dayton assigning her the target. The only catch being that she would have to gather intelligence and then wait. At first, she had been disappointed, taking it as an insult to her skills, but the professional side of her soon won over, and she pushed the thought aside. She was the new girl on her first assignment. Of course they would want her to take it slow.

She reviewed the target profile while she drove. A child molester, a repeat offender about to go free on a technicality. Why had she gotten the job? Was it because of the man she had caught before? The case where her actions had ultimately cost her job? She couldn't be sure, and she sure as hell was not going to ask. She pushed this thought aside as well.

Turning onto the last street, she slowed to just under the speed limit. The neighborhood was the very definition of ordinary. Older Florida-style one-story homes made of cinder block and covered in low-pitched roofs. The vegetation was thick and testified to the age of the area. But the yards were neat, and the cars were on the newer side. Middle class in all directions and on a fairly busy road. Travis was hiding in plain sight. Her camera on the dash was filming the homes as she passed, so she examined the other side of the street. One home caught her attention, and she slowed further to commit some information to memory. A block later, she sped up and found her way to a local grocery store parking lot. She jotted the information down before she forgot it, then made a phone call.

"Ockham."

"William, it's Anna. I have a request."

"Of course."

"There's a home for sale across the street from the target house. I need the four-digit code to the lockbox from the realtor. Also, if you could keep me informed of any scheduled showings she has, that would be great."

"I see. An excellent tactical move. I imagine I can have that information to you within a couple hours. The code may not be documented, and if not, I'll get you the top ten most likely combinations. Would you like me to keep the home empty for you?"

"How ...?"

"A simple raising of the price should do the trick. I'll run the comps on the area homes for sale and arrange for a typo in the listing. I'll also send you a magnetic sign that says Sale Pending. They seem to work very well for this situation. Perhaps you can borrow one from another sign until I do?"

"Oh? Uh, that would be great. What else?"

"I'll hack her cell and have the realtor's emails and text messages forwarded to your secure phone. I'll monitor the owner's email for you as well. If there is any movement, I should be able to warn you in plenty of time."

"That's ... great. More than I imagined. Can you get me a camera inside his house?" She laughed.

"I'm afraid there aren't any that I could find. I hacked a laptop in the home and found nothing other than personal bills and normal web traffic. If he's continuing with his ... activities, it's not by that route. The camera on the laptop is covered and the mic has been disabled.

He's using a pre-paid cell for communication and web access. He's being very careful, for now."

"For now?"

"It's been established that men such as he cannot go long without feeding their desires. Despite the pressure and scrutiny on him, I would not expect him to stay clean for long."

"I see."

"Do good work, Anna. But please, do not delay."

"I will, William. You'll call when everything is in place?"

"Of course."

"Then I shall get prepared on my end. Thank you, William."

"Thank you, Number Twelve."

---

ERIC HELD his head in both hands and groaned.

"Eric?"

The speakerphone had picked it up.

"Yeah, Jack. I'm here."

"Is what I'm asking possible?"

"Well ... yeah, technically. Take me a day or two, and I may have to hack my way into some of these databases if you don't have warrants ..." He let the last bit trail off on purpose.

"I can get them ... but it might take a while."

Eric read between the lines. Get started and Jack would catch up with the paperwork. "Let me see what I can do. Anything you'd like first?"

"Yes, the second properties. I'm thinking storage units would be the preferred choice. Second homes and warehouses after that. Big enough to store a van or two—there can't be many that size out there. We've been looking and most of them are on the small side."

"People with those big-ass RVs?"

"Most of them get stored outside."

"Okay, so you want me to narrow this down by age, race, marital status, and location. What's my search radius?"

"Let's go with an hour driving time from the location of the van."

"An hour? That's a huge amount of LA."

"Okay, half-hour, and we'll expand it as we rule out suspects."

"Better, not much, but better. Do I have the complete list? Is it in the file you just sent?"

"So far, we keep adding to it."

"Okay." Eric couldn't help but let a deep sigh escape. He hated being sick—worse yet he hated having to do anything while he was sick. If he had his way, he would just disconnect from the world and lie on the couch until he was not-sick. Drugs, Netflix, couch. That was all he wanted. He had even bribed the kid next door to walk Bear, something the dog was accepting for the moment. He seemed to understand.

"You all right, Eric? Syd tells me you're sick."

"That I am, but I'm getting over it—kind of. Might be a good thing actually. If you need this as fast as you say, I may need to be sick longer than I planned. This is definitely a work-from-home gig."

"Okay, if you need me or Deacon to say anything—"

"No, no. My boss isn't an ass, but he's not a fan of sharing me either. Even if I do carry three badges around with me. I'll get it done, but my head's kinda foggy, so it might take a bit longer than planned."

"Don't kill yourself. We'll work with what we have in the meantime the old-fashioned way."

"Okay, I'll let you know when I have something."

"Good man. Feel better."

"Will do, boss."

"Thanks, Eric."

Jack hung up the phone and stared at it.

"I'm getting fucking nowhere," he muttered.

---

ERIC THUMBED the phone off and forced himself up. He tugged his sweatpants higher as he made his way to the kitchen. The refrigerator contained condiments, old Chinese take-out, and an empty case of Mountain Dew.

The dog came in and looked as well. He offered a sympathetic look, but no help.

"This is not going to work, buddy."

He dialed the phone without looking. He had the neighbor's kid on speed-dial.

"Andy? Hey, it's Eric. You want to take Bear for a walk to the grocery store for me?"

Bear's tail thumped on the floor in approval.

---

CARTER WALKED the lot examining each vehicle. Like most dealerships they kept the vans in the back, preferring to use the flashy sports cars and luxury SUVs up front to attract the customers. It worked to his advantage as he preferred to be out of sight. Today was the only weekday the dealership stayed open late, and he was hoping to be seen by as few people as possible. He wore business attire and completed the look with a jacket and briefcase sitting on the front seat of the Mercedes-Benz. His pocket contained a stack of fake business cards in the event he should need one. He examined the lot from behind his sunglasses and saw two salesmen checking him out. Both of them were at least fifty pounds overweight and probably waiting for the other to decide if making the long walk to the back row was worth the effort. He pulled out his phone and made a show of doing some calculations until the younger of the two relented and started toward him.

"Take your time, fat boy," he muttered.

The wait proved to be the longest part of the transaction. Carter picked a van with low mileage and minimal upgrades. A work vehicle for his business, one he was rather vague about. The salesman didn't care, just wanted to speed the process up so he could get back to selling higher margin vehicles. He surprised Carter by examining his license closely before copying it and handing it back.

"Sorry, had some fake ones come through, and the boss is all over us."

"Uh-huh," Carter replied with a stone face.

The smaller man quickly got back to the paperwork, not wanting to offend the large man with the bulging biceps any further, and Carter almost smiled at his nervousness. It was different here in California. Back home in Mississippi he had grown up around white people who were proud of their racism. Here they were embarrassed by it, afraid of being labeled as such. Carter had learned to use it to his advantage either way. He let the man work without another word. The dummy account and money transfer set up by William went through without a hitch and in a few days, he would visit the dealership's computers and erase any evidence of the transaction. By then the van would be stripped of its serial numbers, scrubbed down with bleach, and stored safely away until he needed it.

Another day as Number Six. He estimated it would take him thirty minutes to get to the storage unit, ten minutes there maybe, followed by a taxi ride back to the dealership for the Mercedes. If the traffic wasn't too bad, he might make it to the gym just as the after-work crowd was leaving.

---

"So, what do we have?"

Jack paced the room in front of them. Sydney

had laid claim to half the table while Larry and Greg lounged in chairs at the other end. They all had stacks of paper on their laps or in front of them. A computer printout, from a dot-matrix printer on oversized perforated paper no less, sat in front of Sydney. It was at least two inches thick. The department was a bit behind as far as hardware went.

"So far, I've managed to find three suspects with storage facilities. All of them single, although one is recently divorced."

"I imagine this will house his share of the stuff," Greg commented without looking up.

Sydney frowned at him. "Perhaps. We should still check it out."

"Were you able to get the size and shape of the unit?"

"For that one it's ... ten-by-twenty. A bit small I think for what we're looking for."

"Maybe. Our guy could have more than one. What else?"

"The others are twenty-by-twenty. One of them is at the edge of the zone, but I have a former address which is fairly close, so that may be why."

"Any more?"

"My friend just texted me, saying she found three more. She's printing them off for me."

Jack frowned and tossed the papers down on the table before pacing again. His idea wasn't working. The thick printout mocked him. It represented three people. Three. With more on the way. If the list grew to twenty it would amount to weeks of work no matter how much manpower he could find.

"This is taking too long. He could be hiding his gear anywhere. We're in the second largest city in America for God's sake. We need another way."

He got only silence.

"C'mon guys, think. How else can we find this guy?"

"Taxes? Check their records and look for flags?"

"Maybe. We'd need an army of forensic accountants for that. What else?"

"Guns? Cross check the DLs against registration forms? He's got to have a few."

"I'm sure he does, but I doubt they are legally registered. If it were me, I'd have the least amount of paper in the system—for anything."

Larry spoke. "The van?"

"What about it?" Sydney asked. "It's clean. I went over it four times."

"Not that van. The one he's replacing it with. Or the motorcycle, for that matter. He'll need to replenish his supplies if he's going to do this again, right?"

Jack's mouth fell open. The van. How did he not see it? He recovered quickly.

"Sydney, get a list of the dealerships that handle this type of van. I want to know every sale made from a month prior of the shooting up to today. Larry, visit the newspapers and get a list of every classified ad for the same timeframe. Greg, you and Laurie do the same for Craigslist. We'll also need any magazine or weekly published in the area that handles vans. *Wheels 'n' Deals*, that kind of thing. What else?"

"Auctions?"

"Find 'em. What else?"

"Cars dot com?"

"Good, what else?"

Jack was now writing on the whiteboard so fast the marker was giving off an unnerving squeal.

"Okay, stop that please. I think that's enough to start with, don't you?" Sydney asked.

Jack reviewed the list with the marker raised.

"All right, let's start there. If you think of something else, add it. Let's go."

CARTER PARKED the new van right where its predecessor had been. This time the van was black, and he had already decided to leave it that way. Affirmative Action, he told himself. A few changes would be made after he'd sterilized it, but having done it twice before he knew it would take him about six hours. He removed the temporary tag from the bumper and replaced it with a forged plate. The paperwork went into a metal wastebasket, and after deactivating the smoke alarm, he set it aflame. He checked the supplies on hand while they burned and made a short shopping list. Disc for the grinder. Sandpaper. Bleach. There was not enough time to make the changes tonight and he had to get back to the dealership and retrieve the Mercedes. He'd come back tomorrow maybe, or the day after, then spend a few hours grinding numbers off of parts and peeling away stickers.

Satisfied with his purchase, he reset the camera and left the unit locked behind him. He walked out the gate without looking at the office and turned right. The street here was semi-commercial. Paint shops, landscaping supplies, used car dealerships, and pawnshops. He walked a block north to a corner restaurant, sat down on the bench outside, and called for a cab. The ten-minute wait was spent thinking about how he was going to replace the motorcycles. The press had run a few follow-up pieces about the shooting, but it said little about the FBI. He was wondering if they had found the bikes. If so, it would be some time before he could chance replacing them. Two months would probably be safe enough. He'd wait until then, unless he heard something different. He tapped out a secure text to William with his arrival and departure times to the storage unit just as the cab pulled up.

The cab driver was not the talkative type and dropped him in the middle of the dealership lot without a word before driving out past the two salesmen standing in the same spot Carter had found them. He followed a minute later and was barely glanced at before pulling out.

# 10

*"Corruption is the enemy of development, and of good governance. It must be got rid of. Both the government and the people at large must come together to achieve this national objective."*

—Pratibha Patil

It was late. Anna saw fewer and fewer house lights as she jogged her way deeper into the neighborhood. She was actually later than she wanted to be, but the problem of finding a parking spot within range—one that would not call attention—had proven to be harder than she had thought. She had eventually chosen a spot down the street from what looked to be a popular neighborhood bar. She had two hours before it closed to get the job done and get out.

She slowed to a power-walk as she passed the house and gave it a good look from the sidewalk. No lights from the front. No cameras that she could see. A sign from an alarm company she had never heard of. William had reported no security system on the house, so the sign was probably a fake. The faint glow of a lamp from a back bedroom and that was all.

Good.

She picked up the pace and did another lap around the block. Traffic was nonexistent at this hour, so she moved to the street. The fanny pack bounced uncomfortably against her back, and she ignored it as best she could. With any luck, it would be empty soon.

Passing the house again she saw no change, so she turned her attention to the homes on both sides and across the street. Mostly dark. A light two doors down, but on the same side. Nothing that would trigger her to change plans.

She jogged up to the house for sale and squatted in front of the key box hanging on the front door handle. Consulting a piece of tape on her arm, she tried the first set of numbers. No. She repeated the process three more times before finding the right combination. The box clicked open, and a house key fell into her hand.

"Thank you, William," she whispered before moving inside and locking the door behind her.

She paused and listened while her eyes adjusted to the dark interior. The streetlights outside and the half-moon provided enough light for her to navigate without the use of a flashlight, and she quickly determined that the house was indeed empty. The lamp on the timer in the back bedroom clicked off, startling her, but she welcomed the darkness after her initial flinch. She returned to the kitchen and unloaded the fanny pack on the counter. Sorting the items out and checking that they had survived the bouncing travel here took less than a minute. She prowled the rooms facing the street and examined every window.

A small front bedroom provided the best option. The previous owner had covered the south-facing window with heavy curtains, and they had been left behind for the new owners. Perhaps the person had worked nights and slept during the day? For whatever the reason, they were opaque and covered half the window even when it was open. Even better, they hid an electrical outlet on the right side.

"Lucky girl," Anna told herself as she stood on her tiptoes to place the item. She extended the antenna horizontally across the top of the rod, then taped the cord against the window frame, leaving just enough to reach the outlet. She smiled when the little green light flashed three times before going dark. The breaker to this outlet was still on, saving her a search for the electrical box. More luck. She double-checked her placement, then found a dark room to use her phone in. She entered a security code and the view from the camera popped up on the tiny screen, giving her a direct view of Travis's house across the street. She looked for any needed adjustments, but decided the view was as good as it was going to get. She played with the zoom and the brightness for a minute before being satisfied.

Time to go.

She gathered up the trash and stuffed it into the pack before slipping it back around her waist. She rubbed her fingers together in response to the superglue—she was still not used to it. The fingerless sports gloves would prevent any palm prints, and her hair was gelled and tied back. Footprints in the carpet were mixed among many. The house had not been vacuumed since being put on the market. She reviewed her actions inside and found no reason to believe she had left anything behind. The camera would run indefinitely until it was unplugged, and for twelve hours after that on battery. She had removed any identifying marks and serial numbers the day after she had purchased it. The key would be coming with her. Realtors were always forgetting to put them back. Hopefully, it would keep the camera from being discovered until after she was done with it.

"Time to go." She said it out loud this time, urging herself to move faster.

She examined the street in both directions before slipping back out the door. She locked it from the inside and pulled it shut until she felt the click. With a quick wipe of the knob, she jogged back to the street. Thirty minutes later she was at her car. Several others had since joined it, and she heard the music spike in volume when someone opened the door of the bar a block away. Not liking the increase in traffic, she made a quick exit, took the corner without stopping and headed north, away from her hotel.

A block away Dayton watched from the seat of a rental car and nodded approval.

---

JACK RATTLED the ice in his glass before setting it down and the bartender responded.

"Another, Mr. Randall?"

"Please."

The young man poured generously, then paused. He'd recognized his customer but hadn't let on. He'd learned the hard way that it often prompted their exit, and that hurt his tip jar. Not that they got many celebrities in here—the hotel was far from being one of the better ones in town. Mostly he served businessmen who were traveling through, or relatives whose families lacked enough room. Occasionally a hooker would park herself at a table in hopes of working the guests, but the owner would quickly point them to the door. Tonight he had Jack and a couple of men with laptops and papers over in the corner. A slow night; he had time to talk.

"Can I get you something from the kitchen?"

"No, just the Scotch tonight."

"That bad of a day?"

"I'm celebrating a lack of progress—so to speak."

"Had those myself."

Jack swallowed a healthy portion before looking the kid over. His name tag read Herman. He was barely old enough to serve liquor, but Jack wasn't one to judge. He'd been doing far more dangerous things than drinking at that age. Herman had a textbook hidden under the bar. No doubt it would appear once the manager left for the night.

"Herman? You don't see that name much on a guy your age—not these days."

"My mom wanted to be a writer. She read a lot of Herman Wouk."

"Your mom has good taste. Do a guy a favor, Herman?"

"What's that?"

"You have a spare bottle of this stuff tucked away somewhere?"

Herman glanced toward the door and the front desk beyond. Jack produced a C-note and laid it on the bar.

"I might have an extra someplace."

THE ASPIRIN BOTTLE RATTLED, and Sydney ignored the fact that Jack was self-medicating again. The red eyes and pained expression told her the alcohol was back. She wanted to confront Larry, who had left without him the night before, but had not had the chance. Stymied, she dove into the job.

While Jack had been tying one on, she and Eric had been going over the records that had come in. So far, they had found three possibilities. She tossed them in front of Jack, but after taking a look at the size of the font he shook his head.

"Just give me the highlights."

"Okay." She let her frown show. "Number one is a guy from Venice. He fits the description. He's single and has recently rented some warehouse space near the water. He's a software engineer and works from home. No kids and no family that we can find other than a sister on the east coast. We have a unit heading there to look around, but until then we wait.

"Number two. A guy in Hollywood. Same thing as far as description and single status. He's a writer —screenplays and TV. Looks like a Bruce Willis film in the past, but nothing big since. He's managed to invest it wisely and has the money to throw at something like this. Just rented a storage unit last month. We're checking it out as well."

"What does he write?"

"I'm sorry?"

"What does he write? What kind of books?"

"They're scripts, not books. Mostly blood and thunder. Terrorism, cops and robbers, that kind of stuff. Why?"

"Just wondering. Any history in the military?"

"No, he's just making it up."

"Okay. What else?"

"Number three. A security consultant. Has a condo in Van Nuys. Still tracking down his history, but he seems to have a good income. Nice car. Not finding much, so it's raising some flags with Eric."

"If he works security, he may have taken steps to not be found easily."

"True, but we should have found something by now."

"Let me know when you do. What about the vans? Any luck there?"

"Fourteen purchases since the shooting. We're tracking them down and sorting them by private versus not. The private ones we'll check out first."

Jack paced and rubbed his aching head. The aspirin had yet to kick in, but he was treating his hangover with water and hoping for the best. He caught Sydney's look and avoided eye contact. He needed to get out of here.

"Let me see the list?"

Sydney pushed it across the desk without a word. He grabbed a highlighter and started circling items. She watched without a word.

"These are all fairly close together. Larry and I will pay them a visit."

"You're going to visit them yourself?"

"With Larry," he confirmed. "Can I have some DL pictures to take with me, mom?"

Sydney opened her mouth to reply, but a shake of Larry's head behind Jack told her not to go there. She instead fetched the driver's license photos from a nearby file and handed them over.

"Good luck. Enjoy the fresh air."

Jack ignored her snark and gathered the pile. He stalked out of the room without a word.

"You got him?" Sydney asked Larry, her worry showing through.

"I got him."

---

"A YIPPY DOG. GREAT."

Anna watched from her car as Travis left his. Reaching in the back, he pulled forth a small dog of questionable heritage. The dog was set on the hot asphalt and immediately tried to scamper away only to be yanked back by Travis. He donned a pair of sunglasses and with a quick look around set off down a sidewalk. Anna let him get around the bend before following.

It was the weekend, and the park was somewhat crowded. A typical mild and sunny day. A mix of retirees and soccer moms moved in all directions at a variety of speeds. Anna had worn her active wear under her clothes for just such an event and was now blending in with others using the trails. She spotted Travis about fifty yards ahead and, not wanting to catch up, she stopped to retie a shoe.

The dog was a problem. As Dayton had mentioned in training, they tended to bark at everything and give your position away. "Worse than monkeys," he had said. She didn't ask for an explanation to that one. Either way, it was something to factor in. She resumed her pursuit in time to see him yank the dog on their way—clearly they were not here for its benefit.

So what was it for then? To attract kids? To help him blend in? She couldn't be sure. The only thing she was sure of was that Travis was not here to exercise.

She got her answer ten minutes later. The path ended and circled around a set of soccer fields. They were full of both the yells of children and their parents. Coaches screamed instructions and refs blew whistles. The traffic increased ten-fold, and she lost sight of her target for moments at a time as they both weaved through the crowd.

Then he stopped.

A dog park. One with a low fence around it and several picnic tables inside. Travis opened the double gate and yanked the little dog through. They were immediately investigated by a small group of canines and Travis released the mutt to play. The dog was soon running with the pack, and Travis was examining the picnic tables. Most held a few people, but one was empty. She watched him walk over and casually sit down. From his seat he had a perfect view of the boys playing soccer. She circled around and joined the line at the concession stand. A soccer mom made small talk, and she returned it while she waited and watched Travis over her shoulder. He was ignoring the dogs and staring at the kids.

Finding herself at the front of the line she was forced to order something. A menu of junk food was displayed on the overhead sign, and she searched in vain for something she could stomach.

A bottle of water and a pretzel was the best she could do, and she took her purchase to a far table that gave her a profile view of the man she was tracking. She nibbled the pretzel and searched for the opportunity Dayton said was there.

Travis stood and she almost did as well, but he simply fished a cell phone out of his pocket and scanned the screen before working it with his thumbs. A call or text? Something that William could possibly intercept?

No. The pretzel turned in her stomach as she saw him carefully angle the phone and take several pictures of the boys playing. Her fists clenched and she felt her neck grow hot. The Monster roared inside her and it was all she could do to not jump the fence and beat the man to death. She struggled with it, gripping the table until her knuckles turned white.

But there were too many people. They crossed her view repeatedly until she reined the monster in. She watched another dog owner approach him and inquire about the vacant seat. He offered it with grace and the woman parked her ample bottom next to his before releasing her own yippy dog to the pack. She watched him smile and make conversation with her. The phone was now gone. A wolf in sheep's clothing

—the woman had no idea what she was sitting next to.

"I know what you are, you bastard. You and I will meet real soon," Anna promised him. She rose and tossed her trash in the nearby bin before stalking away. The suppressed rage prompted her to pick up the pace, and she was soon running down the path with the others, weaving in and out of the walkers and kids playing.

Dayton watched without following.

MAJOR WESLEY PHILLIPS shook his head and pulled his eyes away from the logbook. His mind kept wandering and that was not a good thing. Settling back in the pilot's seat, he gazed out at the mountains overlooking Incirlik airbase, the tips of which were still glowing in the setting sun. He watched the light climb upwards until the peaks were in shadow. A glance at the cockpit clock told him the sun was right on time. The light would linger long enough for them to take off—a pinky, they called it—but it did little to settle his uneasiness. Even if everything went as planned, they would be back long before the sun made another appearance.

"As planned," he muttered before checking behind him. The loadmaster and engineer were still standing on the ramp, too close to hear him. He scolded himself for speaking out loud and then again for getting himself in this situation. "As planned" had taken on a new meaning.

But they needed the money. His wife was still looking for a job and with the kids, the moving expenses, and the bills from his mother-in-law's recent illness, there was never enough. It pissed him off. He'd tried every way he could of rationalizing the situation, but always ended up at a dead end. Eventually, he had faced facts; there was no excuse. He'd done everything right. He'd pulled the grades in high school and mowed countless lawns to pay for flying lessons. He'd put himself through collage and a commission in the Air Force before marrying Pam. War had come, and they had put off any plans for a family until after, only to find out there was no after. Hundreds of combat missions. His plane shot up twice. His unit broken up and rebuilt only to be broken up again. Eventually, he'd become part of a conglomeration known as the 486th Air Expeditionary Group. From there, they had moved him around so many times he'd lost track. Now here he was, years after the war had supposedly ended, flying tactical airdrops to the enemy of our enemy, while his wife raised their two little ones at home on a shoestring budget. If he'd been smart, he'd be flying a 757 out of Louisville for UPS instead of flying a C-130 out of Turkey for Uncle Sam.

At least that was how he rationalized things.

How the stranger had found him he didn't know. But the man knew all about his problems. He knew his record and where he was being stationed. He knew where and who he flew with and all about them. He knew how much debt he owed. He knew all of those things before that day in the bar when he had sat down next to Phillips and struck up a conversation. A day later, Wes had said yes and then sweated every knock on the door and every ring of the phone for a week after.

But it had proved to be remarkably easy. The pallets would arrive from the rigging shed as they always did. Wrapped and strapped and covered in a nylon net that was secured to the aluminum plate they sat on. Chalk marks marking the center of gravity. He'd watched the loadmaster examine each one carefully and when they raised no alarms with him, he had stopped worrying. Whoever he was working for was inside the system and he decided it was best that he stop thinking about who they were and how they had gotten there and just do the job they were paying him for. The pallets found their way to the ground at the coordinates provided and the money was in his dummy account soon after. And the business of war went on.

A metallic noise brought him out of his reflection, and he turned to see the two men pushing the loaded pallet into the plane. The rollers on the deck made it possible for the two of them to do so despite its large size and weight. A bark from the loadmaster and the load stopped right at the predetermined anchor point, the chalk on the floor lining up with the line on the pallet. Wes watched as they circled it twice and double-checked each pallet lock. The two men spoke with gestures only they knew due to the noise of the flight line outside, but he could still make out the gravelly voice of the loadmaster.

While he couldn't make out the words, he was confident the majority of them spoken by the man were of the four-letter variety. Master Sergeant Billy Harpe had been in the Air Force since Wes was a "punk-ass kid" and had let him know it a few times. Wes had taken the ribbing in stride as he was glad to have him on his crew. Most people on being introduced to the man would describe him as "Crusty." Old School and politically incorrect among his peers, he could switch to a charming southern gentleman a second later should someone's wife appear. He viewed every pilot as someone trying to kill him, and as a result did not suffer fools very well, nor was he afraid to speak up and call out anyone—regardless of their rank —for being stupid. While competent and smart, he had very little use for Air Force protocol and formalities that had nothing to do with mission accomplishment. The ever-present unlit cigar in his mouth went ignored as a result, even by Wes's superiors. The man got the job done, and Wes had long since stopped worrying about the back of the plane. Among the crew he was known as Harpo, and he was infamous among his peers.

The man standing next to the Master Sergeant was also infamous. Flight Engineer John Miller was the opposite of his colleague when it came to speaking his mind but matched him in professionalism at every level. An honor graduate of his school at Little Rock AFB he had found his way to the flight line from the engine shop where he had earned the name Cyborg for his mechanical way of both speaking and performing his duties. Rarely one to show emotion or initiate any conversation, Wes had been on the fence about him for some time before overhearing Harpo boast about his abilities. He soon discovered that the man lived and breathed the plane they flew in and knew every function inside and out, often quoting the technical manuals verbatim while he worked. Their only effort to get the man to relax and open up had required six drinks, and even then, the conversation was about flying. Wes and Harpo had carried him back to the BOQ and dumped him in his bunk to sleep it off, and they had never spoken of it again. Now Wes watched him nod his head in response to Harpo's ever ongoing rant while they examined the load from every angle.

His view was suddenly blocked by the appearance of his copilot. His face was grim as he climbed the three steps into the cockpit and took his seat on the right side.

"Where's the Mattress?"

"I left him in the head. Any problems?"

"Not so far. The wind is picking up and changing direction at the PI, that'll help a little, as long as he doesn't get too curious."

"And if he does?"

"We'll kill that weed when it grows."

The copilot tapped the yoke and frowned. He had wanted to try and bring the new navigator in on the deal, but Wes had vetoed the idea. Yes, it was more money for them and there was always the risk that he would turn them down or even report them, but it would make the mission so much easier if he knew. What the man didn't know was that he had already made such a drop with them twice before, and if necessary, they could use that against him. But the man was not the assertive type, and while technically competent, he was not the sharpest knife in the drawer. As a result he had been assigned to a strong pilot and crew in an effort to even his weaknesses out. The crew had dubbed him "The Mattress" behind his back after the man had made a feeble attempt to assert some authority by writing up the mattress of the crew bunk in the logbook for being too thin. Wes was counting on his weak spine and timid character to not question his authority when he changed the mission tonight.

"You all right with this?"

"Yeah."

Before they could say more, a shout came from the back. Their navigator had arrived, and as usual Harpo loudly accused him of getting lost on the way. The man smiled at the man's joke and nearly stumbled from the clap on the back he received as he walked up the ramp. Wes noticed him frowning at the crew bunk before he climbed the steps and joined them. Tugging on his gear he eventually

landed in his seat, his laptop bouncing once before landing on the flat surface of the navigation
station. He pushed his glasses up his nose and
smiled at his pilot.

"Major."

"Glad you could make it, Jim."

The young captain just nodded at the rebuke
and turned to his station.

Wes exchanged a look with his copilot before
turning back to his logbook and made a quick no-
tation before storing it in his helmet bag. His
copilot took the cue and pulled out his checklist,
beginning the process of starting the engines. He
secured it to his yoke before turning to locate the
engineer. Cyborg was already walking toward him,
but he still made the finger twirl telling him it was
time to go. The man just nodded and climbed into
this seat without a word.

"We're all here, Wes."

Phillips craned his neck around and saw
everyone in their seats. A glance outside showed
Harpo, a cable trailing from his helmet, standing
by with a groundsman. A pair of wheel chocks
were at their feet, but there were more still in
place. As the Aircraft Commander they would not
proceed until he gave the word.

"Okay, let's get this thing off the ground."

"Before Starting Checklist," the copilot commanded.

The arms of the navigator appeared over the head of the pilot, and Wes watched with half-interest as the engineer configured the plane for start-up. Fuel. Bleed air. Auxiliary power. Generators. His hands moved with a fluid grace, and Wes found himself wondering if his engineer could do this in the dark before dismissing the thought and moving his gaze to his copilot. He followed his movements as he cycled through the screens and instruments. When the last one was set and checked, the man turned to see the engineer giving him a thumbs-up. He moved on without missing a beat.

"Forms?"

"Checked."

"Oxygen?"

"Set."

The list continued on. Flight parameters. Flight plan. Waypoints. DZ parameters. GPS. Radios.

"Clear APU?"

Harpo's grave voice sounded in their ears from outside. "Clear."

"EFI and Radar?"

"On."

"Standby ATTD?"

"ISOL DC."

"Lights?"

"Fuel?"

"Checked."

"Ramp and Doors?"

"Neutral."

The copilot paused while he checked the hydraulic panel.

"Parking brake?"

"Set and checked. Remove chocks," Wes replied.

"Removed."

"Before start checks?"

Each crewman sounded off. "Complete."

Wes looked outside and located his loadmaster before proceeding. "Clear on three, Harp?"

"Number three clear."

Wes reached overhead and pushed in the start switch for the number three engine and held it down. "Turning."

Behind him, Cyborg monitored the start, checking the engine bleed air and APU generator switches.

"Remove externals."

"Removed."

The crew repeated the process until all four

engines were running to the engineer's satisfaction.

"Start engine checks?"

They again responded in turn. "Complete."

"Well, all right then. Let's go for a ride."

Wes gave a thumbs-up to the airman on the apron, who saluted in return and with a wave of his wand shooed the plane in the direction of the runway.

"Tower, Forge 858. Clear to taxi?"

"Roger 858, clear to taxi."

Wes slipped the brakes and advanced the throttles, and the Hercules bumped its way over the expansion joints to the thick white strip. Wes applied the brakes and announced their readiness by advancing the throttles.

"Can somebody check on Harpo?"

Cyborg leaned to the side and peered into the rear of the plane. He could just make out the sergeant lounging on the red webbing of the fold-down seats. He already had a dog-eared novel in his hand.

"He's good."

"Tower 858, clear for takeoff?"

"Affirm 858, clear for takeoff."

Phillip's clicked the mic twice in reply before releasing the brakes. The plane responded slowly but built speed at a steady rate. Built for transporting heavy equipment over long distances, its takeoff was anything but exciting. But the massive wings coupled with the raw power of the four engines didn't require much space with so light of a load. At one hundred and twenty knots, he pulled back on the yoke and the aircraft eased into the sky.

"Gear up. Flaps up," the copilot announced as he threw the switches.

"Gear up," his pilot muttered back. It was one of his favorite things to hear.

Phillips waited until the flaps were fully up, then eased the C-130 into a climbing turn to the east. He could just make out the face of his copilot in the green glow of the instruments.

He was still frowning.

# 11

---

*"There is no compromise when it comes to corruption.
You have to fight it."*

—A. K. Antony

"He say why he was buying it?"
"For some business he had. I really didn't ask since he was buying it in his

name. Kind of funny now that you mention it, he missed out on the write-off."

Jack exchanged a look with Larry. So far, they had visited two dealerships and found nothing. The third had provided this man, Marty James, car salesman and aspiring actor. He had headshots on the wall and two different sets of business cards. He had been curiously cooperative once Jack flashed his badge and asked about the van. He described a large black man who fit the description of one of the suspects. He'd narrowed the man down to two of the photos he'd been shown before slipping up and saying they all looked alike to him. He now fidgeted and repeatedly looked over Jack's shoulder at the customers wandering the lot.

"We'll be done in just a minute. You say he drove a Mercedes here? How did he get the van home?"

"He drove it. Came back for the car in a cab later."

"How long was he gone?"

"Oh, I don't know. Maybe a half hour, little more. He might be on the security tapes."

"Might?"

Marty lowered his voice. "The owner's cheap. The front cameras facing the high dollar stuff are real, the rest are fake. We keep the vans in the back row." He shrugged as if the rest were self-explanatory.

"You remember what cab company?"

"United."

"That was awful fast, you sure?"

"Yup, they're the only ones with that ugly-ass green paintjob. Dropped him off right at his car and he pulled out heading north."

"Same direction he went in the van?"

"I ... don't remember. Sorry."

"Okay. This was right before you closed, you said?"

"Yeah. Hey—I want to help and all, but I gotta make a living here. Are we about done?"

"Yeah, sure. We can call you at this number you gave us?"

"Sure, sure. Just give me a call." He stood.

"Thanks."

Marty left them in his glass cubicle and was shaking the hand of an elderly gentleman standing next to a new Lexus a few seconds later. They watched him work for a bit before dismissing him.

"What do you think?" Larry asked.

"I think my headache just got better. Let's go visit this cab company."

"The fifth you say? That'd be a Wednesday!"

The man shouted the question as if he were going to be challenged. The noise of the mechanics working in the garage penetrated the thin walls of the office and made him hard to hear. Larry imagined he'd been shouting no matter where he was for many years. He placated the man.

"Yes, I believe it was. Right around seven p.m., took him to the Ford dealership on Lankershim!" Larry was shouting now too; the man seemed not to care.

The man squinted at the computer as he rolled the mouse with a bony finger. Larry guessed his age at one hundred and ten. He wore an old windbreaker over a spotted company shirt despite the stuffy and warm interior. The radio squawked behind him, and he answered it with a shout before going back to the screen.

"That'd be Duke! You're lucky, he's right outside! Guy in the grey hat! His name's John Wain, but we call him Duke! Get it?"

Larry forced a grin. "Yeah, I get it. Can we talk to him?"

"Until his cab's fixed, then I need him back out on the road!"

"All right, we'll be quick!"

Larry heaved himself out of the chair and bolted for the door. He found Jack pacing in the doorway of the garage with his jacket over his shoulder. The gun and badge were making the workers nervous. Jack pretended not to notice.

"What you got?"

Larry turned himself and Jack around until their target was behind him.

"See the guy with the grey hat? He's the one that drove our suspect. How you want to do this?"

"What do you mean?"

"Well, detective, if you haven't noticed yet, there seems to be a common south-of-the-border theme here. If he runs, I'm sure as hell not chasing him."

Jack looked the man over again behind his sunglasses. "He's not a runner, just curious. I'm sure the FBI is not something they see here every day."

"Okay, your turn."

Jack smiled and walked around his partner and directly at the man. Glancing at the papers in his hand, he approached and stopped. Duke made no move to flee. Jack looked up as if just noticing he was there.

"You must be Duke?"

"Yeah, that's me, but I didn't do it."

Jack smiled his best disarming smile. "Not here for you. Nothing like that. Just have a question about a fare you drove the other night."

"All right. Lots of fares, though."

"Big black guy, huge. You picked him up and took him to the Ford dealership in Burbank?"

"Yeah, I remember him. Dude was big all right —he barely fit in the back. Not a talker. He read the paper the whole way, so I just shut up and drove, ya know?"

"Would you know him again if you saw him?"

"His face? Doubt it. He wore sunglasses and then he was behind the paper the rest of the time. I mean, he wasn't an ass or anything. Paid cash and left me a decent tip. Just wasn't really sociable. Only reason I remember him at all was 'cause he was so big."

"Tell me about where you picked him up."

"Oh, uh, hold on. They all kind of run together after a bit. Was it up in Sun Valley? Right on the edge of the industrial section?"

"Yeah, there about."

"He was outside the corner restaurant there on Roscoe, by the cement company, I think."

"Okay. You remember him carrying anything? Briefcase or a bag of some kind?"

"No, just the newspaper. What did this guy do?"

"Not sure yet. Just need to ask him some questions. You've been a big help, Duke, thanks."

"Sure, uh ..."

Jack disengaged before Duke could ask his next question and walked to the car. Larry got behind the wheel and started it up before asking the obvious.

"Where to?"

"Sun Valley. Roscoe Avenue. Near the cement plant."

"I know it. Maybe a half hour. More if there's traffic."

"Well, let's go. I don't want to lose our momentum."

---

"WHAT'S IN THE BACK?"

Wes pulled his eyes from the instruments and listened closely. Other than heading changes and resetting the radar altimeter, the flight had been uneventful so far. They had checked in with the AWACS bird, which was monitoring and controlling the traffic around them, then maintained radio silence while they flew over the border into Iraq. Now the boredom had prompted questions from the idle mind of their navigator. The inquiry was aimed at the engineer and thankfully not directed at him. He glanced in the reflection of the upper window in time to see the engineer shrug in reply.

"You don't know?"

"Arms for the Kurds, I imagine," Wes answered for him in an attempt to control where the conversation was going.

"So, you don't know what it is?" This time the navigator was looking directly at the engineer, who shrugged again before replying. "I know how much it weighs."

"How much it weighs? Nobody is curious as to what it is we're dropping out of the sky to these people?"

Wes adopted his command voice. "No, I'm not. And I'd advise you not to worry about it, either, Captain. Not only is it above your pay grade, it's probably not something you *want* to know. We're the deliverymen. We don't shake the package before we drop it off."

"But ..."

"Did you ever stop to think you might be better off being in the dark?" the copilot chimed in before shaking his head at the man's naiveté. "It's called deniability in case you're still not getting it."

The navigator swallowed the remark and bit his lip. He was about to say something to help his case when the radio squawked.

"Forge 858, contact Dragnet on Blue."

"Copy Dragnet on Blue."

The copilot consulted a mission card on his kneeboard before selecting the frequency matched to that color. He keyed the mic and spoke clearly.

"Forge 858 up on Blue."

"Roger 858, go secure."

The copilot dialed in a second frequency, this one scrambled.

"858."

"Roger 858. Update: winds at PI now out of the east at seven knots, gusting to ten. DZ secure. Possible AA in the area. Ground signal is Alpha, repeat Alpha. You are cleared to proceed."

"Roger. Good copy all. 858 out."

Wes exchanged a look with his copilot before holding up two fingers. He got a silent nod and flipped his cards to one containing his own notes. The navigator was typing furiously behind them.

"If we come in from the north ..."

"Negative," Wes answered. "Those guys are sitting on the ridgeline, and the wind is always slower in the valley. We learned it the hard way last year. We'll go with option two."

"Two? That puts our approach over ISIS territory."

"They have nothing that can reach us. We drop the package dead into the wind, and hope it stays between the mountains."

"What about the anti-aircraft?"

"A heavy machine gun with no thermal or radar capabilities? They'll be shooting at our noise and never see us. We'll stay above base plus six just to be sure, but we drop into the wind and between the mountains, or we won't even come close."

The navigator wanted to protest further, but he caught the copilot glaring at him in the glass, so he changed his mind and returned to his computer. The copilot let out a sigh of relief when the man gave up. The wind was actually stronger the closer you got to the ground, channeled and guided by the mountains it was blowing into. Luckily, the navigator did not know this yet. Plotting a new course as instructed, he sent it to his pilot. The plane banked right, deeper into Iraqi airspace.

Below them now was ISIS.

"THAT THE PLACE?"

"It's what he described." They both examined the mom-and-pop diner until the light turned green. Since there was nobody behind them, Larry stayed put.

"What now? You want to go in?"

"No, let's cruise the area a bit."

Larry turned left, circling the block. Jack's hunch was rewarded when he saw the storage facility. Larry turned in without being prompted. Through the filthy windows, they saw an elderly woman sitting behind the desk with her feet up. A TV flickered against the wall, and she studied it intently between puffs on her cigarette. She didn't even look up when they entered.

"Rates are on the wall there. I got a ten-by-ten and a ten-by-twenty available, but that's it." She pointed at a dusty sign with her smoke before taking another puff.

Jack squinted at her through the haze. The show was a soap opera—not that he watched them, but it was easy to tell. The loaded ashtray and the condition of the office told him a lot about the woman's priorities. Still, he had spotted two cameras outside, so he was hoping for the best.

With a look from Larry, they both pulled their badges.

"FBI, ma'am. We'd like to ask you some questions."

That got her attention, but only for a moment. She glanced at them for all of one second before opening a drawer and grabbing a card. She puffed again before extending it, her eyes never leaving the screen.

"Call the owner. I just man the office."

Jack took the offered card but said nothing. Obviously, he was going to have to get her attention some other way. He circled around the desk she had her feet up on and examined its contents. Next to the ashtray was a covered travel mug. The stains on the blotter however were not coffee brown. He reached out and picked up the remote. The TV died.

"What the hell?" the woman protested. "I gave you the man's card. Call him. I got nuthin' to tell."

"Oh, we will. Maybe we'll discuss the contents of your desk drawer there when we do."

The woman glanced down to see the neck of

the bottle sticking out of the drawer and preventing its closure. She quickly stuffed it inside and slammed it shut.

"None of your business either."

Jack examined her again. Not as old as he had first thought, just aging rapidly. Her skin and face spoke of a diet consisting of cigarettes and alcohol. Her defiant expression did little to hide the fear below the surface.

"We're not here for you, but if you give me a hard time, I can change my mind. Is that what you want?"

Jack's tone brooked no argument and the woman's bravado quickly faded. Her shoulders slumped, and she sat up to stub the smoke out in the overflowing tray. Jack swiped the pack of Pall Malls off the desk before she could grab another.

"What you want?"

Larry stepped forward with a picture, a blowup of the suspect from his driver's license. "You seen this man? Is he a customer here?"

"Nope."

"That was awful quick, try again. He's big, a bodybuilder. Might be driving a van."

She frowned at them before opening the top drawer of the desk and putting on a pair of glasses. They were a decade out of style and morphed her eyes into large orbs. She examined the picture again.

"Maybe. If he is I haven't seen him in a while. Everyone has a key code for the gate. They come and go as they please. I only see them if there's a problem. And as long as they pay their rent, there's no problem."

Jack examined the filthy windows and the view from her seat. She could see the entrance and the street for a few yards in either direction, but that was about it. Unless she was staring at the TV of course.

"Those cameras work?"

"I think so. They run on a loop. It resets itself every few days. I just make sure it's plugged in, and that green light is showing. Rotate the discs."

"You don't watch the feed?"

"Nope. Used to. Had a TV for that next to this one, but it crapped out months ago. Fourth time. The owner said screw it, he's not gonna buy another one." She shrugged.

"Rotate the discs?"

"Yup." She opened the top drawer again and pulled out two computer discs. They were labeled ONE and THREE. Disc two was obviously in the machine. "I don't know how it works, I just do what he says. Can I have my remote back?"

"Not yet. How late are you here every day?"

"Until five."

Jack gave her a look.

"Maybe four sometimes. Like I said, they can come and go all they want. They don't need me to let 'em in and out."

"Be right back." Larry walked out and headed to the car.

"Where's the owner?"

"Long Beach is where he's living, I think. He owns a few dozen of these places. He or one of his bratty kids drops by every few months. Otherwise, I never see him. What'd this guy do? Last one was storing drugs. They busted him last year. One before that had a couple hot cars. Why they gotta pick this place?"

Jack ignored her as Larry came back in. He handed Jack his laptop before reaching over and grabbing the discs. The woman watched silently as he copied each one, including the one from the machine. She glanced at it long enough to see the green light before turning back to them.

"My remote?"

"A list of the renters, then we'll leave."

She let out a sigh before giving up and reaching in the file cabinet. After scrounging for a minute she pulled a list from a worn and stained file.

"Here's the one from three months ago. Supposed to update it when a new renter comes in but haven't had one since then." She tossed it to Jack, then took a sip of her drink. Jack caught a whiff, and his stomach protested.

"That'll be fine. What did you say your name was?"

"My name? Her Royal Highness Queen Shanequah, ruler of Sun Valley. Anything else you want, G-man?"

"Well you have a nice day, your majesty." Jack tossed her the remote and soft-pack and watched her have a quick battle over which one got attention first before making his way out the door. The TV was on, and her feet were back up on the desk before they reached the car.

"Nice lady," Larry commented.

"Queens usually are," Jack shot back. "Let's head back and see what we have here."

# 12

*"Democracy must be built through open societies that share information. When there is information, there is enlightenment. When there is debate, there are solutions. When there is no sharing of power, no rule of law, no accountability, there is abuse, corruption, subjugation and indignation."*

—Atifete Jahjaga

"Anything?"

"Jack, I swear to God ..."

"Okay, okay."

Sydney tapped the mouse again to restart the footage. Half of it was practically unusable because the angle of the sun was blinding the lens. The rest wasn't much better since the camera had not been cleaned in a long time. Still, she examined every second as it played by at a slightly increased speed. Only two people had come and gone in the time frame Jack had specified. She was an hour past it and the street was starting to get dark. She hit the pause button.

"There's nothing, Jack. I don't think our guy is a customer there. I didn't see any black vans on the street either. How about the records?"

"Larry's running them through the DMV." He paced behind her and glanced at the screen. A frozen frame of the street revealed long shadows appearing as the sun went down. He paced some more, and Sydney used the opportunity to open a Mountain Dew. She watched him with a frown as he rubbed his temples. The Scotch. She kept her thoughts to herself.

"Wait a minute." He returned to look over her shoulder again. "What time is that?"

"Says 8:40. Why?"

"Run it back, high speed."

"Okay." She clicked the mouse, and they were treated to a jumping picture. Cars leaped down the street while the shadows slowly retreated.

"There!"

"What?"

"Back a bit, then forward, slow."

She did as he asked. "What am I looking for?"

"Watch the shadow of that building."

She focused on it just in time to see it jump a few feet. She hit the mouse and played it again. The clock in the corner jumped with it.

"Fifteen minutes."

"There's fifteen minutes of tape missing. Somebody altered it."

"The person working there?"

A mental image of Shanequa smoking at her desk entered Jack's mind and was quickly dismissed. "I don't see it. She can barely run the thing."

"Somebody from outside then?"

"It would have to be ... let's watch it again."

They watched the tape twice more and Jack took some notes.

"What do you think?"

"Tomorrow morning I'm going here." He tapped the screen. "Get me some information on the place and its owners. I may need some leverage."

Sydney squinted at the screen. "Top Dollar Pawn?"

"I'm sure they'll have better cameras than the Queen of Sun Valley. I'm hoping they can fill in the blanks."

"Okay. What else?"

"Call Eric. I want to know how those tapes were erased. See if he can track it back to its source."

"All right." She checked her watch. Eric was probably asleep, but you never knew. He kept odd hours. "Where are you going?"

"To find Larry!" The door slammed behind him.

Sydney saved the file and encrypted it before she put it and Jack's request into a secure email. Hopefully Eric was awake. If she didn't get an acknowledgement soon, she'd call him.

"Queen of Sun Valley?" she muttered as she worked. What the hell was that all about?

---

"CREW, COMBAT ENTRY CHECKLIST," the navigator prompted.

"Acknowledged."

"Altimeters?"

"Set. Base plus 6."

"Ingress?"

"Reviewed."

"Survival equipment?"

Wes frisked himself without taking his eyes from the instruments. The survival vest, flak vest, helmet and oxygen were obvious. Despite the lack of water below them for thousands of miles, they were still required to wear an LPU. His hand found the .45 in its holster, and he gave it a pat for good luck. While the younger members of the crew had opted for the high capacity 9mms, he had stuck with his old-school .45. It was his good luck charm.

"Dump manifold?"

"Purged."

The checklist continued, and Wes followed it with a portion of his mind while the other reviewed their decisions up to this point. Their navigator had once more questioned their approach, and Wes had been forced to overrule him. Fortunately, some small arms fire had chosen that moment to arch into the air in front of them, and Wes had chosen to maneuver the plane in an unnecessary attempt to avoid it. The navigator had then forgotten his questions and focused on spotting the next stream of tracers reaching out for them. It had kept him occupied until it was time to start their run into the drop zone.

"Defense systems?"

"Armed."

This was something new for Major Phillips. In the last decade, almost every C-130 in the inventory had been equipped with defensive countermeasures. Their "trash-hauler" now sported chaff, flares and IR jamming. It gave them some comfort when deployed on such missions. That and the pair of F-15Es circling high overhead, waiting to be given a target to pound into the ground. In all of his experience, Wes had only called them once, and the results had been rather spectacular.

"Lookouts?"

That one required a response from him. He was supposed to assign sectors for each crewman to scan, as if "outside" didn't cover it.

"Left and right," he responded. He wasn't worried about them not seeing any tracers reaching up for them. They glowed like shooting stars in their night vision equipment.

"Combat entry checklist?"

"Complete."

"Standby for pre-slowdown."

IN THE VALLEY BELOW, Burhan strained to hear the sound of the plane he knew was up there, but the wind took whatever noise there was to the west.

"When?" one of his fighters asked.

"Soon. Be quiet."

Burhan ignored the man and walked to the lights arranged in the field. He had drawn them a picture and had made sure they knew in which direction to point it, but he didn't trust their illiterate minds to perform the task correctly. To his amazement, the lights were correct: arranged in the letter A with the apex pointed due east. He avoided the wires traveling to each light from the pickup truck parked under a nearby tree. It idled, and the men were nervous due to the noise. He didn't care; they had no choice. If it failed to start when the time came, they would have nothing, and there would be no second chance.

He looked to the east for the hundredth time since the sun had gone down. The Kurds were close: just across the narrow river and on both sides of the valley. If they had come here during the day, he had no doubt his men would be suffering a mortar attack right now—or worse: foreign planes and their bombs. The Americans and their A-10s were feared the most. His men called it The Devil's Cross as it looked to them like a crucifix. As a precaution, he had men stationed on every approach, both to listen for the plane and to spot any advancing Kurdish forces.

The radio in his hand squawked to life.

"Burhan?"

"I'm here."

"A plane from the west. A big one."

"Turn them on!" he ordered without acknowledging the message.

The lights came to life, and the engine of the Toyota threatened to stall before its driver revved the RPMs higher. Burhan examined the lights, amazed that they all were working after their rough ride to this location. They angled up and to the west as instructed, and after assuring their operation, he scrambled for the relative safety of the wood line.

Some of the men rose to move farther away, afraid that the lights would attract a drone or worse.

"Stay where you are!"

The men reluctantly sank back to the ground, their eyes searching the darkness overhead. This plane would bring them the tools they needed to fight the Kurds, or it would rain death down upon them. Either way, they had no choice but to wait.

---

"THIRTY SECONDS TO SLOWDOWN."

The plane was very close—closer than some of the crew realized.

"Five."

The copilot moved his hand to the flaps controls.

"Slowdown ... now."

"Flaps at fifty percent."

"Auxiliary hydraulic pump?"

"On. Ramp clear to open."

"Flaps at fifty, ramp open. Red light on."

"Slowdown checklist complete."

"Got the PI marker?" Wes asked.

"Dead ahead, a little right."

"It's short," the navigator spoke.

"It's whatever they mark," Phillips countered. "Time?"

"One minute."

THE ROAR of the engines was clearly heard by all of them now. Several raised their weapons by reflex only to be cursed at by Burhan. The lights faded again, and the driver responded by revving the engine higher. Its noise barely masked the four screaming engines overhead.

"Get ready," Burhan shouted.

---

"FIVE SECONDS!"

"Red light on."

The copilot placed both his hands on the buttons in front of him. The engineer was looking aft as Harpo knelt next to the cargo with the release in his hands.

Wes ignored everything else, including the appearance of a second set of lights a mile in front of them. As soon as the first set disappeared under the nose, he gave the command.

"Green."

"No. Wait," the navigator protested.

The copilot pushed both buttons, and the green lights came on over the ramp. Harpo's hands were on the lock handle in the event the mechanism failed to function, but the actuator performed, releasing the drogue parachute. It streamed out the rear of the plane and inflated, its force overpowering the equipment pallet locks and yanking the load out the rear of the plane a split-second later.

"Load clear!"

The Hercules, now free of its heavy load, climbed rapidly, and the pilot let it, while banking away from the second PI marker as the navigator called, "Red light."

The copilot flipped the switch and replied, "On," before exchanging a look with his pilot. The sharp bank and climb had moved their view of the second marker out of their line of sight. There was now nothing but black sky outside their cockpit. But was it in time?

THE NOISE of the plane rapidly melted away into the night, and while Burhan's men continued to search for the plane in the night sky, he ignored it, instead looking up and behind them.

"Turn them off!"

The lights died a second later, and his eyes struggled to adjust. He regained his vision just in time to see a faint green glow fall into the trees to their right.

"Get up! Hurry!"

He pushed through the tall grass toward the sound of breaking branches, and the glow grew and separated until he could make out the individual chemical lights attached to the load. It had landed upright between two small trees, and the parachute had partially snagged on a third. The men grabbed it and tackled it to the ground as instructed, before their leader found and released the riser, deflating it. The lights of the truck now approached, and they attacked the netting in its headlights.

Ammunition. Crate after crate of it. Arms. Mortar rounds. Grenades. Burhan barked orders, and they dug deeper until two long black cases appeared. He pushed the men away and read the stenciled markings on the side.

"Allahu Akbar."

―――――――

"I THINK WE WERE SHORT."

"Not in that wind."

They had performed their combat exit checklist and were now turning to head back to Turkish airspace. The plane was climbing. The loadmaster was back into his novel.

The navigator was still examining his computer screen with a frown, trying to work out the difference between what it said and what his eyes had told him. Wes watched him out of the corner of his eye and waited.

"Will we get confirmation?" the man asked.

"I doubt it. It's over, Captain. Notify Dragnet, then get us back to Incirlik."

"Yes, sir."

"Dragnet, Forge 858."

"Dragnet."

"Forge 858, Rabbit. Repeat, Rabbit. We are RTB."

"Dragnet copies Rabbit. Clear."

The navigator slumped back in his seat before clicking the mouse of his computer with a frown.

"One point two to Incirlik."

"Very well," Phillips acknowledged.

The navigator pulled the laptop off the table and out of sight of his crewmates. A few notes made it into a personal file. He'd maybe add them later to his after-action report, he wasn't sure yet. Something about the drop wasn't adding up. First, he had to think about it, and right now there was plenty of time for that.

# 13

*"The fight for justice against corruption is never easy. It never has been and never will be. It exacts a toll on our self, our families, our friends, and especially our children. In the end, I believe, as in my case, the price we pay is well worth holding on to our dignity."*

—Frank Serpico

"Any word from Eric?" Larry asked.

"Sydney got an 'Ok' in return, but nothing since. He's been sick, so I don't know if he's working on it, or if he's passed out in bed. I'll give him a call myself later. What time is it?"

"It's a whole ten minutes past the last time you asked me. Where's your watch?"

"I forgot it. I left in a hurry."

"They don't even open till ten."

"You always bitch about the traffic out here, so I thought we should leave early. Besides, I needed coffee."

Larry eyeballed the Venti-quad-whatever Jack had in his fist and shook his head. Jack had ordered for them both, and he was just happy not to get something with whip cream or caramel on top. Black and hot was his preferred flavor. Either way, Jack had recovered from his hangover and was even more fired up than yesterday. Their conversation in the bar back in DC had not been brought up, and Larry was content to let it lie for now.

"This is Hollywood. Nobody gets up till noon. I'm surprised these guys are even open this early."

"I'm hoping the owner shows up. If not, we'll have to wait some more. But I didn't want to tip him off."

"You don't think us sitting here in a borrowed bu-car will tip him off?"

"Is it that obvious? According to the file, he's helped the cops twice in the past with stolen property and some other things. Not a bad record for a pawnshop in Hollywood is what I was told. This him?"

Larry eyeballed the man coming down the street. "No, just a local."

"You sure?"

The man strolled past the gated entrance. Jack gave a nod to him though his window.

"Morning, officer." The man grinned as he walked on.

"I guess that answers your first question."

"You're a funny guy."

They sat in silence for another ten minutes. The Queen was visible in her glass cage across the street, just where they had left her the day before. No traffic had come or gone from the storage unit. Jack drained the last of his coffee and adjusted the Browning poking him in the ribs. He found himself hoping the pawnshop had a clean bathroom.

"You miss it?"

Larry pulled his gaze back inside. "Miss what?"

"LA. You have friends here, right? You can retire anytime you want. Thought about where?"

Larry rubbed the stubble on his face to buy some time. He'd never really talked to Jack about quitting. His daughter was in Baltimore with his new grandson, so he figured he'd stick around there or DC when the time came, but beyond that he'd managed to avoid the subject.

"I miss the weather. Most of the guys I ran with are retired already. Some have stuck around, the others are in Arizona or with family somewhere else. Maybe. I'm in no hurry."

Before Jack could follow up a car pulled up to the curb. A large and round man got out and examined them for a second behind his sunglasses before walking to the gate. He unlocked it and the door behind it after checking the street in both directions. Jack spotted a handgun tucked into a holster on his belt. Not unusual for a pawnshop owner. They were a favorite target for robberies. The man entered for only a moment before surprising them by leaning back out the door and waving them inside.

"Don't say it," Jack said before rolling his window up.

The shop was like any other pawnshop. The barred windows displayed a variety of merchandise of varying value. Musical instruments. Stereo equipment. Power tools. Inside, they found larger displays of the same items, many with layers of dust on them. Against one wall were a row of glass display cases. They held the usual guns, jewelry, and collectable items you would expect. The wall behind them sported row after row of long guns. Everything from shotguns to AR-15s. Two large windows with one-way glass reflected the room back at them from the rear of the shop, and a locked door led to the back between them. The owner was standing behind the counter, waiting for them when they entered.

"Morning, officers? Or is it detective?"

"Special agent actually. FBI," Larry replied and badged him.

"What can I do for you?"

"Don't worry. We're not here to give you a hard time."

The man shrugged. "Didn't think you were. If you're here, I'm sure you've checked me out already. I'm Joe Hanson, but you know that already."

Jack shook the offered hand. "Jack Randall. This is my partner, Larry."

"Jack Randall? The guy from the mess in Niagara Falls?"

Jack made a face. The damn press had made him famous. "Yeah, that's me."

The handshake got firmer. "Job well done. My

son's in the Corps, followed in his dad's footsteps. He re-enlisted because of you."

Jack wasn't sure how to take that. "Well, good for him. Tell him I said hello."

"Will do. What can I do for you?"

"Well, we were wondering if your camera there could see the whole street out front?"

"The one in the corner? Sure. There's another one at eye level you can't see. Records the face of everyone that comes in and out."

"Any chance it was running two nights ago?"

"It runs 24/7. It goes to the cloud and is saved for six months. Didn't really need that much storage, but it came in a package offer from the company, so I took it. It's an insurance write-off, so I figured why not."

Jack could barely contain his joy. "You've got six months of tape from two cameras?"

"In color," the man confirmed. "Want some copies?"

"Just like that?"

"For you? Yeah, just like that. Maybe one condition?"

Jack grinned. "What's that?"

"Take a picture with me. My kid will never believe this without it."

"Deal."

A half hour later, they were back on the street. Larry had copies of the video in hand, and Jack had a smile on his face. He'd had to suffer through numerous photos, then wait until the man printed one out for him to sign. A copy of which was already in an email and on its way to his son in Iraq. He imagined the other would be framed and on the wall before the day was through.

"Fame has its advantages, I guess," Larry quipped.

"It just got us what we needed without a warrant. Small price to pay. A friendly civilian. We could use more."

"I guess so." Larry dropped the car in gear and did a quick U-turn. Jack eyeballed the office of the storage facility again. No movement from behind the glass. Perhaps the Queen was napping.

Jack examined the area as they rolled through it, committing it to memory and trying to put himself in the head of the man they were after. He could see why he had chosen it. Low traffic. Populated by people who minded their own business. Quick access to major roads in all directions, and the maze of LA all around to hide in. When he got back, he'd draw a half-hour circle around it, then another around the dealership, and then another around the gym. Somewhere inside them was his guy.

There were close to four million people in LA. Despite that number, Jack couldn't help but feel he was getting closer.

———

"WHAT DOES IT SHOW?" Jack asked.

"Slow down. I'm trying to sync it. Something's not right, though," Sydney replied.

"What do you mean?"

"Well ... it's not the same tape when I sync the time and date."

"Seriously? Why would it be different?"

"I don't know, Jack. I've had it for all of fifteen minutes. Let me play with it a bit. But if what Eric said about the first tape is true, they may have hacked these cameras as well."

"Well, you're just a bundle of joy today."

"Sorry, Jack. Go find something to do and let me work."

"You'll call Eric?"

"If I have to. Go. Please!"

"All right, all right."

Jack waved Larry up and out of his chair. He

led them out to the car where Jack paced for three laps.

"Let's review. We know him from the gym. He matches the description. The car is registered to a company that's not answering the phone. The address on his DL is a fake or former address. The name doesn't come up in any of our computers. He buys a van and disappears with it. He hasn't returned to the gym for the last three days. The storage unit is a strong maybe, but the security camera footage shows nothing, and has been tampered with by an outside source, one that's good at hiding its tracks. And now the tapes from across the street are compromised! What next?"

"We're not even sure this is—"

"This is our guy. It just doesn't add up. This is our guy."

Larry sighed and gave Jack a moment to calm down. "We don't know that for sure. If he works security this may be nothing more than him retaining anonymity. Those guys make enemies. He could just be keeping the people he's pissed off from finding him."

"Then why the van?"

"So he owns a van? So do my kids."

"His name isn't in the system."

"You can legally change your name every month if you want. Deadbeat husbands. Ex-cons. Prince. I went to high school with a guy named Jeff Dahmer. He couldn't change his name fast enough."

"Prince?"

"The purple one himself. You making fun of my taste in music?"

"No. Just ... you really don't think it's our guy?"

"I think it's our guy."

"Then why the hell are you ...?"

"What I think and what I can prove are two different things. Let's say he is. If we go charging in after him, he'll see us coming and bolt. Then we're back to square one. Let's just be careful, okay?"

"Yeah." Jack resumed pacing. Larry watched silently until his phone rang.

"Yeah? Okay."

"It's Syd. She found something."

Jack bolted for the door without a reply. Larry struggled to keep up. So much for slowing down.

---

"OKAY, turns out there was no plot against us, just time zones and laziness."

"How's that?"

"The company that stores the footage is in an area that doesn't recognize daylight savings time, so the timestamp was off by an hour from the place it's being gathered from. On top of that, it was a leap year this year, and the owner didn't bother to change the date on the machine, so we were off a day in the other direction. Once I figured that out, I was able to sync the footage with the video from the storage unit."

"So it was off by twenty-five hours?"

"No, twenty-three."

Larry was confused. "But?"

"Never mind that. What did you see?"

"This." She rotated the screen so they could see it and clicked the mouse. The first thing they saw was a black panel van entering the storage facility. It didn't even pause as it went through the open gate. Sydney clicked the mouse and froze the frame.

"Too distant to read the plate, but I sent some stills for enhancement."

"Okay. What else?"

"This, fifteen minutes later."

They watched the screen until a large black man appeared and walked with purpose through the gate. He didn't pause or look around before heading up the street and out of the frame. Just before he disappeared, he pulled something small and black from his pocket.

"That's the direction of the restaurant, the one where the cab driver said he picked the guy up," Jack said.

"That's probably a cell phone in his hand."

Jack watched the footage. A passing car every once in a while, but nothing more. Sydney recognized the look and let him think.

"Think it's enough for a warrant?"

Larry made a pained expression. Sydney frowned as well.

"No. Sorry. Maybe if the judge owed you a big favor. Otherwise, it's too thin."

Jack frowned.

"Is this our guy?"

Sydney didn't hesitate. "Yes."

"Larry?"

"Maybe. Definitely worth checking out."

"All right. I guess the next question is, do you have any?"

"Any what?"

"Judges that owe you a favor?"

"I've been gone a long time, Jack. I don't even know who to ask anymore."

"Would your friends at Robbery-Homicide?"

"Maybe. But it's going to take more than that."

"You make your call, I'll make mine."

# 14

*"Revolution is the festival of the oppressed."*

—*Germaine Greer*

L ieutenant Andrew "Archie" Bunker took one last look at the picture of his wife and newborn son he had stuck between two gauges before moving his gaze outside and returning the salute of the CAT officer. Setting his head back against the rest, he waited, the engines screaming their readiness behind him. The man glanced up the deck before twirling his wand, tapping the deck and pointing at the bow.

The familiar jolt of the hold-back bolt parting set them free, and the plane hurtled off the bow at just over one hundred and fifty-five knots. Sixty feet off the water and climbing, Bunker raised the gear and fed in enough back stick to initiate a climb before leveling off at two thousand feet.

"How we look, Mike?"

"It would appear we have survived liftoff intact."

"All right, coming around to the east."

Bunker tugged on the ejection seat harness before bringing the plane around to an easterly heading. The straps had been as tight as he could get them before the CAT shot, yet were always loose after. He had no doubt that his Weapons and Sensors Officer, Lieutenant JG Mike "Hassle" Hoffman, seated a few feet behind him was doing the same. He settled the plane into its rendezvous heading and held it when it centered on the ADI.

"Ready?"

"Steering is good."

"How's your ass?"

"Fine if you must know. I'll be sure to tell Jen of your concern."

"Oh, she already knows," Bunker shot back with a laugh.

His partner had suffered from hemorrhoids recently, a common ailment among fighter crews due to the G-forces they dealt with. On their last rotation, Hoffman had required some surgery to treat his. Bunker wasn't to that point yet, so he gave his partner hell about it every chance he could. The two men were friends both at work and at home. After being paired up, they had discovered that they lived only a few miles from each other at home in California. Every weekend since was spent at the other's, usually around the grill with their kids playing in the yard.

"Checklist," Hoffman prompted.

"Stand by."

While his pilot got ready, Hoffman warmed up the onboard radar jammer.

"ALR?"

"On and checked."

They both watched their screens as the plane performed a self-check. Missile alerts, chaff dispenser, terrain clearance, radar, FLIR, and the armament panel itself. After a few minutes, the lights stopped.

"All tests passed. All CBs are in."

"Roger that. We're at the rendezvous."

Since they were alone on this mission, there was no actual rendezvous, but the term had yet to be replaced. Bunker leveled the plane off at fifteen thousand feet, still heading east, and throttled back to conserve fuel. They cruised in silence for a few minutes while each of them checked and rechecked their gauges.

Twelve minutes later, they reached their first waypoint. They listened in silence as other planes called in. Some heading into the zone and some heading out. They had a ten-minute window to stay in to prevent blue-on-blue conflicts—none of them wanted to get shot down by their own colleagues. The seconds ticked by slowly.

"Viking Five-Oh-Eight clear inbound. Webster is clear."

The communication from the E-2 Hawkeye high and several miles behind them started their mission. Webster being clear told them there were no enemy aircraft on their screens.

"Coming down," Bunker said. "Radar altimeter at four hundred." Hoffman replied with a click on the ICS—he was already busy with the computer and data link, getting the plane dialed in for the mission. Bunker eased the aircraft down until the shimmering water of the eastern Mediterranean raced by beneath them. The coastal mountains appeared in the distance, a wave of grey shapes sitting on the black water.

"TC is intermittent, RADALT looks good."

"Roger." Bunker pulled the plane out of its dive and leveled off at just over four hundred feet letting the airspeed bleed off until he reached a fuel-conserving three hundred and sixty knots again.

"Coastline in sight. You ready to strangle the parrot?"

"I got it. CBs are checked in. Lights are off. Twenty seconds."

Bunker keyed the mic and spoke to the airborne radar plane: "Viking Five-Oh-Eight is feet dry, feet dry."

"Viking Five-Oh-Eight, roger feet dry. Good hunting."

With a flick of the switch, Bunker turned off the IFF. With it disengaged, the plane would no longer radiate a signal in response to civilian radars. Only an active military search or targeting radar could see them now. They would no longer transmit any signals; no radio or radar of their own that would give away their presence. They became a black hole in the sky.

"Hawkeye acknowledges. We're five seconds

early," Hoffman relayed after seeing a message on his screen.

Bunker gave one last tug on the straps of his harness before easing back on the stick. The F-18D responded accordingly and eased up from its current altitude of four hundred feet. The beach disappeared below the nose and was replaced by patchy desert. To the south, the lights of the city of Tripoli in northern Lebanon could be seen in the distance, but it was the only manmade light for miles in any direction. He followed the heading on the VDI and leveled off at one thousand feet—just enough to get them through the gap in the coastal mountains. The plane plunged into the clouds only to come out a few seconds later. The broken clouds were exactly what the weatherman had predicted for a change, and for a brief moment Bunker saw the grey line of the M1 highway below them.

"Sixty miles to the IP. FLIR coming out."

Bunker felt the slight yaw as the forward-looking infrared camera came out of its stowed position. The clouds parted, and he glanced outside in time to see a narrow strip parting the desert.

"I've got the M1."

Behind him Mike acknowledged him with a

grunt. His head was down and on his instruments, so he had no time to look outside. He examined the data link from the E2-Hawkeye several miles behind and thousands of feet above them for any threats, but the sky was clear.

"Looks clear. Steering update."

The VID slipped to the left, and Bunker followed with the stick. He nudged the aircraft lower until the radar altimeter kicked in and started giving him readings. He was both pleased that the reading matched the pressure altimeter, and angry for staying so high. Despite the lack of aircraft in the sky around them, and the brutal beating the coalition had given the enemy air defenses already, he hated being an easier target. But the mountains had dictated it; once they were on the other side, he could drop back down.

The Hornet was on offense, as it had been since arriving in the eastern Mediterranean, striking deep into ISIS territory. With the enemy lacking radar and surface-to-air missiles, their biggest threat now was a radar guided anti-aircraft gun. The best defense for that was flying as low and as fast as he dared, using the darkness and the earth itself to keep them out of the enemy's gun sights. Over the years, Bunker's personal definition of low had become legendary.

On a previous mission they had taken a bird strike, and after limping back to the carrier on one engine, Hoffman had explained to his squad mates that it had been "standing in the way." Bunker had laughed it off and taken the flak from his shipmates, successfully hiding the fact that losing the engine at that altitude had almost cost them their lives. The truth was that it had rattled him; he'd been shaking so badly during the landing that he ended up diving for the deck to catch the two-wire. The LSO had graciously given him an even grade and a "Don't do it again" look.

The grey shapes of the mountains soon passed below, and Bunker wasted no time in dropping the nose. Easing the plane down, he leveled off at four hundred feet and nudged the throttle forward to a speed of five hundred knots. Like a finely tuned race car, the plane settled into its comfort zone. Even with the weight of the bombs and missiles under its wings, the aircraft became very sensitive to his every input. He let it drop another hundred feet before deciding he was happy. At this speed, he would be past any enemy gunners before they could train their weapons on him. Even if they did hear him coming, he would be nothing but a dark shape hurtling across the equally dark sky. The clouds were now overhead, shielding them from the sliver of moon.

Bunker kept his gaze on a steady scan. Compass. Horizon. Airspeed. His hands were steady on the throttle and stick, and he blinked the sweat from his eyes rather than let it distract him. A break in the clouds reflected moonlight back at him from the ground ahead.

"I've got the lake, Mike."

"Update."

Another steering command from the ADI, and Bunker followed it immediately. They were now skirting around the city of Homs, heading northeast. The terrain rose and fell beneath them. As the clouds thinned, Bunker caught sight of their shadow leaping up and down as it kept pace with them out the right side.

"Ten o'clock," Hoffman prompted.

Bunker's eyes immediately looked in the direction indicated and saw small flashes of light from a ridge top. A few tracers arched through the sky, but he determined they were off target and made no move to avoid them.

"Small arms fire. They're shooting at the noise."

"Yeah, must be no football game tonight."

Bunker smiled. Every man and boy in the

country had an AK-47, and at the first sound of a
jet engine they would fire randomly into the air.
They had no way of seeing them, nor any training
in how to properly lead them even if they did, so it
was little more than a wish thrown into the blackness. A morale booster, one made at little cost for a
potentially large payout. Something to let little
Haji think he was fighting the Great Satan and all
that was unholy. The chances of them actually
causing damage were about the same as the bird
they had struck. What he couldn't let them do was
distract him enough to fly his plane into the
ground.

"Some more at one."

Bunker had already seen them, and with the
clouds thinning he used the moonlight to fly even
lower. The tracers passed harmlessly overhead.
They skimmed the earth now at just under three
hundred feet, and he kept his eyes outside, preferring this input to the one from his instruments.

"Thirteen miles. We're on time."

"Got it."

More tracers reached up into the sky ahead of
them, and Bunker evaluated each threat before
staying on course. Out of the right side he could
see Highway 42 in the distance. It would lead them
right to their target, just outside the small village

of Shuheeb. Intelligence had placed an ISIS leader there, hiding in a home surrounded by a wall and a small orchard. It had also warned them of an anti-aircraft gun in the area. A bulldozer, one that had been taken out by one of their squad mates two nights before, had managed to dig several shelters for such a weapon in the area before they had reduced it to a pile of smoking metal—courtesy of a Hellfire missile. Drones had failed to find the gun after the strike, and it was thought to have fled the area to the east, where more airstrikes had been happening over the last few days.

"Come right three degrees."

"Coming right."

In the back, Hoffman watched his pilot follow the commands. Once they had leveled off again, he reached out to check the armament panel. He turned on the master armament switch, then checked the position of every toggle one last time. The five-hundred-pound bombs were ready to be unleashed.

"Master arm is on. No reselects. Your stick is hot."

"Roger." Bunker flexed his thumb, making sure it was not on the red button that would send the bombs under his wings into the night sky. Soon though.

"Cycling IP."

Bunker's steering jumped thirty degrees to the right. He followed, and they were both pressed back into their seats by the Gs. He ignored it and kept his eyes traveling from the threat display to the ADI and to the tracers outside.

As they passed over the last small ridge, the sky lit up with tracers. Big ones this time. They marched across the sky in slow motion only to speed up and zip past as Bunker banked the wings between them. He immediately dropped back down to the deck.

"Shit! That gun's still here!"

As if to answer the ECM panel lit up, the warbling scream of the alarm telling them a fire-attack radar was trying to find them.

"Fuckers were just waiting for us. Two miles."

Soon.

"Come back right more."

Bunker pulled back on the stick and, using their airspeed, increased their turn to the right. This was their most vulnerable time. Committed to the bomb run and presenting their largest silhouette against the sky, he waited for the impacts of the incoming rounds. He let the plane climb to five hundred feet before grunting against the Gs.

"Anything?"

"Stay on course, little left, yeah, I got it. Stepping into attack."

Bunker was momentary distracted by the AT-TACK indicator lighting up in his VDI and the high warble sounding in his ear, but he stayed on heading. He jammed the throttles forward and climbed to six hundred feet. The bombs had to fall a minimum of five hundred feet to arm, and he wanted to make sure they all cooked off. Duds became IEDs in the hands of these guys, and he wasn't going to give them the opportunity.

The VDI was alive now, full of symbols and numbers telling him the time to weapons release, drift angle, position to target. Bunker centered his attention on the steering to release, ignoring the tracers reaching out for them. The stick quivered in his hand, responding to the slightest input. The airspeed topped out at five hundred knots, and Bunker held it there, giving the computer time to gather its needed information. His heart thumped so hard in his chest that he felt sure that it would burst at any second.

"I've got lock."

Bunker didn't reply; he was too absorbed in the plane, wearing it like a suit of armor, his every movement translated instantly to its control surfaces. The wings rolled right between a stream of tracers and snapped back to level flight without him giving it thought. His whole being focused on guiding it to a specific point in the sky, where the bombs would leave his aircraft and visit death on those below. He pushed the stick forward to duck under a stream of tracers, and the radar altimeter beeped at him until he brought the plane back up above three hundred feet.

"Two miles. Hammer, I'm committing."

The release indicator, or Hammer, on the VDI turned yellow as it marched down the screen and Bunker gritted his teeth against the approaching tracers again and froze the plane on a solid heading. Outside, the buildings came into view under his nose. The hammer disappeared off the bottom of the screen, and the plane gave off a series of shudders as the bombs were kicked loose in rapid order. The ATTACK light went out, and Bunker immediately banked left and dove for the ground. Hoffman grunted against his harness as he grabbed a handle and twisted his body around to look behind them.

The first explosion lit the night and provided him with a fleeting glimpse of the target building before it was obliterated by the next three a split-second later. Bunker squinted against the flash in his rearview mirror as he leveled off and jammed the throttles forward. Without the six-thousand-pound weight of the bombs, the plane leaped ahead, but he held it back and again banked farther left.

"One secondary, but that's it. Are we done?"

"No, arm the Hellfires. I think I know where that gun's at. Besides, he's nice and hot now."

"I'm on it."

The forward-looking infrared camera now dominated Bunker's display. He banked the plane harder, and it tracked across the face of the ridge from which they had been shot at.

"There. He's dug into the side of that ridge."

"Looks like a tunnel. They're trying to pull the gun in."

The twin barrels of the anti-aircraft gun glowed white-hot in the picture, and Bunker shook his head. They should have been shooting, but instead they were trying to hide. Clearly, they had no idea of the plane's capabilities. Well, that's what you get when you recruit with a century-old book, Hoffman thought, as he worked the armament panel, flipping switches by feel, as he kept his eyes on the display. He pushed a button and told the Hellfire where to go.

"You're hot."

"Another pass. How we look?"

"Threat board is clear."

Bunker took the information without a reply. These guys were toast as soon as he got his Hornet pointed at them. He banked hard again, and the radar altimeter protested when they went past sixty degrees. This time, he ignored it and lined them up for another pass, one which would aim them and the missile seekers right at the cave.

FARTHER DOWN THE ridge and in a much smaller hole, Amed had watched in silence the destruction of the leader's newly commandeered home. He had warned him against making himself a target, but the man had chosen the luxury of his new home over the cold of the desert. It was not his concern anymore; the plane in the night sky circling his position was now his only focus. He waved the boy hiding behind him away as he pulled the weapon to his shoulder.

The fact that he spoke and read English was all that had mattered to them, and they had presented him with the weapon as if it were made of gold. He had accepted it without question, and then traveled all night to this position. The boy had dug the hole and brought meals for the last few days, but other than that they had done little else but wait. They had provided pages of information downloaded from the internet for him to read, but it was mostly of little use. The instructions were printed right on its side. Power on. Aim. Wait for the weapon to lock on its target. Shoot. The boy could have done this himself, but he didn't voice any objections.

BUNKER HAD JUST LEVELED his wings and placed his finger on the red button. The Hellfire was screaming its readiness in his ear, and he obliged it. The missile leaped off the rack and streaked into the target. The flash of the explosion overloaded the FLIR and caused spots to appear in Bunker's display. He was about to pull up when Hoffman screamed on the ICS.

"Missile!"

"What?"

"From the ridge!"

With no warning from the sensors, he labeled the missile as a heat seeker. Bunker reflexively banked into it and squeezed the chaff and flare button repeatedly. Unfortunately, he was pulling out of his run, bleeding heat and airspeed in the process.

"On our six!" Hoffman yelled through the ICS.

"Where the hell—"

Bunker slammed the stick into the corner and the throttles to afterburner in an attempt to put the ridge between his plane and the incoming missile, but it was not fast enough. The SAM flew over the right engine and exploded against the horizontal stabilizer, shredding it and sending the plane yawing sharply to the right. Bunker reached for the ejection handle between his legs but was blasted free before he could pull it. The chute had barely opened when he impacted the side of the hill, shattering his leg and taking his breath. His plane followed in a fiery explosion a second later, cartwheeling into the earth only a few hundred meters away, the blinding flash sending a wave of heat over him. He reflexively turned away only to see the still form of his WSO lying a short distance away.

"Mike?" he croaked before coughing a mouthful of blood.

A secondary explosion sounded from the crash site, and he flinched. The expanding cloud of fire dissipated over his head, swallowed up by the

black sky. It was the last thing he remembered before slipping into unconsciousness.

---

AMED and the boy quickly crested the ridge to see
the impact site. They watched as the flames
roared, lighting the small valley in all directions.
Secondary explosions followed, first slowly, then
more rapidly as the cannon rounds cooked off. He
pulled the boy down to a seat beside him and they
watched the plane burn.

"There!" the boy pointed.

Amed followed the boy's finger and saw the
fluttering shapes of two parachutes on the side of
the ridge. Attached were two dark motionless
shapes. He fingered the knife tucked in his waistband before standing.

"Run. Fetch a truck."

The boy stood rooted in place, mesmerized by
the burning plane.

"Quickly!"

The boy snapped out of it and ran toward the
burning village. Amed drew his knife and started
down the ridge toward the dark shapes.

# 15

*"It's not unpatriotic to denounce an injustice committed on our behalf, perhaps it's the most patriotic thing we can do."*

—E.A. Bucchianeri

"Hey, Eric. How you feeling?"

"Better, boss. At least my stomach

is. I've never been so hungry. Did I wake you up?"

"Glad to hear it. I've been up for a while. You have any good news for me other than you're hungry?"

"Not yet. I wanted to catch you before you got started today. I'm actually calling to warn you about something."

"What's that? Is somebody not happy with you working at home?"

"No, I told them I was still sick. Evidently, now my boss is too, so I'm not getting any push back. It's about the tapes you sent."

"Okay?"

"Well, without getting all technical on you, I've been trying to track the source of the computer that made the changes. I'm not having any luck."

"Okay."

"Any luck at all."

"I guess I don't follow."

"Boss, not to pat my own back here, but if I can't find this guy, it means one of two things: he's either very good at what he's doing, or he's inside."

"Inside? You mean in our system?"

"I can't rule it out. If he's inside our system, it means he's definitely inside the LAPD's system. Which, frankly, isn't that hard, but still."

"So, I should assume the guy we're after knows we have his description and maybe even the area we're looking for him in?"

"I can't rule it out. Have you been using LAPD's communications?"

"As little as possible."

"Might want to stop—at least until I get a better handle on who's watching. Can you keep the investigation confined to your team?"

"It would mean a drop in manpower, but if I have to ..."

"Any good suspects yet?"

"One that's pinging my radar, but he's one of many we're looking at."

"I can see the group. My suggestion, keep the list big; the bigger the better. Let whoever is watching think you're still searching for that needle. When you rule one out, don't delete him; keep your own list and not on a computer."

"All right. Anything else?"

"If the guy who's watching is still inside, you might want to refrain from using any LAPD people."

"That's going to be hard. What if we locate a suspect or need help with a tail? Or surveillance?"

"I can't help you there, boss. Isn't Deacon sending you some people?"

"Yeah, but not for a day or two."

"Well, until you get more of your own people. I'd be careful using theirs."

"All right. You'll stay on this for me?"

"You know it."

"Okay, thanks, Eric. I'll talk to you soon."

---

CARTER EYEBALLED the other members of the gym as he made his way to the squat rack. He was at gym number three, a small place stuffed into the basement of an old office building. He had found the place through a friend, and it had quickly become his favorite. If it was closer to his home, he would have used it exclusively. His job required that he stay mobile however, so he rotated his time among the three.

This gym had no name. It also had no air conditioning. No mirrors on the wall. No Spandex-clad housewives gawking from the stationary bikes. This place was for serious bodybuilders and power lifters only. The machines were old and rusting in places. The plates were of several different brands. The rack he aimed to use was stocked with manhole covers. All around him men grunted and sweated, and the smell was as foul as one could expect. Another room sported a wrestling mat surrounded by boxing equipment; the sounds of fighting could be heard as he passed. It was not uncommon to find men with syringes in the small locker room. Steroids of all kinds could be had from the man manning the door. The only way in was with cash and a password. Nobody knew anybody else's name, and that was the way they preferred it. Carter would be here for a least a week.

He ducked around a man doing pull-ups off of an overhead pipe. He loaded a bar on the rack. A work light had been clamped to an overhead beam to provide a shadow of the person lifting. It was the next best thing to a mirror. Carter actually wished there were mirrors, since they would make watching his back easier. Here he made do. Despite the dim light, he still wore his sunglasses, his lightest tint, ones that shielded his eyes but allowed him to look around without others knowing.

His skin had crawled for two sets before he finally saw him. The pull-up guy. He was looking a little too long for it to be professional admiration or something sexual. Carter took a good look when the man resumed. He spotted a military tat on his calf—Army, not Marine Corps. He wasn't anyone Carter had served with. The hair was the second thing he noted—that and the farmer's tan. The left arm was darker than the right. The man spent a lot of time in a car.

Like a cop.

He did another set before tossing his towel over the bar and heading for the locker room. It was a sign that he meant to return. Pull-up man ignored him as he passed, and Carter headed for the exit as soon as he was around the corner. A fist bump to the doorman was all he slowed for until he was in his car. He pulled the car out of the lot and circled the block before selecting a spot in the shadows just down the street. Examining the cars around him, he didn't see anybody sitting and watching—nothing that screamed unmarked police car. Still, his radar had pinged, and until he knew better, he would watch.

Pull-up guy appeared less than a minute later, looking in both directions carefully before moving to the parking lot and strolling its length. Shaking his head, he pulled out a cell phone and spoke into it as he walked back inside.

"Hello, cop. Looking for me?"

He dropped the car in gear and drove away.

His blood was pumping, and it was not from the abbreviated workout. The man was clearly watching him. He replayed the last mission in his head, looking for where he had slipped up, but he soon dismissed it. It didn't matter how they had found him, only that they had.

Or had they?

If they had, William would know. Maybe they had nothing but a description? William had erased him; of that he was sure. The cars, the houses, the documents, all of them had passed scrutiny without fail.

A sudden thought had him pulling into a parking garage. He went up to the second floor and slowly cruised the middle of the structure until both the GPS and the satellite radio lost signal. He sprinted to the stairs and checked them before glancing over the side. There was grass below, and he was confident he could get out in any direction if needed. He returned to the car and began a very thorough examination. Every inch inside and out got checked twice before he accepted there was no tracking device attached. Sitting in the front seat again, he toweled the sweat off himself and considered his options.

Was he being paranoid? Was the man really looking for him? Was he being paranoid enough? If they knew it was him, then why not a whole team of cops? If they had something, he'd have never made it out of the parking lot. So what did they have? Just a description, maybe? Or were they looking for someone else who looked like him? Another thought jolted his brain: what if they did know it was him and were just following, waiting to see who he worked with?

He started the car and pulled it to the edge of the garage until he had signal on the cell phone. It rang once.

"Ockham."

"William, it's Carter. I have a question."

"Of course."

"Is there any traffic out of the LAPD or the Fibbies about me? Or maybe someone with my description?"

"Nothing new since they found the van. Not that I have caught, anyway. You have reason to believe there may be?"

"A guy at the gym. He was a little too interested. I ducked out after I fingered him, and he tried to follow, I think."

"You don't sound too sure?"

"I'm not now. My car is clean, and I haven't noticed anything else, but I thought I would check, ya know?"

"I see. I'll do some checking myself. May I suggest you stay away from your primary for a few days?"

"I've already planned on it. I'll be at alternate one until I hear from you."

"Very well. Perhaps this would be a good time for a vacation?"

"Any work in the area coming up?"

"Not that I'm aware."

"All right. I'll consider that, too, then."

"Anything else?"

"No. You'll get back to me?"

"I should know if there is anything by tomorrow."

"Okay."

"Stay hidden, Number Six."

"You too, Mr. O."

Carter punched the phone off and settled back. The guy could have been watching him for a number of reasons. It had happened before. He'd been offered drugs, had been asked for a date, had even been offered to audition for a part in a movie. None of those people had pinged his radar like this guy though. Maybe he was just being paranoid. He watched a car travel by in the rearview before putting his car in gear and making for the entrance. He was soon back out in the Hollywood traffic, heading west. He kept an eye on the rearview more often than usual, while he formed a plan.

Alternate one was a condo in Reseda. He would stay there for a few days and let William do his thing before returning to his place in Hollywood. He didn't like it, being forced to run. Some of the Shepherds took a trip after every job, just in case. Others were like him and faded back into their surroundings, their normal lives, with barely a ripple. He could go on a road trip, maybe a few days in Vegas or a drive up to Oakland. Maybe go camping for a few days in the mountains up in Tahoe?

He dismissed the ideas as soon as they entered his brain. Despite William's information about there being no work coming, he knew he was not mission-ready even if there was. He had to restock. The new van needed to be cleaned and sterilized. The bikes would need to be replaced as well as the rifle. He had work to do. There would be no more jobs coming his way until he was ready. He would never say it out loud, but it was his priority. The possibility of work was what kept the monster at bay. Without it, he was tempted to create his own. It had happened only twice before, and if Dayton ever found out, it would be his last day as a Shepherd.

Carter ground his teeth in frustration at the idea of being forced into a defensive mode. But discipline won out this time, and he forced himself to slow down. He'd grab something to eat and hide out at the condo. He'd watch TV and do push-ups until he heard from William, then he'd stay a few more days just to be sure. Maybe work on the van while he waited.

He found himself nodding, trying to convince himself it was a sound plan. The debate was harder than he thought.

———

"NEW FOOTAGE OBTAINED today of what appears to be an errant airdrop into ISIS's territory. This video came to us from Al Jazeera. And although unverified, it appears to show members of ISIS gathering around a large pallet of materials attached to a parachute."

Haney's eyes jerked up from the paper in his hand, and he thumbed the volume higher as Harper stood and walked closer to the screen. The screen showed a number of men—most of them toting AK-47s, dressed in the traditional dishdasha with the beard of ISIS fighters—dancing and cheering around the stacked crates lying in the back of a small truck wrapped in netting. One of them produced a large knife and began cutting the netting away.

"You fools!" Haney spat at them.

Harper glanced at his boss, but he quickly returned his eyes to the small screen. The footage was jerky and often showed nothing but the dirt at a man's feet or the blue sky. It returned to the crates in time to see the man on top cut away the last of the netting. The crowd of men surged forward and began hoisting their prizes over their heads and the camera panned around to gather the action. The crates were now being gathered up and hauled away to other waiting pickups. Eventually two men emerged, a long black box on their shoulders. The stenciling on the side was in English. It only showed for a half a second, but it was enough.

"You idiots! Now the world knows what you have! How do these shitheads keep living!" The former VP railed against the TV with balled fists. The screen returned to the talking head reporter.

Harper reached out and took the remote from the man's desk. Rewinding the footage, he stopped it at the black crate.

"Is that what I think it is?"

"You know damn well what it is!" Haney

fumed. "They were supposed to use them on the Turks! Idiots! Now we have a new problem."

"I don't understand."

Haney held up the file he'd been reading before the broadcast had interrupted him.

"We lost an F-18 over Syria last night. It's not public yet. It was *supposed* to be a Turkish plane. If they killed the crew—or worse yet, captured them and behead them on the damn internet—it'll enrage the public here."

"Isn't that what you want?"

Haney gave his man an evil look. "Yes, smartass, it is, but we wanted it on our timetable. If they do it too early The President may use that to end this ISIS issue quickly—a full on invasion! If that happens, it'll be hard to drag out. This is what you get for dealing with amateurs! God, I miss the Russians!"

Harper wanted to ask how one controlled who someone shot at—especially if you just handed them a gun—but he thought better of it. There was nothing to gain by pissing the man off further.

"So now what?"

"Now we wait and see what our President says. This F-18 business will leak; there's no stopping that. To control the story, he'll have to get out in front of it. If there are pilots on the ground, he'll have to either get them back quickly or not at all. Either way, it's bad for us. If they're alive the smart thing to do would be to use them as shields, something to stop the rain of steel that keeps landing on their heads, but we just saw how bright these holy warriors are!"

Harper sat back down and made himself comfortable. He didn't see a place for him in this mess. He was in the business of making them, not cleaning them up, but his brain automatically processed the options.

"If they have captured them, wouldn't it be to our advantage to drag that out? At least until it's time to get the public fired up?"

Haney thought about the option. Yes, it could work. They'd have to find the men first, and if they were still alive find a way to keep them that way, at least until he no longer needed them.

"That might work."

Harper smiled and put his feet back up on the table.

"Don't get comfortable; get the hell out of here. I have to make some calls!"

Harper went.

# 16

*"To oppose corruption in government is the highest obligation of patriotism."*

—G. Edward Griffin

G reg walked in and held up a paper. Jack was eating at his borrowed desk and raised an eyebrow before swallowing.

"What you got?"

"Good news and bad. One of the locals saw your guy last night. He may need us to cover his ass a little."

"How's that?"

"Seems he's into MMA and found an underground gym where he can do some fighting—for real. It's in the zone, and the guy fit the description to a T."

"Why'd he need us to cover for him?" Sydney asked. "Did he come to you with this, or Larry?"

"Me. Larry's still at a gym somewhere; he'll be along in a few. The report was off the record—way off. Seems there's a bit of gambling going on when they fight. Also a lot of drugs around, mostly steroids and whatnot, but where there's one kind there's usually others. The gym runs on cash, and I doubt it pays any taxes." Greg shrugged. It didn't matter to him, but he understood the cop's worry.

Jack cared even less. "Whatever he needs, we don't talk about Fight Club. What's the bad news?"

"The guy may have spotted him. He left in the middle of a set of squats and disappeared."

"Seriously?"

"Yeah. The guy feels bad enough, but he said it's tight quarters in there and no way to keep his distance without losing sight of him."

Jack tossed the report on the table. He paced for a bit before asking a stupid question.

"Prints?"

"Nope. He didn't even try. If he had, he'd not have made it home. Besides, he said the guy touched nothing but the plates and the bar, and there was already someone using them when he went back inside. I doubt anything could be salvaged, anyway. Said he thought about it all night before choosing to tell us."

"That may be a good thing. I got a call from Eric this morning. We may have a problem with LAPD." He went on to explain Eric's concerns.

"So what now?" Sydney asked.

"If he saw our guy, he'll go underground. We won't see him again."

"Maybe. I doubt it, though," she replied.

"Doubt what?"

"That we won't see him again. I don't think he'll abandon the area just because some guy at the gym looked at him funny. If these guys are as trained and prepared as you think they are, he may just hunker down in the area and wait. The Shepherds are still running in other areas. He may think he can wait until we move on to something else. If LA proves to be a dead-end, we'll have to.

Deacon and the suits aren't going to let us just sit here."

Jack considered it and determined she was right. "The Tampa crew has nothing new to work with. I talked to the local SAC again last night. Same in Texas. The others are old. This is the only Shepherds case with a suspect description and material evidence. We have to stay here until we have something better."

"What about the other suspects?"

Sydney was keeping the list. "Ruled out save for two, maybe one. We found a flight to Atlanta on his credit card and a trade show convention for his occupation. It's over tonight, so we expect him home soon. The other is a charter fisherman and his boat's out to sea right now. The Coast Guard is tracking it down. I imagine it's down in Mexico somewhere for the weekend. Either way, they both look clean. Our guy from the gym is the last unknown."

They took the news in silence. Jack shoved the remains of his sandwich away and put his feet up on the desk.

"One break. That's all we need. Ideas? Anybody?"

Laurie chewed the last of her Caesar salad in

silence before closing the Styrofoam container and tossing it on the table. She'd stayed silent throughout the conversation, slowly digesting the information.

"We still have one possibility to find him."

"What? The storage place? You really think he'll go there if he thinks we're on to him?"

Laurie wiped her face with a napkin and sat back. Jack pulled his feet down and spun around to face her.

"C'mon, new girl. Use that big brain of yours."

"I think the question is: how bad does he want to stay?"

"I would think any risk of getting caught would demand he leave the area. That's sniper 101, never stay in the area you just fired a shot from."

"Maybe. To you, it might. But to this guy, I'm not so sure. He's gotten away with it before, as have the others. Maybe he thinks he can beat us."

"The entire LAPD and the FBI? That's pretty ballsy."

Laurie shrugged. "Again, maybe. He's done it so far. Wouldn't be the first time complacency has taken down a guy like this."

Sydney watched Jack twirl a pen through his fingers as he often did while thinking. She had tried it herself a few times only to flip it into her own face. At that point, she had given up. Now she waited.

"Okay, let's run with that in mind. What—"

Greg interrupted. "You really think he's still in the area?"

"I have to," Jack shot back. "The alternative says we're done. So, with the theory that he's laying low in the area, what do we do next?"

---

CARTER HAD AWAKENED AT FIVE. The California night chill was still making itself known, and he tried to ignore it and get a little more sleep. It was a losing battle.

The condo was in a different kind of neighborhood than the one of his primary house. The noises were different. The sun came in from the other direction. The neighbors were close. All of these things had combined to wake him at odd hours throughout the night, and he had gotten little sleep. A barking dog and a garbage truck eventually forced his surrender, and after a quick check of the front and back doors followed by a long look outside in all directions, he made it to the shower.

The freezing cold water cleared his mind, and he let it chill him until he shivered before shutting it off. He wandered to the closet and selected clothes from the limited supply. Not that it mattered much; one could wear almost anything if the plan was to do nothing but watch TV all day. He had binge-watched an entire season of something military which he'd vaguely heard of before. It wasn't bad, just far from realistic.

The refrigerator held leftover Chinese and a half gallon of milk. He took the container to the couch with him and thumbed on the TV looking for the news. No newsflash with his picture on the screen, so he hit the mute and checked the phone. A coded message from William telling him that he'd found nothing so far but was still looking. Carter sighed and drained the milk.

The right thing to do was to stay in place for a few more days, but Carter wasn't the sit-still type. One could only do so many push-ups and sit-ups before boredom took over. He could go for a run, but the end result would still be him sitting right where he was now. The news went off the air and was replaced with *The Price is Right*. He remembered watching it as a kid whenever he was at home sick. It was a good memory, despite the illness part. Just him and his mom sitting on the couch together. Sometimes he and his sister were sick at the same time and would shout guesses at the tiny screen for things they could never even hope to have. He watched silently as the people bid on stuff they would never buy themselves, his thoughts in a former life, one that was long since gone and never to return.

A wave of anger forced him to his feet. He threw the clothes he had just put on in the corner and replaced them with a pair of jeans and a T-shirt. Heavy boots were soon on his feet, and he was out the door heading for the storage garage. He couldn't take care of his little sister by sitting on his ass. It was time to get busy. Tools. He needed tools to do his job, and they weren't ready. Paranoid or not, they wouldn't wait any longer. If he moved now, he could spend some time grinding off serial numbers before the real heat of the day set in.

———

"I MISS THE AREA."

Jack pulled his eyes from the rearview mirror and fixed them on his partner. Larry had his seat reclined and his head to one side. The California sun was full in his face behind the sunglasses.

"You're going to burn."

"Maybe."

"Maybe," Jack repeated. "That seems to be the word for the day."

"Fits. You don't like it?"

Jack frowned and returned his gaze to the mirror. "Better than others I guess."

They had been in the alley for two hours, parked in a spot reserved for the pawn shop. Jack was restless. They didn't have enough for a warrant, but Jack had asked Deacon to apply some pressure in places and hopefully change that. They had game-planned for a short time and then finally driven over to sit on the storage unit.

"Why did you veto the surveillance team? They're good. I mean, they do Internal Affairs investigations. If the cops can't see them following them, I doubt this guy would."

"I want this kept as compartmented as possible."

"I can see that, but why?"

"Something Eric said."

Larry pulled his head up and out of the sun and gave Jack a look. "What?"

Jack squirmed in his seat and kept his eyes on the mirror. These were some of his partner's friends he was talking about. "He thinks the LAPD computers are compromised. No, he basically said they *are* compromised."

"Do I want to know how he ...?"

"No."

Larry chewed on the information for a moment.

"Okay, since I can retire at any time and really don't give a damn, I'll ask. Is it us watching them, or somebody else?"

"No way of knowing for sure, but the Bureau has access to most of their traffic already. A left-over from, well, you know."

"Yeah."

Since the corruption issues a decade ago the FBI had kept a close watch on the LAPD. Something they had despised, but had to admit was of their own doing. Most of them had developed ways around it. Private email servers and sterile phones mostly. The new Chief had cleaned house, but the workarounds still remained in place. They were far from being the only depart-ment to do so.

"You think the Shepherds are in the system?"

"I can't rule it out. Neither can Eric."

"Is that why we're printing stuff off at Kinko's now?"

"Yeah. Printers are especially vulnerable to

hacking. Something I've learned. Anyway, Eric is on it, but he says it's a needle in a haystack."

"So no help from PD?" Larry deadpanned.

"Not unless we have to."

Larry sighed and placed his head back into the sun. "How long until Greg and Laurie get here?"

"Two hours."

"Wake me up then."

———

CARTER MOPPED his forehead and tossed the towel aside. The temperature was rising, and the inside of the storage garage was leaking the cool air it contained when he had arrived. He grabbed another bottle of Gatorade out of the cooler, the ice that remained was small. He sat down and eyeballed the checklist while he drank.

Engine block. Transmission. Frame. Window plate. Door jambs. Two hours of work and he was only halfway through. The Tyvek coverall he wore was covered in metallic dust from the hours of grinding. He had hammered over the existing numbers with a number eight punch before grinding them down to smooth metal. The stickers full of numbers and bar codes had been scraped away with a putty knife. He found himself wishing he'd purchased an older van—the newer they were the more identifying numbers they had. He estimated another two hours of grinding and then another two hours of cleaning before the van was sterile. It was anything but enjoyable work, but it had to be done.

He got up with a grunt and walked to the drain in the center of the floor to pee. Shedding the Tyvek, which didn't breathe at all, was a huge relief. His clothing was saturated with sweat. What little moving air there was felt wonderful, and he considered knocking off for the day. Maybe another hour. At that point the heat would be dangerous—if he passed out in this garage they wouldn't find him for weeks. The woman who ran the place never came out of her office unless it was to go home—one of the reasons he liked the place. They had only spoken once since he had rented the place, and Carter had no desire to change that.

He pulled the soaked shorts back in place and then tugged on the Tyvek. It had stuck to his sweaty back and required some persuasion to get back in place.

"C'mon," he bitched, shrugging his massive shoulders. It was the biggest suit they made, and he had ordered a few dozen when he'd first gotten set up here, only to find them a tight fit. But they were necessary to prevent leaving physical evidence behind while he worked. Still, they were extremely uncomfortable.

The suit responded by splitting across the shoulders, the seam parting into a two-foot opening. Carter cursed it and then ripped it further, shredding the garment as he took it off and then wadding it up.

"Damn it." He shoved the suit into a plastic bag and left it by the door. He paced a bit and slapped a handful of ice water on his face from the cooler. He eyeballed the stack of suits in the corner and counted them. He'd have to be more careful, he was getting low.

Deciding to call it a day, he changed clothes. The old ones he tossed into his backpack and made for the car.

His eyes fell on the remaining electric motorcycle parked on the other side. This one a street version. The charger was in place and giving off a friendly green light. He checked his watch. It was too hot to keep working. He couldn't go home or to any of the gyms. He loathed the condo. Maybe a ride out to Malibu on the bike would make the day go faster?

"Larry!"

"What?"

"Wake up, he's leaving!"

"Oh, sh—where?"

"On that motorcycle! Let's go!"

Larry tried to drop the car in gear, but it wasn't running. He slammed it into park and quickly got it going.

"Where?"

"He turned west, that way."

"Hell, Jack. A little warning!"

"He came right out and turned, he didn't even stop at the road."

"You sure it's him?"

"No, just a huge black guy on a motorcycle, but I'm going with the odds."

Larry grunted and sped up. The bike was visible two blocks ahead over the top of a small car in front of them.

"Close enough," Jack warned.

"Thanks, Jack, I have done this before you know."

"Sorry. Where you think he's going?"

"Right now? West. Nope, make that south." He worked the turn and made it through the light just in time.

"Funny. Where do you think he's going?"

"No telling. Let's see where he goes when we come to the 101."

Jack drummed his fingers against the dash before stopping after a side look from Larry. They pulled up at a light a block from the 101. The guy was two cars in front of them. Jack kept his gaze forward and neutral as he watched the man scan the traffic around him.

"Big dude. It has to be him. You want to call in some back-up?"

Jack struggled with the question. He could get on the phone and have a few units and a helicopter overhead in a matter of minutes, but that would involve the LAPD communication network. The warning from Eric rang loud in his ears.

"Not yet. How close are Sydney and Greg?"

"About fifteen minutes behind us."

"Crap, just stay with him. But if he gets on the highway he's gone. He'll split through the traffic, and we'll lose him within a few miles."

"Okay."

The light changed and they edged through with most of the traffic veering to the right to enter the 101. To their dismay he got on and headed west. Jack pulled out his phone, but the man chose to merge with traffic and match their speed. They passed the 401 and moved into the right-hand lane. Jack put the phone down.

"Ideas?"

"None yet. He's not moving too fast, so maybe he's getting off soon."

As if hearing them the bike exited the freeway at Topanga Canyon Road. The biker headed south and stayed in the middle lane without slowing. The traffic thinned and Larry dropped back.

"Woodland Hills," he announced.

"What's in Woodland Hills?"

"Nothing. Houses. He may cut up into the hills though."

"What for?"

"No telling. He may be just out for a ride, Jack. From here it heads over the hills to the other side and meets Highway One. Then it's either south to Santa Monica or north to Malibu."

As if he were reading Larry's mind the bike pulled to a stop at Ventura. He stayed in the middle lane. The light lasted only a few seconds before turning and the bike accelerated away into the open space in front of it.

"What if ...?"

"Shhhhh." Larry held up a finger and craned his head out the window.

"Hear that?"

"What? No."

"Exactly. He's on an electric bike."

Larry slowed to let some cars get between them and then kept pace until the biker disappeared behind a bend. The road became steeper and began to twist and turn after they passed Mulholland Drive. They craned their heads to see in both directions before speeding through.

"Can we get somebody on the other side to pick him up when he gets to the One?" Jack asked.

"There's a million options once he's up in the hills. If he really is just out for a joyride he may take the long route. For all we know he's going to ride up and take in the view before coming back down. Or he may go to Malibu for a beer and then circle around. We need a helicopter."

"No, not yet. Just see what we can do."

"Okay, boss." Larry floored the accelerator, and they made good progress before getting behind a pair of cars stacked up behind a flatbed hauling some digging equipment. Jack frowned at their pace and the numerous side roads they passed before they finally were able to get around the slower traffic. He punched up a map of the area on his phone only to see a tangled mess of back roads and residential areas between them and the beach. He estimated the range of the bike with his fingers and drew a mental circle on the map before looking up. The bike was nowhere in sight.

"Malibu. Let's head there and hope we spot him."

Larry watched Jack out of the corner of his eye. It wasn't long.

"Son of a bitch!"

# 17

*"It is the duty of youths to war against indiscipline and corruption because they are the leaders of tomorrow."*

—*Ifeanyi Enoch Onuoha*

"**S**ir, I need that warrant. The longer we sit and watch this guy the greater the chance of us being seen. If that happens this guy is *gone*."

"Alright, Jack. Calm down. The judge said no last time, you'll need to give us something new, something concrete."

"We followed him for a bit, he was on an electric motorcycle. The plate comes up as stolen but done very well."

"Very well?"

"Stolen from the exact same make and model of bike, only this one belongs to a teenager in Santa Monica. When we contacted him at his parents' house, he didn't even realize the plate had been switched. And that plate was stolen as well, off a bike in Ventura. Who does that? Who would go to such efforts to hide their identity? I'm telling you, this is our guy!"

Deacon was scribbling notes but gave up. "You sure you don't want to follow this guy instead? He could lead us to the leadership."

"I've been weighing that, but I think we're better off bringing him in. At least then we'll have a link. Once we figure out who he really is we can hopefully make the connections we need to the rest of the Shepherds. If we follow, and he catches on, he'll bolt and we're back where we started."

There was no reply for a moment, and they all held their breath, waiting.

"Okay, Jack. I'll go with your call. Send this

all to me and I'll get it to the people you need. They'll make the calls to the judge this time. I've already pushed this enough and we need some new blood. You still watching the garage?"

"24-7 now. He didn't come back."

"Alright, give me a couple hours. But Jack ..."

"Yes, sir?"

"There are ways around a warrant." Deacon hung up before Jack could respond.

Jack tossed the phone on the table. Sydney came in and posted up some shots of the man on the motorcycle taken from the dash cam. She had borrowed the LAPD lab gear to blow them up and enhance them.

"Anything?"

"Not really. No scars or tattoos that I can see. The clothes are just clothes. Other than his size he's just a guy on a bike."

Jack's gut rumbled and he reached for the bottle of antacids on the table. Sydney frowned but held her tongue. Jack crunched them loud enough for them all to hear.

"This is our guy. I *know* it. I want a plan to raid that storage unit without calling attention. Get a rental truck or something big enough to hide a whole team and we'll use it to get in and block the entrance view from the street. What other ways out of there are there?"

Greg added another printout to the wall. An overhead shot of the entire facility.

"The rear side backs up to this warehouse for the full length, there's a fence up against it. Must have built it after, waste of money now. Anyway, there's that and the open area to the east. Again the fence and on the other side a row of junk cars. To the west it's another fence and a row of garage type businesses. They have dogs at night."

"Size and shape?" Larry asked.

"Big Rottweilers."

"Thanks."

"Okay. What do you think, Greg?" Jack asked. Greg was a former leader of the FBI's Hostage Rescue Team. If anyone knew how to take down a suspect like the one they were after it was him.

"I think we should use the place. Let him come in and then cut off the exit here in the front. Stage some people to the east since that's the only remaining exit; over the fence and into the junkyard lot. After that he can move in any direction. The neighborhood that way is a bit of a maze as well. It's where I would want to go since it would give me the best chance of losing a pursuer."

Jack eyeballed the picture, seeing it through Greg's eyes. He had to agree.

"How tall's that fence?"

"Eight foot, with some old barbed wire on top. Nothing a guy like this can't handle."

"Okay." Jack turned and smiled at Larry.

"What's so funny?"

"Her majesty's not going to like this."

CARTER CAREFULLY CRUISED the streets in the pre-dawn traffic. Reseda was a bedroom community and there were plenty of commuters on their way to work, not like Hollywood where everyone slept till noon. He had to be careful not to fall prey to a zombie driver, still asleep and sipping a coffee while at the wheel. Between the silent bike and the darkness of his skin he knew he was not easy to see.

After his ride to the beach and a few beers the day before he'd determined that he had enough of a charge left to make it to the condo. The garage would have been cutting it too close and he didn't feel like pushing the bike for blocks if it decided to die on him. He'd parked it in the dining room without anyone noticing and plugged it in for the night.

He'd showered the grime off of his frame and wolfed down a sub he'd picked up on the way home before binge-watching another TV show. He'd dozed off before it was over, and the TV had awakened him at four AM with a loud action scene. He'd jerked awake and rolled off the couch before getting his bearings. Thumbing it off with a curse he decided to head for the garage and get some work done before it got too hot again. So now here he was, an early morning commuter.

The street was void of traffic when he turned, and he cruised the entire length before turning in. He slowed to a stop at the sight of the rental truck parked in the entrance. Reaching a hand out he felt the hood. It was cold. The truck had been there for some time. He glanced inside and saw a sparse interior. A rental agreement lay on the passenger seat. Warning stickers about the height and weight limits adorned the dash. It looked like every rental truck he had ever used. Still, he walked the bike forward until he could see the rear end. Locked. He listened. Nothing.

He didn't like it. Sitting next to the truck he scanned the area. Nothing looked out of place. The office was dark. Even the trash stuck in the fence was still there. Drawing his gun he tapped it on the skin of the truck. It echoed back. The truck was empty or close to it. He debated busting the lock and looking inside, but decided that might call too much attention, especially if he was the only one here and making noise. Someone might knock on the door to ask if he had seen anything. Maybe he should just go home for the day, come back tomorrow, the truck might be gone by then.

His mind rebelled against the idea of another day stuck on the couch. He was being paranoid. It was a stupid rental truck, left there by a new neighbor. Time to quit screwing around and get to work.

He opened his garage and pushed the bike inside before shutting it and throwing the lock closed. He hooked up the bike to a charger and changed into a Tyvek suit. The grinder fired up with a sequel and he soon had sparks flying across the concrete floor.

---

"Okay, people, you can all breathe. He's inside," Larry whispered from across the street. He was sitting in front of the pawn shop windows with a pair of binoculars. The owner had donated both the space and the lenses after seeing Larry's much smaller ones. The chair was from his office and actually quite comfortable. He had definitely gotten the better end of the deal. Sometimes being old had its advantages.

"About time," Jack radioed back. "Think he's on to us?"

"No, not unless he pulls out in the car in the next minute and hightails it out of here. What's that noise?"

"Sounds like a metal grinder. You can hear that?"

"Yeah, there's nothing else making noise. Is the door open?"

Sydney turned from her peephole in the back of the truck, shook her head and made a hooking gesture.

"No, he closed and I'm sure latched it behind him."

"So I guess it's option two then, sorry guys."

Jack clicked the mic in response. After game-planning this for hours they had come up with two options. One was to surround the place after he had gone in and demand his surrender. Since they suspected the target had numerous weapons and possibly even explosives inside, they hoped not to have to do that. Option two was confronting him while he was coming or going. Larry had waved them off when he pulled the gun and never got off the bike on the way in—they didn't want a moving gun battle on the streets of LA.

"Sorry, guys, I guess you'll just have to get comfortable."

"We're here until we get a warrant? Could be a long time."

"We don't need a warrant if he runs," was Jack's answer.

Sydney opened her mouth to question that, but the look on Jack's face changed her mind. She exchanged a look with Greg who offered a quick smile. If Jack was tired of waiting, he evidently had no problem with it. A look at Laurie got the same answer.

She decided that neither did she.

---

BUNKER FORCED HIS EYES OPEN.

Pain. His leg was on fire. His hand reached for it but was stopped by some unknown force. A hand was on his forehead, and he squinted against the light to make out the face. A bearded face with a pair of curious eyes behind a pair of broken eyeglasses. His head was wrapped in black. The ceiling overhead fluttered in the wind. Tent, his brain labeled it. He was in a tent. Trying to speak produced no sound, his mouth was too dry.

"No speak," the man whispered.

The man reached behind him and produced a cloth dipped in water. He squeezed a few drops into Bunker's mouth. He sucked it in too fast and choked, coughing forcefully and sending waves of pain through his chest and leg. A hand was slapped over his mouth in an effort to silence him.

"Silence," he hissed.

"Wh-where?"

"No speak." The man gestured behind him. "They will hear you."

Who was they? Why was he in a tent? He craned his head to look down at his body. His flight suit was gone, and his chest was wrapped in torn strips of cloth. His leg was also wrapped in layers of bloody sheets and held straight by two pieces of lumber, one of which had a nail still protruding from it. His boots were gone as well. The man pushed him back down to the ground and held up a finger. *Stay*, it said. As if he had a choice.

Then it all came flooding back. The mission. The bombs. The gun that had tried to kill them and their attack on it. Hoffman screaming. The missile. The ejection. Pain. Blackness.

He looked at the man staring down at him. There was a stethoscope around his neck. A doctor?

"Where am I?"

The man leaned down and whispered in his ear.

"You are in Syria, in the hands of ISIS."

Bunker's eyes widened. He looked for an escape. His eyes traveled in all directions. There was the tent. The remains of his flight suit cut up and lying in a corner. A couple of backpacks covered in dust. A medical bag with US Red Cross printed on it. That was all. His flight vest with the beacon attached was gone.

"Hoff? Where's my friend?"

"They took him away."

"He's alive?"

"I don't know."

Bunker squeezed his eyes shut. His mind raced through the possibilities before a hand on his shoulder brought him out of it. The man with the glasses.

"Who are you?"

"I am not one of them."

Before he could ask more, they heard voices approaching. The man brushed his eyes closed and sat back. Bunker did his best to feign sleep, but his heart threatened to leave his chest.

---

THE VAN WAS READY. He'd stamped and ground off every number he could find. After that he'd replaced the air and fuel filters, given it an oil change and then wiped everything down with bleach. The fumes were harsh, and he was tempted to open the door and let them out, but instead he adjusted the fan, hoping it would help. Deciding the van was as dry as it needed to be he shut the doors and pulled the tarp over it. He cleaned up his trash while thinking about what was next. New bikes. A rifle. Maybe he'd go shopping for that today. Somewhere south. There were gun shows almost every weekend in San Diego. Maybe it was time for a little road trip.

He toweled the sweat and grit off as best he could before tossing it aside. The bike was charged. He could drive it to his primary residence and exchange it for the car and then head south or use the car at his third residence. That would be the safer choice, even though he preferred the Mercedes to the very plain Jeep SUV. He tucked his gun inside his belt in front and pulled the shirt down—doing so in the back was not an option when riding a bike.

---

BUNKER GRIT his teeth as the man adjusted the bandage on his leg. The men had finally left after screaming at him for several minutes. One had kicked him, drawing an involuntary cry, and the men laughed. The doctor had spoken harshly only to be shoved aside. A conversation had ensued, very one-sided and with several threatening gestures. It ended with the doctor being slapped across the face, sending his eyeglasses flying. The man took several pictures of their captive and laughed again as they walked out.

Bunker watched the man search for the glasses and then carefully examine them for further damage. He bent the frame carefully back in place before placing them back on his face.

"Are you alright?"

The man smiled at the question. "For now. How is your pain?"

"It hurts," Bunker admitted. "Are you really a doctor?"

"An orthopedist."

"What's your name?"

"I am Dr. Waqas ul Haq. I'm from Pakistan."

"Pakistan? How did you get here?"

"That is a long story."

"Well, I'm not going anywhere."

"Let's hope not." He pulled the bandage away as he spoke. Bunker looked down expecting to see bones protruding. Instead he found a leg he barely recognized. His once pale skin was now several shades of blue, the tissue mottled with bruising. A ragged line of sutures traveled across his thigh. He reached down to move the board wedged in his crotch, but the man pushed his hands away.

"You don't wish to move that, it applies traction, and it's keeping the pain away."

"How bad?"

"It's bad. A compound fracture of the femur. I was able to set the bone, I think. Without an x-ray there's no way to be sure. The traction is crude, but effective. I apologize for the sutures. I am in short supply. Fortunately for you I have antibiotics. For some reason they are plentiful. Russian made, so most likely from a Syrian hospital. Pain meds, not so much. You will have to make do. You have some cracked ribs and a head injury as well, but other than that you seem to be intact."

"My WSO? Did you see him?"

"I only saw you. I know they took him some-where else, where I do not know."

Bunker grimaced at the news. There was nothing he could do about it.

"Why are you here?"

The man offered a half-smile. "Not by choice. I was in Syria with my wife. ISIS raided the city, and we were separated. The Russians came with their planes. I returned three days later to search for them. I found a note telling me they went to Jor-dan. I have no idea if they made it. Later that day I was treating people at a makeshift clinic. They captured it and took me and two others east. I've been forced to treat their soldiers ever since."

"You're Muslim," Bunker stated.

"Yes, but I am not one of them, and it is they who are not Muslim."

Bunker wasn't sure what to make of that state-ment. Was the doctor really a fake, a man trying to get information from him? Was the slap just a show? He didn't know, and he was too tired to wrap his head around it.

"What will they do?"

"With you? I don't know. I imagine those pic-tures will be on the internet very soon. You are a trophy, something they can use to inspire others to their cause."

"And when that's over?"

"I don't know." The man gestured to his flight suit in the corner. "Your name is Bunker? I have never heard that name."

"It's my last name. My first name is Andrew."

"A pleasure to meet you, Andrew."

"I wish I could say the same."

The doctor finished rebandaging the leg and reached for a bottle of water. He held his patient's head up so he could drink without choking.

"Are you hungry?"

"No."

"Very well. You should eat though, even if you are not."

"Maybe later."

The doctor nodded and set about cleaning the area. Bunker watched him.

"How many of them are here?"

The doctor seemed confused by the question. "About forty, sometimes more, they will leave soon to join the fighting to the east. We are miles away from the Kurds, even farther from the Turks. You cannot walk and even if you could, there is nowhere to hide in the desert."

"Oh, I know. I was just thinking."

"Well stop, you need to rest."

"Yeah." Bunker closed his eyes, but sleep would not come.

# 18

*"It isn't the young who corrupt the old, rather it's the inverse. The aim of the old should be to ensure that the young grow up incorruptible."*

—Justin K. McFarlane Beau

"You hear that?" Sydney whispered.

Jack shook his head. Years of shooting and blowing things up had taken a toll on his hearing. It was one of the reasons Jack had placed her by the door.

"The latch," she hissed.

Greg got to his feet and grabbed his rifle before walking to the door. He knelt down and placed his hands on the mechanism. Jack and Laurie creeped over as well.

"We may have some movement, Larry," Jack whispered into the mic.

"Got it, I'm moving."

"Wait till he's out and the door is shut and latched again."

Laurie nodded and got down on the floor. Drawing her .44 she lay prone with it in front of her. Jack nodded in agreement. She would have a clear shot the second the door was raised, the rest of them had to stay on their feet in case he bolted. The gun looked outrageously huge in her small grip, but there was no denying she knew how to use it.

The sound of the storage unit door sliding open reached their ears. After a slight pause they heard it shut and the metal-on-metal sounds of the lock being worked.

"I'm in the east lot," Larry whispered in their ears. Jack clicked the mic in response. He held up three fingers, then two. The sounds stopped.

Jack nodded and Greg raised the door.
"FBI! Don't move!"

---

"YOU SAID YOUR WIFE WAS SYRIAN?"

The doctor was sharing a meal of thin vegetable soup with pita bread and water with his patient. A young boy had brought it and quickly disappeared.

"Yes, we met in school in England. We have two children. I was here to try once again to gain favor with her parents. It did not go well."

They don't approve of you? A doctor is not good enough for their little girl?"

"Their little *Christian* girl," he corrected.

"Ahh, I see now. This is why they treat you that way."

"Yes. If I were not useful to them, I would be separated from my head and buried on the side of the road."

Bunker nodded, it made sense now, even if it did not.

"I have a new son. Four months."

"You're just getting started." He offered his patient a fig and he nodded in the affirmative.

"This is good."

The doctor nodded. "Something they do well here."

Bunker remembered the orchards surrounding his target. He was now in a tent. Had they not moved him?

"Do you know where we are?"

"Somewhere in the interior, west of Homs. They blindfold me when they move me. I cannot be more accurate than that."

Bunker thought of a test question.

"Are we near where I was shot down?"

"Yes, very."

"You were here when it happened?"

"Yes, you almost took my life as well."

"As well?"

"The leader you targeted, you were successful."

"Not sure I'd agree with you a hundred percent. The missiles, I didn't ..."

"They have missiles?"

"A heat-seeker of some type, I'm not sure. I just hope they don't have any more." Bunker stopped before he said too much.

The doctor nodded. "They were boasting before. Hoping you would come. I thought them very foolish to wish for such a thing, but I understand now." Another thought emerged and he looked to his patient, whose face confirmed his suspicion.

"Will they come for you, Mr. Andrew?"

"They don't know where I am." Bunker waved the idea away. "Without my radio or beacon they'll never find me."

"But they are looking?"

"Oh, they probably are. Especially if that picture they took goes viral. But unless I get moved there's nothing to see, even if the drone was right over the top of us."

The doctor chewed slowly, deep in thought.

"Mr. Andrew, I wish to go home. I wish to see my family again."

"I do too, Waqas, I do too."

"If I tell your drone where you are, and they come for you, will they take me too?"

Bunker turned and looked the man in the eye. "How?"

"Leave that to me."

CARTER FLINCHED when the door to the truck slid up. Caught off guard, he dropped the bike and ran. His eyes had caught sight of at least four people inside the back, but he wasted no time looking further.

"Syd, get the entrance!"

Greg hit the ground running with Jack right behind. Sydney bolted out and around the corner to cut off the entrance. Laurie jumped out and examined the lock on the unit. It was secured. She tugged on it, and it held. Their suspect couldn't get back in without it costing too much time. She checked the bike laying in front of it. The keys were in it, and she quickly pulled them before taking off after the men.

BASTARD'S FAST, Greg thought as he raced after him. The calf was complaining, but he ignored it as he came to a corner. He threw his body up against the wall and stuck his head out for a look just as Jack arrived.

A bullet caromed off the steel just as he pulled back.

"Shots fired, he's armed and heading east, just like we thought."

"Coming to you, Larry!" Jack yelled into the mic. He dropped to his knees and stuck his own head out and saw nothing. He moved around the corner in pursuit with Greg hot on his heels. The storage facility split, and Jack waved Greg to the left while he went right, both of them pausing at every corner before moving on.

Where did he go?

LARRY SCANNED the fence over the barrel of his .357 resting on the hood of a parked car. He had an open view of the entire fence line and had no intention of letting the guy get across it. After hearing the crack of a pistol inside he was ready to shoot the man on sight. If he tried climbing the fence maybe he could put one in his leg. He heard Jack or someone breathing heavy into the mic and realized he was doing the same without any exertion.

"He should be here by now," he said. He keyed the mic. "Jack, I got nothing. He's not here."

Jack paused at another corner and keyed his mic. "What? He was heading right to you."

"He's not here! Check your six."

Jack turned and caught sight of a giant fist just before it snapped his head around.

GREG STUCK his head around the corner and took a mental snapshot before pulling back. The fence line. Some cars on the other side. And some open space. He bolted around the corner and scanned again over the barrel of his rifle.

Nothing.

Larry rose from behind a car. "He didn't come out! He's still in there!"

"Shit! Stay there!"

Greg spun and ran back the way he had come, keying the mic as he went.

"He's still in the complex, he's still in the complex. Jack, where are you?"

No answer.

"Jack?"

Greg ran faster.

---

CARTER STUFFED the gun in his belt and ran full speed at the fence, leaping as high as he could and grabbing the links with his ham-like fists. He reached the top in under ten seconds and yanked at the barbed wire. It fell away with little resistance. He had cut it soon after renting the unit and simply bent it into a weak link in the event he needed to get over the fence quickly. The roof of the garage next door was almost within reach, if he could get to it and down the other side he could escape into the surrounding buildings. He could feel the heat reflecting off the metal skin of the building only a foot from his face. He gripped the top bar and got ready to swing his foot up.

*BOOM!*

A large hole appeared in the metal wall inches from his face. He felt the passing of the round on his cheek. The report was loud, and his brain instantly categorized it as a large caliber handgun.

Drop. Roll. Draw. Return fire. The programmed response was already loading into his brain and—

*BOOM!*

Another hole appeared next to the first, this time on the other side of his head.

"The first was no accident! Come down that fence and do it slow or the next one is center mass!"

Carter froze. A female. One that could shoot.

"Do what she says! Now!"

A male voice. The guy with the rifle?

His brain searched for options.

KIMBERLY VOGL WAS A GAMER. She'd spent many of her twenty-four years side by side with her brother on the couch with a controller in her hands. It seemed natural for her to work toward a degree in computer science. It was something she was still working on.

In order to pay for her degree she had joined the air force. After a few entrance exams and a security clearance, she'd been offered the ultimate video game. Drone pilot. She now spent her days operating an airborne platform worth millions of dollars from a comfortable chair on the other side of the earth. The joystick was not much different than the one she had grown up using.

She punched in the grid coordinates of the terrain the intelligence department wished to see, and her global hawk responded with a right turn. Monitoring the strength of the data link was her only task until it reached the area. She initiated a grid pattern search and activated the camera pod.

"It's a desert!" she exclaimed to her partner with a grin.

"It's not funny anymore," he answered.

"Or maybe it's you that's not funny," she shot back. "Prob'ly why you're single, just sayin'."

"Ha-ha. What grid you running?"

"Ladder. North to south for BDA on target 60489."

"Got it. You're green."

"Copy."

She watched the screen as the drone tracked its way south. After three turns she saw it. A small town bisected by what was accepted as a highway in that part of the world, running from the north-east to the southwest. A few orchards to the south. Growing what? She didn't know. Some smaller buildings.

"Whoa. That's a big hole."

Her partner craned his neck around to see. The center of the town was gone, reduced to a pile of rubble.

Kim keyed her mic and addressed her commanding officer. "Sir, I've got visuals on 60489."

"On my way."

They watched the drone move over the town. A few tents were set up to the south. A few more among the rubble. Shapes moved around and over it, salvaging what they could. Her boss appeared and watched over her shoulder without comment. It was all being recorded and watched by the intel squad a few rooms away. Their job was just to go where they were told and take pictures of what they wanted to see.

"Well, if the target was in that building, I'd say they got it."

The screen lit up with a text command. Kim acknowledged it and canceled the ladder search in favor of a spiraling one outward from the impact area.

"Look on this ridge, is that a cave?"

"With smoke. Cavemen?" she quipped.

Her boss didn't comment on her attempt at humor. His best pilot had yet to understand that those were real live people under her drone, ones that had been alive the night before. She was insulated by the distance and the technology. To her this was little more than an elaborate video game. Someday it would dawn on her that this game was for real, but until then she'd always be on an intelligence platform.

"Look here, to the west," he ordered.

She zoomed the camera in on the black smudge. It was if someone had spilled an ashtray across the ground.

"Farther."

She went in tighter and adjusted the resolution. A cone shaped object appeared, followed by some pieces of its twin. She was trying to wrap her head around what they might be.

"To the east, halfway up the ridge," her partner prompted.

She zoomed the camera and looked for what had caught his eye. Some fabric, fluttering in the wind. Its orange and white color identified it immediately.

"A parachute, sir! Two of them."

"Bodies?" He leaned over so far, she thought he was going to fall in her lap.

"Um, negative. Just the seats and the chutes."

The screen was suddenly framed in red, and a secret clearance code was plastered at the top. The footage had just been classified by the intelligence dweebs.

"Oh my god," she breathed. "Those things, I didn't know ..."

"The afterburner cowling, they tend to survive the impact and fire intact," her partner informed her. He watched her face as she stared at the image.

"You alright, Kim?"

"Yeah, yeah, I'm good. What do you think they'll want next? I mean, where are the pilots?"

"I imagine we'll be trying to find that out. Let's continue on this pattern until they tell us otherwise."

"Yes, sir."

Kim wiped the sweat from her hands on her pants before grasping the joystick again. Her boss left to visit with the men down the hall.

# 19

*"A system is corrupt when it is strictly profit-driven, not driven to serve the best interests of its people."*

—*Suzy Kassem*

Carter planted his second foot on the ground and waited, keeping his hands high up on the fence. If the guy with the rifle got close, maybe.

But he didn't. He stayed far enough away to take away that option. The girl with the cannon in her fist moved left. The guy with the rifle to the right. He heard more feet approaching.

"In his belt," Greg warned.

Sydney holstered her H&K and walked up behind the man.

"On your knees, you know the drill. One move toward that gun and I put one out your chest."

Carter slowly complied. The woman snapped a set of cuffs on one wrist before guiding his arms down behind him and joining them. She then reached around and liberated the Sig from his waistband and tossed it away. She grabbed a handful of his pant leg and crossed his ankles before roughly shoving him over to land on his side. Carter saw it all coming and rolled with it in silence.

More footsteps. Carter looked up to see a fat man with a revolver in his fist jogging up. He was sweating profusely. The man scanned the situation once before asking a question.

"Where's Jack?"

RASHAD AVOIDED MAKING EYE CONTACT. Little Infidel they called him. They used him for labor, and twice for other things he tried not to revisit. This morning he had avoided being hit, and as long as he kept working, he hoped that would continue. The crates where heavy, but he managed to carry some and drag the others. The damage from the bombs was great. The leader's dwelling was now little more than holes in the ground surrounded by rubble and the splintered trees of the surrounding orchard. He had been stacking anything worth saving inside the courtyard. Its walls providing some protection should the planes come again. But the space was getting tight, something he was counting on to hide the task the doctor had given him.

He weaved the crate through the narrow gap and added it to the final pile, arranging it just so. He checked the shapes against the drawing made by the American in the dirt. He had memorized them and then redrew them for both the doctor and pilot before they were satisfied. Now they were spelled out in the courtyard. But how would anyone see them behind the walls?

Retreating to the entrance he piled more crates in its place. Now no one could enter without moving them and he was confident his ISIS captors would not expend the energy to do so. He was done.

---

"You sure you're alright?"

Jack rubbed his jaw and then the back of his head. The first was blue and the second had a nice knot growing under his hair. He accepted the ice pack and debated where to put it first.

"Yeah, guy caught me just right. Just glad it was a fist and not the gun. Dude is big."

"Sure you don't want the doc to look at you?" the medic asked.

Jack pointed to Sydney. "She's my doc."

Sydney exchanged a look with the medic and threw up her hands. "He won't go, just let me steal a couple more of those ice packs and I'll keep an eye on him."

"Ok, just sign here then."

Jack scribbled his signature on the tablet and pushed himself off the back of the car. Sydney walked next to him for a few paces before deciding he wasn't going to fall over, and they ducked the crime-scene tape together.

"So, how'd you stop him?"

"He was trying to climb the fence at the rear of

the complex. Looks like he had it pre-cut to make things faster. Laurie stopped him."

"Laurie?"

"She put two rounds past both his ears with that .44. It convinced him to stop. We might need to apologize to the guy next door though. There's two big holes in his building."

Jack waved the thought aside as they got to the storage unit. Greg was standing in front with a shit-eating grin.

"What do we have?"

"What don't we have is more like it. Two vans, one looks like our brand new one and it's been sterilized. The other one looks like a bug-out vehicle. It's got food, water, a tent. There's a few guns inside. Extra fuel. Enough to live out of for days. There's the motorcycle you saw him on, but there's chargers for two others. What do you want to bet they match the bike we found on the mountain?"

"What else?" Jack pointed to the lockers.

Syd asked, "Did you ...?"

"We just opened them and looked. Nobody's touched anything yet, Syd. I told them to wait for you, but it looks like he was prepared for anything. There's some military hardware. Some explosives and a few grenades. Tools and wire and whatnot to make it all go boom. That box over there has a bunch of passports and other ID in it. This is going to take days to go through."

"A computer? Laptop maybe?"

"Not yet."

Jack scanned the unit while adjusting his icepack. Their chance had paid off. But would it lead anywhere? That was the question.

"I need to call Deacon."

---

"WHAT ARE THE TREES?" Kim asked her partner.

"Olives, I think. Figs maybe. About the only thing that will grow in that area. Why?"

"Just curious. I see a lot of people out there working them."

"It's harvest time."

"Even when bombs are falling all around you?"

"People still have to eat."

"True." Kim shook her head at the thought of working outside while steel fell from the sky.

"You seeing anything new?"

"Not yet. But I just fly where they tell me to." She worked the joystick a bit and then punched a button to send her drone on another search pattern. She had just settled back into her seat and reached for her giant insulated cup of caffeine when a command appeared on her screen—the intelligence guys down the hall again.

"Circle on current orbit," she mumbled before commanding the drone to do so.

"What did they see?"

"I dunno, take a look."

He punched the feed up on his own screen and examined it. He picked out the impact craters, the ridgeline they had heavily photographed the previous day, and the crash site, which the wind was slowly spreading to the north-east. The parachutes were gone and now serving as makeshift tents next to the destroyed buildings.

"What's that?" He pointed.

"What's what? A little direction might help."

"Inside that courtyard to the south of the impact zone. You see it?"

She followed his directions and saw a courtyard full of crates. Evidently, the people working the trees had more than they needed as these were just sitting empty. She examined the courtyard, but didn't see where he was going.

"I don't ..."

"Bottom left corner," he prompted. "What was the call sign of the F-18?"

She saw it and jerked up to view it closer, knocking her drink over in the process. She cursed it and tore her eyes away just long enough to up-right it before examining the screen again.

Numbers. There were four of them spelled out in the crates.

"Five ... oh ... oh?"

"The last one's an eight I think."

She watched the shadows change their angle as the drone circled. A moment later she saw it.

"I agree. Five-oh-eight. What was the call sign?"

"Viking five-oh-eight."

The light in the corner of her screen was blinking repeatedly, telling her the intelligence guys were grabbing numerous stills of the footage.

"How?"

"No idea. But it's there. Our guys are alive, or at least one of them is."

"How can you ..."

"The call sign is something only the crew would know. Since I doubt they are running around the area freely it's one of two things. Either they have someone helping them or ..."

Kim waited. He was waiting for her to put it together, but it wasn't coming.

"Or what?"

"They beat the information out of them, and this is bait."

Kim's mouth went dry as she swallowed the information. They watched silently as the red light continued to blink.

"Hold on, guys," she whispered.

---

WILLIAM WAS READING the files as fast as they could be decrypted. As near as he could tell the man saving the communications worked for a high-level government official. Whether or not the actions were officially sanctioned he couldn't tell. Breaking the code did not necessarily give him their identities. A code name here and there, but little else. Despite his skill and endless supply of hardware, he would have to figure it out from context. Not as easy as it sounded.

Another document announced its readiness with a polite ping and William loaded it onto the largest monitor. He had barely begun when the computer pinged again. A red dot began flashing in the corner of the screen. William clicked on it.

A police report. From the LAPD. A highlighted section drew his attention. It was an address. One that the computers were programmed to watch for.

"Oh, no."

He immediately placed an alert to Number Six and another to Dayton before returning to the screen. He speed-read the report and scribbled notes and then searched for the dispatch report for the day. The address popped up there as well. First a report of shots being fired and units being dispatched. Then another a half hour later.

A request for an evidence recovery unit, from the FBI.

"No, no."

The phone rang and he clicked the answer tab. "Ockham."

"Dayton, William. You called?"

"I have some troubling activity out of LA. The police were called to Mr. Carter's storage facility. Shots fired at around ten this morning, and a second call a half hour later for an evidence recovery unit. The request was from the FBI."

"You've tried contacting him?"

"Just before calling you. I've yet to hear from him."

"Anything else?"

"I'm checking the news broadcast next, and then I intend to run a search through the LAPD computers. I've only had this for about five minutes. Give me some time to confirm and I'll call you back."

"The General?"

"Not yet. I thought it best to call you first."

There was silence while Dayton thought it over.

"Send me the Citation, to Miami. I'll be on my way as soon as I can. Keep trying to contact Number Six and put out an alert to the others. Inform the General and update me every thirty."

"Yes, sir."

<hr>

DAYTON THUMBED off the phone in disgust.

What happened? Somehow they had found Carter. Was he in custody? Did they just have his storage unit? Was he on the run? There were too many unknowns.

He spun the car into a U-turn at the next intersection and got a few honks which he ignored. He floored the accelerator and traveled the ten blocks in record time. He pulled right up to the door and screeched to a halt. He saw the curtain move as he exited the car and walked to the door. It opened before he could knock.

Anna stood before him with one arm behind her back. She scanned the parking lot behind him, and seeing no threats gestured him inside.

"What the hell ...?"

"Pack your stuff, we have to leave." He grabbed her suitcase off the floor and started loading it.

"I'm still in recon," she protested.

"You're aborted. We have a new problem."

"What?"

"A Shepherd may have been captured."

She nodded twice before grabbing her clothes and throwing them on the bed next to the suitcase. Dayton packed them without stopping.

---

CHARLIE REVIEWED his notes from his last talk with the General. The man was putting some steady pressure on him to learn this economics and business stuff, especially the ins and outs of how banks operated. He was doing his best to please the man. He understood why, sort of. Finance was something they weren't taught in school, at least not the school he had attended in DC. The only money those kids saw was government checks or cash, usually with drugs attached. He doubted anyone in his school had ever had a checkbook, or even a savings account. His mother had three sources of income. A paltry check from her job cleaning offices in a government building. Despite working over forty hours a week they still needed an EBT card to supplement that. Occasionally a wad of cash would appear if things got behind. He had found a strange package once in the floorboards of their tiny apartment. Once a man had come late at night and his mother had shooed him into the bedroom before handing it over to the man. That was before the other men had come, before he'd gone to the orphanage and then to the Corps.

He understood it now. His mother had done what she had needed to do, using the only options available. The economics of the drug trade and chronic poverty were simple. Much simpler than what he was reading about now. The crime was the same really, just on a much larger scale. Added zeros. People feeding off of other people.

Accountability though, that was certainly different. If you were busted selling crack your door would be broken down and you had a fifty-fifty chance of being executed, whether it was from a rival dealer or the police it made no difference, you'd be just as dead. White-collar crime was different. If you got caught you were asked to appear, placed on house arrest and, on the slim chance you were found guilty of anything, they *asked* you to report to prison. And don't forget to bring your tennis racket. Amazing.

Why was the General so adamant that he learn this? Was he grooming him for something? Or just making sure he could defend himself from such people? Or was he trying to justify what they were doing?

He'd been giving it a lot of thought lately, what they were doing. Up till now he'd always thought of himself as being in the General's employment. He did not consider himself a member of the Shepherds. Why was that? He was part of the inner circle, he had the knowledge to bring the whole thing crashing down if he should decide to.

But he hadn't, and he was not really sure why. Was it because of his own experience with the law? He'd seen it ruin families, tear them apart and force them into even more dire straits than the ones that had driven them to crime in the first place. By the age of ten most kids in his neighborhood viewed the police as the enemy, something to avoid at all costs. Certainly not someone to go to for help. The General had asked him what he thought justice was; he'd replied that it was authority, the rules. The General had frowned and corrected him. Now Charlie read the man's words at the top of the page where he had jotted them down: *The Law and Justice are two different things, one represents authority and the system, the other integrity and the truth. Never forget that.*

Were the Shepherds fighting for the latter, or trying to become the former? He wasn't sure yet, and he felt the General knew it.

His thoughts were interrupted by the phone.

"Yes, William?"

"Charlie, I need to see the General immediately. It's about an old friend."

Charlie's eyes widened at the use of the code phrase.

"I'll get him right away. Should I call for the plane?"

"No ... not yet. I'll know more soon."

"Alright, five minutes."

Charlie tossed the books and papers aside and sprinted from the room.

## 20

---

*"Weak men cannot handle power. It will either crush them, or they will use it to crush others."*

—*Jocelyn Murray*

"Did he say what happened?"

"No, sir. He just said to bring you down right away."

"Well, you're just a fountain of information today, Charlie."

"I do my best, sir."

Charlie looked down at the man in the chair. Despite his cool exterior he was clearly agitated. The ring on his finger knocked against the padded armrest. Whatever it was it was bad. He glanced at the floor indicator and willed the elevator to drop faster.

Charlie rolled them through the opening doors and William was already buzzing them through the security airlock. The clicking of the keyboard was audible from across the room as William pounded the keys. The screens danced in front of him with data. His muttered cursing became clear as they got closer.

"William?"

William spun to face them, sweat dripping from his brow. Charlie set the brakes on the General's chair before stepping back. William signaled him to stay while he formed his words. The General's ring knocked louder.

"Sir ... Number Six is in custody."

"What? How?"

"I received an alert from the LAPD dispatch this morning. The address of Mr. Carter's storage unit came up. Since it's one of many I couldn't be sure. A half hour later a request for an evidence recovery unit was called in. This was from the FBI. I sent out an alert to Number Six."

"And?"

"I've yet to get a reply."

"Confirmation?"

"None as of yet. The feds, however, are holding a John Doe as of one hour ago. I have no mug shot or other means of identifying the man, but I have to assume it's Mr. Carter."

"They must get several of those a day," Charlie ventured.

"LAPD does. Mostly homeless people or drunks. This is the FBI," William shot back.

"Anything on the news?"

"Negative. The facility has a history of housing stolen property. I'm not sure they would deem that newsworthy enough to send out a crew. I have the computers searching though, just in case."

Charlie watched the ring stop knocking. The pulse in the General's neck could now plainly be seen and his jaw tightened.

"What will he do?" Charlie asked.

"Nothing. He won't even give them a name. He'll wait until we can make contact with him. You've contacted Dayton?"

"He's on his way. The Citation will pick them up in ... twenty minutes if they're there."

"They?"

"I'm assuming he'll bring some help. I have not confirmed that."

"Can we get him back?"

"I don't ..."

"Hold on." The General held up a hand silencing them both. "We don't even know for sure if he's in custody. He may be extracting himself and not be able to make contact yet."

"So, what do you wish to do, sir?"

"Dayton is eight hours away. In the next few hours we need to confirm that Carter's being held and where. Determine if anything in the unit will lead them to us. I doubt that, but we have to consider it until it's been ruled out. Do we not have safeguards in place?"

William took a deep breath. "Yes."

"Initiate them, now."

"Sir, I ..."

"Carefully, Mr. Ockham."

"Yes, sir."

William spun back to the screens and selected one. He pulled up a menu and carefully input a code twice. The screen flashed red a few times and asked him if he was sure that he wished to proceed. He held his breath and clicked the YES key.

---

A THOUSAND MILES away Sydney was cataloging another box of items from the lockers inside the unit. The temperature had risen, and despite the open door, the breeze was minimal. They had spent the last few minutes photographing everything. Now they were planning the removal process. It was going to take some time.

A loud clicking noise drew her attention to the ceiling. She looked up to see the corrugated steel panels offering nothing by way of an explanation. The noises stopped.

She turned to find her partner, a tech on loan from the LAPD, also looking aloft. She held herself frozen with a plastic evidence bag in front of her.

"You hear that too?"

"Yeah, I—"

Before she could answer an alarm sounded, drowning out her reply. Sydney clamped her hands over her ears and rose just as a cloud of thick smoke spewed forth from the ceiling. It fell to the ground and quickly dissipated, filling the room from the bottom up.

"Out!" Sydney yelled before clamping her jaw shut and sprinting for the door. She made it just as more clicking sounded and a deluge of liquid fell to the floor. She pushed the tech out the door and into the clear air before it caught up to them. The others outside were already backing away from the smoke as it began to fill the alleyway between the units.

Out of breath Sydney dropped to a crouch and took a sip of clean air. Her nose fed her information. It was just smoke, not CS or some other gas. Then she smelled something else.

"Run!"

She pushed people and they caught the look on her face and ran before her. More loud clicking and the fuel caught fire with a deafening whoosh. Sydney dove forward, knocking two of her crew to the ground. A wave of heat blew over them.

She gasped for air and clawed at the hot asphalt. Hands grabbed her and dragged her to her feet. She stumbled a few yards before shaking them off and turning.

The unit was fully engulfed in flame. Black smoke pushed the previous white cloud away and rose into the sky to be carried away on the westerly wind. The suction of air now feeding the fire blew her hair around her face and she spit it out in anger.

Everything was gone. She could make out the burning tires of the van sitting inside. The lockers were feeding their contents to the flames. The motorcycle fell over with a crash, its body melting onto the floor.

"You alright?" a voice asked.

Sydney turned to see Laurie staring up at her; she reached out to touch her face. She beat her to it and felt a tender spot, one that would no doubt be worse later.

"Yeah, I'm okay. Everybody get out?"

"It looks like it. Fire department is on its way."

Sydney looked back at the growing fire; it had already moved into the units on either side.

"They're already too late."

---

"I HAVE calls for a fire at the address ... no ambulances requested," William reported before collapsing in his chair.

"Well done," the General said. "The safeguards you insisted on worked then. I should not have questioned you."

"Thank you, sir."

"So what now?" Charlie asked.

"We gather intelligence, after that we consult with Mr. Dayton. How long, William?"

"Give me an hour, sir, I'll have something by then. Do I have permission to use HUMINT?"

The General frowned. Human intelligence. Real people as opposed to cameras and eavesdropping. It was obviously more dangerous.

"Use the press first, then we'll reevaluate."

"Yes, sir."

William spun back to the keyboard and typed furiously. The General rubbed his temples and motioned to Charlie.

"Let's leave him be, he'll call if he has anything," he whispered.

"Yes, sir."

Charlie unlocked the chair and pulled the man back. They silently headed for the gate. The General continued to rub his temples. William buzzed them through the gate, and they entered the elevator.

"Are you alright, sir?"

"That spiked my blood pressure for a bit, Charlie, but I'm alright. Take me back to my study. I'll wait to hear from William there."

"Sure you wouldn't want to relax a bit, sir?"

"I was reading, can't get much more relaxed than that. Why, what were you reading?"

"A book about hedge funds."

"Well, you'll soon have a headache of your own then."

"Yes, sir." Charlie painted a smile on his face and in his tone, but he was worried about the man. Nevertheless, he deposited him behind his desk.

"So, what's it look like?"

Jack and Sydney stood outside the shell of what had been the storage unit only a few hours ago. Fireman patrolled the interior looking for hot spots and water dripped from every overhead beam. The smell of melted plastic and burnt insulation permeated their noses. Helicopters from the area news stations hovered overhead but were kept back by a pair from the sheriff's office. They had to speak up over the noise.

A fireman held a charred piece of metal and plastic. His name was hidden under his coveralls, but ARSON SQUAD was printed across the back of his coat. To their amazement he lit up a cigarette before answering them.

"Looks like at least a thirty-gallon tank with

some kind of remote valve in place. Next to that we've got a pair of smoke grenades with similar triggers. Cute set-up actually, haven't seen anything like this in some time."

"Locally triggered?"

"Can't say for sure but looks like a cell phone was the receiver. Hardwired into the building's electrical system. Always charged and waiting. Your guy could have phoned it in from China. What I can't figure out are the smokes."

"To clear the area," Jack said.

"What?"

"The smoke triggered first, right?"

Sydney nodded. "About twenty seconds before the rest."

"Long enough to drive you out of the place before the gas hit the floor. They didn't want to hurt anybody."

"Didn't want to hurt anybody? That's not really how arsonists work," the fireman commented.

"These guys aren't arsonists. What kind of smoke grenade, was it military?"

"Looks military. I forget the designation, HC ... something."

"HC-White," Jack informed him. "I'll need the serial numbers, if they still have them."

"Yeah, sure. Just give my guys a few more minutes. How'd you know what kind they were?"

"Just a guess." Jack tugged on Sydney's sleeve and led her away before the man could ask any more questions.

"You knew already, Jack. What's going on?"

"Deacon's theory. The smoke grenade used in Miami was the same kind." He eyeballed the crowd at the tape line a half-block away. Among them were some TV cameras. He led her around a corner and out of sight.

"Was the press here before the fire?"

"I don't know, I was inside. Laurie might know. Why?"

"I'm getting the feeling someone is watching our every move. Anyway, were you able to salvage anything?"

"We'd just finished shooting everything and were starting to process it when the fire came down. The pictures are all we have."

"Not all."

"How is our suspect?"

"I parked him in an interrogation room to stew for a bit. So far, he's said nothing."

"Nothing?"

"Zero. No name, no address. Nothing. No

phone request. No request for anything really, not even for a lawyer or a glass of water."

"Are you keeping him off the computers like Eric said?"

"So far."

"So, what's next?"

"I'm not sure, but this guy is our connection. I'm not going to let him deny me that. This guy is going to talk, or he's going to wish he had."

Jack spun away, stalking out of the complex and ducking under the tape. The press badgered him all the way to his car, but he ignored them before pushing his way through and driving off.

Sydney watched him go with a cloud of worry in her heart.

---

WILLIAM MONITORED the information from his bots for another ten minutes. He had to be sure. The fire had triggered a general alarm with several trucks responding. Per protocol ambulances were dispatched as well and he'd found himself holding his breath while waiting to hear calls of the injured, or even worse, the dead. He had monitored the battle for over twenty minutes without hearing any ambulances leave the scene. One had been dispatched back to its station and ten minutes later the other was placed on stand-by at the scene. They would leave when the fire chief released them. William had allowed himself several deep breaths at that point. He had just committed arson; if that had somehow resulted in the death of an agent or fire-fighter, he was not sure if he could handle it. Still, the situation had called for it. He would force the thought aside now and revisit it later. Right now there were more pressing issues to attend to.

Number Six. Where was he? He scanned the information he had: no change. How? Were they keeping the information off the system somehow? Were his bots functioning? He started a series of tests to be sure. While they performed their self-check he called Charlie.

"Yes, William?"

"Please inform the General that the device functioned as planned. No injuries. I have no fur-ther information on Number Six, but I'm still dig-ging. Dayton will arrive in five hours, and he does have Number Twelve with him."

"Got it. Anything else?"

"Did you call for the plane, Charlie?"

"For us? No, he told me not to."

"Charlie, you need to know when to ignore orders. He needs you to do that for him."

"Easier said than done."

William was taken aback. He thought Charlie understood this already. "No, Charlie, it's not. He may be in charge, but some things are not up to him. He can't be the President who refuses to go to the bunker because of how it might look. It's not his decision to make, it's *yours* now. You understand what I'm saying?"

Charlie was a bit shocked by William's tone—he'd never spoken to him like this before. But the wisdom of his words could not be denied.

"I guess I do. Maybe I wasn't ready to admit it yet."

"Alright. Let's focus here. Tell him my message and then call for the plane. He doesn't need to know you did, but if he finds out I doubt he'll say anything."

"I understand. I'll call you when it's done."

"Atta boy."

---

CHARLIE STARED at the phone for a moment while he thought about William's words. Was he failing the man? The thought sparked fear in him. He owed him so much. Why hadn't he seen it?

He snatched up the phone again and placed a call.

"Higgins."

"It's Charlie. I need the Falcon to home."

"Got a when and where for me?"

"Now. And, John, I mean right now, get here as fast as you can."

"Okay, be about an hour, maybe a bit more. Destination?"

"I'll know more by the time you get here."

"Charlie, I—"

"Just get here." Charlie hung up before the man could protest. He redialed. The phone rang repeatedly and after the sixth ring he hung up.

"Probably in the bathroom."

He threw himself to his feet and walked down the hall. The General had a bathroom off of his private study. It had a phone and an emergency pull in case he fell but the man often refused to answer while he was in there. "Some things are best not interrupted," he would say.

He found the room empty and the door to the bathroom shut. He could hear water running so he waited.

He checked the time and made a mental note

to track the plane in an hour. He would check on Dayton as well. Should he call him? Was he too busy? No, he'd wait, let William and the General decide their next move.

The water was still running. Charlie moved to the door and listened closer.

"Sir?"

Nothing.

"Sir? Are you alright?"

Nothing.

Charlie tried the knob, and it turned. He swung the door open only to have it abruptly stop. He squeezed his head around it to see the General on the floor, his chair overturned and blocking the door.

"Sir!"

Charlie shouldered the door open, shoving the chair and the man across the tile until he could enter. He dropped to his knees and shook him before planting his ear on his chest.

"He's breathing," Charlie told himself. He reached up and yanked the chain on the wall. A long second later a voice answered.

"Do you need assistance, sir?"

"It's Charlie! The General's down! I need the medics here now!"

"On the way!"

Charlie scanned the man in front of him. What was happening? He struggled to remember his training and the lessons came back. Airway: the General was breathing. Slowly, but he was breathing. A. B. B was breathing. C, circulation. He felt for a pulse in his neck, but his own heart pounding in his ears made it difficult. He found it just as the medics rushed into the room. One of them grabbed the overturned wheelchair and dragged it out of the small space. His partner took it and threw it aside.

"Get out of there, Charlie."

"But—"

"Get out of the way!"

Charlie scrambled to comply. The medic checked the man's breathing and pulse simultaneously before prying his eyes open.

"Blown on the right, he's stroking!"

The nurse appeared in the doorway. "What happened?"

The medic in the room was moving furniture to make room for the stretcher. He said, "The General's having a stroke, call for the helicopter!"

To her credit she didn't ask any questions, she just stepped around him and yanked the phone off the desk while he was moving it.

"When's the last time you saw him, Charlie?"

"When?"

"The last time you saw him, be accurate!"

"Um ... maybe, fifteen or twenty minutes ago, a little less."

"Shit, how far to the hospital?"

"In the bird? Maybe thirty."

"It's going to be tight. Let's head for the pad, we can work while we're waiting."

They arranged and hoisted the General onto the stretcher with little effort. The General stirred with the activity, reaching out blindly and grabbing at the air. One of his hands found the medic's sleeve and he latched on tight.

"Stop Angler! Get to Ramadi!" he yelled. The speech was slurred and barely coherent.

"He's altered," the medic exclaimed. "We gotta move."

The medic grabbed the General's flailing arms and tucked them under the straps of the stretcher. The General squirmed against the restraint and continued to yell.

"Haney! Stop Haney! He's killing my boys!"

The lead medic ignored the man's ravings and raised the end with his head while his partner placed a hissing tube of oxygen in his nose.

"The file?"

"In my pocket."

"There's aspirin," the nurse pointed. An open bottle was on the desk blotter, overturned and scattered by their activity.

"Was he complaining of a headache, Charlie?"

"Yes, right before I left him here."

"Okay." The medic scribbled on his glove with a marker while his partner strapped the General to the stretcher. He glanced at Charlie and saw the look on his face.

"Not your fault, Charlie, there's no way to see this coming."

The sound of the helicopter landing outside canceled his whispered reply and they all moved toward the door. Less than a minute later they were strapping in.

"Slow altitude changes!" the medic yelled to the pilot. The man nodded and they were airborne, skimming the ground as it dropped beneath them. Charlie gripped the overhead handle and willed the bird faster as he watched the medics work. One grabbed his partner's harness and steadied him as he examined a catheter before deftly inserting it into the General's arm. A bag of fluid was soon dripping overhead, swaying with the movement of the bird. Once it was secure the medic reached out and stripped the man of his shirt with the aid of some shears. He applied leads and the man's heartbeat appeared on a small screen. The medic's hands moved in concert, never interfering with the man next to him and never slowing down.

"ETA?" one of them shouted in his ears. Charlie winced but didn't wish to let go of the handle and find the volume button.

"Fourteen ... Hold on."

Charlie's stomach rose into his throat, and he struggled to keep his lunch down as the helicopter plummeted over the last ridgeline and into the valley. Despite the wild ride, the medic was speaking slowly into his mic. Charlie couldn't hear him, but he guessed that he was talking to the hospital.

The other medic wrote on his glove. He looked up and noticed Charlie looking. It was as if he had forgotten he was there.

"What's happening?" Charlie asked.

"He's having a stroke."

"I know that! How bad?"

"I don't know, he needs a CT scan. It's the only way to tell."

The General's arm jerked, and the medic reached out to stop it so the IV stayed in place. He rubbed the man's chest hard with his knuckles. The General stirred and grabbed at the air.

"Sir!? Can you hear me?"

"Ramadi!" the General yelled. "Get to Ramadi!"

"Sir! You're in your helicopter! We're taking you to the hospital!"

"Dust-off! Send dust-off from Fallujah!"

The General lashed out again and the medic caught both arms this time, pinning them down. His partner grabbed some restraints.

"Find Haney! Don't let him ... Angler. Stop Angler!"

"What's he talking about, Charlie?" the medic asked.

"I—I don't know," Charlie lied.

# 21

---

*"The whole point about corruption in politics is that it can't be done, or done properly, without a bipartisan consensus."*

—*Christopher Hitchens*

F allujah, Iraq. April 2004
The convoy was small considering

what it was transporting, but the General preferred to travel light. Just four Humvees and a pair of LAVs, including his own C2 model with its half-dozen radios. They moved at high speed, their drivers barely slowing down for turns on the dusty and broken tarmac of Highway One. The General had almost been ejected more than once.

Despite the added dangers of moving by ground, the General preferred it. After being hit by three IEDs and a half-dozen ambushes, his staff had pleaded with him to use the helicopter. Most of them warned that the General was being targeted. He had shrugged off the warning and continued as he had. If the insurgents were targeting him, it must mean he was doing something right. He added a second LAV to humor them and got on with it. In the LAV, he could move around and actually see his troops, stopping here and there without announcing his presence and coating them in dust. If his officers couldn't see the advantage of that, he'd find new ones. He preferred the company of Lance Corporals, anyway.

The one sitting next to him driving had brown skin, a shade darker than the coat of dust they all wore. A young man from the streets of DC, Lance Corporal Wilk had found his way to the General after breaking his ribs in a firefight in Fallujah a month ago. Finding out they wished to medivac him to Germany he had promptly gotten up off the gurney, policed up his weapon, and walked back to his unit. The General had happened to be hunkered down with the men eating an MRE when Wilk appeared out of the darkness. After an asschewing from his Lieutenant, who had threatened to send him back, the General had stepped in and made him his driver instead. The young Marine had taken to the job immediately, his only request being that he go back to the line when he was all healed up. Doubting he could stop him from doing so, the General had smiled and assured him that would happen. Since then, he had learned that the boy was an orphan, his father long since disappeared and his mother dead, a victim of the drug war. The Corps was the boy's family now, and there was nothing that was going to change that.

The trip was quieter than usual, both internally and externally. The troops were on high alert and only spoke when necessary, while the General was deep in thought about what he had just learned and how it might affect the coming days.

The chances of attack were low. The area had been swept in the last few days by Task Force Ripper, a column of 168 LAVs, Hummers, 7-ton trucks, Amtracs, and Abrams tanks. All in an effort to crush the insurgent uprising in Anbar province. So far it had worked; the two-faced sheikhs and twenty-year-old imams had been smacked down hard. Sadr was negotiating for his life a hundred miles south of them in Najaf, and the Iraqi teenagers with rifles who had been fired up by their rhetoric had quickly seen the folly of taking the fight to the Marines. Now the General was returning to his headquarters outside of Ramadi to get back to the original job at hand.

Ramadi, and its neighboring city Fallujah, were the centers of the insurgency in Anbar province, with the latter being a growing problem. Foreign fighters from every corner of the Muslim world had found their way into its twisted maze of streets and bombed out buildings. Encouraged by the sheikhs and former Baathists who had been made wealthy under Saddam, the imams broadcasted daily calls for jihad from their mosques inside the city. Their claims were a mixture of twisted truths and outright lies designed to turn the population of young men into the soldiers they needed to facilitate their own ambitions. Their crazed rants spoke of American forces destroying Bagdad, demolishing mosques, and raping their women. Of foreign companies stealing their oil and shipping it to Israel. They denounced the Iraqi Governing Council, calling them traitors and enemies to Islam. Without any other source of real news to counter this, the population believed the propaganda, prompting ignorant Sunni gangs, urged on by an influx of foreign fighters, to pile into taxis and pickups, roaming the streets and firing their rifles and RPGs at the Marines outside before racing back into the cover of the city.

IED attacks had tripled in the last few months, and sniper fire was now coming from several different weapons, all of them rare in Iraq. There were rumors circulating that Abu Zarqawi was being sheltered there by the Sunni cleric Janabi, although Janabi had denied the existence of any foreigners in the city at their last meeting. The General had reluctantly let the cleric go back to his city, something he had since vowed never to let happen again.

Janabi. The General cursed him under his breath. He'd been nothing but a businessman before the war. A man who saw the opportunity to make a dollar everywhere he looked. With the defeat of the Baathists and the capture of their leader, Saddam, the opportunist now sought to fill the power vacuum. Janabi had made himself a cleric and now broadcasted his sermons from a mosque in the area the Americans called the Jolan District. It was a hotbed of insurgent activity.

Corporal Wilk pointed silently to the north-west where Fallujah was coming into view. The crump of impacting mortar fire could be heard on the wind, and a loud droning sound had filled the air. Chatter on the radio was picking up as night-fall set in. A high ceiling of cloud cover made the sky inky black.

"Slayer," Wilk said.

He had barely spoken when a tongue of flame shot out of the sky and connected with a spot in-side the city. The mortar and machinegun fire ceased. The AC-130 gunship, which the troops had dubbed Slayer, had reached down from its orbit over the city and obliterated the threat. He listened closely and soon picked up the annoying whine of a predator drone overhead as well. The nightlife in Fallujah was getting underway early.

"Let's stop and find Colonel Tucker."

"Yes, sir."

Wilk grabbed a mic and announced the change in destination with the rest of the column, before speeding up and heading toward the cloverleaf east of town. The Marines had taken over Fallujah's makeshift base there from the 82nd Airborne Division a few months ago. Little had changed as they were being forever told that the assault on the city was to happen any day now. Months later, they still sat while the politicians talked. In the meantime, Marines died from sporadic shelling, sniper fire, and IEDs. The General was not at all happy about it.

He turned and tapped the man behind him on the leg. An NSA man who had simply appeared one day and announced he was at the General's service. The General had looked him up and down with barely held amusement before shooing the others out of the room.

He had gotten right to the point.

"Who are you and why should I trust you? You sure as hell don't belong here."

The man had looked down at his attire. Dressed in dirty khakis and a button-down shirt, he looked more like a reporter than an NSA operator. He set his laptop down and pushed the glasses back up his nose before replying.

"To be short, sir, General Land thought I could be of some service. He said to tell you 'three before and three after.' I spent the whole flight here trying to figure that out, and I'm still at a loss. He also sends you this." The man reached in a pocket and removed a crumpled but still sealed envelope before handing it across. The General opened it to find a short message from his old friend the Joint Chief. It was all he needed.

"Very well, Mr. ...?"

"Ockham, sir. William."

"Well, Mr. Ockham, let's see what you're made of."

In the weeks that followed, Mr. Ockham had become a close advisor. Always on his computer, pulling information from a variety of sources. He had quickly proven himself to be a great asset. The General had scrounged him a Marine uniform with rank to match his age, buzzed his hair high and tight, and kept him in disguise. Based on their boss's actions, his soldiers had accepted him without question. Now, wherever the General went, Mr. Ockham went as well.

"What's happening?" he shouted.

"Word of the meeting has leaked. The lid's coming off."

"Not if I can help it. We're going to the cloverleaf," he informed him.

"Great," Ockham deadpanned.

The General smiled at Ockham's usual response and turned back to look out the front. Flashes of light came from inside the city, lighting up the faces of the taller buildings before they disappeared back into the night. Tracers again walked

across the sky in a vain attempt to reach the gunship overhead. They were answered by the 25mm
chain gun of an LAV sitting behind the bulldozed
berm of earth surrounding the city. It was gearing
up to be an active night.

The convoy sped past the turn that would have
taken them across the guarded Fallujah dam and
headed north. The Marines didn't question the
change in plans; they simply deployed their night-
vision gear and rolled with it.

The General pushed the sounds and sights to
another part of his brain, one that would monitor
them and sound a warning if needed but let him
focus on other things while doing so.

Politicians. He had just left a group of them
back in Bagdad, including the current Vice President of the United States. The man had flown in
unannounced and demanded a meeting. Like a
good soldier, he had obliged the man, though he
had suspected the meeting would not only be a
waste of time, but counterproductive as well. He
had to keep it to himself, but it was not hard to see
that the two men despised one another. The General thought Haney too eager to send troops to
solve every problem the administration found,
and Haney thought the General thought too
much. Haney would have pushed for his dismissal

years ago if not for the guaranteed backlash from his fellow generals and the entire Marine Corps. If it were not for the war, the General would have retired before serving under the man. He stayed for his men, too afraid of letting Haney have his war without someone to check him. His stars carried a lot of weight, but he could only do so much.

The war had changed from a military operation against a government-led force to one of an insurgency as others sought to fill the vacuum of power. They saw a chance to rule and had stepped up attacks against the fragile new government. On top of this new threat, the politicians had quickly made the mistake of appointing too many chiefs. Now he had his immediate boss, a three-star who commanded the First Marine Expeditionary Force, who reported to a four-star army general named Adams, who commanded CENTCOM, who then reported to the Secretary of Defense, the Chairman of the Joint Chiefs, and finally the President. Added to this now was an ambassador to Iraq who led the Coalition Provisional Authority, whom had recently been given responsibility for policies, plans, and the budget for rebuilding the country. The ambassador bypassed the whole chain and reported directly to the President through the National Security Advisor and the

Secretary of State. Somewhere in the middle of all of this, you had another three-star general by the name of Sanchez, who commanded Joint Task Force 7, he directed the coalition forces throughout Iraq and reported to the Chairman of the Joint Chiefs.

The whole thing became a mess as orders were issued by one party only to be countermanded by another. Intelligence came from both higher up the chain and well below it and was often in conflict to each. The fight for shares of the budget had grown in intensity and now rivaled the battles being fought on the ground. The soldiers couldn't convince the politicians that the battle wasn't over yet, and the politicians couldn't shove the soldiers out of the way fast enough so they could start "nation building."

As a result, his Marines had been forced to withdraw from their initial assault on Fallujah, an attack which had cost the lives of many men, and now were holding in place while the city filled with homegrown insurgents and foreign fighters. The General was now surrounded by Monday morning quarterbacks with no choice but to listen to one ridiculous idea after another on how to take back the city—everything from the Iraqi national guard, who had fled from every fight they were sent to, to the outright insane notion of trusting the local imams to quell the violence. Tonight's meeting was just the latest version, and he had sat and stewed through an hour of circular arguments before losing his patience and demanding an answer.

Again, he was told to hold in place and take no action, or move into the city unless under significant attack. The talk then turned to infrastructure contracts and who should get them. Haney's former corporation seemed to be heavily favored, and it wasn't hard for the General to see the true reason for his visit. He left an hour later too angry to speak. His driver had wisely let the matter alone as they headed back up Highway One to Ramadi. Now they were stopping in Fallujah, which was never a good thing.

---

KARMA, Iraq. Eight miles northeast of Fallujah.

Dayton and his partner Jamie communicated without speaking. They had entered the town under the cover of the previous night and hunkered down in the vacant building all day. Now they sat back to back as the chill set in, waiting for their contact to show. Jamie elbowed his partner, and he turned to look over his shoulder and up the road. Pulling his binoculars from his loose robe, he trained them on the approaching vehicle. A small pickup truck. White with an orange stripe down the side. They were popular in the area for some reason, as if a company had once had a fleet of them here and then suddenly abandoned them, leaving them all behind for the locals. For whatever the reason, it was not the first they had seen today.

"Not slowing down," Dayton said.

"If it's not him, how long you want to give him?"

"If he doesn't show by midnight, I think it'll be time to go. Maybe our guys stopped him when he tried to get out of town?"

His partner shrugged and offered no comment. Informants were never punctual, but Abu had been more reliable than most. They both watched the approaching truck for a moment before he spoke.

"You got it?"

"I'm on it."

His partner turned his own binoculars away from the truck and scanned the fields in all directions. If their informant had been caught and persuaded to talk, this truck could be a distraction. It was the reason they had chosen the bombed-out house on the hill in the first place. There was no way to sneak up on it without being seen.

"We're still good."

Dayton just grunted in reply. Still good. It was a relevant term. Two Americans all alone in the boonies of Iraq were never a good situation, but that was the job they had signed up for.

The truck was now close enough for him to determine that it was manned by one person. The red blob of heat in the driver's seat had both hands on the wheel just as they had instructed.

"One guy, slowing down now."

"Still clear."

Dayton watched as the truck came to a stop in front of what remained of the house across the street. The courtyard wall had been destroyed by a vehicle of some kind many months ago, and what was once a two-story structure had been reduced to a pile of rubble by direct tank fire. Only one room was still standing. He watched the man examine the graffiti on its wall before smiling and parking the truck off the road. The man was very careful getting out, making sure not to make any sudden movements. He stepped out in front of the vehicle and opened his coat, slowly turning in a circle before leaning back on the hot steel of the hood. Dayton zoomed in on his face as the man lit a cigarette.

"It's Abu. Any company?"

"Nothin'."

"Okay. You on the mic?"

His partner stuffed an earbud in one ear before returning to his scan. "Test, test."

"You're ugly and your mother dresses you funny," Dayton replied.

Before Jamie could reply they heard distant thunder from the south. His partner swung the binos in that direction in time to see another flash in the distance.

"Fallujah's heating up."

Dayton just nodded at the news; it was nothing surprising. He patted himself down, making sure he had all of his toys before tapping Jamie on the shoulder.

"Be right back."

"Be right here."

Dayton crept across the concrete floor silently, and then worked his way down the stairs. He avoided the tripwires of the flash-bangs they had set out and moved through two rooms before exiting out the back of the building. Circling around, he approached the truck from an angle that would give Jamie a clear shot if the need arose. Dayton was only a couple meters behind the man when he spoke without turning.

"You write this?" Abu gestured at the graffiti with his smoke.

"Yeah." Dayton joined him on the hood and contemplated his work. "Why? What's wrong with it?"

"'Yes to Saddam.' That is a bit old, no? Perhaps 'Yes to Islam,' and your handwriting is that of a child." He tossed the butt aside and pulled a new one from a pack hidden inside his shirt. Dayton fought the reflex to reach inside his own.

"I'll work on it. What did you hear?"

Abu dragged on the butt hard before replying. "Zarqawi is close. He has people in Fallujah, but I'm not sure if he is still there. Perhaps Ramadi or even Baqubah. There is no way to be sure, but he is close."

"How do you know this?"

"There are more foreigners every day. They think we are all stupid and uneducated, so they speak freely in other languages in front of us. One of them is a Frenchman. He—"

"Wait. A Frenchman? What does he look like?"

"A small man. Balding. He wears glasses, and his beard is shorter than the others. He has, how you say, soft? Yes, soft hands."

Dayton pulled a stack of photos from his pocket. The size of a deck of cards they were well worn. He held a small red-lens flashlight with his teeth and thumbed through them with Abu watching closely.

"Him?"

Abu examined the face. A smiling man, clean-shaven, wearing a suit and tie.

"Perhaps."

"Look at the eyes." Dayton arranged two cards to block out everything else.

"Yes, that is the man. Who is he?"

"Ali Mahadaai. He's a Syrian. Educated in France. An electrical engineer turned bomb maker. We want him. You know where he is?"

"Yes."

Dayton pulled a map of Fallujah from a pocket and spread it out on the hood. The red-lens flash-light only illuminated a few inches at a time, but the man traced streets with a finger until he found the right house.

"Here. He is in the basement most of the time. Several porters have visited."

"Can you get inside?"

Abu smiled and the scars on his face gave him a joker-like grin. "I already have."

Reaching in his pants, he pulled out a cell

phone. Dayton held his breath as the man punched it on and selected an app. A video. The view was narrow, as if looking through the entrance of a tunnel, and bounced with the steps of whoever was carrying it. Whoever it was, he was crossing a courtyard, one of thousands in the city. A box was in his hands and the camera bounced on his chest with every step. There was no audio, and Dayton saw others passing and silently greeting him as he made his way inside. A stone corridor led to a room that had a hole crudely punched in one wall.

"Did you film this?" Dayton whispered.

"No, the camera is in an AK. I will explain." He gestured Dayton to keep watching.

The man moved to step through the hole and the picture gyrated wildly as the rifle bounced off his body. A sweeping view of the ceiling followed, and Dayton struggled to interpret the shaking view. A stairwell now, turning two corners, then leading down a narrow hall. Overhead bulbs were ducked with each passing until the hall widened into a basement room. There he was shown two large tables, each of them full of electronic parts and tools before the picture swept right. A balding man briefly came into view. Bent over a table, holding a soldering iron, he looked up at the intrusion with annoyance before pointing to a spot on the floor. Dayton's finger twitched; he wanted to stop the video and go back, but he let it run. Whatever the cameraman had been carrying was set down, and the rifle was adjusted again before he spun to leave. The picture retraced the previous path before emerging back onto the street. The view then went dark as the man entered a car and the camera was covered up. Abu stopped the video.

"How ...?"

"I used the magazine you gave me. They use the wounded who can still move, and the older men like myself to carry things. I swapped the magazine with the camera in it for one of theirs. They search everyone, but they never check their AKs. The man made two deliveries before I could get the camera back. The second time the camera was blocked. I recognize the courtyard wall; it has odd holes in the side from your ugly plane."

Dayton could not believe the man's gall. If he had been caught, he would have been tortured and killed. He shook it off; the man had his reasons. The ugly plane comment referred to the A-10 Warthog, a close-support/anti-tank airframe, and while it lacked the sexy lines of an F-16, it was still a thing of beauty to an infantryman.

"Let's see this again."

They watched the video twice more. Dayton confirmed the man he saw as Ali Mahadaai, then set about sketching a map of the interior of the house. Abu corrected him twice, and together they placed as much detail as possible on the paper. They were running out of time.

"What else?"

"The Muhammudia Mosque. Janabi has it now. I believe they are moving arms to it."

"What kind of arms?"

"RPGs mostly. Ammunition. I saw an RPK once. Several artillery shells. Some mortars. I overheard one driver say that he needed gas before he went if he was going to make it there. They stole some from a generator. The trunk was very full. He made three trips, and I timed them; it was about right each time."

The thunder from the south intensified, urging them along.

"Where are they mounting their defense?"

Abu was confused by the question. "I ... I do not know. You did not ask me ..."

"No, I didn't, but this changes things. I think the attack will happen soon. That's not my job, but if Zarqawi is in the city, it becomes my problem. I want him and Mahadaai. You haven't seen him yourself?"

"No, only others talking. I believe he is there, but he could also be gone."

Dayton swallowed the information. They were close. His group had covered most of the province looking for the Jordanian terrorist. He was running out of places to hide, but until the day came he was no longer a threat, Dayton's job was not done.

"I have someone else for you to watch for."

"Another bald Frenchman?" Abu asked.

"No, a girl." He pulled a small photo from his shirt and handed it over.

Abu gazed at the girl's face. Her eyes betrayed the fear hidden behind her false smile.

"She's young."

"Fourteen in the picture. She's sixteen now—just turned."

"Who is she?"

"Her name is Isra. She's Zarqawi's fourth wife. We believe she's in the country with him."

Abu read his tone. "What else?"

"She'll be traveling with an infant, just over one year old. Zarqawi's son."

Abu tapped the photo and looked away. "I see."

Dayton changed the subject. "Go home, my friend. Stay out of the city."

"They expect me back."

The thunder increased and the scream of jet engines passed overhead. Dayton pulled a bundle of cash from his pocket and stuffed it in Abu's hand, along with a pack of cigarettes.

"They'll be too busy tonight, and by morning it may not matter. If you have to run, use this and the code word we set up. We'll get you out."

Abu frowned at the statement. Dayton was telling him something he didn't wish to hear.

"You've done enough, Abu. Let us finish this."

Abu turned to gaze at the flashes of light coming from his city, while he finished his smoke.

"For me, Mr. Dayton, it will never be enough." He pulled the SIM card from the phone and handed it over, before stuffing the phone and the photo back down his pants. He walked to the truck without another word and was soon lost from sight.

Dayton watched him go until Jamie silently appeared next to him.

"What now?"

"Now? We get out of here."

"East?"

Dayton turned and examined the flashes Abu had stared at only a moment ago.

"Nope, south."

Jamie spat on the dusty road. "Why did I know you were going to say that?"

---

FALLUJAH, Two hours later.

The General watched the screens as the reports came in. Fourteen of them glowed in the ops center. The days of chalkboards and sand tables were long gone. The hushed tones of operators speaking into headsets and the tapping of keyboards had replaced the hisses and the squawks of the radios. He glanced at the large map on the wall and saw the blue designators of the 3/1 move a block south. The insurgents had been probing the Marines' lines on the north side of town, and the Marines were pushing back.

"We have an opportunity to push south at the graveyard."

The General turned to find Colonel Tucker standing next to him. One of his best battlefield commanders, he had been straining at the leash to take the fight to the insurgents for months.

"I hear you, Colonel, but I'd hold to the north

and not give up the buffer. It's an excellent field of fire. You can tidy up the lines, but the orders are still hold in place."

"Yes, sir."

Before he could give the orders, the door opened and they saw Major Leonard, the regimental intelligence officer, leading two men into the room. One of them was tall with piercing grey eyes over the top of his deployment beard. They swept the room and missed nothing before finding the General. The other was shorter, stocky, and repeatedly checked behind them as they moved. Both of them were dressed in grey jumpsuits over which hung basic Iraqi ankle-length, long-sleeved robes called dishdasha. Around their necks were faded kaffiyeh and peeking out of the folds of their loose clothing were several weapons. The dust of the desert coated them from head to toe.

"Evening, General. My name's Dayton, and this is Jamie. Do you have a minute to talk?"

The General smiled at the polite tone and slightly southern accent. He knew who they were, but not much about them. Special Operations Forces. They were known among the troops as the Z squad and they roamed the country at will, hunting for key players in the opposition. Several cards in the deck had been taken out by their men, including Saddam himself a few months prior. Now they hunted Abu Zarqawi and his foreign terrorist fighters. "Dayton" was a lieutenant colonel and "Jamie" was a major, but beyond that he knew little else. The men appeared and disappeared at all hours and without warning. When they did appear, it usually meant trouble.

"In my office." Colonel Tucker pointed.

The Marines in the room watched silently as the men filed into the room. The Z squad was the varsity—the pinnacle of their profession—and they commanded respect everywhere they went. Their presence also meant action. Before the door closed behind them, the word went out on the lance corporal hotline: "Some serious shit is about to happen; get ready."

"I swear the tall one had a lightsaber."

"Shut up."

"WHAT CAN I do for you, Mr. Dayton?"

"We were wondering when you might be ready to move into Fallujah."

"I've been ordered to hold in place while the talkers talk. I can respond to attacks and strengthen the lines, but little else."

Dayton exchanged a look with his partner before going on. He pulled a photo from his pocket and set it on the desk.

"This is Ali Mahadaai. We have good intelligence that he's holed up in the city. He's a Frenchman of Syrian descent who was radicalized after 9-11. He has a degree in electrical engineering, and since he's entered the country, he's become Zarqawi's chief bomb maker. The uptick in IEDs over the past month is due to him."

"I see. This is good intelligence?"

"I feel it is."

The General nodded and examined the picture. If the Z squad felt the information valid, then he did, too.

"Where?"

Dayton pointed to a nearby laptop. "May I?"

The Colonel waved to the affirmative and Dayton reached into his robe to pull out a flash drive. He inserted it into the computer and soon had a detailed map of the city on the screen. He counted streets and zoomed in and out a few times to confirm before showing the two men.

"Right here. The house faces south, and the courtyard wall is knocked down here, and here, from some A-10 fire. This door here leads east for five meters, then there's a wall here which has been knocked open into the next room. A stairwell to the basement here, then it drops to the south before leading about twenty meters to the basement next door. There, Mahadaai has set up shop. He has two tables in the middle of the room, and several shells on the floor here and here. He's also making vests. We counted at least three ready to go. The house above was knocked down a couple months ago in the first assault on the city. We don't know of any other exits, but they may have dug one. From what we know, he lives there, eats there, sleeps there, never leaves."

Tucker shook his head. "That's right in the middle of the Jolan district, a couple blocks from the Muhammudia Mosque."

"It's not a mosque anymore; Janabi is using it to warehouse weapons. Our intel suggests about a hundred RPGs, a couple heavy machine guns, and plenty of ammo."

The General grimaced at the news. "Fucking Janabi. Should have ended him when we had the chance."

Dayton stayed silent and let the men think.

"Your target is in the middle of the lion's den. Our closest units are seven blocks to the north. That mosque will have a hundred men in it, and it's only a few blocks to the east. You think Zarqawi is in there with him?"

"It's a real possibility. He's been spoken of by several sources, but I have no firm intel that he is."

The two Marines examined the map, weighing angles of approach and the means to get there. It could be done, but at what cost? Outside, the rumble of mortar fire continued, and the scream of a chain gun soon answered.

"This is the noisiest ceasefire I've ever heard," the General commented.

While said as a joke, the men knew it was anything but funny. Marines were dying while the politicians wasted time. The General was all in favor of talking if there was something to gain. What the politicians didn't understand yet was that the time to talk was *after* you had taken the city.

The General made a decision and fixed his gaze on Dayton.

"So there's a good chance Zarqawi is in there?"

Dayton opened his mouth to reply, but there was something in the man's tone that stopped him. He exchanged a look with his partner, who considered the unasked question before nodding to the affirmative.

"Yes, sir."

"And you want us to assist you in raiding the place?"

Tucker unconsciously nodded at the direction of the conversation.

"Yes, sir."

The General turned to Tucker. "Considering the location of the target and the strength of the insurgents' positions, it'll take at least three battalions. If we do this, hundreds of men will pick up their AKs and rush toward the raid site. Doesn't matter anymore if they're Wahabbi wackos or Baathists or former Iraqi military; these foreign terrorists have them all on the same side. This will be a unified front. It could become an all-out battle for the city."

Tucker couldn't help his grin. "Yes, sir. It's definitely a possibility."

"Maybe you should make sure we're ready, just in case that happens?"

"Yes, sir." Tucker grabbed a short stack of paper off the desk and returned to the ops center, leaving the General alone with the two SOG soldiers plus one.

The General had risen and was now pacing the room.

"If my Marines are going to die, then they're going to do so fighting, not sitting on their asses!

Politics be damned; they'll like us when we win!" The windows rattled, and it was not due to the explosives detonating a mile away. The two men waited for the General to collect himself. Eventually, the chair reclined as the man sat back down and examined the map on the wall.

"Tell me your plan to get this guy."

"No problem, sir." Dayton replied. "But do you mind if I call in some friends first?"

The two men shared a grin.

"Please do."

# 22

*"When the law no longer protects you from the corrupt, but protects the corrupt from you—you know your nation is doomed"*

—*Ayn Rand*

The word went out quickly. Fallujah was happening. Serious men in gray jumpsuits appeared out of the darkness, some walking out of the desert while others drove up in battered Mercedes. They gathered at the op center to speak quietly with Dayton. Hummers full of Delta operators, medics, and snipers divided themselves up among the Marines, giving them both a needed boost in moral and the assurance that the attack was really happening this time. They had been in and out of the city's perimeter so many times, gaining ground only to give it back when the politicians reined them in, few of them could believe they were actually going to finish this time.

The General watched as preparations were made. The city was small by American standards —barely five kilometers wide and the same in depth—yet it contained forty thousand buildings with an estimated four hundred thousand rooms. Each one would have to be searched and cleared before the job was done.

The number of enemy inside the city had grown while they had waited through the months of endless talks. What was once estimated to be five hundred hardcore fighters and two thousand part-time soldiers, was now close to double that. They had positioned disabled busses in the major avenues of entry, dug trenches and rigged explosives along the streets and alleyways, bulldozed earthen berms in front of the open areas, planted landmines and IEDs on previous entry points, and stocked weapons and ammunition on every block. The only positive number was the civilian population; it had dropped to an estimate of less than one hundred. There were now whole sections of the city which had not shown any laundry on the lines for months.

Many of the insurgents welcomed the battle, eager to die as martyrs after being programmed to do so by the imams who supported the insurgents. The Marines and Delta soldiers were more than happy to fulfill their wishes. It was long overdue.

The plan to take the city had been drawn up months ago, and its overall tactic had not changed in the slightest.

Overwhelming force.

The General and Dayton had worked out a two-phase operation. He and his SOG team, supported by a pair of Abrams tanks and a couple Bradleys, would knife their way into the city in a rapid attack, converging on the targeted house and hopefully snatching Zarqawi and his bomb maker in quick order before withdrawing. The Marines would support the raid with the help of even more tanks and LAVs. The insurgents would no doubt converge on the invading forces, who would attempt to lure them out of their fortified positions with a delayed retreat. Once in the open, the Marines would launch their attack on a five-kilometer front, four battalions of pissed-off Marines would push the insurgents south, out of the crowded residential areas and into the more open industrial sections, where they could be more easily targeted by indirect fire and air support. The plan was to rapidly become so deeply engaged with the enemy that, by the time word of the attack reached Bagdad, it would be too late to withdraw again.

Preparations were short. Knowing that insurgents could attack convoys at will, the planners had stocked up for the attack months ago. Several "steel mountains" had been built around the city. Munitions, fuel, water, medical supplies, spare parts, arms, and food. Enough to last a week or more. The attack would go on without relying on resupply from outside the zone.

The only thing left to obtain was air support. For that, the General made a call of his own. Fortunately, the current commander of the air wing was an old classmate from the War Collage. After some quick pleasantries, he got right to it.

"What you got on the schedule tomorrow, Jim?"

"In your zone? One gunship and a pair of 16s on loiter as usual. The rest are working the towns south of Ramadi and patrolling the highway to the west. Why?"

"Getting some noise out of Fallujah. I may need some help, say about an hour before sunrise?"

There was a long pause while his friend read between the lines.

"Okay ... I suppose I could keep a few birds closer to home. Would this be a good time to move some A-10s into the area?"

"I think there will be enough fun for everyone. Would your medivacs crews want to train with my Marines tomorrow, too?"

"I think that's a good idea. I have four here that I can spare. Of course I'll have to send a pair of Cobras with them to keep them safe."

"They're welcome, too."

"I'll make it happen. Sunrise, you say?"

"Around 0400. My Marines will be awake."

"Got it."

The General hung up and called for the captain in charge of his forward observers.

"A pair of 16s, some A-10s, four medivacs, and a pair of Cobras. Have your commo set up and ready to go but do it quietly."

"We keep Slayer, too, sir?"

"Twenty-four seven."

"Yes, sir." The man was reaching for his radio before he left.

The General drummed his fingers on the desk and stared at the map. What was he missing?

"Any word?" he asked.

William, sitting silently in the corner with his ever-present laptop, had been monitoring communications out of Bagdad since the operation had commenced.

"Nothing yet. They're still in the dark."

The General spun and looked at him. "Can you keep it that way?"

William frowned at the request. Was it possible? Maybe. Was it something they could both end up in Leavenworth for? Yes.

"I don't wish to lose more Marines on a job that we're not going to finish," he added.

William considered the statement. It was what he had come to expect from the man. To hell with the politics; take care of the soldiers.

"I'll see what I can do, sir."

The General spun the chair back around and once again stared at the map.

"Hoo-rah," he muttered.

AN HOUR LATER, the office doors opened as Dayton and his silent partner Jamie burst back in, followed by Lance Corporal Wilk. The General had loaned them his LAV and driver.

"Everything is in place for the raid, sir. Were you able to arrange air support?"

"We'll have a cap overhead, starting an hour before dawn. Slayer is refueling and loading up. You'll have whatever you need. Anything else?"

"The natives have noticed. The roadblocks are reporting a steady stream of people bugging out. So far, the insurgents are letting them, but pretty soon they'll figure it out and keep them in the city for human shields. One of my informants made contact with me; the rumors are flying. Most of them think this is another show of force, the others want the fight. Either way, the field is too small for a diversion to last long. They'll know it's for real pretty quick."

Before the General could answer, Colonel Tucker entered.

"We're ready to take the bridges and the hospital. The SF advisor at the national guard unit will keep his guys inside until it's over. By then, he says they'll be ready to move in and occupy the city."

"All right. All units in place?"

"Yes, sir."

"We close the highways in one hour. Soon as that's done, take the bridges and the hospital. Start the attack at 0400."

"Yes, sir." The men filed out, save two.

The General frowned at the two men. "What is it?"

Dayton hesitated, but after a look at Wilks, he forged ahead. "Sir, Charlie has requested that he be allowed to join the raid."

William's head came up at that, and he exchanged a look with his boss. Evidently, Lance Corporal Wilks had made some friends while out driving them around the city's perimeter. They had already adopted him and were using his first name to address him.

The General eyeballed the young man. "You're still on profile," he stalled.

"I'd just be driving, sir, and my profile is up in a few days anyway. I know the city, and if I drive, then it's one more shooter you won't have to pull from the assault team."

The Marines on the perimeter were no doubt jacked-up for the fight—leaning forward in their foxholes was the euphemism. Charlie had caught the bug. Going on the raid might kill him but keeping him here would do the same thing. The General couldn't do that to the boy.

"You drive for the raid and then report back here. No hooking up with the assault battalions. Stay in the damn LAV."

The young man's face split into a wide grin and the General almost retracted his order, but he let it go.

"You're under Mr. Dayton's command until you get back here. Now go suit up."

"Yes, sir!" the door banged open, and he was gone.

Dayton was surprised. "Sir? I thought—"

"I'd reject the idea? Maybe, but he makes sense. I need every rifle I have for the assault. Besides, he drives like a New York cabby, and he's got an internal GPS that's never wrong. He'll be an asset to you. Just tell him what you need, and he'll do the rest."

"Alright, sir." He turned to leave, but the General called out.

"Mr. Dayton? If you can manage it, I would like him back."

Dayton just nodded at the request before disappearing out the door.

The General rocked in his chair and drummed his fingers some more.

"A ship in harbor is safe," William offered.

"But that's not what ships are for," the General finished the quote.

It didn't help.

---

THE FIRST SHOT came from the air. The drone overhead had been scanning the city for hours, and it had picked up a group of men on the roof of the building overlooking the Brooklyn Bridge. It was the name the paratroopers had given the steel span crossing the Euphrates river, and it had stuck. They had watched them tote the heavy gun up the external stairs and then position it carefully in the corner of the roof where it could cover both the bridge and the road in both directions. Only when they were done did they erect a tarp over their position and hunker down beneath it.

"Really? Do they think we only watch them during the day? Why didn't they set up inside? Stupid."

"Have they done anything smart yet? I hope they stay stupid; makes it easier for us." The lieutenant checked his watch. "Two minutes. Slayer ready?"

"Affirm."

"Light 'em up."

The Marine piloting the UAV, circling over the southwest side of the city, focused the cameras on the building once more.

"Looks like they have company. I count ... three more on the ground, around the corner." He confirmed the location before glancing at the upper left portion of his screen. He typed the grid coordinates into a message to regiment and sent it off. Within seconds, he got a reply.

"Slayer is inbound."

The Marines gathered around the screens and watched the dark blobs of heat laying on the roof around the machine gun. The tarp did little to hide them. The lieutenant counted to thirty before the corner of the building turned into a cloud of black. Another puff exploded in the alley before more walked across the building's front. The sound reached them a moment later and continued as the AC-130 gunship pounded the position with 105mm shells. The Marines grinned as the building came apart, each round delivering fifty pounds of high explosives with a deafening punch. It was no wonder the insurgents referred to it as "the finger of God."

"Two stragglers heading east."

The camera followed the two men as they fled

the scene. One of them at a dead sprint, the other limping along on an injured leg. The first disappeared into a storefront, while the other collapsed in the street. A warm glow began to surround him.

"He'll be cold soon. What about the other one?"

"He's deaf for sure. Let him go; Slayer's needed elsewhere. Steer north, while I call this in."

The Marine circled the UAV north as ordered and shopped for more targets, while the lieutenant got on the radio.

"Bridge looks secure, you're go for the hospital."

ACROSS THE BRIDGE to the west, the Special Forces advisor to the Iraqi National Guard unit got the words he had been waiting for. He gave a hand signal to the tank on his left and that was all that was needed. The unit moved as one, storming their way down the boulevard and fanning out in three directions. They quickly had both bridges and the parking lot secured. Troops stormed the structure and cut down what few insurgents remained. After taking some sporadic fire from across the river, he had his gunner answer it with a few 120mm rounds. The rifle fire quickly ceased.

The battle for the hospital was over in under ten minutes. The advisor sent the word up the chain on the secure net before hopping out to congratulate his troops. It was their first real victory, and while a small one, it had been badly needed. When this battle for the city was over, it would be them taking over, so they needed to be confident in their abilities. A perimeter was formed, and the men settled in to watch the coming battle.

---

"SIR, report that both bridges and the hospital are secure."

"Very well. Start phase two."

---

THE ROAR of the diesel engines was enough to draw the fire they wanted. The tanks and Bradleys raked the berm south of town with their chain guns and 120mm cannons. The insurgents swarmed out of the buildings and raced to the berm to return fire, only to be targeted by Slayer as soon as they were out in the open. The Marines

held their fire until they were receiving a steady
rain of unaimed RPGs and machine gun fire, before giving the green light. Pre-sighted artillery fire
soon walked up and down the berm, erasing the
resistance or sending it fleeing back into the buildings. Colonel Tucker waited for word from the
UAVs. He didn't wait long.

"Activity heading south."

"Slayer confirms. At least two large groups and
several smaller."

"Hold fire. Let them come," Tucker ordered.
He walked the room and found the screen with
the datalink from Slayer showing him the insurgents moving through the city. He estimated over a
hundred, many of them coming out of the
mosques. A tempting target, but they had to hold
their fire.

"When this last group gets below Highway 10,
launch phase three. Give them a five-minute warning, then keep an eye on what goes west of phase
line Henry. Time?"

"Twenty to sunrise."

"All right, call in the hogs. Nothing goes back
north once it's across ten."

The forward air controller smiled as he keyed
his mic. It was about damn time.

"WHERE AT IN DC, CHARLIE?"

"Southeast. Birney off of MLK. By the Parkway."

"Bad?"

"Pretty bad. Not the worst, but enough to make me want out."

A rumble from the south interrupted them. Charlie turned his head toward the noise, while Dayton ignored it.

"So how'd that happen?"

Charlie couldn't believe the man's cool. They were about to attack into Fallujah, the heart of the insurgency, in an attempt to snatch their leader, one of the most vicious men on the planet, out of a basement full of bombs, and the leader of the Z squad was passing the time by asking him about where he grew up? It was the strangest conversation he had ever had.

"Uh, I made friends with this store owner after my mom died. He had a brother in the Corps, and he helped me get in."

"Gonna stay?"

"Long as they'll let me. The General says I should go back to school, but I don't know. Maybe when we're done here, I'll think about it."

Dayton repositioned his feet on the wall of the LAV and adjusted his rifle accordingly. His partner Jamie snorted awake and scanned the interior before closing his eyes again. The Marines just shared a silent grin, too keyed up for battle. How the man could sleep right now, they had no idea.

"You should think about it, Charlie. The Corps would pay for it, and you can always come back."

"True, I—" He was cut off by the squawk of the radio.

"Five-minute warning. Five minutes."

"2/7 actual, roger." Dayton reached out and shook his partner awake before picking up a second mic. "We go in five."

---

THE EXPLOSIONS WERE DEAFENING. All along the berm north of the city the engineers had snuck forward and planted their charges. Whether by design or coincidence, they blew them all at once, sending geysers of earth skyrocketing. The Bradleys and Abrams opened up on the first row of buildings, drowning out the yells of the Marines as they charged forward through the gaps. The LAVs streamed through like a flowing river and got online. Once the last was in place, the order went out and they advanced rapidly on the city.

Charlie let his mouth fall open to lessen the effect of the shock waves reaching through the skin of the LAV. He was happy to be inside for once, his fellow Marines trailing the armor on foot were getting beat up by the guns. Not only were they an assault on the ears, but the entire body as well. The shock waves caused the liquids in their bodies to vibrate, and the blood vessels to dilate. Troops had actually passed out from repeated exposure. Some were dazed enough to freeze in place or stumble out from behind cover. The platoon and squad leaders kept a careful eye on their men as they moved forward.

As they neared the first intersection, they began taking fire from a three-story building. An RPG skipped off the armor of the tank in front of them, but the commander was buttoned up and could not see where it had come from. The Marines trailing them lit the target with tracer rounds, and the gun soon followed their lead. The Marines ducked and covered up just before the tank rocked back. The concrete face of the building exploded, and the Marines stuck their heads back up to see the corner of the building crumble in slow motion.

"Form up!" the call sounded in their ears.

The two tanks slowed and lined up with two Bradley fighting vehicles followed by several LAVs. Two abreast they smashed through the makeshift roadblock and tore down the boulevard. Charlie tensed in his seat as they rolled over it, waiting for the IED he was sure was there, but they made it through unscathed. The tanks continued at their best speed, leaving the infantry behind to secure their escape. The main guns fired at anything that looked threatening, while the Bradleys and LAVs raked the buildings on both sides with their chain guns. The radio became clogged with traffic as drivers, gunners, and commanders called out targets in every direction.

In the middle of all this, Charlie saw something. Barrels. There were 55-gallon drums at every intersection. Most of them spouting flames. He was wrapping his head around the mystery when the tank in front of him took an RPG round to the turret. The commander slumped forward and was quickly pulled down by the gunner. The tank lurched to the side and stopped behind a burned-out car.

"It's the barrels! They're using them to site in!"

"What?" Dayton shouted.

"The barrels! Tell them to take out the barrels!"

Dayton gazed out his viewport and saw what Charlie was seeing. He snatched up the mic and calmly spoke. At the next intersection, the lead tank paused long enough to take out the barrels burning a block ahead of them.

"Do it on the run! Let's go!"

They lurched forward, and Charlie frowned as they snagged on some wire. Downed lines were everywhere, and the lead tanks were already dragging several. It was impossible to tell which were ordinary wires and which were trip wires. At least the power to the city had been cut; they didn't have to worry about being electrocuted.

The radio squawked again, and Dayton held it tight to his head while he listened. Charlie did his best to ignore him and stay on the road. The incoming fire was increasing as the insurgents got over the initial shock of their attack.

"Wolfpack says we got activity on both sides. A lot of traffic leaving the mosque."

"If they have weapons, it's a safe house. Light it up!" Jamie yelled back.

"Slayer's already inbound, but we're going to get hit on the left soon."

Charlie automatically turned his head left and

was treated to a tongue of tracers reaching down and peppering the mosque. Its tower shone bright in the rising sun. An A-10 suddenly appeared, and its nose clouded as the gun fired, strafing a target to their south. It disappeared behind some buildings, and Charlie was sure it had crashed only to see it pop up again to the east. Its engines screamed as it banked away, giving him the profile the enemy called "The Devil's Cross."

"Crazy mother," he muttered.

He glanced behind him to see Dayton already working the radio with the forward air controller.

"One minute!"

"This thing will be over in one minute! Tell them to hurry up and be ready to support us on the way out!"

Machine gun fire pounded on the armor, and Charlie flinched before steering the LAV right at it to reduce their profile. Their gunner opened up with his chain gun and walked the tracers in. Another joined him, and they soon had three guns raking the face of the building. It vanished in a cloud of concrete dust.

"Shoot at me again, Mo! I got your address!" the Marine yelled.

They had just turned their attention elsewhere

when a building a block in front of them began spouting green smoke. Slayer had marked their target for them.

"One more block! Break it off here! Assault team move up!"

Charlie took a deep breath; this is where it got interesting. The tanks in front of them sped past the target and stopped in the next intersection. They began blasting any position that might hold a shooter.

Dayton smacked Charlie's shoulder, and he stomped on the brakes. The rear doors were already open, and Jamie piled out with two Delta operators and a pair of Marines.

"On the ramp!" Dayton yelled before disappearing out the door and into the smoke.

"What?" Charlie didn't know what he was talking about. How could he drive if he was on the ramp? The LAV had doors anyway, but it was a figure of speech he understood.

Checking around him, he turned the LAV around and positioned it exactly where they had stopped. The turret swiveled to aim first down one street, then another as the nervous gunner looked for targets. Marines fanned out in all directions. Charlie glanced behind him at the open doors. He didn't like it. An insurgent could fire an RPG right up their ass and end this really quickly. But the assault team would be in a big hurry when they were coming out, and the doors would slow them down.

"Screw this!"

Charlie pulled himself out of the driver's seat and grabbed his M4. He took up a position just inside the rear door and scanned the area behind them. A black-clad Delta operator was repositioning Marines and had them facing down the side streets. The ones behind them scanned the buildings on all sides and over their heads. Most of them had M-203 grenade launchers. He glanced at his watch.

Four minutes? The raid was only four minutes old? It felt like an hour.

The boom of a breaching charge sounded behind him, and he forced himself to ignore it as he switched sides to see down the alley behind them. Shapes moved in the distance. He rubbed his sore ribs and spit out a mouthful of dust.

*Four and half minutes. Hurry up, Mr. Dayton. They're coming.*

The sound of rifle fire, followed by an exploding grenade, came from inside the house. The chatter of the radios was constant and only drowned out by the roar of the A-10s overhead. One of them strafed the street parallel to theirs. Charlie shared a "that was close" look with the Marine on the corner.

*Let's go, Mr. Dayton.*

# 23

*"Another word for corruption is injustice."*

—*Auliq-Ice*

The smoke round was still burning in the courtyard when they blasted the door open with a well-aimed shotgun round. They tossed two grenades over the wall while machinegun fire from the nearest Bradley peppered the front of the building over their heads. They stacked three-high and kicked the door open as soon as the grenades had done their thing.

Jamie charged in low with Dayton high. They each pumped two rounds into the bodies lying in the doorway before stacking up again at the next door.

"Rear secure!" a voice sounded in his head. "No back entrance."

Dayton didn't bother with a reply. He was too busy examining the house. It looked bigger than expected and had a different roof. Most homes in the city had a similar layout, a foyer with a large common room to the right and left, the kitchen, and one-hole toilet were in the back. The stairs up were either on an outside wall or up one of the common room walls and led to a central corridor which had three to four bedrooms off of it. The roof was bothering him for some reason he couldn't identify, but then he had spent his time going over the inside layout more than he had the outside. Either way, he had no time to dwell on it.

He nudged Jamie with his knee until he looked back over his shoulder.

"Rabbit?"

Jamie grinned and nodded. He slung his rifle over his back and pulled his pistol from his belt. Dayton handed him his, and he held them both ready and to the floor as he took up a starting position. Dayton nodded to the operator across from him.

What they were doing was a classic CQB, Close Quarters Battle, technique. They were going to "Run the Rabbit." Jamie would sprint across the room to the next doorway and distract the enemy, while the men stacked behind them did the shooting. Dayton used hand gestures to establish rear security, and then stacked men behind him. He planted a booted foot behind Jamie's to give him a starting block on the smooth concrete. With a nod from him, the man beside him kicked open the door.

As Jamie leaped into the room an insurgent appeared with an AK in the doorway right in front of him. His eyes widened at the charging man, but before he could react, the pistols in Jamie's fists slammed two rounds out the back of his head. Jamie was past him and in the room before he hit the ground. He tumbled onto the floor and rolled to the side as bursts of AK fire filled the room behind him. A boy about the age of twelve stared wild-eyed at him as he rolled to a crouch. Seeing the AK in his hands, Jamie dispatched him with a single shot to the head before turning back to the door.

"Clear!"

He saw Dayton shake his head, but before Jamie could pull back, AK rounds chipped concrete from the wall next to him, cutting his face and blinding him with dust. He cursed and withdrew back into the room. Dayton fired a burst over his head at the second floor.

"Son of a bitch!" Jamie cursed and reached for a bottle of water in his combat pack. He flushed his eyes with it until he could see again. He looked across to see Dayton still in the doorway.

"What the hell?"

"There's a balcony!"

Before he could say more, a pair of grenades bounced down and across the floor. Jamie dove back into the space behind him, while Dayton did the same. The blasts deafened Jamie, and he felt hot metal burn his leg. He groped for the wound, and his hand came away with blood. Rolling to a sitting position, he checked the door before pulling a knife and slicing into his jumpsuit. He wiped the blood away twice before determining it was not life-threatening. His ears cleared, and he heard Dayton returning fire.

"Jamie!"

"Yeah?"

"Okay?"

"Yeah, just give me a second." He reached out and wiped the blood on his hands off on the dead insurgent's shirt, for the first time noticing that he wore a vest under a green camouflage jacket. His pants were black and looked military in origin. He was light skinned and wore a red bandana. Pulling the cloth aside Jamie examined his face. Not Zarqawi. He yelled the news to Dayton, while he worked on a pressure bandage for his leg.

"My buddy here is a foreigner. Looks Chechnyan."

"I'm shocked," Dayton replied. Another burst of gunfire pounded the walls. "Anytime you're ready."

"Coming, mother. What do we have?"

"Three of four on the balcony. Can't frag 'em as they'll just duck back into the rooms."

"Screw them; we gotta get downstairs! Quit fucking around and get over here."

The Delta man with Dayton stuck his head out long enough to get a look. The insurgents were taunting them and screaming to Allah. He had to speak up to be heard.

"Couple of SAWS and some flash-bangs would get us across."

"I like that," Dayton agreed. "Hang on. I'm coming," he shouted to his partner.

"Well hurry the hell up!" Jamie had switched back to his rifle and was now trying to watch two doors at once. The hole in the wall led into darkness, and he was not about to stick his head around the corner yet.

The operator appeared again with two Marines in tow. They each sported Squad Automatic Weapons, light machine guns with an extremely high rate of fire. The gunners even carried interchangeable barrels so they could switch them out when they got too hot. Dayton explained what he needed, and the gunners changed their gas settings before moving up to the door on either side. Dayton palmed a flash-bang grenade, and with a nod he sent it up and over the balcony. The yells changed in octave, then faded just before the grenade went off, but the SAW gunners were already sweeping the balcony with 5.56 rounds at one thousand rounds per minute. Dayton and the operator sprinted across unhurt.

"Be back soon!" he yelled back to the Marines.

They nodded and began taking turns, sweeping the area over their heads.

Dayton put his back to the wall facing the opening before eyeballing Jamie's leg. "That still work?"

"Dunno." Jamie got to his feet and tested it. "It hurts," he deadpanned.

"Suck it up, princess. Gimme my pistol back. We're behind schedule." Dayton holstered the handgun in a cross-draw rig, palmed another grenade, and walked to the hole in the wall. The two men stacked behind him without a word.

Jamie nodded his readiness, and Dayton pitched the grenade inside. As soon as it went off, they stormed in. The air was thick with smoke and the stench of gunpowder. They split right and left and hunkered down to let it clear. The stairwell was right in front of them, just as they had seen on the video. Dayton duckwalked across the room and took a look over the barrel of his rifle. He saw an insurgent leaning out, doing the same. They fired at the same time, the insurgent's rounds passing Dayton's head by inches, while his own punched the man in the chest and neck. A spurt of arterial blood showered the far wall, and the man fell forward onto the steps, his legs kicking as his heart emptied its supply onto the dusty floor. Yells were heard, then the sound of the man being dragged away.

The ringing in his ears subsided enough for Dayton to hear cursing behind him. He looked to see Jamie holding pressure to the operator's head.

"Just a crease. You're fine."

"Tell me you got that fucker?"

"Yeah, but he's not alone."

Jamie finished tying a bandage around the man's head before picking his rifle back up. He wiped blood from his own cheek where the chipping cement had cut him.

"You got one on each cheek. They're nothing."

He shrugged off the news. "What's the plan? Can't frag 'em; there's bombs in there."

"No."

A hail of gunfire, grenades, and pounding feet sounded behind them, and they turned to see three more operators entering the room.

"Fuckers are dug in up there. They keep changing position and popping up. Dangerous, but they can't go anywhere. You need some help?"

Dayton assessed the situation. The target was downstairs and trapped. The insurgents on the balcony were as well. There was no talking them out and the longer they took the more time the terrorists outside had to get to their location. They had to do something—and quickly. The two operators had brought some borrowed SAWs with them.

"Listen up. Here's what we're going to do."

---

OUTSIDE THE SITUATION was getting worse. RPGs were arcing in over the buildings from the side streets in a desperate attempt to reach the Marines dug in around the house. Small groups of insurgents were probing their defenses, popping up on roofs and out of distant doorways to loose a few rounds before ducking back out of sight. When they were seen, the Marines answered with machinegun fire and grenades. The forward observers had called in the A-10s twice: once to level a tall building to the east which offered too many covered firing positions; and again to silence a mortar tube off to the south.

Now the planes were busy, dropping out of their overhead cloverleaf pattern to strafe the highway south of them as the insurgents tried to cross back over and join the battle at the bomber's house. Despite their efforts, some were leaking through. Slayer reported several cars and trucks heading toward them. They were beginning to take a few casualties.

Charlie leveled his rifle and covered two Marines as they ran from a nearby alley. One of them had a pronounced limp. He was unceremoniously thrown aboard the LAV, where the medic immediately sliced open his pant leg. Charlie grimaced at the sight; the man's calf muscle was a mess. The medic stuffed gauze into the entrance wound with one hand, while squeezing the man's leg just below the knee.

"Will you shut the hell up!" he scolded the wounded Marine.

The man did as he was told, surprised by the blunt rebuke. He craned his head around to see his wound as the medic rotated it. The bullet had not exited out the other side; instead, it lay just under the skin in a clearly defined outline. The medic shook his head and tied off the dressing over the wound before slicing the laces off his boots. He tapped hard on the man's ankle bone. The soldier didn't react, still looking at the protruding bullet tenting his lily-white skin.

"Hurt?"

"Naw, kinda numb now."

"I don't think it hit the bone; just took a chunk of meat. You're fine."

The man nodded at the news and turned to see Charlie watching. He rotated his leg, so he could see better.

"Check it out. Kinda cool, huh?"

"You're a dumbass," Charlie told him with a smile.

"Yeah, I know. Scoot me over there, so I can cover that AOA."

They did so, and the medic gave Charlie a nod, which meant "keep an eye on him," before moving off back into the fray. Charlie watched him until he disappeared around a corner. All medics were crazy; he had learned that a long time ago.

"Time to go yet?" the Marine asked.

"They're still inside," Charlie answered.

"Doing what?"

A loud explosion followed by machinegun fire sounded from inside the building. Charlie didn't bother with an answer. They both resumed scanning the streets around them.

"Hurry up, Mr. Dayton. Past time to go," he muttered.

---

DAYTON HAD LAID out the plan quickly. Who was going to corner, how they would slice the pie, who stacked where, and when they would fully enter. When he got nods all around, they shuffled to the stairwell, Jamie low and Dayton high with the Delta boys behind them with the SAWs.

Each had one in either fist, making it difficult to pull the pins, but they managed. The grenades were equipped with five-second fuses, and Dayton counted down silently before tossing them inside at the three count. Two left and two to the right, they both jumped back and covered their ears, mouths wide open to compensate for the over-pressure. The screaming of Iraqi voices could be heard before the blast erased them.

Dayton's head felt like it had exploded, and he struggled to breathe as the shock waves beat their way through his body. A wave of nausea spiked and was fought down in time for him to open his eyes and see that they were all in a cloud of dust. The Delta guy stepped on him as he moved to the corner and sprayed the interior before drawing back. Dayton watched him, as if seeing him on TV, before Jamie grabbed his vest and yanked him up.

"Okay?"

He was clearly yelling, but Dayton could not hear him. He shook his head to clear the fog and then nodded to the affirmative. Jamie made sure he could stand before letting him go. Bullets ricocheted off the wall and peppered them with cement chips, waking him up further. He instinctively ducked to the opposite wall and hunkered down.

"One straight ahead and another at three o'clock!"

Dayton gave a single jerk of his head in acknowledgement. The concussion grenades had been a risk. The room he had seen on the small screen had explosives in it. He and his three companions could all be mist and pieces of meat on the walls right now if any of them had decided to detonate. They had ditched the basic technique of storming the room right after the grenades, in favor of locating the targets inside first and not walking into a death trap.

A hand signal conversation had them repositioned in seconds. Another grenade found its way into his hand, and he tossed it into the center of the room. This time, the SAWs opened up as soon as the deafening blast and flash of light flooded the room. Jamie broke into the room and ran the wall to the left, while Dayton did the same on the right. Through the dust and noise, he saw one of the benches overturned in the middle of the room, its surface scarred by the grenades and numerous rounds that were impacting it. What was left of a desk sat in the three o'clock position and was being steadily splinted by the rapid fire of the SAW. An insurgent sat behind it, jerking with the impact of the multiple rounds. Dayton dismissed him as the gunfire stopped and focused on the top of the metal bench.

A head with a pair of crazed eyes stuck itself up over the barrel of an AK. Dayton's brain focused on the hair and eyes, a split second before his finger caressed the trigger, sending a three-round burst through both. The man fell behind the bench out of sight.

Dayton spun around and checked the three other bodies in the room, pumping a round into each before rolling them over and checking their faces. Jamie kept his rifle pointed at the bench, while Dayton took care of business. Once he had determined they were all dead, they approached the bench from both directions.

Two men lay behind the bench. One still and missing his face, the other holding what remained of his abdomen in while he rapidly bled onto the floor. The man raised his head and cursed them, blood leaking from his mouth and ears.

"He in the deck?"

Dayton examined his face, focusing on the eyes. No, the man was nobody they were after. He looked the man's wounds over and quickly determined he would be dead soon.

"No, he's nobody." He stepped back and Jamie sent the man on his way to Allah.

"Clear!"

One of the Delta operators entered and scanned the room. Dayton and Jamie were emptying pockets and pulling papers out of what remained of the desk. He watched them for a moment before looking up at the Al Qaida flag on the wall. He reached down and pulled a suicide vest from the rubble. It was wired and rigged with a remote detonator; all it lacked were the explosives.

"Shit. Is he here?"

"I don't see him," Dayton said, clearly not pleased. He ignored him and continued searching the desk, stuffing whatever he found into his vest.

The man flung the vest aside, and it landed with a thunk. They all spun at the noise. Dayton brought his rifle up and gestured to Jamie. They circled the vest on the floor.

Jamie saw it first. A hole, about one inch round and centered on the edge of a plywood floor panel. He searched the wall and found a rod with a hook bent into the end. He lay down and rolled to the opposite side, while Dayton and the Delta operator respectively took up positions at the top and at the bottom. Jamie lowered the hook into the hole and gave a tug, rolling away as the trap door opened.

Two men stared up at them, one of them holding an AK. He swung it around toward Dayton but was dispatched by the operator with a three-round burst to the back of the head. The man next to him flinched as he was showered with the contents of his companion's skull and reached for his belt.

"*Oogaf!*" Dayton shouted, but the man couldn't hear him. Like the others, his ears had been rendered useless by the concussion grenades. Dayton turned the rifle in his hands and butt-stroked the man across the head before reaching down and yanking him out of the hole. The man continued to struggle until Dayton ended it with a knee to the gut. As he gasped for air Dayton quickly flex-cuffed him. Flipping him over, he wiped the dust and blood from his face before examining it closer.

"Ali Mahadaai," he spoke loudly. The man either heard him or read his lips as his eyes widened with a start. They knew his name.

"Zarqawi?" Dayton yelled. The man turned away, and Dayton bounced his head off the floor.

"Zarqawi!?"

The man attempted to spit at him, but Dayton stopped him with a punch to the face.

"There's nobody else here, D. Let's go," Jamie urged.

"Damnit!" Dayton grabbed the man by his neck and half-carried, half-dragged him to the stairs. The gunner nodded that they were still clear before leading them up to the room above. They grouped around the opening and got the attention of the gunners across from them.

"Still at least three up there!"

"Can you keep them down?"

"I think so."

"Let's go then!"

Dayton wiped his eyes and spat out a ball of dust. The room was full of the smell of cordite and gunpowder. A heavy haze hung from the ceiling, helping to conceal the insurgents when they raised their heads or stuck a rifle over the top of the balcony. The room was a death trap. The insurgents knew it. Never mind that there was no escape for them as well; they had obviously been radicalized to the point of not caring anymore. Ready to die for Zarqawi and his twisted version of Allah, they had volunteered to defend the building till death. Dayton was more than happy to grant them their wish, but first he had to get across the room. He tightened his grip on the shirt of his captive and watched as the SAW gunners stacked up in the opposite doorway. He shared a look with Jamie as they ducked behind the cover of the doorway.

"You first. I'm last," Jamie said.

Dayton had time to nod once before a yell came through the sounds of battle outside. Two grenades arced through the air, one of them made it over the balcony rail while the other bounced back down into the room. They went off a split-second apart, and shrapnel whistled into the room inches from his head. Dayton waited just long enough for the SAWs to cut loose before sprinting across the room, Mahadaai bounced off the floor like a rag doll as he was dragged behind. The sound of the SAWs was deafening as the two gunners emptied their 200-round boxes at the balcony above. Dayton ducked under the bullets and dove through the doorway just as one of them yelled, "Grenade!"

Dayton tried to roll, but the weight of the operator behind him knocked him back down. A second later, the grenade went off behind him, followed by a loud grunt and a round of cursing.

"Jamie!"

Dayton rolled to his feet and saw Jamie flat on

his back in the room firing his rifle at the balcony as he tried to kick his way to the door with one good leg. The other left a trail of blood in the dust. The gunners continued to spray the balcony.

"Son of a ..."

Dayton dove between the red-hot barrels and grabbed his partner by the collar. Jamie never stopped shooting as he was dragged out of the kill zone and into the hallway.

"Fall back to the entrance!"

The Delta operator was already rolling Jamie over. He sliced his pants open to reveal several wounds from shrapnel in Jamie's legs and buttocks. One of the wounds pumped bright red blood, and the operator slapped a gloved hand over it.

"Motherfucker—that hurts! How bad?"

"You took some in the ass. Hold still!"

Dayton watched as the man planted a knee into the wound hard and got out his medic pack. Grabbing a large roll of Kerlix, he began stuffing it into the wound as fast as he could. Jamie pounded the ground with a fist against the pain. The man ignored it and kept working. The gauze went red as fast as he could stuff it in. He shared a silent look with Dayton. Not good.

"We gotta go!"

Marines appeared with a stretcher and loaded Jamie up on it. He refused to give up his rifle and scanned the buildings outside over clenched teeth. The operator grabbed Dayton by the arm before he could follow.

"What about them?" He jerked his head toward the building they had just left. It was still full of insurgents and bomb-making supplies.

"Fuck 'em. Blow it in place."

Dayton left him there and made for the LAV, still holding Mahadaai by the neck. The Marines they passed took a quick look, but after seeing it was not Zarqawi and the look on Dayton's face, they quickly went back to their rifles. Most of the perimeter was now engaged with the insurgents. The chatter of rifle fire combined with the booming rhythm of the fifty-cal machine guns, and the buzz saw of the cannons aboard Slayer over their heads, made it impossible to hear anything else. A pair of engineers with a satchel charge sped past him in the direction of the house, and he ignored them.

Charlie appeared in front of him. "Heavy fire from the west and south. Slayer reports seeing activity on our route as well."

"Charlie, you're supposed to be ... never mind. What's the best option?"

A senior officer asking a Lance Corporal what the best move was? Charlie shrugged it off, remembering that rank meant little to the special ops guys. He filled him in as they made their way to the LAV.

"The way we came in, I think. That way we still have the presets."

"Okay, then. Let's go. Find a place for this." He dropped Mahadaai at his feet and entered the LAV. He found the Marine Lieutenant in charge, a guy named Lee, on the radio. Behind him, a pair of medics worked on Jamie. He gave him a hand signal; it was all he needed.

"Yeah, yeah, shut up! Second and first pull it in. Third and guns one and two cover them. We're leaving." He paused and shot a questioning look at Dayton.

"North, route one," he replied to the silent question.

"Egress will be route one. Repeat: route one." He checked to see if the forward observer had heard him, but he was already calling in air support to cover them.

Dayton slid into a seat and took off his helmet long enough to mop the sweat from his head and eyes. He watched as one of the medics shot a syringe full of something into the IV now in Jamie's arm. His cursing became more subdued. The other medic slid over and got in Dayton's ear.

"The shrapnel tore through his pelvis. I can't stop the bleeding. He needs a surgeon, and I mean right now."

"Fifteen minutes," Dayton told him.

"Maybe." The man went back to work.

"Charlie! Get us out of here!"

# 24

*"Corrupt judicial practices in Russia, America, China, Great Britain, and other countries only vary by a single degree: the cost of services."*

—*Christopher Mart*

The General listened to the chatter and watched the display on the wall from Slayer. The insurgents were flowing to the northeast section of the city. Communication came to them in the form of loudspeakers mounted on the towers of the mosque. Normally used to call the faithful to prayer, they were now used to direct the insurgents into battle. The General had given the planes overhead permission to silence them, but it was already too late. The PsyOps forces that had accompanied the troops on the north side of the city were now blasting AC/DC at one hundred and ten decibels as the Marines moved forward. While it made verbal communication more difficult, none of the troops asked for it to be silenced. It was unnerving to the enemy. He remembered how the troops had scrounged stereo equipment from the rubble during the first Gulf War and hotwired it into the tanks and Bradleys they rolled in. He had looked the other way then, and now the practice was a part of their doctrine.

He looked up in time to see the camera light on the target house again. The troops had pulled back, retreating to the north. Insurgents poured into the space left by the departing Marines with several of them entering the house itself.

"Bad decision," one of the controllers voiced. He thumbed the record button just in time.

The screen went white as the camera was

overloaded by the heat from the exploding charges left behind by the Marines. The software quickly compensated, and the General was treated to a view of the house slowly imploding. Before it could finish, another explosion and then a third shot concrete and steel skyward. Secondary detonations from the bombs inside. The building and the ones around it were now little more than piles of rubble under a cloud of dust.

"Homey don't play that," the General commented. It had been a popular saying among his Marines in Gulf One. Now only half of them got the joke and smiled. God, he was getting old.

"Word from Mr. Dayton?"

"Coming out with one, sir. He's requesting medivac at entry one with a critical. Nothing further."

Before the General could inquire, the air ops man said, "Already in place and informed, sir. Colonel Jackson is on his way to meet them."

The General frowned at that, but let it go. His surgeon was a little too aggressive for his comfort. He insisted on being as close to the front line as he could, the argument being that the sooner he got to the men bleeding-out the more he could save. While that was true, it didn't void the fact that they had only two of them. If he got killed, who was going to save the others?

He dismissed the thought and returned to the battle at hand. The easy part was over, the insurgents had expected an all-out assault from a broad front. Instead, they had been fooled into moving south while a raid was struck deep into their territory from the north. Now they were on to the ruse and responding. The fight to get out was going to be a bloody one.

He examined the map again. Constantly updated, it showed the positions of the advancing troops in the north as well as the reported positions of the raiding party. The two were moving toward one another, but at a snail's pace. His trained eye estimated fifteen minutes, maybe twenty, until they linked up. A distance of maybe a dozen blocks. Despite the stars on his uniform, the battle was out of his hands now; the lance corporals, their sergeants, and the lieutenants on the ground would now decide the outcome. Twelve blocks was a long way to travel in an urban environment where others were doing their best to kill you.

They would have to fight for every one of them.

HANEY WAS JUST FINISHING another meeting, this one with the civil affairs leader. The man was painting a bleak picture. Despite orders to spare as many key infrastructure sites as possible, the war had destroyed more than half. The electrical grid of Iraq was down to less than fifty percent. Water treatment facilities about the same. Highways. Bridges. Dams. Food storage and processing. All were heavily compromised. Then there were the oil fields. Output was down to thirty percent of its pre-war capacity. Mostly due to pipeline disruption and the loss of drilling hardware. Two air bases were up for expansion after Haney's lobbyist had pressured enough congressmen to approve it. Two more runways plus several hangars and support buildings, all of them to be built right next to the existing and underutilized structures already in place. The contract was worth three billion dollars, and Haney had already secured it for his former employer. If he and a few of his backers could drag this war out, they stood to make billions. He'd already lost track of the potential profits and now struggled to keep a look of genuine concern on his face as the man rambled on.

Harper appeared in the doorway and scanned

the room before crossing it and standing behind the civil affairs man until Haney noticed him. He held up a finger to silence the man before beckoning him over.

Harper got close enough to whisper in his boss's ear.

"General Marr has launched a full attack into Fallujah. Word is that they had a possible location for Zarqawi. A raid was launched, and the troops are now fully engaged deep inside the city."

Haney's jaw tightened at the news, but he kept his composure. He nodded to the man across from him.

"If you'll excuse me?"

"Certainly, sir."

Haney rose and signaled to his Secret Service detail. The man walked over.

"I need a room."

"This way." He eyeballed Harper but said nothing as he led them both to a small sitting room away from the main gaggle. Harper shut the door behind them.

"Say that again," the VP ordered.

"I'm getting word of a large battle in Fallujah. My men inside claim the General went straight there after the meeting you had and shortly after arrival launched a full attack into the north side of the city. Evidently, the Z squad was there and had reliable intelligence that Zarqawi and Mahadaai, the French bomb maker, were in the city. They launched a raid to capture them and are now engaged on a broad front to extract them. My guy says they're several blocks into the city with over eighty percent of their available forces in the fight. They may be too engaged to order a withdrawal."

Haney spun and slammed his glass down on a table, sloshing its contents onto the floor. He ignored it and began pacing the room.

"General Marr is getting to be a pain in my ass. I just ordered him *not* to become engaged! The Fallujah mess is what we need to keep this thing going long term! Now he's fucking that up!"

"Sir!" Harper gestured for the man to lower his voice and walked closer. "We need to look at options—and quickly."

Haney nodded. His number two man was right. Think it through. He began pacing again.

"If I order them to withdraw, I'll have the entire Marine Corps calling for my head. If I slap Marr down, it'll be the same. Not like I have a valid reason to do so in the first place. Janabi is starting to think too much, but I'm not ready to get rid of him yet."

General Marr was the problem. A man he

could never figure out. The rich son of a rich family, born with a silver spoon worth billions. Yet, instead of following the family tradition, he had gone to Annapolis, and joined the Marine Corps. Haney had tried on three separate occasions to subtly pull the man into the circle he led, but the man had refused. His entire focus was on the Corps. The fact that he had taken the time to find a wife and have a son was a miracle to those who knew him. The son had also joined the Corps, only to be killed outside Mosel a few years ago. The VP had attended the funeral, making sure his picture was taken. The General had gone right back to the front the next day. Haney could just not figure the man out. Now he had become a major problem, one it was time to deal with.

He stopped pacing and faced the Blackwater man.

"You have people in the area?"

"Yes, sir?"

"You say General Marr is in Fallujah? When this is over, I'm going to order a meeting at his headquarters in Ramadi. I want you and your men to be ready for when that happens."

"Which is ...?"

"Our friend the General refuses to fly. He likes to stay on the ground with his men." The VP let the statement hang until the man caught its meaning.

"I understand, sir. I think I can arrange that."

"We'll communicate as usual. Put things in place but wait for my order."

"Yes, sir." Harper turned to leave.

"Mr. Harper?" the VP called. Harper spun in the doorway, his hand still on the knob.

"No loose ends. I mean zero. You understand?"

The man swallowed at the hidden order but nodded to the affirmative. "Yes, sir."

The VP picked up what was left of his drink and drained it. Harper left without another word.

CHARLIE SWORE REPEATEDLY as he weaved the LAV around the rubble. His cursing was echoed by those in the back hovering over the man on the stretcher. Charlie had glanced back only once to see them all working feverishly to save the Z squad soldier. IV lines swayed and hands held the medics in place so they could do their job with blood-soaked gloves. Their boots made rasping sounds as they were repeatedly peeled off the floor and repositioned, the blood attempting to glue them in place. Charlie vowed to not look again.

The tank in front of him blew a hole in the wall of a building and Charlie was forced to brake as the Marines darted out in front of him. The commander opened up on the wall facing them with the fifty-cal, and the surface turned to one of dancing dust—as if an invisible hand were shaking it, forcing it to shed its coat of dirt. He watched as the fire lifted from the ground floor to the second and finally to the roof. Insurgents appeared and sprinted for the neighboring building, jumping the gap in an attempt to escape the rain of lead. A couple of them made it, but most fell or disappeared through a cloud of red mist. The tank's turret swung left to engage the next building until Charlie screamed at the lieutenant. He was on the radio and ordering the tank to continue on a second later.

"Let's move, Charlie!" Dayton yelled.

Charlie didn't waste time with an answer. He floored the accelerator, and the LAV responded with a lurch that sent them all tumbling. They had barely moved a few feet when an RPG skidded down the right side of the LAV to impact the building behind them. The Marine walking in front of them saw where it came from and used the radio on the back of the tank he was following to direct its fire. He gave a wild arm signal, and the

Marines cowered where they could before the main gun fired. The top floor of a house a block away crumbled. Charlie didn't wait for the dust to clear; he weaved around the next pile of rubble and fell in directly behind the tank.

"Tell him to move! Stop shooting everything and let's go!"

The tank lunged forward, and they made it to the next intersection before stopping again. Charlie was about to scream in protest until he saw a fresh smoke grenade in the street. A building half a block in front of them began to come apart under the repeated impact of heavy shells. The Marines cheered as it collapsed into the street, the bodies of a few insurgents sticking out of the rubble. Slayer's engines roared as it passed overhead. The tank moved again, directly through the smoke, and Charlie followed. Marines on both sides sprinted from cover to cover to keep up. Every side street they passed brought the chain gun to life, and it shook the LAV as it fired at darting shapes. The Mark-19 on the LAV behind them joined in, peppering the alley on the other side with explosive rounds. Charlie ducked out of habit and gripped the wheel tighter, his mouth dry and full of the grit of the street. The ringing in his ears was almost constant now; he could barely hear the cursing from the back. He found the hulking shape of the tank in front of him through the dust and followed. The remains of the building had created a choke point, and they now had to pick their way over it before hitting flat ground again. Charlie was forced to pause again as the tank forced its way through. The Marines caught up and worked their way down both sides of the street.

The muzzle of an AK poked out of a small hole in the wall and sprayed the street in front of him. Marines dove for cover behind the LAV, and Charlie watched as three of them crept up to the hole and tossed a pair of grenades inside. They had barely gotten back when they exploded. Charlie flinched when a sneaker with a foot still inside landed on the front of the LAV before slowly sliding down to get stuck behind the left headlight.

"Holy shit!" He stared at it in disbelief.

The rattle of the chain gun literally shook him out of it, and he got the LAV moving again. He followed the two tracks left by the tank over the mound of debris and made it without losing control. The LAV rocked as he set it back on firm ground, his relief cancelled out by the shouts of protest from the back. He ignored them as best he could and worked the wheel until he caught up to the tank at the next intersection. Charlie parked the LAV between the tank and the smoking remains of a car. He struggled to see down the side street to the east, and the Marines waved him back for reasons only they knew. Before he could shift gears, a blue BMW appeared out of the dust, sliding to a halt. Four men spilled out and were immediately met by a wall of bullets. Three of them dropped like ragdolls, but the fourth struggled on, spilling his armload of ammunition and a large quantity of blood onto the pavement as he made for a doorway. Charlie watched as the man would crumple only to be picked back up by bullets passing through him. He eventually dropped just feet from the door. He didn't even have a rifle. One of the Marines took the hint and gestured wildly behind him. A Marine appeared toting a SMAW, a Shoulder-Launched Multi-purpose Assault Weapon. It looked like an old-fashioned bazooka right out of World War Two. The thirty-pound rocket created an enormous overpressure on detonation and could take down a house from the inside. The rocket jumped through the doorway and exploded, throwing clouds of dust out of every window as the roof jumped up and then crashed back down in pieces. A Marine crept up on the doorway and listened before throwing in a frag for insurance. The Marines stacked up and then charged in. A flurry of AK and M-16 fire followed, and two Marines staggered back out. One limping and leaving a blood trail, the other shot in the neck. Marines caught them before they fell and dragged them off to the LAV behind them. A Marine with a grenade launcher fired a smoke grenade down the alley to cover their retreat. The gunner on the LAV followed suit and soon the Marines poured back out of the house. There was a lot of gesturing and yelling before cooler heads intervened, and the Marines moved off to the north. Charlie caught sight of a man with a stick of C-4 moving toward the house before he moved the LAV forward. Problem solved. He put the house out of his mind.

Out of the smoke appeared a motorcycle. On it was a teenager holding an AK. It was thirty meters away before they saw each other. The boy's eyes widened at the sight of the Marines so close, and he swung the bike into a U-turn while firing at the men. The Marines returned fire, but the boy miraculously disappeared back into the smoke unharmed. Charlie watched as the Marines shared looks of amazement with each other. One of them gave the boy a thumbs up before they moved off.

The buzz saw sound of Slayer met his ears, and lead rained from the sky as the gunship worked the buildings to the east with its 25mm cannon. Charlie struggled to pull his eyes from the sky and focused on the road in front of him.

"To the west! To the west!" the radio screamed. The turret rotated behind him as they came up on the next intersection. Charlie glanced that way to see a car keeping pace with them on the next street over. Where the hell was Slayer? The car was gone by the time they passed the next street. Was it behind or in front of them? He didn't know. He felt his butt clench as they approached the next corner. Burned out cars had been shoved into a pile creating a choke point. The tank nudged the first car as it passed through, creating a wider path, but Charlie still had to slow before he could navigate the gap.

"Holy shit! Are they that stupid?" he heard the gunner ask.

He turned to see the car speeding toward them. Marines began firing, but the driver kept the car coming behind the shattered windshield. The LAV's chain gun opened up on it and the front of the car burst apart under the impact of the shells. Both tires blew, and the nose ground a shallow ditch as the car came to a halt. Men spilled out and were quickly cut down. The Marines stopped firing, and when they did the driver reappeared, and to their shock, sprinted *toward* them. Charlie had time to see the man's bright white Adidas tennis shoes, dark pants, and bulky vest over a western style shirt. He was un-armed. A pair of tracers passed through him, and he staggered only to regain his footing and stumble in a circle. He paused long enough to gaze in their direction, a confused look on his face, before he detonated the vest. The Marines had already found cover, but it didn't save them from being showered in the red mist.

"Let's go, let's go! Leapfrog, dammit!"

The street was wider here, so the tanks and LAVs began leapfrogging up the street. The Marines on the flanks were encountering ragtag gangs of insurgents at irregular points. Most fights lasted no more than a few seconds as AKs and RPGs rained in from corners and roofs only to be driven back by the overwhelming firepower of the column. Three blocks later, the attacks suddenly stopped.

"Go firm! Go firm!"

They had reached the advancing battalions. Marines dove into the surrounding buildings on both sides, and the tanks attempted to turn around, but Charlie didn't wait this time. He sped past them and ignored all the other radio traffic. The map in his head said they were only a few blocks short of the city's edge. Beyond that lay safety and medical. He had to get there. Fast.

He took a look behind him. The men were still working frantically on Jamie. Charlie caught sight of a pale arm sticking out of the mess. Dayton met his look for a second; his face spoke of fury and checked rage. His captive lay on the floor in front of him, his head pinned to the floor under Dayton's bloody boot.

Charlie turned and willed the LAV faster.

---

"LOCATION?"

The man at the screen pointed to the red dot. "They just passed the front of 2/7, a block north of Phase Line Olson, sir. They should be out of the city in a few minutes."

The General took the news silently. The raiding party was out, now to see what they had with them, and what it had all cost.

"3/5 is reporting light resistance. He wants to push past the cemetery?"

"Negative, hold until the others are on line and

then back sweep. Do not get overextended," Colonel Tucker ordered.

The General nodded in agreement. There were forty thousand houses in the city—any of them could be hiding a group of insurgents. The plan was to jump forward three blocks, establish a line, then back sweep every one of them. Resupply and medical would do the same behind them. But they had to get deep enough into the city to keep the politicians from calling them off again. Time was not on their side. Sooner or later someone would notice there was a battle going on. At that point, the General's phone would ring.

He hadn't decided whether to answer it yet.

CHARLIE HALTED the LAV next to the doorway. Shouts and scrambling bodies came from the rear as the doors were flung open and he had time to see the face of Colonel Jackson among them before they all disappeared into the building. The medic struggled with the stretcher, IV bags hanging from clenched teeth, as they all tried to fit through the door. Charlie watched them go before extracting himself from the seat and picking his way through the blood and debris of the interior.

From the looks of it, the battle inside the LAV had been as hard fought as the one outside. The blood sucked at his boots as he made his way free.

Exhausted Marines stumbled around looking for water and ammo. Others watched the streets behind them for any insurgents dumb enough to approach. Charlie policed up his rifle and gear and did a walk around his vehicle. Burn marks told him where the RPGs had hit. Two of the tires were shredded. A section of the back looked like it had been on fire at one point. Bloody handprints coated the sides and rear doors. Eventually, he reached the front and found the shoe. He pulled it free and looked around for a place to toss it.

"Nice trophy," a passing Marine commented.

Charlie just grunted a reply, too tired to come up with a witty comeback. Finding nowhere to dispose of the foot, it went under the vehicle. Deciding the LAV was still able to move, he crawled back in through the gore and drove it around the corner. From the sound of it, there would be more wounded coming soon, they would need the space.

COLONEL JACKSON REGLOVED for the tenth time and examined the man before him. The medics around him worked to cut the remaining clothing and gear away, most of it soaked and turning a dark brown. Like most soldiers, his patient sported a farmer's tan, but what was not stained by blood was whiter than normal, even in the half-light of the abandoned store they were using for triage.

"Hang the O-neg, two units."

"That's half our remaining, sir."

"I know."

"He took shrapnel from the rear. It sliced his femoral somewhere. I tried to clamp it, but I couldn't get a hold of it. Knocked him down and tubed him early but ..."

"Hespan?"

"Five hundred in."

"What's his pressure?"

"Seventy over forty."

"Not enough. Infuse another five hundred. Flip him over and get on the chest." Hands reached in, and they did so being careful of the IV now infusing the last of their O-neg blood. The man immediately started CPR. Jackson pointed to the soaked bandage on the back of Jamie's leg.

"Release the pressure. Let me see."

The medic took his hands and the bandage in

them off the leg, and Jackson found what he had suspected. Kerlix stuck out of the wound, but it still pumped a stream of blood with every push on the man's chest. Next to the wound were the bloody tracks of another piece of steel. Its trail gave him an idea of where the other piece had traveled.

"Betadine and a ten blade!"

A medic reached over his shoulder and emptied a bottle onto Jamie's pelvis before dropping a roll of Kerlix on top. Jackson grabbed it and mopped the area for a total of four seconds before holding his hand out. The scalpel appeared in it without delay.

"Light!"

Two men with handheld flashlights jockeyed for position between the medics. Jackson didn't wait; he found his landmarks by feel, planted a finger and thumb to mark the spot, and cut between them. Once deep enough, he spread the opening with his fingers and searched.

"Suction."

The medics had caught up; one of them had the catheter in before he was done ordering it, and Jackson could finally see what he was looking for.

"Damn thing is shredded." He worked to make the opening deeper. A pair of hands planted a re-

tractor and pulled one side away, freeing the surgeon's hand. He probed higher.

"Got it. Somebody clamp this thing."

Hands reached in and carefully slid the instru-
ment over the surgeon's fingers. If they bumped
him, he could lose his grip on the artery, letting it
snap back up into the pelvis again. If that happened, they might not have another chance.

"Easy, easy, you got it? Okay, get another one
on it. Pressure?"

"No change."

"Package him up, he's going to the box. What's
next?"

"There's a chest in the other room that needs
you and a partial amputee coming in."

"On my way."

The surgeon stripped off his gloves as he
turned away, only to be stopped by the steel grip of
Dayton. Jackson opened his mouth to protest, but
he changed his mind when he saw who it was. The
fact that he held another man, flex-cuffed and
hooded, in his other fist, spoke volumes.

"What happens to him?" Dayton asked, indi-
cating Jamie with a thrust of his jaw.

"He needs to get to the box and get that artery
repaired. Major Neil can do it, if he's not too busy."

"And if he is?"

Jackson grimaced and shrugged. "He'll probably lose the leg. Do you mind?"

Dayton looked down at his hand gripping the man's arm as if seeing it for the first time. He quickly let go. The man clapped him on the shoulder before moving off.

Dayton paused for only a moment, watching the medics secure the clamps protruding from his partner's legs.

"Is there a helicopter?" he asked them.

"First birds took RPG fire, so the Colonel cancelled dust off. Everyone is going by ground."

Dayton was already out the door, dragging the man behind him.

"Charlie!"

# 25

*"The only thing I'm afraid of about this country is that its government will someday become so monstrous that the smallest person in it will be trampled underfoot, and then it wouldn't be worth living in."*

—*Harper Lee*

"I don't give a damn how many stars he has! He was told not to get engaged! Are you saying you don't know what the hell is going on in your own backyard, General?"

General Kasel stood with his arms crossed and let the smaller man rant. Homicidal thoughts entered his mind as they usually did every time he was in the same room with him. He often wondered if the Secret Service men present would lift a finger to stop him if he ever decided to put those thoughts into action. It wasn't worth it, but he'd about had enough.

Haney had worked himself up for the show he was putting on. He'd already flung his tie across the room and kicked a chair after it. Now red-faced and sweating, he was cussing up a storm, as if the Marine in front of him had never heard worse. Kasel cut him off mid-sentence.

"General Marr had reason to believe that Zarqawi and three other high-value targets were in the city! He acted on that intelligence under standing orders to get them! The nature of the resistance required whatever he felt was needed to counter it and ensure the success of the raid!"

"And I'm supposed to believe he never contacted you first? Or did you approve of this without sending it upstairs?"

"He didn't need my permission! This isn't some game of Mother-May-I we're playing here! Zarqawi is leading the insurgents! He's beheading people on the fucking Internet! You think Marr's going to waste time in debate when there's a target like that right in front of him? This isn't some fishing trip they just went on; it was a raid against a heavily armed target, and I'm not going to second-guess the judgment of the man on the scene from miles away ... sir!"

Kasel had steadily walked toward the VP while he spoke, his hands balling into fists. Haney held his ground but was sufficiently cowed. He had pushed the man too far. Vice President or not, he could only get away with so much, and the President liked Kasel.

Haney shook his head and stalked away. The fishing trip comment was a veiled insult. His Secret Service name was Angler, after his love of fly fishing. The joke among the Service was that it was the only sport his fat ass could perform. He shrugged it off; the act was more important right now. He'd deal with Kasel down the road when the time was right.

"I want to hear him say that. Right now, tonight. I want to hear it."

"He can't leave. He's in the middle of a battle!"

"As soon as it's over I want to see him. Where is he now? How long to get there?"

"He's outside Fallujah, sir. You can't go there," another voice said.

Haney eyeballed his Secret Service man. He was from the command group, not the head of his usual detail. There was no way in hell he would let Haney near the city.

"Where's his headquarters then?"

"Outside Ramadi."

"There, after dark." His tone said it was an order. He shot a look at the Service man, who reluctantly nodded.

Haney stalked out of the room. It had gone just as planned.

THE HELICOPTER DROPPED HARPER OFF JUST west of Habbineeyah lake, just south of Ramadi. He was met by a group of five men sporting beards and dressed in various black or tan clothing, all of them well-armed with a variety of weapons. They had driven out of the city in a pair of Mitsubishi SUVs and now waited, watching the sky for drones and scanning the desert around them with high-powered lenses. One of the SUVs sat a bit lower than the others. Harper took all this in as he sprinted through the downwash to meet them. Off to the east, the distant rumble of battle could be heard.

"Who knows you're here?" he asked without any preamble.

"Nobody. We left out the west side and circled back. All the drones and other air are over Fallujah. Everyone's eyes are pointed that way—no way to tell for how long, though. You going to tell us what we're doing out here?"

He ignored the question. "You bring what I said?"

"Two of them. With the proximity switches. I've got the laptop, too; just need the tracking codes." Harper produced a thumb-drive from his pocket and handed it over.

"Good. Here's what I want done."

CHARLIE PUSHED SO hard on the accelerator he lost feeling in his booted foot, but the LAV was already maxed out and would go no faster. He could see the lights of the camp just east of the cloverleaf, but it seemed to take forever to get closer. He chanced a look behind him to see no change. Dayton and the Delta man were working to keep Jamie in place in the bouncing rear end. The various IV lines swayed violently and threatened to tear themselves loose from the man's arms. Their prisoner, bound and lying on the floor, had managed to slip his gag and was now cursing them repeatedly. The two men were too busy keeping the Z squad soldier alive to shut him up.

"Time, Charlie?"

"Two minutes!"

The noise of the shredded tires suddenly lessened by half as the remaining rubber left the rim. Charlie ignored it and drove on, taking the last turn at the edge of the compound and roaring toward the secure gate. The Marines were expecting them and stood aside. Charlie turned twice more before stopping in front of The Box. It was the name which had been given to the sandbag bunker with the plywood interior that had become the medical center.

The doors opened before he had the brake engaged, and a group of Marines reached in to extract the patient. Dayton let go of the stretcher and punched Mahadaai in the face, shutting him up before dragging him out by his neck and tossing him to the ground. The Marines paused for only a second before a bark from their gunny got them moving again. An army captain stood waiting to one side.

"You the alpha?" Dayton asked.

"Captain Moore, this for me?" He looked down at the now silent man lying in the dirt.

"Secure him for now. He'll be coming out with me."

"Roger that."

Dayton turned without another word and followed the medics into the bunker. Charlie scrambled out just in time to see them disappear.

"Hey, Charlie."

He turned to find the Delta man standing next to him. He held Dayton's combat vest in his bloody hand and a dirty rifle in the other. Charlie realized he didn't even know his name.

"Yeah?"

"That was some good driving. Where can I get some ammo around here?"

"Other side of that berm. He going to make it?"

The man shrugged. "No telling; he lost a lot of blood. If they get him stable, and the surgeon can repair the artery, and get some blood flow to that leg in time, he may not lose it. He's in a world of hurt either way." He patted himself down while he spoke and examined the interior of the LAV for any lost items. Charlie glanced in as well, but he quickly looked away; it was going to be an hour at least to clean that mess up.

"Gotta go!" The man punched him in the arm before jogging off in the direction Charlie had pointed him. He was quickly lost from sight.

Charlie turned around twice, trying to decide what to do next. Everyone else seemed to have a job, and he was suddenly without one and exhausted. He was examining the damage to the LAV again when a familiar voice spoke behind him.

"That the General's LAV?"

Charlie turned to see First Sergeant Skiles behind him, his arm in a sling and his head wrapped in Kerlix.

"It is, Top. I ... it's got some damage."

The man examined the damage before he glanced inside and made a face. "Get it to the motor pool and get those tires changed out. You can clean it up while they're doing that. He might need it soon."

"Yes, sir," Charlie mumbled, his eyes on the bloody trail the foot had left.

It was the wrong reply to make to a man of his rank, and it prompted the Marine to examine the younger man.

"You all right, Charlie? You injured?"

Charlie pulled his gaze away and met that of the first sergeant. "Yeah, Top, I'm good. I'm on it."

"All right then, get it moving. There's more wounded coming in, and you're in the way here."

Without a word, Charlie did as ordered. The LAV drew several looks from the Marines about to join the battle. Some grinned stupidly, while others frowned. Charlie ignored them and drove off in the direction of the motor pool. The stench from the back end turned his stomach the whole way.

---

TWO OF THEM worked feverishly on the hole, while the rest of them scanned the sky in all directions. They had adopted traditional Iraqi dress for the satellites that were sure to be watching, but if anything closer spotted them, they would be targeted immediately. They could not afford so much as a radio inquiry as to what they were doing. Their only saving grace was the terrain, a natural dip in the earth shielded them from any eyes on the ground.

Harper checked his watch. "One minute."

"I'll be done in a few seconds. Get ready to cover this up."

Harper pointed to two men. "You and you. The rest keep scanning. Anything on the radio?"

"Nothing but traffic over Fallujah."

The man lying prone on the hot asphalt ignored the conversation and concentrated on the task at hand. He'd only have one chance. He made the final connection and tested the circuit. It was good. He placed the device back in its plastic bag and wedged it in the narrow hole. The two men immediately began shoving dirt and rock over it. What was leftover was scattered into the wind. The large chunk of asphalt they had pried up was now carefully placed in its previous position. The man finished the process by cutting the antenna wire as close to the remaining crack as he could.

"That's it. Let's go."

"You guys take this heap. I have to go back. Stay off the radar for a few days."

The men didn't question. They crowded into the small truck and left in the direction of Ramadi. Harper headed west, out of the depression and over the small rise. There, he stopped the vehicle and got out, walking back in the direction he'd come. Dropping to his belly, he crawled to the top of the rise until he could see the cloud of dust following the truck. When it had traveled a sufficient distance, he pulled out his phone.

The delay was longer than he expected, but he soon saw the flash of light and the debris flying through the air. The truck continued to roll on, belching flames and black smoke until it left the road and flipped on its side in the soft earth. The rumble was lost in the noise of the battle to his north. Harper examined it through the scope of his rifle. After a full minute of not seeing any movement, he withdrew and climbed back into the truck.

The trap was set. Now all he needed was a diversion. He sent a coded text before slipping the truck in gear and heading east. He would rendezvous with the helicopter in twenty minutes.

---

DAYTON SHOVED the door open with a foot and glared at the Marine guarding it. He was not in the mood for delay.

He had watched for ten minutes while the surgeon and his team worked to stabilize his partner. The fight had been loud and full of activity, but eventually they all calmed and watched the numbers on the tiny monitor settle into a range they approved of.

"He's stable for now," the surgeon had told him.

"His leg?"

"If I have time," was the only answer he'd received. The surgeon had been over his next patient before Dayton could ask more. He swallowed the information and with one last look at Jamie lying on the stretcher he made his way out of the box and to the command post. The blood on his fatigues and the set of his jaw worked to clear a path for him. He ignored the stares from the seated soldiers as he crossed the room.

"Is he okay?" one of them whispered to his neighbor.

"It's not his blood," the older Marine had answered.

The revelation only widened the young man's eyes further, and he had followed Dayton's figure as he went by until the older Marine nudged him back to his screen.

"Mr. Dayton?" Colonel Tucker acknowledged him. "Were you successful?"

The General turned at the comment and took in the man's appearance, his hand still resting on the phone. He waved Dayton silent before he could answer and asked a question of his own.

"Are you alright?"

"Yes, sir. My partner is with the surgeon; he's a critical, but stable. We had three injured on the raid and several on the ride out. I don't know all of their statuses. Charlie is fine."

The General nodded a thank you for the question he could not ask. Dayton returned it and drove on.

"We found Zarqawi's bomb maker and took him alive. He's with the intelligence guys at the moment. There was no sign of Zarqawi himself."

"The house?"

"A bomb factory. We found several in production, and a few ready to go. I imagine any others are out there, in the city. A few artillery rounds being rigged for IEDs. Some remote detonators. Cell phones. I have plenty of pictures."

"Still standing?"

Dayton shook his head. "There was too much pressure from the south. I had them blow the building in place. There's another hiding place out there somewhere; I didn't see the room from the internet videos. No bloodstains on the floor. No flags or other backdrops on the walls. Wherever they did the beheadings, it's somewhere else."

Dayton watched as the two men shared a look of disappointment. Not nabbing Zarqawi was a big one, but the looks spoke to more than what they were talking about here.

"Something I should know ... sir?"

"I've just been ordered to my regional head-quarters in Ramadi. The VP himself is flying out to chew my ass for launching the attack. Colonel Tucker will take over the operation here."

Dayton couldn't believe what he was hearing. "How could he not want to get Zarqawi? What—"

"Ours is not to wonder why, Mr. Dayton," the General cut him off. "What will you be doing with your prisoner?"

"I'll secure him until I can get him to Bagdad. Once there, it's above my pay grade."

"Perhaps you'd like to accompany me? You and your package can hitch a ride back with one of the escort birds."

Dayton read between the lines. The presence of Zarqawi's bomb maker could not be overlooked by the VP. It might even prevent the man from re-taliating against the General. The decision wasn't a hard one.

"When do we leave?"

---

CHARLIE DIDN'T LIKE IT.

They were speeding down a broken road well south of the city. Highway One, north of Fallujah, had suffered a large IED attack on a convoy resulting in them being rerouted. The LAV had crossed the Euphrates a few miles south of the city, and they were now striking out west over the barren desert. Lake Habbineeyah could be seen to the north, but Charlie had no time to look. He concentrated on the road in front of him, keeping the armored Hummer they were following just in view in the cloud of dust ahead. The road was rough, and Charlie silently cursed both the rapid pace, and the million hiding places for an IED that appeared and disappeared in front of him. They were number five in the column, the LAV supported by a half dozen others and with a Bradley bringing up the rear. An A-10 had flown over them a short time ago, the pilot examining the road ahead from his inverted position. Despite the pilot's report of a clear road ahead, Charlie was still tense. What could the man really see at that speed?

The General sat behind him, clearly agitated by having to leave the battle. The Marines had advanced farther into the city than they had planned, and before they had left, Colonel Tucker was giving orders to halt the advance and find hardened positions so they wouldn't get overextended. Back sweeping the overrun buildings, resupply, and removal of the wounded were now the goal. The attack would recommence before dawn, unless they were ordered not to. The General hoped the politicians would see that they were too engaged to withdraw, but you could never count on a politician to see anything. The General had already sent a communiqué to his superiors, copying it to the Secretary of Defense, in the hopes of adding as many voices of reason to the debate as he could. Not that Haney would listen. He and the SecDef did not like each other, one of them pushing for more action while the other always favored a slow response. Each knew the other's motivation. The simple answer was that one of them was rich enough, the other wasn't. The General was not looking forward to this meeting.

Next to him sat Dayton, his gear still bloody and coated with dirt. He reeked of cordite and death. His eyes focused on nothing. Clearly exhausted, he had said little, but the pressure of his bloody boot holding Mahadaai to the floor did not let up. William had raised an eye at the treatment, but the General had shaken his head to the negative. William let it be and turned back to his screen. He was following their progress via satellite. Miraculously, the communications gear had survived the battle intact, and he was using it to relink with the GPS tracking unit. It would show anyone with the proper code exactly where they were in case something happened. He now measured the distance between their current location and the base. Forty minutes, maybe less. The sun was already going down, and the night chill had started.

HANEY LOOKED up as his aide presented him with his phone. The message on the small screen was scrambled and required him to put in his code. He kept his face neutral while reading its short message. Checking his watch, he estimated he would be back at the airbase within the hour.

CHARLIE CAUGHT sight of the top of the lead vehicle rising up the other side as he made his way into the depression. They were getting close; thirty more minutes, and he could finally relax. The LAV needed another hour of attention to be fully free of blood, but he was hoping to have some help with that. All he wanted right now was his place in the bunker and a couple of poncho liners, but he knew these would have to wait as well. Whenever this meeting was over, the General would want to return to Fallujah. He'd be lucky to get any sleep until tomorrow or the next day.

---

THE RECEIVER in the hole woke to the signal of the coming transmitter. Accurate to three meters, it broadcast the shrinking distance with blind accuracy. Waiting patiently until its target was within its programmed distance, it sent a measured voltage to the detonator, not caring that its actions would destroy it.

---

THE HIGH SPEED of the LAV meant the detonation occurred under the rear end. Charlie had no time to react as the LAV was launched skyward by the charge. The vehicle flipped once, then rolled down the grade into the depression, its shredded carcass stopping on its side with the wheels still spinning. He woke from his daze to the screaming from the back end. A sticky film covered half his face, and he wiped it away in order to see. Hydraulic fluid, his brain classified it before screaming at him to move. His hearing returned, and he began to sort the voices yelling from the back.

The General, he couldn't hear him.

He scrambled from his seat and twisted his way to the rear. The rear doors were hanging open, and the occupants were piled on what was now the floor.

"Charlie!"

Charlie followed the voice and found Dayton lying on the floor with the General underneath him. The ruptured hydraulic lines spewed the last of their pressure out onto his back as he shielded the man. Dayton's face was a mask of blood from a head wound Charlie could not see.

A hand grasped his arm, and he swiveled to see William holding him with one hand while the other held what was obviously a fractured leg. He was yelling and pointing at the smoke coming from an overhead panel.

Fire. The LAV was on fire. It jolted him into action.

Grabbing William by the collar, Charlie dragged him toward the rear. Ignoring his screams, he lunged repeatedly until he was at the entrance. Marines appeared and grabbed them both, but Charlie tore himself away and dove back inside. Dayton had managed to extract himself from the pile, shoving his now dead prisoner and what was left of a young Marine off of him in order to reach the General. Charlie saw that the man was unconscious, and he grabbed Dayton's arm in an attempt to help. Dayton roared in pain and shook him off, tucking the broken appendage away from Charlie. He grabbed the General with his good arm and braced his feet on the body of his dead prisoner before pulling again. They both fell back, pulling the General up their bodies far enough for the Marines outside to grab him.

But there was only so much room.

The smoking panel flared up, shorting out and sending sparks across the inside of the LAV. Dayton's oil-soaked back instantly caught and Charlie shoved him out just before his own uniform was set ablaze.

The pain was like nothing Charlie had ever felt before. His scream was cut off by the thick smoke, and he flailed about in an attempt to escape it. He blindly stumbled in the direction of the door only to be grabbed and flung into the sand by his fellow Marines.

The stars in the ink-black sky were the last thing he remembered.

# 26

*"The level of corruption in a country is determined by the value systems of that country."*

—*Sunday Adelaja*

S enator Lamar pounded the marble floor of the capitol building. Secretaries and aides scrambled to get out of his way as he rounded corners without slowing. His aide was forced to run a few paces to keep up.

The group outside the door turned their collective heads as he approached and quickly parted. The door opened just in time for him to pass, and he ignored the others in the room while he addressed the woman in front of the inner door.

"Is he in, Carol?"

"Yes, sir." She knocked on the door twice before opening it. The senator's aide stopped outside. Carol shut the door behind him.

Senator Maxwell Bunker pulled his head from his hands and looked up to see who had entered. His face was one of shock.

"Rem. Thanks for coming."

"I've just heard. What the hell happened?"

"They've just informed me he was shot down. In a few hours they're sending a DOD officer to brief me on what else they have."

Lamar scanned the room. Two of the senator's aides sat against the wall. A young man in uniform stood behind the door, nervously fingering the band on his hat.

"Can we have the room, please?" the senator asked. The aides looked at their boss, who nodded. They rose to leave, and the officer made to follow.

"Not you. You stay," Lamar ordered.

The officer shut the door behind the departing pair and resumed his stance against the wall.

"What do you know?"

"Sir, Colonel Conner will be here later to brief—"

"Don't give me that, Lieutenant. I don't care if he has to write it up first. Tell me what you know and do it now!"

The lieutenant swallowed and thought about his options, but a look at the senator's face told him he had none. The man was the head of the intelligence committee; he was going to get the information anyway and making him wait would only piss him off.

"Lieutenant Bunker was shot down over central Syria last night, sir. The ejection seats were fired. We've scanned the area with drones and discovered their parachutes, but we're not seeing them ... sir."

"They've been captured?"

"It's too early to say, sir. I—"

"Beacons?"

"Um, no, not yet, sir."

"Oh my God, what am I going to tell Susan?" the senator whispered from behind his desk.

Lamar turned from his interrogation of the young officer and focused on his friend. "I'll go with you, and I'll bring Rita."

"Yeah, yeah, that would be good."

Lamar pulled out his phone and called his aide. "Pull the car around. We're going to pick up my wife, then go to the Bunker house." He hung up without waiting for a reply. His friend was now staring out the window, playing with his shoelace. He let him be and turned back to the lieutenant.

"How?"

"Sir?"

"How was he shot down? We've destroyed their anti-aircraft abilities. They have no radar, no aircraft. How did it happen?"

"Sir, I'm not sure I'm at liberty to—"

"Bullshit! How did it happen?"

"Radio traffic and data link from the aircraft suggest ... suggest a missile."

"A missile?"

"Yes, sir."

"How in the hell ... from the airdrop? Is this what I'm being told? Did one of our planes just get shot down by one of our own missiles?"

"Sir, I'm very junior and—"

"Get your boss on the phone with me, Lieutenant! Now! I want to know how that airdrop went so far off target. I want to know everything that was in it! I want to know why Stingers were even on that plane to begin with! And I want to know yesterday!"

"Yes, sir." The man made a hasty exit. Lamar slammed the door behind him and paced the room.

"Max, I'll get to the bottom of this. I promise."

The man just nodded.

A tentative knock sounded on the door.

"Yes?"

"Your car is ready, sir."

"Come on, Max. Let me get you out of here. Let's go see Susan."

"Yeah ... okay." The man allowed himself to be led out the door. Senator Lamar kept his rage in check as they passed through the halls. Something stank about this whole thing. He shared a silent look with his aide as they walked out. He loaded his friend in the Lincoln, then grabbed his aide's shoulder as he rounded the back end.

"This is tied to that errant airdrop. I want the raw data on this. If they send over a glossy report, let me know right away. I want the NSA feed from that night, as well. I want to compare it to what DOD gives me. Keep it as quiet as you can."

"Yes, sir."

———

DAYTON REWOUND the footage and played it again. The helicopter avoided the rising smoke as the camera zoomed in for a better shot. The entire north end of the building was on fire. They had watched it twice already without finding anything new, but it was all they had, so they worked it to death.

"It went up so fast."

"That's the idea."

Anna sat back and rubbed her neck. The last few hours had been hectic. First Dayton had dragged her out of her motel room only to sprint them back to Miami and straight to her storage unit. They had quickly loaded items into two large bags and set out for the airport. The Citation was ready and waiting, and they were in the air minutes later. Dayton had shut the cockpit doors after they reached altitude, and together they had inventoried and organized an arsenal of weapons and other gear while they raced the sun west. She had started to load each weapon, but Dayton had stopped her.

"Not a wise thing to do on a plane," he had said.

She realized her stupidity: one misfire and they would depressurize, possibly killing them all and ending their current mission real fast. They had stowed everything back in the bags for departure and settled in to read and watch what William had sent so far. The storage unit fire was all over the news.

"So we don't even know if they have him?"

"They have him. He would have checked in by now, if they didn't."

"So what do we do?"

"We find out where and do it quickly. Once we have that, we can make plans."

"Plans for what?"

"Getting him back."

"You think he'll talk?"

"Number Six? No, he knows better. He'll only talk if he sees an opening he can exploit. If there's an opportunity to help us, he'll take it. We just have to be there to capitalize on it when it happens. He knows we're coming; just not how long it's going to take us to get there. I'm hoping he stalls them for a while, then makes his play."

"How's he going to do that?"

Dayton looked away from the fire replaying on the screen. "I'd planned on getting to that lesson after your current job. Consider this a crash course."

---

JACK LOOKED through the one-way glass at his prisoner. The man sat calmly, his mountain of bulk threatening to overflow the chair. His legs and bare feet stretched out underneath the metal table between him and the bench on the other side. His cuffed hands were in his lap and his head was on his chest, which rose and fell with his steady breathing. A rivulet of sweat formed on his brow and traveled down his face and neck to be absorbed by his t-shirt. A pair of flip-flops two sizes too small sat on the floor. He seemed unfazed by the heat or the bright lights.

"Only the guilty sleep. It's the innocent who stay awake and worry." It was a common saying among cops, even though they all knew it to be false. This man was guilty, but he was a man responding more like a soldier, banking up sleep for when he would need it.

"Nothing?" Jack asked Greg.

"Nothing. Asked to use the bathroom once and a nod of thanks for the water. That's it."

"Why's he still in his clothes?"

"They didn't have a jumpsuit which would fit him downstairs. The guy's a frickin' mountain."

Jack dismissed it as irrelevant. "It's been six hours, and he hasn't talked."

"Yeah, you'd think a phone call, or maybe a lawyer, would be on his mind by now."

"I think he's following procedure."

"Whose?"

"Well, that's the million-dollar question, isn't it?"

Jack watched the man sleep and sweat for another few minutes.

"He's in the chair?"

"Yeah. Soon as we put him in there and shut the door, he swapped it for the bench and got comfortable. Evidently, he has some experience in this type of room."

Jack nodded. The bench in an interrogation room was altered to lean slightly forward, making it uncomfortable for the person using it. Evidently, their suspect wasn't up to playing such games. The room also had its own temperature control and double the needed lighting, all in an attempt to keep the person being questioned awake and un-comfortable.

"This isn't going to work."

"What?"

"The lights and heat. The bench. This guy's been trained. That stuff might work on street crim-inals, but it won't on this guy. Find me another chair and turn the air back on."

"You sure?"

"Yeah. I'll talk to him in a bit."

"Okay, boss."

---

CHARLIE JUMPED to his feet when he saw the doctor enter. The man motioned him to a private room nearby, and Charlie's heart sank. It was the same type of room he had become an orphan in. He had to force himself inside.

"Charlie, I'm Doctor Cassidy, the neurologist on call. I've been taking care of your boss. I under-stand there's no family?"

"No, his wife died several years ago, and his son was killed in Iraq. I'm his power of attorney for medical issues."

"Good. Sorry, we just have to establish these things up front and—"

Charlie waved it away. "How is he?"

The doctor pulled out a CT scan and held it up to the light, while searching for a pen to point with. Charlie handed him his.

"Thanks. He's had a moderate stroke. Fortunately, it's not hemorrhagic. The CT scan showed a blockage in the left parietal lobe, and it's blocked the blood flow to the posterior middle cerebral artery here and here. This is what's altering his mental status."

"Is this permanent?"

"It depends. You got him here fast, which gives us some options. But there's a risk involved."

The doctor pulled out a second set of pictures, this time of the General's legs. "We see some clotting here, in the left quad area. There's still flow, but it's diminished. This may be where the clot that caused the stroke came from."

"So, what's the risk?"

"I can give him a drug known as Trans—never mind—we call it TPA, for short. It's a thrombolytic, a clot buster. It'll hopefully break up the clot in his brain and restore the flow where it's needed."

"So give it to him!"

"Not so fast. It can also break up this clot in the leg more. Those clots can travel up to the heart and cause a number of problems. Pulmonary embolisms, heart attacks. They can even travel to the brain and cause more strokes. We may fix one problem, only to make more. It's a pretty big risk."

Charlie deflated and sank back into the chair. He needed help. Where was Dayton? Or William? He wanted to call them, but he knew he couldn't. He saw the doctor check his watch.

"How fast do I have to make this decision?" he asked.

"Right now. The window for TPA is narrow. If you add up his down time and add the time to transport ... we need to make a decision now."

"What would you do?"

"Charlie, I can't ..."

"He's a soldier, doc. Risks are something he's used to, but I don't know this stuff and I've got no time to learn it. What would you do?"

"It's a tough call. His condition makes him prone to this. He's on thinners already, so we can start without waiting for a bunch of tests. His heart's strong, and if that file you brought is current, he hasn't had any surgeries or head trauma lately?"

"No, the file's current. You're avoiding the question, and we're wasting time." Charlie fixed him in his gaze and held it.

"If it were my dad ... I'd go with the TPA."

"Do it."

Without a word, the doctor closed the file and walked out. Charlie waited until the door shut behind him before sinking into a chair and burying his face in his hands.

---

JACK OPENED the door and kicked the chair in. It rolled to a stop against the desk and stirred the man awake. He'd been faking, Jack saw. Yes, he was resting, but not fully asleep. He squinted up at Jack. Jack dropped the file on the flat surface and spun the chair around so he could sit. A paper cup was still in his hand, but he kept it off the table.

"Coffee?" he offered.

Carter shook his head. He sized Jack up. He scanned him top to bottom, even glancing under the table to see his lower half. He then sat a bit straighter, wiped the sweat from his brow with his sleeve, and placed his cuffed hands on the table.

"Sorry about the heat; it's their standard tactic. I should have told them it was useless for you."

Jack opened the file, reading whatever was on top. Carter scanned the room, lingering on the door for a moment before glancing at the mirrored glass and back to Jack.

"It's open. But you know that."

Carter did. It was to allow someone—usually someone with a weapon or Taser—quick access to the room in the event he tried something foolish. He wouldn't. He was actually surprised not to be cuffed to the metal ring in the middle of the table. The leg shackles were a problem, though. He cocked his head at Jack, waiting.

Jack stopped reading. "You know who I am?"

"You're Agent Jack Randall of the FBI," Carter stated.

Jack's heart leaped. The man had spoken. But would he continue?

"Why now?"

Carter shrugged.

"You've been silent for six hours. Why you talking to me?"

"Felt like four."

"And?"

Another shrug.

Jack tapped the file. "What we found the first hour. Weapons. Explosives. Military hardware. Bomb-making materials. Sterile vehicles. It's some interesting reading."

Carter examined the file, cocking his head to

one side, then leaning over to see its thickness. He sat back up and leaned over the table before drawing a deep breath through his nose.

"This file. It smells well done."

Jack kept his face passive while cursing himself at the same time. His clothes smelled of smoke, too. He had just screwed up.

Carter sat back and smiled before shaking his head.

"You disappoint me, Agent Randall. I was told you were better than this. Now, how about you find us another room, one without a camera on the other side of the mirror? Somewhere we can speak alone, without all the watching eyes and recording equipment, and dispense with the bullshit."

# 27

*"Corruption is never compulsory."*

—Sheldon Vanauken

Six. There were six different bags of fluid hanging on the pole. Little blue pumps with numbers flashing on them. Numbers he didn't understand, but they seemed to please the nurses, so he didn't ask. Oxygen flowed to the

Generals nose through yet another tube. The bubbling humidifier provided a background noise he was familiar with. The line of his EKG traced a path across the small screen. Green for heart. Blue for respirations. White for oxygen. Red for $CO_2$. They rose and fell within their accepted zones.

"We'll know something within the hour. If he wakes, have the nurse page me."

"All right," Charlie answered, without taking his eyes off the man on the bed. The General's chest rose and fell, his breath fogging the mask with each repetition. His finger would twitch every so often, and he would stir briefly. It was enough for the nurse to apply some tape to keep the $O_2$ sensor in place.

The doctor finished scribbling in the chart and flipped it shut. He studied Charlie for a moment, before exchanging a look with the nurse behind the desk.

"Charlie? When was the last time you ate anything?"

"Um, this morning."

"It'll be a while before he wakes. You should get something while you can. Is there anyone you should be calling?"

Charlie jerked at that. William, he needed to call William. He stood and pulled out his cell.

"Not in here, out in the waiting room," the nurse ordered. Her tone brooked no argument. The doctor shrugged and offered a look of surrender. The nurses run the floor, it said, don't piss them off.

Charlie took one last look at the General before walking out. He punched the button to open the door and checked that his visitor pass was still stuck to his shirt before walking out and down the short hall to the waiting room. There was a family sitting there, with two kids watching TV while the parents spoke softly under its volume. Charlie gave them a sympathetic look before traveling on. He needed privacy.

Two doors later, he found it. A small chapel, currently unoccupied. He walked to the front and turned so he could see the door before punching the call button.

"Ockham."

"It's Charlie."

"Charlie! What the hell? Where have—"

"Been a little busy, sorry."

"Okay, okay. How's the General?"

"We won't know for an hour or so. It was a stroke, just like we thought. They gave him something to break up the clot in his brain. If it works, they think he'll be fine."

William exhaled loudly into the phone. "Okay, I guess that's as good news as I could ask for."

"There's more. There are still clots in his leg. If the drug breaks them up, they could float around and cause other problems. Maybe a heart attack or a pulmonary ... something."

"Embolism?"

"Yeah. Sorry, I'm a bit foggy. It was a lot to absorb in a short time."

"It's okay. It's a clot in the lungs, it prevents the exchange of oxygen. Is the doctor worried?"

"Yes, but he couldn't say how bad the risk was. William, I ..."

"What is it, Charlie?"

"They needed me to okay the treatment. What ... what if I made the wrong decision? What if I've killed him?"

"Charlie, you made the best decision you could, based on the information you had. That's all any of us can do. In my opinion, you made the right one. Don't beat yourself up over it."

"But ..."

"What would the General say?"

Charlie sighed. "He'd say worrying about decisions once made is a waste of time."

"And he'd be right. So what happens now? What can I do?"

"Umm, nothing. We're just waiting. Anything on the ... other thing?"

"No."

Charlie read through the short answer: they would discuss nothing about the Shepherds over this line.

"Wait. There's one thing. Can you review the security footage and see if you can pin down the exact time this happened? The doctor keeps asking. Something about down time before administration of whatever he gave him."

"I'm waiting for more information on some other things, so I'll do that right now."

"Okay, thanks, William."

"I'd be there if I could, Charlie."

"I know you would."

"Call me if anything changes."

"Will do."

Charlie flipped the phone off and stuck it in his pocket before leaving the chapel. The waiting room now held more family members. A different doctor was there talking to them. It looked like bad news. The husband held his wife, while the kids looked puzzled that mommy was crying. Charlie looked away. He felt guilty, as if he were invading their privacy. Luckily, a nurse exited the ICU door just as he was arriving, saving him from having to wait for someone in their presence. He slipped down the hall past the glassed-in walls, trying not to look inside. Some family members sat in chairs, some of them shocked by his face, others looking but not seeing him at all. He wiped a tear from his eye as he entered the General's room. The man was just as Charlie had left him. He rearranged the sheet covering him before sinking into a large chair.

A wail sounded from the waiting area. The mother. It cut like a knife through his head, and he covered his ears in a vain attempt to block it out.

---

WILLIAM SEVERED the connection with a heavy sigh. He was both relieved and concerned at the same time. The General lived and would hopefully recover. Charlie would fight that battle. William's job was to manage the fight they were having here.

With a few taps on the keyboard, he had the mansions security software up on his screen. He selected the archives and quickly found the file for that morning, fast-forwarding it until he saw the General wheel himself into the room. He made a note of the time displayed in the upper left corner before watching it at normal speed.

The man went straight to his desk and was soon into a file. He read quietly for a full minute before rubbing his head. He then pulled his reading glasses off and massaged his temples before reaching into a drawer and pulling out a bottle of aspirin. He shook out two pills into his hand, unlocked his chair, and went to the bathroom. The door was shut, then it was popped back open a few inches. William could make out his hand reaching for the medicine cabinet. It was opened and shut without him seeing anything retracted. There was suddenly nothing to see.

"Dumbass," he labeled himself. He fed a command and a password into the computer, and the audio of the event clicked on. He turned it up and listened. Running water. Some movement. Silence. A low moan, then a crash. The door slammed shut. He listened hard, but he heard nothing more. He jotted down the time again and fast-forwarded the footage, hitting play again when Charlie appeared not even ten minutes later.

He had seen this already, so he pulled up another screen and composed a secure text message to Charlie with the times he needed. The audio continued to play, and William shut it out as best he could.

"Stop Angler! Get to Ramadi!" he heard the General yell.

It stopped William in his tracks.

He watched and listened intently as the medics worked to save the man while Charlie stared down at him open-mouthed from the side of the picture. The words coming from the General had obviously triggered him, too.

"Haney! Stop Haney! He's killing my boys!"

"He's back in Anbar," William whispered.

Angler? There was that codename again. Haney. Vice President Haney? It was who they had been traveling to meet that night.

Angler. Haney. Were they one and the same?

It came to William in a flood, and he struggled to comprehend it all. The file he had found. Orders from Angler. At the same time they had all been in Anbar province. The second battle of Fallujah. The raid on the city for Zarqawi and his bomber. Dayton. Charlie. The meeting ordered by the VP. The convoy. The IED.

He spun and pulled up the files he'd been slowly decoding. He knew the date by heart. He would never forget it. Like the General, Charlie, and Dayton, he carried a constant reminder of it with him everywhere he went. The leg now ached as if to remind him, and he ignored it, searching frantically for the date he wanted.

There. Two transmissions. He moved the files to the front of the list and hit the decode button. The computer chewed on them quickly. His mouth went dry as he read, and his fingers collapsed on the keyboard.

Haney was Angler.

Angler was Haney.

He had tried to kill them.

---

HANEY BALLED a fist and struggled not to pound the desk with it while he watched the man speaking on the screen. The transcript of the speech had arrived just minutes ago, and he'd not had time to read it before the man appeared. He was speaking from behind the Resolute desk in the Oval Office, which sent a message right there as this was often interpreted as something put together quickly. Haney knew it was just to keep the press out of the small room. Off camera there were over a dozen people present, most of them senior staff. The rest were camera, light, and sound people. They were controlling the message—the same thing he would have done.

ISIS had released the pictures of the downed pilot just hours earlier. They had then been plastered on every news outlet around the globe. The fact that he was the son of a junior senator had complicated things. Chief among them was the copy of the inquiry on his desk from Senator Lamar, demanding to know how the missiles had gotten into the hands of ISIS. He needed to do something—and fast.

He thumbed the mute button and tossed the remote aside before pacing the room. On the leather couch was his number two, calmly reading the transcript.

"How can we counter this?"

The man frowned and flipped the page before answering.

"We should have used the Verbas."

"Russian missiles? Don't give me that! It would open the door for a Russian response, and I don't want them involved. Putin already caved to us halting him in the Ukraine. He's not going to let us use him as a scapegoat for this! There has to be a way to fix this!"

"MANPADS were a mistake. I don't care which country they're from."

Haney spun at the rebuke—nobody talked to him that way. Before he could open his mouth,

Harper kicked the coffee table over and stood, pointing a finger at the shorter man.

"No. Don't even go there! These things are second only to nukes, and you know it. Giving them to these nutcases was too much, and now the heat is coming down on us. You've been sitting at that desk too long! You can't just throw these things out there and hope they shoot at what you want them to. You just denied the U.S. air superiority over that whole battlefield! And now I'm supposed to just clean it up? How do you propose I do that *Mr. Vice President*? Should I hop over there and ask them nicely if we can have them back? Something tells me I'd be the next YouTube star if I tried that!"

Haney bit off his words and stared Harper down. The man threw the speech against the wall and walked to the wet bar through the falling paper, ignoring his boss in favor of a shot of amber liquid. He slugged it down, then poured another. It was his first time letting his boss have it like that, but the man needed it. What was he going to do? Find someone else to fix this for him?

While he drank, Haney stared at his subordinate's back. Was he becoming a problem? If so, he'd have to wait to address it. Right now he needed him, and the man knew it.

"Options?"

Harper downed another shot and slammed the glass on the bar before turning around. He took a deep breath and rubbed his nose with a thumb and finger.

"There's only one missile left. We'll never get it back, so just forget about it. We'll have to stop the senator from finding anything that leads to us."

"How?"

"We only have to break a link in the chain."

"Okay. How do you—"

Harper cut him off. "You don't need to know." He snagged his coat off the couch and headed for the door. Haney watched him go and said nothing.

Two flights down, Harper stopped on the landing and reached in his pocket. He thumbed the recorder off before descending the rest of the way. Once outside, he pulled out his phone.

"Yes, sir?"

"Call the plane. I need it now."

"Destination?"

"Spokane."

---

WHILE HIS BOTS watched and waited for information about Number Six, William paced the area behind his desk. He ignored the pain in his leg and scribbled in large letters on the glass before stepping back and examining his work. While he had a whiteboard nearby, he had switched to the large pane of glass soon after discovering it to be the size he preferred. He now had its entire expanse covered in dates and times and file numbers. Lines connected them and pieced the occurrences and their origin together. A circle in the middle held the name of the former Vice President, and the lines left and returned from several directions. Other names occupied other circles, including his own. The lines crossed and recrossed into a tangled web of confusion. One circle remained unnamed, the owner of the file. Who was he? He clearly worked for Haney, or Angler— whatever he was being called, they were one and the same now. The fluorescing lines glowed under a black light, searing the information into his mind.

"Who are you?" he asked the mysterious man.

The glass offered no answer, so William spun away and returned to his desk. He needed information. If he couldn't find the identity of Haney's man, he'd skip over him and address the threat directly. But how to reach him? The man had Secret Service protection—not something easily penetrated, even for a soldier like Dayton.

William stopped himself. He clenched his fist over the mouse and forced himself to stop. He needed to think. What would the General say? Did he already know? What about Dayton? Would he agree? Was this revenge, or was Haney a legitimate target for the Shepherds?

The pain in his leg flared again, and he automatically reached for the bottle of pills. Shaking one out, he slipped and spilled them all over the desk and keyboard. They tumbled over the edge and scattered across the floor. He cursed and began sweeping them up before stopping.

These pills. They ran his life. They were a part of him now. No different than the General's chair. Charlie's face. Dayton's back. The pain was everlasting. With them until they died.

The decision made itself. He gathered the pills and placed them back in the container before setting them aside. The pain continued, but he now welcomed it. He brought up a search engine and typed in the Vice President's name. Every man had a weakness, and he recalled that Haney had a unique one.

CHARLIE PACED past the desk again, and the nurse looked up from her paperwork long enough to give him a smile of encouragement.

"He should be back soon, Charlie."

"Yeah, sorry."

"It's okay."

Charlie forced himself to go back to the now empty room and sit down. The nurses were busy, and he was distracting them. He gazed across the room at the daughter of another patient. The man's heart had stopped this morning, and she'd been a front seat witness as the ICU team fought to save her father. The battle had raged for several minutes before being won. The woman now held his hand and silently wept. She felt Charlie's eyes and turned to see him watching her. He offered a smile of encouragement, and she returned it. They were on the same team. They even had matching uniforms, right down to their blue booties.

The door hissed open on its pneumatic hinges, and the bed holding the General appeared. Charlie scrambled to his feet as the man was backed into his previous space. The various lines, tubes, and wires were reattached to their previous connections, and the General was propped up in a semi-reclined position. His nurse brushed his hair back, then swabbed his mouth with a special sponge. Charlie remembered them from his days in the hospital. Not allowed to drink for a few days, he had used them in great numbers. They had a lemon flavor, which he quickly got tired of. His head jerked up when the General responded to the sour taste and clamped down on the stick.

"Well, hello, sir. Are you awake?"

The General opened his eyes and looked at her for some time. She wiped his mouth and mussed his hair again.

"You're in the hospital. My name's Terra, and I'm taking care of you." He blinked and offered nothing. Terra motioned Charlie over to her side of the bed. He moved into the General's line of sight.

"Hello, sir."

The General's eyes focused on him and became sharper. He glanced around, taking in the machines and their flashing lights, the bed, the wall of glass, the departing transport team, before returning to Charlie's face.

He smiled.

"There you are. Can you tell me who this young man is?"

"Char ... Charlie."

"Excellent."

The General nodded and drifted off to sleep again.

"Sir?"

"Let's let him sleep, Charlie. Did you see that smile?"

"Yeah?"

"It was even on both sides. His face has lost its droop. The muscles are back in play."

"What does that mean?"

"I think the results of the new CT scan are going to be good. I imagine the doctor will be up to see you soon."

Charlie sank into the chair with a heavy sigh. It was the best news he'd had since they had arrived. His first thought was to call William.

"How long until the doctor comes?"

"I'll let him know that his patient was awake. I'm sure he'll want to see how he's doing."

"Thank you." Charlie decided to wait until after the doc came. He was sure William had other things to worry about. His thoughts went to Number Six and Dayton. Where were they holding him? Was he talking? What was Dayton doing about it?

# 28

*"The job of a leader isn't just to diagnose the disease but to treat it."*

—*Narendra Modi*

"Do we have confirmation?"

"No, Mr. President. We have more assets overhead. We can watch the area

24/7 now, but we have yet to see any further evidence that the pilots are there."

The President ignored the eyes on him and examined the photos again. Different angles of the same objects. There was no doubt they had been arranged deliberately. The only question was the reason.

"How do we know this isn't bait for a trap?"

"We don't," the man to his right said.

The President shot a look at the man before returning to the photos. He cycled through them again. The answer was blunt, one he had come to expect from his Joint Chief.

"The other Stingers?"

"Stinger, sir. Singular," his Chief of Staff corrected him. "We believe they possess only one now."

The President nodded and cycled through the photos again. The men at the table shared silent looks and waited.

"Who's got a cigarette?" the President asked.

A junior aide stepped forward and placed a pack in front of him. The President shook one out, and the man lit it before stepping back. He took a long drag before setting the photos down.

He pointed the cigarette at the colonel doing

the briefing. "You have a plan? What am I saying— of course you have a plan. Tell me the plan."

The Joint Chief nodded, and the man quickly changed the large display to include a map of Syria and the surrounding countries. There were icons in Iraq, Turkey, and the eastern Mediterranean.

"Operation Agile Retrieval. A team of SEALs will deploy from Incirlik airbase in Turkey and HALO into the drop zone here, just north of the target. They'll be supported by F-18s off the carrier Reagan and A-10s out of Bagram in Iraq. A pair of Ospreys will also deploy from Bagram to extract the team, with the hostages, once they have been retrieved. They'll then return to Bagram with the A-10s providing cover. While this operation is commencing, we will launch a diversionary strike here to the west. It will commence at sunset, with the intent of drawing the anti-air threat away from the target. We'll have a new moon in two days' time, plus favorable weather. The assets can be in place in time."

"And if it doesn't?"

"Sir, I ..."

"If it doesn't draw them away from the target?"

"Sir?"

"This is thin. You haven't got it. How do you

know this isn't a simple bait and switch? I need something more than a few crates in the sand before I risk the lives of that many men and that much hardware. I want to know where that Stinger is. I want to know for sure that the pilots are where we think. I want to know if we're walking into a trap of our own making! You haven't got it! Call me when you do!"

The President finished his rant and punctuated it by tossing the cigarette butt in a glass of water. The hiss silenced any thought of a reply from the men at the table. They rose when he did and watched him stalk from the room.

The White House Chief of Staff held up a hand before the Joint Chief could speak.

"I'll talk to him, but he's right. You'll have to get something concrete if you expect him to green-light this."

The Chief walked out to catch up with the President. The Admiral turned to his men.

"You heard the man. Let's get him some answers."

JAMES COOK FOUND the President sitting on the

steps with a Secret Service man hovering nearby. He waved him away and sat down beside him.

"You okay?"

"He wants me to send them, even with what little intel we have. I understand the whole 'leave no man behind' thing, but I can't just hand them more bargaining chips."

"They understand, and they'll work on it."

"You'll tell Lamar something?"

"I'll take care of it."

"Yeah ... okay. Have them put the assets in place, but nobody moves without my order."

"Yes, sir."

"But, James, so help me, if that boy's head leaves his body ... I'm ready to—"

He threw himself to his feet. The Secret Service men fell in behind as he navigated the stairs. Cook watched him go until he was out of sight before returning to the Situation room.

---

"OCKHAM."

"William, Dayton, we're on the ground. What do you know?"

"He has yet to appear on their computer system. I

took a facial profile of Agent Randall and Agent Whitcomb, and I'm using the department surveillance cameras to try to track their movements. I've seen them both inside police headquarters twice. I'm fairly certain that's where they are holding him."

"Okay. Any traffic about moving him?"

"Oddly, no. I think they may be staying off the net."

That made Dayton pause. "Were you detected?"

"No, I don't believe so. They may be, I don't know, just being paranoid. I did plant a bot in the motor pool computer. They have regularly scheduled transports to and from the county jail, as well as the area prisons."

"Federal?"

"Those seem to be random, but they use the same vehicles."

"All right. I need locations of the federal destinations and the routes they take to get there. I also need the make and the type of the vehicles they use. Pictures would be nice. How do they man it? Is it armored? Is it tracked by GPS? That kind of thing."

"I can have that within the hour."

"Good. We're going shopping. Anything else?"

William hesitated for the briefest of moments. "No, nothing else."

"All right. Inform the General for me. You're running the show here. We'll be pretty busy for the next few hours."

"I—I will."

Dayton terminated the call with a frown. William seemed ... off. What was going on?

He quickly forgot about it when Anna asked a question.

"Shopping? Where?"

He smiled. "Home Depot."

BUNKER LAY AS QUIETLY AS possible, feigning sleep, and listening to every sound. The doctor had left him in the care of the boy while he went scrounging for more food. The boy watched the pilot with wide eyes from across the tent. His body was wrapped in loose clothing, and dirt streaked his face. Bunker guessed his age at ten. The heat of the tent seemed to have no effect on him. He, however, was losing valuable fluids in the form of a never-ending sweat. He almost longed for the return of night when the temperature had plunged and the ground beneath him had sucked what little body heat he had away. The doctor had given up his own blanket to keep him warm. Bunker had thought the sun would never arrive.

Bunker offered the boy a smile and got one in return. The doctor reappeared. He held a handful of bandages, but no food.

"Food will come later, I've been told. We must wait." He flopped down on the dirt floor and stowed the bandages in a plastic bag.

"Hoffman?"

The doctor shook his head. "Nothing."

"Any planes?"

"Planes?"

"Did you hear any?"

"No."

Bunker was almost sure he had heard the distant buzzing of a propeller earlier, but it had always faded. Now he wasn't so sure. Maybe he had just imagined it.

"Will they have seen the crates?" the doctor asked.

"I don't know. It may not even matter."

"Not matter? I don't understand."

"They're just crates. It may not be enough."

The doctor searched his mind, trying to wrap his head around the problem. What was this pilot telling them? That the Americans would not come? If they did not come, how could they escape?

"They need proof of life. It's what they call it, anyway," the pilot said.

The doctor examined the man, then their surroundings. The tent flapped in the breeze, a triangle of sun knifed into what little shelter it offered.

"Then we shall give it to them." He rose and grabbed Bunker by his shoulders.

"What are you—"

"Do not cry out," the doctor warned.

Bunker clenched his teeth as the doctor picked him up and dragged him across the floor. He set him down, then tugged him a bit farther. The pain knifed through his leg and chest, but he bit it off before a cry could escape his mouth. After several deep breaths, he opened his eyes only to be blinded by the sun. He waited and panted until the pain subsided, before looking again.

The sky. Blue and free of clouds. How he longed to be in it. Closing his eyes, he let the sun warm his face.

The doctor examined his patient and the sun's angle. If the drones could see the crates, they could surely see this man lying in the tent's door. He positioned the boy where he could warn him of approaching ISIS fighters and sat down at his patient's feet. If they came, he would have to pull the man back inside by his fractured leg.

He decided it was best not to warn him.

---

"OKAY, IS THIS PRIVATE ENOUGH?"

Jack had listened to his prisoner for ten minutes before agreeing to his demands. A cell block had been cleared, and Jack had stripped himself of all of his electronics before escorting the man down the stairs. Every camera on the wall had a towel over it, and the man seemed to be counting them as they moved. Jack had deposited him in the cell and allowed him to examine every inch, before he finally moved to the chair and sat down. Jack pulled up a folding metal chair and faced him on the other side.

Carter said nothing. He just turned his head and examined Greg.

Greg's face did nothing to hide his opinion. He didn't like this, but it was not his call.

"I'll be watching through the window."

Jack and Carter watched him and listened to the sound of his boots on the concrete as he made his way to the other end of the hall and pushed his way through the heavy steel door. It slammed shut behind him, and his face appeared in the small window.

"Satisfied?"

"Your shirt ... please."

Jack rose and unbuttoned his shirt, peeling it back, then turned around once before slipping it back on.

"You've seen some action," Carter said.

"They're just scars. If you want to see more, forget it."

A smile. "Very well."

"So what is this? Why all the cloak and dagger?"

"My employers are *everywhere*."

Jack said nothing while he thought the statement over. Carter let him chew on it for a moment.

"Employers? This is a job for you?"

"Yes and no."

"And you're telling me they have the system here compromised, that they can see what's going on here?"

"I don't think you're surprised by that information."

Jack's face revealed nothing, but in his mind his thoughts were racing. Where was he going with this? What was he trying to accomplish?

"What do you want?"

Carter smiled at the blunt question. "A man of action. I was told this about you. What do I want? To live, first. After that has been secured, we can talk further."

"You think you're a liability now? Is that it?"

"I know less than you hope I do, Mr. Randall, but it may be enough. It's certainly enough for them to be concerned."

"Enough to kill you?"

Carter shrugged. "That I cannot say for sure, but I will say this: until you get me somewhere I feel is safe, our conversation cannot continue."

Jack did his best to appear as if he were considering the request.

"And if I do this?"

"We can talk and hopefully come to some kind of arrangement."

"And if I don't?"

"Then I imagine I will be quite dead, and we will never talk again."

"They have that kind of reach?"

"Yes."

Yes. A one-word answer. Delivered in a way that dismissed any argument. The man in front of him was not voicing an opinion, he was stating a fact.

"I'll see what I can do."

Carter watched him leave, waiting for the man to reach the end of the hall before speaking.

"Agent Randall?"

Jack turned.

"Whatever you are going to do, I would do so quickly."

Jack said nothing. He just turned and walked through the opening door. Greg closed it behind him.

"Well, what did he say?"

"I'll fill you in later. For now, let's keep him where he is."

"All right. I'll have to talk with the guys here about—"

"No, no PD. Just our people."

Greg was caught short. "What are you saying?"

"Nothing yet, but keep the locals out of this, for now. We'll be moving soon. I have to make some calls."

"So, I'm stuck here?"

"Sorry, but yeah. For now." Jack looked up and over his shoulder at the camera as he said it. Greg read between the lines.

"Okay. I'm on it."

"I'll get you a partner. We'll have you both out of here soon."

PARKER READ the warning order twice before kicking the chair back and standing. His boots shed puffs of desert dust as he stomped his way to the door and out into the heat. The sun blinded him as the temperature hit him, a double tap from the desert he had come to hate.

He made his way to the hangar and past it to the barracks housing his team. They had permanently borrowed the barracks from the air force, and they were plush by SEAL standards. Complete with a stocked refrigerator and a pool table. One that now sported spots and stains from them using it to clean their weapons. The air force liaison had frowned, but wisely had said nothing.

Parker kicked open the door and entered to find his team in various stages of undress. Most of them were shirtless and sweating, despite the air conditioning. They were circuit training to pass the time—it was their name for cycling from the weight room next door to the pool table and back. Whatever it took to pass the time and stay mission ready. Parker didn't really care.

"On me, guys!"

The team dropped their cues and steel and

gathered around the table. Parker set the warning order down and waited until they were all present.

"Got a warning order. There's a downed pilot in Indian country they want us to be ready to retrieve."

"How deep?"

"Right in the middle. Now shut up for a damn minute and let me talk. Looks like a Navy puke got himself shot down near Al Sukhnah. They have some drone pics which suggest he's there, and we're waiting on confirmation. If it's a go, we'll HALO in and extract him, then ride out of there on the 22s to Bagram. That's the short version."

"They plan the whole thing for us, or do we have a say in this?"

"It's pretty broad at this point, but so far, the outline looks good. Let's take this and see what we can do to improve it. I want us ready to go in six hours. Get everything checked and loaded. Repack the chutes. I'll have more for you when it happens. This is it."

Parker left, leaving the papers behind on the table. His second followed him to the door.

"What do you think? Will this one actually happen?"

Parker frowned, but he didn't blame his skepticism. They'd been alerted too many times to count only to be told to stand down. Despite being told to keep the information quiet, he wasn't going to do so. He would have to be subtle about it.

"Maybe Google the pilot. Find out everything you can on him," he answered before pushing his way back out and into the heat.

The SEAL's eyebrows rose. A few minutes later, he had the information on his screen—including who the pilot's father was. It shouldn't have mattered, but it did, and he knew that the chances of them going had just increased a great deal. He hurried back to the team to fill them in.

WILLIAM MUTTERED a curse when the computer beeped at him. He tore his eyes away from the main screen to determine its origin, deeming it more important, but he quickly changed his mind. Working the keyboard, he was soon speed-reading his way through the information that scrolled up the screen.

"They're moving him." He reached for the phone.

"Dayton."

"It's William. They're moving him."

"Where?"

"All I have is a coded address. Stand by. I'll cross reference." The keyboard clicked, and Dayton waited while William accessed the data-bank of another government's agency.

"You can't hide from me," he whispered.

"What?"

"Nothing. It looks like Mr. Randall is at-tempting to hide from me by using a different agency. He's contacted a friend in the US Marshal's office. They're providing a van and one of their safe houses."

"Location?"

"Lancaster. Just north of you."

"Lancaster? There's nothing there, unless ..."

"Hold on. I thought of that, too. It looks like they'll have a plane fly into Edwards, the day after tomorrow."

"Day after tomorrow? Damn, Jack's not wasting time. Anything else?"

"I got this through a bot I left in the Marshals' office network, not the FBI. Nor did I get anything from the LAPD system."

"That's Number Six at work. He's following option one, it sounds like."

"So, what does this mean?" William asked.

"It means they'll be moving him in secret, hopefully with minimal escort, which is good for us. Unless we miss their movement. Do you have anything as far as route or vehicle?"

"Checking."

Dayton covered the phone and motioned to Anna, who was listening as best she could.

"A map."

She scrambled to find it, then spread it out on the desk. Dayton traced a finger to LA and, from there, north to Lancaster. There were only two options, and one was out of the way by more than a few miles.

"Looks like there's a van scheduled to depart from LA tomorrow."

"Size and shape?"

"Patience." The keyboard clicked, and Dayton stewed.

"Huh, looks like a brand-new Ford PTV. What is a PT—oh, a Prisoner Transport Vehicle. How original. I'm sending the specs and photos to your email. It has a locator, which I'm now tracking. If it moves, I'll be able to watch it in real time. I'm impressed by the design. It's our tax dollars at work."

"I'm sure Number Six will be impressed as well. Anything on departure times or escort vehicles?"

"Nothing yet, but I will watch for them."

"Okay. Have you kept the General informed? Is he okay with a rescue mission?"

"He's unavailable at the moment, but he has voiced no opposition," William dodged.

"Sorry, that was a dumb question. I'll keep you advised."

"As will I."

"We've got work to do. I'll call you back in a few hours."

"Very well."

Dayton severed the connection, and William let out a long sigh. He'd almost told him. Why hadn't he? He didn't want to distract him from what he was doing, he told himself. But that was only partially true. Was he afraid of Dayton stopping him? Of the General stopping him? The man had tried to kill them! But this was revenge, not something they did. Or was it justice?

It was justice, he told himself, not only for them, but for countless others. He cast his doubts aside and attacked the keyboard with renewed vigor. On one screen, the rescue of one of their own, on the other, the end of their greatest enemy.

CHARLIE SQUINTED and held the phone away until the whine of the scrambler ceased. A secure call from William. His wait wasn't long.

"Charlie?"

"I'm here."

"Any news?

"They brought him back from CT, and he was awake for a few seconds. He recognized me, tried to speak, then faded back out. The doctor has just left. He showed me the scans, and there's blood flow back to the brain. He looks better."

"Excellent."

"How's things on your end?"

"No change, yet. They may be moving our friend soon. Number One is taking steps. I'm worried about something else though."

"What's that?"

"We have to be ready for any contingency, and the General being in the hospital is something we didn't plan for. I need you to do something, Charlie, and I can't help you."

"I'm not sure I see where you're going?"

"You may have to move him."

Charlie immediately thought of the six bags of fluid and the various machines hovering over the General in his glass room. The nurse who was never more than six steps away. The cameras and coded access doors. The six stories between them and the street below.

"I'm not sure I can. He's in no condition to travel, William."

"Find a way and have it ready."

"That bad?"

"We may be running from more than the government soon."

"I don't ..."

"Charlie. Just do it. Be ready to get him out of there, somewhere safe, as soon as you can. Hide your tracks like we taught you, and don't call me until you are there. Okay?"

"I ... okay."

The line went dead.

HARPER GRIMACED as he stepped out of the plane and onto the wet tarmac. The rain was cold and showed no sign of letting up. He pulled up the collar of his coat and hoisted the bag over his shoulder before sprinting to the small FBO. He gave a quick wave to the girl behind the counter before moving toward the bathrooms. She dismissed him as the pilots appeared and was quickly into the paperwork necessary for the plane's refueling. She didn't notice Harper sneak out the door.

The cab dropped him on the corner, and he paid cash before moving off to the east. As soon as the cab was gone, he reversed himself and walked the three blocks to the fenced-in lot. The truck was right where they had told him it would be, and he paused long enough to scan the area before moving to its rear. The keys were in the locker under some chains. The engine started without complaint, and he examined the gauges before flipping the lights on. The tank was full. The needles all in the green. He found the wipers and flicked them to high before moving off. He played with the gears and brakes before being satisfied. It was a tow truck, one like any other found throughout the nation. What it lacked in acceleration and handling, it made up for with power. The big V8 handled the added weight of the rigging and the heavy front bumper with ease, and he climbed his first hill without slowing or slipping on the wet pavement.

Checking the time, he found himself thirty minutes ahead of schedule. He sped up to further cushion that number.

THE TWO MEN ran awkwardly through the rain, their legs still stiff from hours in the cockpit. It had been a silent flight, neither of them wishing to talk in front of the new navigator who had joined them for the final leg back to Fairchild Air Force Base. Tomorrow, they would have to meet with their CO and rehash the flight. They had spent the majority of the days after, and the trip home, getting their story together, and they were confident they would pass the examination if they stuck to it. The load master was in the dark and would stay that way. There was no reason to bring him into the loop.

They made it to the car in record time, but it did nothing to lessen the amount of water that soaked them. Ahead of them lay a forty-minute drive, longer with this rain, which seemed to be intensifying. The senior man slid into the driver's seat without hesitation or protest. A combination of habit and the fact that the car was his. Their green pilot bags landed on the back seat, and they raked the water from their hair. The windshield immediately fogged, and he started the car while the co-pilot adjusted the vents.

"Nice welcome home, eh?"

"Yeah, wouldn't be the same without it raining. Damn cold, though."

"Just get me home, Wes, that's all I ask."

The pilot eyeballed his passenger. "You sure you're okay with all of this?"

"Yeah, I'm just tired. Don't worry, I'm still with you. Kind of late now, anyway."

"She'll be happy when you tell her you can afford the daycare now."

"True."

The windows were clear, so Wes dismissed the conversation and slipped the car in gear. It was already dark, and the mountains were fading into the rain. Since rush hour was over, the streets were fairly clear, and he used the high beams as much as possible as they climbed into the mountains. The drive was another result of their low pay. Homes close to the base were out of their price range, and their wives had wanted some distance between them and the air force. He didn't really mind it. The drive was usually a pleasurable one, and it gave him time to think without the kids' interruptions. It did cut into his sleep time, though. Maybe when the payment for this last mission came in, they could consider something closer. He'd work on it when the time was right.

"Hungry?"

"Yeah."

He pulled the white Honda across the road and into a McDonald's long enough for them to fill up on junk food. By the time they got home, it would be past dinner time, and both of them had other plans, anyway. It had been a long two weeks. They waited in the drive-through and listened to the rain drum on the metal roof.

A BLOCK DOWN THE ROAD, Harper sat in the tow truck, sipping a coffee he had bought from the same drive-through window thirty minutes earlier. He could clearly see the bumper sticker on the back of the Honda, and the small dent in the rear quarter panel. It was them. He kept the window cracked enough to prevent it from fogging and watched them pull out through the splatter of rain. Once they disappeared around the bend, he flipped on the lights and wipers and followed.

THE PILOT NOTICED the headlights behind him but ignored them in favor of the twisty road ahead. The asphalt was slick, and the streetlights were nonexistent this far out of town. To his right was a guardrail, but it would intermittently disappear the higher they climbed. His co-pilot thumbed the defoggers a notch higher as they gained altitude. The headlights behind him flared in his mirror, and he squinted against them. On the next straight section, he adjusted the mirrors.

His co-pilot glanced behind them. "Looks like a truck. A pickup maybe."

"He's got his high beams on. He's dazzling me."

"Maybe. He looks like he might be lifted, or maybe he's just scared of the rain."

"Or maybe he's just an asshole."

"That, too. At least he's hanging back."

"Nowhere to pass for a few miles, especially not in this weather."

The rain increased and the darkness was complete now, clouds covering what little moon was present. The tires squealed twice on the wet pavement as they rounded curves, and the pilot slowed to keep them on the road. The truck was closer now, and the headlights were bouncing off the cliff face to their left, its wet surface shining the light into their faces.

"Asshole," the pilot muttered.

"Prob'ly some kid. Just let him by at the overlook."

"If I do, he's getting my high beams the rest of the way."

"Whatever."

The pilot glanced in the rearview as they rounded a curve. A pickup? Maybe a tow truck? He thought he saw something sticking up from behind it. Maybe that was why he was in a hurry? Was he on his way to a call?

"It's a tow truck, I think. I'm going to let him by."

The overlook was a few curves ahead and the truck was on his ass the whole way, the headlights sweeping left to right and back on every turn, lighting up the interior and killing his night vision. He squinted against the glare and focused on the white line.

The overlook appeared out of the dark in front of them, and he eased the car to the right, off the road and onto the gravel.

"Here you go, asshole, the road's all—"

The truck slammed into the rear of the car. The pilot struggled with the wheel as they leaped forward.

"What the hell!?"

The roar of the truck's engine sounded again, and the car was once again struck. The co-pilot spun in his seat, but he was blinded by the head-lights only a few feet away.

"What the hell is this asshole doing!"

Any answer the pilot may have had was cut off

when the car was hit again, and this time the truck stayed in contact. The two men felt the car accelerate, and the pilot instinctively hit the brakes only to have them lock up. The car's rear end was pushed down into the loose gravel, and now it made ruts as it was pushed forward. The pilot pumped the brakes and attempted to steer but couldn't find any bite in the loose stone.

Then they stopped. Both men peered out the windshield and saw nothing but a pitch-black hole. Their heavy breathing filled the space.

"Holy ..."

The roar of the truck sounded again, and the car was struck once more. The pilot struggled with the door and managed to open it, only to be held in by his seatbelt as the car pitched over the edge. The front end caught on something unseen, and the car lurched to the right and began to roll.

A kaleidoscope of blurred shapes and the sound of twisting metal filled their eyes and ears as they tumbled down the mountain. It seemed to go on for hours, until suddenly stopping with a terrific crash.

Wes stirred and fought the darkness. He found his hand still on the wheel and tried to pull himself up. He lay on his side with his head against something hard. The one remaining headlight provided just enough for him to make out what it was.

A tree. There was a tree where the windshield should be. He turned his head to find his co-pilot, but Wes could only see his legs. His upper body was slumped over and out of sight. The driver peeled his hand from the wheel and wiped the blood from his eyes. Glass came away with it, and the blood flowed faster.

"What the hell? John? You okay?"

No answer. Noise outside. He closed his eyes and summoned what strength he had. The seatbelt, first take off the seatbelt. He fumbled for the latch.

A smell hit his nose. Gas? He struggled with the latch with both hands. His face suddenly burned, and he was soaked.

Gas! The stuff was soaking him! He had to get out. More noise outside. He gave up on the latch and tried to pull the belt over his head. He saw a shape, some movement in the dark.

The mirror. It had survived intact. He peered at it and saw a man outside the car. He was carrying something.

"Hey! I need help! I can't get the seatbelt off." His only answer was the pounding rain.

More gas leaked down and burned his face

where he was wounded. He wiped it away with a sleeve before peering at the mirror again. The man was there with a can of some kind.

Then it hit him.

"What are you doing!?"

The man reached into his pocket. The pilot caught sight of a familiar face in the pale light of the match before it was tossed inside the car.

---

"Charlie?"

Charlie's head came up and he shook off sleep. The glass door was closed. The light over the desk was the only source in the room outside of the glaring screens over his head. The nurse glanced at one in front of her before returning to her paperwork.

"Charlie."

He turned to find the General looking at him.

"Sir?"

"Where the hell ... am I?"

"Are you alright, sir? Should I get the nurse?"

"No, no. What happened?"

"You had a stroke. We flew you here, and the doctors treated you. They say you'll be fine."

"Fine? How the hell ... What did they do?"

"They gave you a drug that broke up the clot."

The General pondered the information and looked around the room and up at the monitors. Some motion caught his eye, and Charlie turned to see the nurse approaching. She slid back the door and walked to the bed.

"Are we awake?"

"I hope so," the General replied. "Mouth is dry."

The nurse helped him take a small sip of water before withdrawing the straw. She carefully watched him swallow. When the General did so without choking, Charlie let out a held breath.

"And with our sense of humor intact, that's good. My name's Terra. Do you know where you are, sir?"

"A hospital?"

"Okay. How about telling me who the President is?"

"Kitarović."

"I'm sorry?"

"She's the president of Croatia. Smart as a whip and much better looking than ours."

"Okay, I guess you don't need any of those questions. Can you smile for me? A big grin please." The General obliged her, making her laugh before she grabbed his hands. "Squeeze my fingers."

Charlie watched while she performed her test of his nervous system. To his untrained eye, his boss was passing it.

"How do you feel?"

"Bit of a headache. Tired."

"All expected. Do you remember what happened?"

"Well ... I was at my desk. Then the bathroom, then ... nothing."

"Excellent." She flashed a smile at Charlie, clearly pleased with her patient's rapid recovery. "I'll let the doctor know you're awake. Do you need anything?"

"Some more water?"

"I can't until they do a swallow study, but I can give you some ice chips to chew on until then?"

"That—that's fine."

"I'll be right outside." She slid the door shut, but she left an inch open so she could hear him if he needed her. They both watched as she made a quick phone call before settling in behind the computer.

The General turned to Charlie. "Is it safe?" he whispered.

"Yes."

"What's happening?"

Charlie pulled his chair closer and whispered. The General's eyes widened, and his heart rate rose a touch at the news.

---

"You sure this is how you want to do this?" Greg asked for the second time.

"I don't have a choice but to believe him."

"What did Deacon say when you told him?"

Jack checked up and down the hallway before looking Greg in the eye.

"I didn't."

"Jack?"

"I know, but if the guy says they are inside, then any communication is a potential problem. He said they were everywhere. I don't know if by everywhere he means LAPD, FBI, or the whole damn government, but until I do, I'm keeping this small and off the radar."

Greg paced in the small area. "Jack, you sound ... sorry, but this is paranoid. You think they have someone in all the computers and commo systems. It's just a bit much."

"You should come to the NSA with me some

time and see what Eric and I see. You wouldn't think so then."

Greg continued pacing. He knew Jack would disappear for a day or two and travel to Fort Mead. Greg never asked what Jack was doing. Maybe it was time for Greg to start, but not now. Right now, he'd have to trust the guy he worked with.

"All right. How do you want to do this?"

"I already arranged for some transport. Not FBI. I called in a favor. We move tomorrow afternoon. Just you and our guest followed by me and Sydney. We go to Lancaster, then to a plane which will arrive at Edwards the next morning. I'll need you to stay up with our mystery guy until we leave. I don't want him to have any contact with LAPD or anyone else. Okay?"

Greg sighed. He was in for a long night, but there was no other way around it.

"All right. Do I have to taste his food too?"

"I'll send you some pizza."

"Gee ... thanks."

———

DAYTON SLOWED the van after the car passed them and examined the terrain on both sides of the road. It was a canyon, a winding pass cut through the mountains to facilitate the two-lane road they were on.

He spoke into the radio. "Right here, this is it. Pull off behind me."

"All right," Anna answered from the truck behind him.

Dayton slowed to a stop after the curve and pulled off enough to enter and leave the cab safely. Traffic was light, and he hoped it would stay this way. He rubbed the stubble on his face as he waited for her. The map came out of his pocket and was spread on the hood before she could get out.

"Here." He circled a spot on the nearby ridge-line. "This is you." He circled another spot on a dirt road that intersected the highway at a right angle. "This is me."

"Okay, that's a long way from you. What if you need me?"

"I shouldn't. Even if I do, you're better off keeping them away from me."

Anna measured the distances on the map and compared them to the terrain around them. She didn't like it.

"We need at least two more people."

"Too late for that. Two will become three as soon as we get him out. We'll make up for the lack of personnel with toys. What's your phone say?"

Anna reached in her pocket and pulled out her cell and two others. They were all on different networks, and she examined each one before answering.

"It's a dead zone, I got nothing."

"Me neither, but we'll make sure just the same."

Dayton drew a few lines on the map before looking up at the ridgeline again.

"Grab your gear. It's time to get set up."

Twenty minutes later, the two vehicles were hidden on the side road, and they were scaling a narrow path. Anna struggled up the loose rock trail with almost a hundred pounds on her back. Dayton had that and at least forty more.

The only good thought she could come up with was that at least she wouldn't have to carry this load back down.

---

HARPER SAT in the cheap leather chair and watched the planes taxi by outside. He'd driven through heavy rain for several hours before ditching the tow truck in the industrial section of

Missoula. He'd then walked until he had found a Denny's that was open all night and settled into a corner booth. The waitress had attempted small talk twice before giving up. Still, she had kept his cup hot and full, while he had passed an hour in the window seat reading a paper and watching the sun come up. After seeing the traffic pick up outside, he left enough on the table to cover his tab, plus a healthy tip, before walking outside and heading west. A block later he hailed a cab, and ten minutes later, he was at the small terminal, waiting for his flight to be called.

Eventually, the old man and his trophy wife sitting across from him left to board their plane, and he was as alone as he could get. Checking his watch, he did a quick time zone calculation before pulling out his phone.

"Yes?"

"It's done."

"You're sure?"

"Check the local news out of Spokane. Two pilots and their car went off the road last night. No survivors."

"All right, then. It should make this damn meeting easier."

"Meeting?"

"The brothers wish to know what our exposure

is. Exposure—it's how they worded the question. I hate when amateurs try to use our language. I'm meeting with them this afternoon to calm them down. Right after I see the damn doctor."

Harper dismissed the issue, instead wondering about the man's tone. He seemed to be adopting a ... friendlier approach. It was something to factor in when dealing with him, but for now he would pretend he hadn't noticed.

"I'm on a plane within the hour. Six or seven hours until I return. Anything I need to know?"

"No, just come back. I have an idea on how we can improve our situation."

"How's that?"

"Not now, no time. When you get back."

Harper severed the connection and uploaded the call to the secure file before slipping the phone back in his pocket.

Something had changed. He didn't know what, but something was happening. His gut was telling him to not get on the plane, but another part of him was intrigued. He had cancelled the plane which had brought him here, just for that reason, and booked a commercial return flight under one of his secure identities. His boss didn't know where he was—only that he was coming back to DC.

It would give him several hours to think.

---

LESS THAN A HUNDRED MILES AWAY, William tapped the desk impatiently as the file was decoded. A pleasant beep announced its readiness, and William opened it and read it twice.

Spokane? The man was close! Could he possibly find him? Did he have time? Haney was seeing his doctor? Which doctor? He didn't know which way to go.

"Stay on target," he told himself.

He pulled up a list of the former VP's doctors and checked their schedules. He got lucky on the second try.

A heart surgeon, just outside DC. Haney would be there in less than six hours. William had to hurry.

His stomach growled in protest, but he ignored it. He may only get one chance like this. He had to be ready. He split his screens: on one, he brought up the security camera footage from the doctor's office; on the other, he brought up a textbook. He quickly scrolled to the sections he had highlighted earlier and reviewed them.

It would happen fast. He had to be faster.

"Just us? Are you sure?" Sydney asked.

"Yeah. Four is enough. I don't want any more in the loop until I figure this out," Jack assured her.

At Sydney's and Laurie's urging, Jack had given in and included Laurie. Now it would be her and Greg in the van with the prisoner, and Jack and Sydney following in a Bureau car. Greg had added body armor, a pair of additional shotguns, and his own rifle to the package. He'd also taken the van on a long test drive until he had been satisfied that he knew its strengths and weaknesses.

"It's like I've got a ton of bricks in the back. Why not just get me a Bradley?"

"Too much paperwork," had been Jack's reply.

He now eyeballed the interior of the vehicle. It was divided into three separate compartments and they all looked equally uncomfortable. The two that were accessible from the back were built to transport two and six respectively. Jack determined that their prisoner was not going to fit in the smaller compartment. They would have to put him in the large one on the right side where he would have his choice of seats on the long metal bench. The inside was stark white, broken up only by the strap of black webbing that served as a handhold. Seatbelts were nonexistent and the bench had no padding to speak of. Prisoner comfort and safety were obviously the last thing on the designers' minds. If the ride was rough, they would have to hold on with their cuffed hands as best they could. At least there was ample headroom, and the air-conditioning seemed to be adequate. The inner doors were steel with thick glass windows covered in expanded steel mesh, each of them held shut by a simple one-way lock. The outer doors were stock from the factory. It was all very plain and very ... washable, he realized. Something the designers had also kept in mind.

"Those seat dividers will be the first thing to go," Greg commented over his shoulder.

"Why?"

"Because American prisoners come in many shapes and sizes, not to mention each one is held down by a few bolts, something we try not to give prisoners access to."

Jack eyeballed the dividers. The man would be back here, cuffed and shackled, for a few hours. Would the bolts be a problem?

"Leave them in or take them out?"

"In, no time now, and one of us can check on him with the mirror while we're moving."

"Okay, let's go get our boy."

LAURIE ROSE from her chair and rubbed her ass. She'd been parked on its metal surface for a few hours. Her .44 went from her lap back into its holster and she stretched.

"Are we leaving?"

"Right now," Jack answered before turning to peer into the cell across from her. He found his prisoner sitting calmly on his bunk, watching their exchange without reaction.

"Time to move."

"To where?"

"Someplace safe, like you asked."

Carter nodded at the half answer and rose to his feet, shuffling across the cell to the door. Jack examined the civilian clothes he still wore and frowned. They had been unable to fix that, and Jack had chosen not to push the issue.

Laurie said, "They quit looking for a uniform that would fit. I think we've overstayed our welcome."

"We have," Jack admitted.

Greg stepped forward and raised the items in his hands. Carter eyeballed them but said nothing before stepping up close to the bars. Greg secured the chains to each ankle and then rose to duplicate the task on the man's wrists before joining them together.

"Am I going to have a problem?" Jack asked him.

"Not from me," Carter replied.

"Then let's go."

The door opened with a metallic clang. Carter ducked his head to get through and allowed himself to be led out.

WILLIAM'S HEART leaped and he struggled to calm himself when he saw the man enter the building. The Secret Service men parked the Suburban right outside the door and then stood in front of it once the man was inside. The cameras were high quality and numerous, all courtesy of the taxpayers. It seemed a bit extreme for a doctor's office, but right now William simply did not care. He already had the software loaded and ready to launch, he just needed the final connection.

He switched from screen to screen as Haney stalked his way down the hall, shedding more security men as he went. The doctor appeared and they shook hands. Haney even offered a rare smile, the same one the public loathed. The doctor returned it and then clapped him on the shoulder before motioning him inside. He and Haney seemed to share a joke, and a moment of shared laughter and William was a bit surprised at his friendliness. But then again, the man had saved his life. First with the installation of a pump to keep his failing heart alive and then again with a transplant. The latter had made a pacemaker necessary, something that required frequent checks.

William switched cameras and saw Haney doffing his suit jacket and shirt. His pasty white skin glowed in the fluorescent lighting, and he kept up a light banter with the doctor as the man pasted leads to his chest and then a set of colored wires. Finally, he rolled the pacemaker computer over and reached for the communication cable. He fixed the donut shaped device directly over the bulge of skin on the man's upper left chest. Haney reclined back and laced his fingers over his stomach.

William wished he could hear what they were saying.

THE DOCTOR POWERED up the machine and waited

for it to boot. He eyeballed his patient while they waited.

"You weigh the same as your last visit," he said accusingly.

Haney frowned. He was guilty and knew it. The man was calling him out as he had expected. It was the reason he had chosen him. The man wasn't afraid to speak to power. Out of all the doctors he had met, this man was the only one who had told him it was his way or go find somebody else. Something that Haney understood and respected. So far it had paid off. He'd survived the assist device and then the wait for a donor heart, and he had survived the transplant. Most new hearts lasted only five years. Haney was on year four, so the visits had become more frequent. The doctor and he were in it for years to come.

"I've been eating on the road a lot."

"By that you mean restaurants. What did I tell you about that? You're going to catch some bug and ruin my good numbers. Stop being a damn politician. You can't go out shaking hands and working the crowds anymore. You get so much as a cold it could be enough to make your body reject the heart."

"I hear you."

"You don't listen though. Next time you better

be down at least ten pounds or I'm referring you to that quack Oz. You can try one of his bullshit miracle pills."

"Didn't you work with him once?" Haney countered.

"At Columbia, before he sold out to the pseudoscience industry. Now hold still."

The doctor inputted the time and date into the program before checking the link between the man's device and the computer. A glance at the other screen showed him that the two readings matched. He started a diagnostic program.

"Any issues?"

"I get winded on stairs still. Have to slow down when I'm eating sometimes."

"Probably because you're talking while you're doing it. Politicians never shut up."

Haney had to laugh. The man was probably right.

"Maybe."

"All right. Well sit still and be quiet for a minute while I check out your friend."

Haney did as he was told. He relaxed and slowed his breathing and again laced his fingers to keep himself still. The doctor frowned at the screen and clicked the mouse again.

"C'mon. What the hell's wrong with this thing?" he muttered.

---

WILLIAM STARED at the screen and held a shaking finger over the mouse. He closed his eyes for a moment and was immediately back in Iraq. The noise, the shock, the heat, the screams—it flooded his brain. He shook the memories off and opened his eyes to see Haney grinning on the camera.

His finger clicked the mouse. Hard.

---

THE PRESIDENT WAS STRETCHED out on the couch with his shoes off, reading a brief in the Oval Office. It was the hour he had demanded and finally received for himself every afternoon. It had taken a few Presidential F-bombs to get the message across, but he was now confident that the door would stay shut barring a building fire or cataclysmic national emergency.

But there were many doors. One to his secretary, one to the hall, one to the outside and one to his private study that also led to his Chief of Staff's office. He now heard the signature double knock before the man stuck his head in.

"Sir?"

"Is the building on fire?"

"We have a situation. They're on their way up."

The President got to his feet and donned his jacket and shoes before leaning on the desk. Cook waited and fidgeted.

"You know what it is?"

"Syria."

"Lamar called me again this morning. I stalled him."

"It's all you can do."

"Let's hope not."

Before Cook could answer there was a knock, and his secretary stuck her head in.

"Send them in, Mrs. Lancaster."

The door opened wider to reveal the Joint Chief with a young lieutenant in tow. They carried files with red borders. The President's eyebrows rose a tad at the sight of them. The junior officer stood aside while the President shook his Chief's hand. They all sat down.

The admiral wasted no time. He opened the file and pulled out a set of photos.

"Sir, about an hour ago we obtained these photos from a platform orbiting the site. As you can see, the crates are still stacked as they were. Some rubble has been cleared and a few vehicles have moved, but nothing else. I'd like you to look at this tent in the upper right of the frame. It was there the morning following the bombing and hasn't moved. We've seen one man and a small boy utilize it, but nothing else. We were classifying it as temporary shelter. That changed after the last pass."

He handed another set of photos over. The President leafed through each before passing them to Cook.

"There's a man barely visible in the entrance of the tent. We didn't notice him at first, but as soon as we did, we took some more shots. This is the highest resolution photo we were able to obtain before he was moved back into the tent."

The President found himself looking at a grainy face shot. The features were a blur, but the blond hair, pale skin, and lack of a beard clearly identified him as a foreigner in those parts.

"Who is it?"

"We're ninety percent sure that this is the pilot, Andrew Bunker. The sun will be down soon, and we intend to fly lower and obtain some IR images when it does, but we believe he's wounded and being held in that tent."

"Wounded?"

"We reviewed the footage and the man with him appeared to be carrying what looked like medical supplies into the tent. The man inside hasn't changed position, he remains on his back at all times. We also feel that if he were healthy, they would have him in a more secure location."

"And the other man. Hoffman. Do we know where he is yet?"

"Location still unknown, sir."

The President sat back and riffled through the photos again. He tried to imagine what the man he was looking at was thinking.

"Chances of a successful retrieval?"

"The area is not strategically important to them. It's little more than a supply dump. Their fighters pass through on their way to the fighting in the east. Right now, there is only light activity. But there is some motion coming out of Homs and traveling east."

"What does that mean?"

Cook answered that one. "The trucks will be full on the way east, empty on the way back."

"And you think our man will become a passenger on one of those trucks?"

"Yes, sir."

The President shuffled through the photos again, this time stopping on the young man's face.

"You didn't answer my question."

"We estimate a seventy percent chance of getting him back, sir."

The photos were shuffled again before being carefully squared and stacked. The President handed them back.

"Work on that number."

---

HANEY FELT HIS HEART SLOW. It had been an odd and somewhat frightening sensation the first time he had done this, but now it was one he accepted. He had given control of his heart to the tiny machine implanted in his chest, and so far, it had not failed him. He waited for the next phase of the test and was a bit surprised when it failed to arrive.

"I'm—I'm a bit dizzy."

"Hold on," the doctor said as he rapidly clicked the keys. Haney's heart was suddenly racing, and he clutched at it as the fog lifted from his brain. The beating got faster, and he felt it thumping in his temples.

"What are you ..."

"Hold on, I'm making adjustments."

Haney looked up at the man's tone. While it was one of quiet confidence he detected a bit of doubt. The man was frowning at the small screen and clicking away with the mouse. Haney began to breathe deeper.

"A problem?"

The doctor ignored the question. More clicking.

Haney felt his heart almost stop. A wave of nausea swept over him as his blood pressure plummeted. Something was wrong. He pawed at his pocket.

"What the—Janet!"

Haney struggled for breath as the door was flung open. A young woman appeared.

"What's wrong?"

"It's not accepting my inputs!"

"Should I call the rep, I don't ..."

"Get the crash cart."

"What?"

"Get the damn crash cart!"

Haney grasped the device in his pocket and pressed the button. A second later the door slammed open directly into the woman's face and knocked her to the ground. Secret Service men quickly filled the room with guns drawn.

"What ...?"

"Get the hell out of the way! The man's crashing!"

The Service men hesitated. Janet jumped to her feet. Wiping the blood pouring from her nose, she ignored the guns and pushed the men out of the way before sprinting down the hall for the needed equipment.

"Susan, I need you!" she yelled.

Another nurse appeared from a doorway and watched open mouthed at her colleague racing down the hall.

"What's happening?"

"Patient crashing in room two!"

She stepped into the room. Sizing up the scene she waded in.

"Put that damn thing away and go help her!" she ordered the closest agent. The agent glanced at his partner before holstering his weapon and running down the hall.

She joined the doctor at the console.

"It won't respond, Sharon, no matter what I put in!"

Sharon examined the screen just in time to see the numbers take another rapid rise and fall. The external monitor matched it and sounded an alarm when it reached 140.

"What's it doing?"

"I'm not sure, I ..."

His voice trailed off as they watched the screen. Every piece of patient information was now slowly being replaced by a three-letter sequence.

TTS. TTS. TTS.

Haney forced back the blackness and raised his head. He saw the screen as the doctor repeatedly clicked the mouse in vain. The three letters burned into his memory before his vision again tunneled. His hand fell, dropping the device on the floor with a clatter.

The noise shook Sharon out of her shock. She turned to find their patient pale and losing consciousness. She grabbed the cable on his chest.

"No, wait!"

With a violent yank, she tore the cable away, severing the connection between man and machine. The monitor went to flat line, the alarm screaming for their attention.

"Call for an ambulance!" she screamed before throwing Haney flat on the table and climbing up to straddle him. She began pumping on his chest with all 110 pounds of her weight.

WILLIAM WATCHED with a mixture of satisfaction and horror. His thoughts were a confused mass of emotions, and his hands shook from the adrenaline. Was this what it was like for the others? Despite working for agencies that specialized in the task, he had never taken a life before. He wasn't sure what to feel. Haney disappeared behind a wall of bodies on the screen, and he watched as they worked on the man.

With a shaking hand, he reached out and slowly turned the monitor off.

---

DAYTON SAT BACK against the rock and drained another bottle of water. From this point just below the ridgeline he could see the highway in both directions for over a mile. Anna lay prone in front of him. He watched as she tracked a car through the scope and wondered what the occupants would think if they knew. He dismissed the thought; he had other things to worry about.

They were exhausted. The entire area had been climbed and explored before repeating the process with several items. Now they were all strategically placed and tested, waiting for them to be needed. The chill desert night had both hidden their movements and made their tasks harder. Twice he had almost tumbled down the mountain after misplacing a step, and once he had dropped an item that was not in favor of sudden movements. With the aid of the moon and a pair of night-vision goggles they had completed their list before the sun rose. Now he watched Anna, her head and hands poking out of the desert camo poncho liner to grasp the stock and grip of the Barrett. She tracked another vehicle as it rambled by, and Dayton watched the barrel move left to right with a nice steady motion. He set down his water and pressed on his throat mic.

"Tsk-tsk."

"I hear you," she whispered back.

"I'm going to head down. What's the sequence again?"

"Confirm, trigger the box—"

Before she could speak further, they were interrupted by Dayton's cell phone. The black box they had set up on the ridgeline was doing its job, albeit for them only.

"Dayton."

William said, "They're moving him."

"Time?"

"I'm estimating you have about forty minutes. Two vehicles: a van just as I mentioned before, white in color, and a car, blue or black. At least four, but maybe more."

"Only four? Jack opted for stealth. That's good for us. Anything else?"

"Our man is in the back, right side, most likely dressed in orange."

"Right side. Good, that fits as well. The other assets are in place?"

"As of 0300. Do you have a destination?"

"Yes. We'll check in once we are there."

William swallowed the answer. Dayton was right, there was no need for him to know.

"William? You still there?"

"Yes, I ..."

"What is it?"

"Are you sure this is ..."

"We're getting him out, William. I'll tell you when it's done."

"Very well. I'll let you know when they're close. Good luck."

"Thanks, we'll need it on this one."

William severed the connection before sitting back with a worried sigh. His eyes traveled to the blank screen of the neighboring monitor.

"Indeed. We all may need some luck before this day is over."

---

SHARON PUMPED as hard as she could on Haney's chest and craned her neck around to see the face of the overhead monitor. The spikes were there, and she slowed her pace to the proper rate. Her adrenaline was making her go too fast.

"Where's the damn cart?"

As if in answer the door was shoved open, striking an agent in the hip, and sending him across the room. Susan entered behind it, her nose dripping blood, and smiled briefly when the man shot her a look.

"Make a hole!" She shoved her way into the room, pushing others aside, even the doctor. She put two fingers in Haney's groin.

"We have a pulse, your CPR's working."

Susan turned her attention back to the cart and noticed the surgeon still messing with the machine.

"Forget that thing, drop a tube!"

The man was startled but shook it off. He caught the items that Susan shoved into his hands and moved around the bed.

"Who knows CPR?" Sharon asked the room.

"We all do, just never ..."

"Doesn't matter, one of you get over here. I'm going to count down from ten and when I do you take over compressions, you just go and go, don't stop unless we tell you to and even then, don't take your hands off the chest, you got it?"

"Yes, ma'am."

The agent stripped off his jacket and got into position just as the doctor slid the lighted blade of a laryngoscope into the VP's mouth. Sharon began her countdown.

"Hold still!" the doctor complained.

Sharon stopped and planted a hand on the agent's chest, holding him in place while the doctor manipulated the tube.

"Out of practice," he muttered but she saw the tube advance just after he said it.

"I'm in," he announced.

"Secure it first, bag's behind you on the wall. Get on the chest!"

The nurse and the agent swapped places. The doctor found and connected the bag. He squeezed it twice before Susan could stop him but ignored the error and placed her stethoscope on the belly and then the chest.

"You're good." She ignored his reply and turned to her partner.

"Is there an ambulance on the way?"

"Couple minutes out," the other agent answered. He had shoved himself into the far corner and had a phone to his ear.

"Susan?"

"I need help, my hands ... damn it!"

Sharon saw her partner trying to start an IV in Haney's arm, but her hands were covered in blood from her nose and making things difficult. She hung her head to one side so the blood dripped on the floor and not her patient.

"I got it, fix your nose!"

Susan dropped the IV catheter and pulled herself away to let Sharon in. She turned and slammed the drawers of the toolbox until she found what she wanted. She tossed the items to the agent who had slammed the door in her face.

"Open those!"

Grabbing a 4x4 piece of gauze she took a breath and then wiped her nose. The pain shot clear up her face and to the back of her head. Broken, her mind informed her.

"Broke my nose, you asshole! Gimme those."

The man stammered an apology as he handed her the open packages and she steeled herself against the pain before cramming one ball of Kerlix up a nostril. A deep breath and she repeated the move on the other side. She stripped off her gloves and donned another pair before turning back to the fight.

Sharon had managed to clean up her mess and get a line started on the other side. She was securing it in place and Susan quickly tore off more tape for her. Sharon did a double-take on seeing her face and she realized she must look ridiculous with Kerlix sticking out both nostrils.

"What next? Another line?"

"No, get the pacemaker, we have to try and override his."

"There's nothing?"

"Stop for a second!"

The agent stopped and they gazed at the green line on the screen. Flat. No spikes at all.

"Keep going!"

The surgeon said, "It makes no sense, why did it just ...?"

Susan cut him off. "It did. Solve this problem first." She pulled a set of pads from the back of the portable pacemaker and peeled the first one free. Reaching over the agent's pumping hands she slapped it down on Haney's right chest. Susan did the same on his left ribs. The automatic blood pressure cuff began to cycle when she powered the machine on.

Sharon twisted knobs and pushed buttons, dialing up the voltage to its highest setting. There was no reason to play around at this point.

"Seventy over thirty-two," the agent in the corner read out loud.

"Not enough, where's that damn ambulance?"

As if it heard the question, a siren could be heard outside. Susan turned to her assistant and shoved him toward the door.

"Go out and escort them in, try not to hurt anybody."

The man frowned at the rebuke but did as he was told. Susan turned back and saw Sharon checking the pads. The agent was sweating now, his shirt soaking through. He looked at the pads right next to his hands and asked a question.

"Is this going to shock me too?"

"No, don't stop, whatever you do!"

Sharon looked at the doctor and then her partner.

"Ready?"

"Ready!"

She pushed the button.

"DAMN, just lost signal again. I give up."

"We'll be out of these mountains in a few more miles," Jack said.

Sydney tossed her phone on the console and twisted her hips to relocate her weapon. It kept migrating into her ribs. She gazed at the passing scenery and then up at the blue sky before returning her eyes to Jack.

"Prisoner transfer. Not really what I signed up for, Jack. You really know how to ruin a nice drive in the country."

"Thanks. I try."

Jack smiled but kept his eyes on the road. The two-laner they were currently on was never straight for very long, winding its way through the mountains north of LA until it reached the valley. There they would find Lancaster, a mid-sized town on the edge of the desert containing their safe house. From there it would be a short overnight stay until the plane arrived to take them east. Jack was pissed at the delay, but there was little he could do. DOD contract planes were limited. Most were also air-medical, and they had taken a financial beating with the economic crash a few years ago. Start-up costs were high, so the number of newcomers was thin. As a result, the planes were in demand.

"Think of it as hauling gold. This guy could be our key to busting this whole group."

"You really think so? I thought you were agreeing with Doctor Wong, that these guys were compartmented, lone wolves with instructions from on high."

"Maybe. They still have to have steady contact with someone. And what about training? Someone had to do some, you just don't find these guys in the want ads."

"You used to. I remember seeing ads for 'Farm Workers' in the *Herald-Tribune* overseas. Lenny says they still do that. It's just on the internet now."

"Any luck on an ID?" Jack asked.

"Nope. No prints. No facial profile on record. No tattoos or other markings that correspond to the data we have. Nothing. Like he's never been here."

"I detected a southern accent."

"Oh, well, that narrows it down."

"DOD get back to you yet?"

"Nothing. That was just an electronic check though. I have a call into Benjamin Harrison for a paper check. Can't believe they want to do away with all those files."

"Anything to save a few bucks. The AG is dead

set against it and so is the Director and the Joint Chiefs. Hopefully that will be enough."

Sydney grunted. She had no faith in Congress making any correct decisions anymore.

Jack worked the wheel as Greg and the van disappeared around the curve up ahead. Jack was keeping a distance just wide enough to allow for surprises and also to discourage cars from passing. So far, the traffic had been so light it had not mattered. He had timed it so they were traveling after commuting hours and before it got dark. With any luck, they would get there ahead of schedule.

"So, what's Lenny up to these days?"

Her reply was drowned out by a high-volume burst of static from the radio. Sydney reached for the knob to silence it.

ANNA FELT for the button on the box next to her without taking her eye from the scope. The magnification was great, and she could clearly see the occupants of both the van and the car following it. She moved the crosshairs to the point she had marked earlier and waited.

"They're here. Van in front and the car about a

hundred meters behind. Two in each. No other traffic. I'm ready," she said.

"Ready here. Your call," Dayton said.

"In ten," she answered before throwing the switch.

## END

I welcome any comments, feedback, or questions at randall.wood@scribecount.

I also welcome any input pertaining to mistakes I may have missed, not necessarily typos or grammar, as they are self-explanatory, but mistakes about procedures or content. Mistakes of this nature tend to pull the reader out of the story and make it less enjoyable. If you should find such an error, please fire off an email in my direction. The beauty of e-books and print-on-demand books is that they can always be updated to fix such things.

I also welcome any and all reviews, with one small request. With the controversy over fake reviews garnering so much attention, it gives your review greater credibility if you do so in your real name and with the verified purchase icon. Doing so helps readers call honest attention to their favorite writers and keeps the integrity of the online review process intact.

Who knows? Your review may end up on the back of the next book.

You can find links to purchase all the Jack Randall Thrillers, including links to purchase directly from me at a discount, at http://randall woodauthor.com/universal-link.

## What happens to Jack?

Jack and his crew venture on in the subsequent books in the series. The best place to find out more, and get those books at a discount, is by visiting my website at https://randallwoodauthor.com/books/. There you will find the complete library of my works, bonus content such as short stories and character bios, cool swag, books that are unavailable anywhere else, and an inside look at how I create these stories.

## What happens to Danny?

Sign up for my email list at https://randallwoodauthor.com/newsletter/ and you'll get a free novel with Danny's latest adventure plus additional content, previews of coming books, discount offers, and a whole lot more.

## Want the latest book the minute it's ready?

We can do that too. Just opt-in to the subscription option at https://randallwoodauthor.com/subscription/ and get the latest book automatically delivered to you the day it comes out, months before it hits the shelves anywhere else.

## Want to know even more?

You can also learn about the places, organizations, government workings, weapons, gear, and law enforcement tactics used in the books, by visiting my Facebook page at Randall Wood Author.

## Stay in touch!

Sign up for my email newsletter at https://randall woodauthor.com/newsletter/

Subscribe at https://randallwoodauthor.com/ subscription/

Follow me on Facebook at Randall Wood Author.

I welcome any comments, feedback, or questions at randall.wood@scribecount.com.

## Want a sneak peak at Jack's next adventure?

Read on!

# A SNEAK PEEK AT BOOK 7:
# RUBICON

"This book is riveting. The flashback is so well done it seems to be in the present. The whole series is relevant to the present times." —*Barbara Chandler*

"The Twelve Shepards are intoxicatingly good while doing bad things in the name of justice."

**ru•bi•con**
to commit oneself irrevocably to some course of
action.

# RUBICON: CHAPTER 1

*"America will never be destroyed from the outside. If we falter and lose our freedoms, it will be because we destroyed ourselves."*

—*Abraham Lincoln*

C arter shifted his ass on the hard metal bench for the hundredth time since they had left the station, but it did little to lessen the impact of the mountain road. The van only augmented the discomfort with its lack of outside stimulation. Every surface was white. His view out the tiny observation window could only be achieved by awkwardly leaning forward, and with this came the risk of being thrown into the opposing wall by the next bump or unseen curve. The drone of the tires on the highway prompted sleep, but this wasn't an option.

His view out the back window was not much better. The picture was distorted and hidden by the three panes of glass and the expanded metal covering them. He could make out the shape of a trailing vehicle through the layers of dust, but little else. Still, it was enough for him to determine the angle of the sun, and from this he knew they were headed somewhat north-east. To where, he had no idea.

The car behind them most likely contained agent Jack Randall. Carter had identified him the day before just before his fist had connected with the man's jaw. Carter was not surprised to see him on the case; it was expected. During his initial training, Dayton had handed him a file on Jack, and Carter had read it with interest. The man who had caught their founder was no amateur. After learning of Jack's military experience, and then his

FBI record, Carter had no problem labeling him as someone to avoid. While the Shepherds did not classify the FBI as the enemy, they were not stupid enough to call them a friend, neither. Knowing who was pursuing you was equal to knowing who you were pursuing yourself. Carter had spent the last twenty-four hours trying to dredge up as much of the file as his brain could remember.

He turned his attention to the two seated up front. The driver, Carter knew. Greg Whitcomb. Former leader of the FBI's Hostage Rescue Team. An elite SWAT team which trained at the same level as Delta commandos and Navy SEALs. A formidable adversary. Carter had seen him on TV. The woman in the passenger seat was a stranger to him, but her skill with the cannon she carried was not to be denied. Her FBI windbreaker was a size too big, but then again, she was probably hard to fit. She turned to check on him every few minutes, and he had been caught trying to hear their conversation. Now the air-conditioning blasted as well as the radio. It was enough to defeat his eavesdropping.

He turned his head back forward, only to face the white wall in front of him. It offered no input, so he turned his attention to his bonds. The shackles were standard issue and installed correctly. Almost. His size gave him some advantages. He had already determined that he could twist the wrist restraints back onto themselves. With enough pressure applied in the right direction, he might be able to break them. That would free his hands, but not his feet. He was still hobbled by the chain connecting them. He estimated it would limit his stride dramatically, to the point that a fast shuffle would become his top speed.

The van hit a pothole large enough to lift him off the seat. He landed awkwardly on the seat divider and let out a curse at the road. The woman turned to gaze back at him, and he shrugged off the pain before giving her a nod. She turned away without a word.

To avoid further discomfort, Carter scooted to the end of the bench seat and then slid off it and onto the floor. With his knees bent, he had just enough space to lay down on the hard surface. He looked up to see the cloudy sky out the back window trailing behind them. Occasionally, the canyon wall they were traveling past would blot out the corner. He let out a sigh and wedged his shoulders in to prevent him from being tossed around. It was only slightly better than the bench.

"WHAT'S HE DOING?" Greg asked

"He made himself a spot on the floor," Laurie replied. "Can't say I blame him; that bench had to be killing him with this road."

"If it's not potholes, it's falling rocks. I was told it's because of the fires they had last year; now there's nothing holding the rocks to the mountainside."

"The other side has a lot of cover. Not that I can see much through this glass." She reached out to tap the windshield. The bulletproof glass was thick, and it distorted their view at times. She had tried rolling down the window, only to discover this was not an option. Good thing the air-conditioning worked.

"Maybe the fire didn't jump the road." Greg ventured.

"What do we have, an hour left?"

Greg glanced at the GPS he had mounted to the glass on his side. It was his personal one that he traveled with.

"Little more than that: an hour and ten. We should be—"

The GPS rebooted. He now had a blank screen with the words SEARCHING FOR SATELLITE SIGNAL displayed. *Odd*, he thought. The sky was pretty clear. Perhaps the steep terrain had cut off the signal? He then noticed that the radio had gone to static. Laurie reached out and thumbed through the pre-sets, but he had no luck.

"This is a serious dead zone."

Greg just grunted as they rounded another curve. Maybe when they cleared the canyon?

---

"I give up."

Sydney tossed the phone down in disgust. Signal had been patchy since they had entered the mountains, and she had now lost everything.

"Thought this was southern California, the tech capitol of the world. You would think I'd have some frickin' signal here."

"I doubt it's profitable enough to put up a tower way out here," Jack replied. "Wait until we're on the other side."

"Fine." She reached out to turn the radio back up, only to find it playing nothing but static. She tried a couple of presets without any change and was about to turn it off when Jack's hand stopped her.

"What?"

"You hear that?"

"I don't—"

"Wait." Jack held up a finger for silence. The radio gave off static that waxed and waned and Jack listened closely before reaching for the portable FBI radio. He had just keyed the mic when something impacted the car. The engine died with a sharp bang and a cloud of smoke. Jack slammed on the brakes before steering it into the wall of the canyon.

"Jack!"

Jack kicked his door open and grabbed Sydney by the shoulder, yanking her out behind him.

"Take cover!"

"WHAT'S THE CALL?"

"Pacemaker something-something. They dispatched it as a cardiac." His partner replied over the sound of the wailing siren. He checked the screen again as his partner weaved the ambulance through another intersection.

"So, we don't really know?"

"You got it. We'll see when we get there, I guess. You been here before?"

"Just once. Guy collapsed during a stress test, and we took him in. It's a doc for the rich and famous. Fancy office, nice nurses."

"Nice?"

"One was real nice."

"Well, okay, then. Here we are, let's go find this nice nurse."

The siren died as they entered the parking lot, and the medic eyeballed the two black Suburbans parked on the curb as they pulled up next to them. They loaded their gear on the stretcher, and the medic examined the vehicles again as they pulled it around the front. They looked familiar to him.

"What?"

"Nothing, let's go."

"Before they got to the door, a woman in office attire opened it and held it wide.

"Down the hall, on the right." She pointed.

The medic followed her lead and stepped into the doorway. He found a room full of men in dark suits crowded around an examination table. On the table was an older man, unconscious and intubated, with a doctor bagging him. A nurse was up on the bed and had straddled him to pump on his chest in a steady rhythm.

"What do we have?" he asked.

The nurse of the man's chest turned to look at him, and he flinched at the sight of her face. Both nostrils were stuffed with Kerlix, and blood was dripping from both sides. Her eyes were watering and already starting to bruise. Despite this, she never stopped pumping.

"Pacemaker failure! He's a full arrest. We need to move him!"

"Frickin' dispatch."

"What?"

"Nothing. Let me get in there, guys."

---

ANNA LET OUT the breath and spoke into the mic before the sound of her shot had echoed off the cliff.

"They're down. Go!"

She took another half-breath and scanned the car. It had abruptly turned and softly impacted the cliff after her round had punched straight through the radiator and into the engine block. The driver's actions and the collision had spun the rear end enough so that it now blocked a good portion of the road. Both steam and oily smoke now poured from the cracks around the hood and traveled across the road blocking her vision. She spotted shapes moving behind the car. She counted two. Opening her other eye, she checked the road behind them only to find it empty.

Good.

Returning her gaze to the car, she spotted a head peeking out from behind the engine. It was there for only a second. Her job was to keep them there. She centered her scope on the canyon wall a few feet over their heads and stroked the trigger again.

---

CARTER'S HEAD snapped off the floor at the sound of the shot. A rifle? Or just a car backfiring? The drone of the road and the thick walls of the transport van had muffled the sounds from outside to the point that he couldn't be sure. He listened for chatter from the front and was soon rewarded by the woman's questioning tone.

Another shot. His brain labeled it a rifle—this time for sure. A big one.

"Get ready," he whispered to himself. He quietly gathered the chain between his fists and held on.

# RUBICON: CHAPTER 2

*"A hero is someone who understands the responsibility that comes with his freedom."*

—*Bob Dylan*

C harlie stepped off the elevator in time to hear the end of the overhead page. Another code. What kind, he didn't know; they seemed to have several. All of them colors.

He'd asked a nurse last night and had gotten a hurried explanation. Pink for missing babies, red for fire, yellow for bad weather. Bad weather? Evidently, they had battery back-ups which were activated when a storm came. Charlie had just nodded and had then left her alone. She had the ever-present stack of charts in front of her and was busy, so he'd wandered on.

His trip this time had been altered by the storm outside. He'd ventured out to the edge of the awning over the front entrance and watched the dark clouds move in along with the valet and security guard. Neither of them looked very happy, and Charlie didn't blame them. The distant thunder and lightning were rapidly approaching. He bid them both good luck and resumed his trip.

His reasons for wandering were two-fold. The first was to learn his surroundings. Something Dayton had drilled into him. Standard security. Charlie wasn't just a body-man for the General: he was also his first line of defense. As such, Dayton had drilled him of how to be a bodyguard. So he now roamed the complex whenever the General was sleeping, but only after the doors were checked and a back-up guard was in the waiting room.

The back-up man had brought a handgun for

Charlie and had simply walked it past the hospital's security, tucked in his belt, before handing it over to him in the stairwell. The handgun was now stuck in the back of Charlie's belt, and he took comfort in its weight. If anyone tried anything, Charlie now had thirty 9mm reasons for them to change their mind. He took care to keep it hidden as he wandered and memorized the various floors and endless corridors. He now knew where surgery suite was, and the cafeteria. The loading dock. The Emergency Room. The Cath lab. The administration offices. Sterile processing. The laundry facilities. Maintenance. And, of course, the coffee kiosk. He was now on a first-name basis with its elderly operator and had a cup in his hand right now.

His second reason was purely selfish and something he would never admit to, but he couldn't be with the General, not in his current state, for very long. It raised thoughts and possible futures he feared to contemplate. Charlie had lost both of his parents already, the thought of the General dying ... was a place he refused to go.

Coming to an intersection, he paused. It had been less than an hour since he had left. One direction led to the cardiac floor, the other back to the ICU. Should he head back? His feet told him no. He entered the cardiac ward instead.

"Hello, Janet." He greeted the charge nurse. She looked up, and smiled, and then frowned on seeing who it was.

"Charlie? What happened?"

"What do you mean?"

"The code? It was the General's bed number. Was it a false alarm?"

Charlie gripped the coffee and sprinted back down the corridor.

---

DAYTON TUGGED THE STRAPS TIGHTER, but they were already at their limit, and then squeezed the sweat from his eyes without taking them off the approaching van. The hash marks he had spray-painted on the cliff face now served to tell him the van's speed, and he counted under his breath until it reached the go-point.

With a practiced motion, he popped the clutch and floored the accelerator. The truck lurched forward, dragging its coat of branches with it and then shrugging them off as the vehicle gained speed and barreled down the steep, dirt road. He worked the gears without moving his gaze from the target. Five more seconds.

---

GREG NEGOTIATED the curve only to find the sun in his eyes again. He averted his gaze and moved it to the GPS, hoping it now had a signal. Laurie was still punching the pre-sets, one by one, attempting to find a station.

"What was that?"

"All I heard was static."

"No. It sounded like a rifle?"

"I didn't—*look out!*"

Greg looked up in time to see a boulder in the road. He reflexively hit the brakes and slowed the van while looking for a path around it. There was enough space between the rock and the side of the cliff maybe? His foot was still on the brake pedal when he caught motion out of the corner of his eye.

---

DAYTON ADJUSTED the trucks path slightly left before pulling both hands from the wheel and grabbing the harness holding him in place. His last sight of the van before it disappeared under the hood was of the open-mouthed look of shock on the driver's face. He cataloged the man's identity just before impact.

---

"Jack! What the hell?"

"Stay down! That was a rifle what took out the engine!"

As if to punctuate his words, another round chipped rock from the cliff over their heads to rain down on them. The sound of the shot followed a moment later.

"That's a big rifle." Jack said. "They're trying to get him back!"

"How did they—?"

"I don't know! Can you reach the shotgun?"

Sydney coughed on the acrid smoke, before crawling to the open door of the car. Reaching across the seat, she retrieved the Remington from its holder. She holstered her handgun in favor of the shotgun, but she couldn't see how this would change their situation. She duck-walked forward to join Jack behind the engine block. It was the best cover they had. Maybe.

"Will the block stop that rifle?"

"If it's a fifty? Not really. Trade me." He gestured for the shotgun, and she gave it up.

He rolled to the ground and looked under it in both directions.

"Can you see Greg?"

"They're around the bend. I—"

His words were cut off by the sound of a heavy impact. First the sound of one, tearing metal and screeching tires, followed by a second, a large thud. Then nothing.

"Try the radio!"

———

"WHAT'S HAPPENING?" the agent asked when the ambulance's doors closed.

"We have to pace him!" the medic answered.

"What's that—?"

"It means shut the hell up and let me work!"

Ignoring the man, the medic stripped off the pads applied in the doctor's office and replaced them with the ones for his own machine. The siren came on and they were moving. The vehicle chose to give a lurch to the left, and with conditioned reflexes the medic managed to plant a hip against the seat and stay upright. The agent, who'd refused to belt in, struck his head on the overhead cabinet. Fortunately, the edge was padded, but it still worked to sit the man down. If the medic noticed, he didn't react. His job was hard enough without the three men crowding the back of his rig, but he had no choice.

"Don't stop," he told the nurse. She shot him a look and kept pumping on the VP's chest.

"Really?"

"Sorry."

The medic planted his butt in the seat, before yelling to his partner on the front, "Time?"

"In this traffic? Fifteen, at least."

The medic caught the look of the agent. "It's rush hour." He turned on the monitor, selected the pacing option, and cranked the milliamps as high as they would go.

"Rate at seventy. Here we go."

The agents leaned back with wide-eyed stares as the muscles of the VP's chest began to twitch at regular intervals. The nurse eased up on the chest compressions, and then stopped to check the man's pulse.

"Faint, but it's there."

The medic wrapped his patient's arm in a BP cuff and hit the button to activate it before addressing her.

"We need volume; hang a bag." He couldn't

reach it, so he pointed. The nurse found what they needed and went through the motions.

"Infuser?"

"Not in the new budget; just wrap it in that spare BP cuff."

The nurse did so and pumped the cuff up until it was squeezing the fluid into the line in the man's arm. She handed it to the agent across from her.

"Keep this inflated—not too much; just until you see a steady stream," she instructed him. The man braced his feet and did as he had been told. The medic eyeballed the monitor, all the numbers were green, but not by much. He checked his patient's pulse to see if it did match the number on the screen before looking the two men over. He noticed a holstered automatic tucked inside one man's suitcoat. A black Suburban kept pace behind them with a light bar of its own flashing.

"Just who are you guys, anyway?"

The one next to him pulled out an ID card and flashed it to him. "US Secret Service. That's former Vice President Haney you're taking care of."

The medic looked down at his patient. His face was upside-down and covered by an endotracheal tube and the clamp holding it in place, but he saw enough to recognize him.

"No shit?"

AT THE SOUND of the impact, Anna took her eyes off the scope long enough to look at the mirror sitting next to her. She could just make out the truck sitting in the road. The heavy plow blade had the van pinned to the cliff's wall. Smoke and dust swirled around it, and she found herself holding her breath until the door of the truck opened and Dayton's shape emerged. He turned and reached back into the cab before climbing down and moving toward the van.

He looked to be okay, and she let out a heavy breath before returning her gaze to the car. She now saw the barrel of what looked like a shotgun sticking up over the hood.

"No-no. You stay put." She centered her scope and sent another round into the cliff, this one a bit lower than the last one.

DAYTON SHRUGGED and cracked his neck before opening the door. One side of his body protested, and he knew he'd be sore in the morning. He dismissed the thought and turned his gaze to the van. He could see down and into the cab through the cracked windshield but saw no movement. It prompted him to move.

He pulled the rope holding the door shut loose and kicked it open. He had tied it shut after wedging the floor mat into the opening, out of fear it would be jammed shut by the impact. The hinges protested as he pushed it and let out a squeal. Stepping out of the cab, he stopped on the diamond plate step to reach back inside. Gathering what he needed, he hopped to the ground.

The van was pinned. The plow blade had bit into the side and lifted it up and forward, slamming it into the wall and crumpling both sides. Dayton gazed out through the helmet's tinted visor and checked the road in both directions. Smoke from the car could be seen in one direction, an empty stretch of highway curved away in the other. That wouldn't last for long, but he had a plan to prevent it.

Lugging the heavy tool belt up onto the bumper of the truck, he pulled himself onto the hood. There, he slung loose his first tool, one that was a personal favorite.

The Milkor MGL was a lightweight 40mm six-shot grenade launcher that had been around since the 1980's. Nowadays it was found in almost every army and police force over the world. Where the one currently in Dayton's hands had come from, he didn't care; it was its rapid rate of fire and flexible ordinance that he needed now.

Taking aim to the east, Dayton launched two smoke and one CS round as far down the road as he could. The combination of thick smoke and tear gas should persuade anyone approaching to stay clear. He checked the wind again and placed the same three rounds in the other direction before discarding the weapon and leaping up onto the roof of the van. The heavy tool hanging from his belt almost cost him his footing, but he steadied himself on the cliff-face before stomping on the roof three times.

"Get clear!"

Not sure if he was even heard, he dropped to one knee and pulled a tool from his belt. The cutter screamed its eagerness when he pulled the trigger, and he eased its spinning blade into the sheet metal of the roof. A shower of sparks arched over the windshield.

# RUBICON: CHAPTER 3

*"All the great things are simple, and many can be expressed in a single word: freedom, justice, honor, duty, mercy, hope."*

—*Winston Churchill*

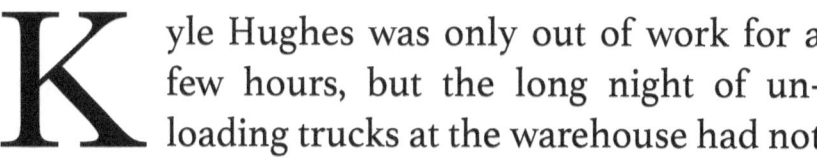 yle Hughes was only out of work for a few hours, but the long night of unloading trucks at the warehouse had not

tired him enough to go to bed. Not with the sun shining like it was. He parked his motorcycle at his parents' house, just long enough to run inside and change, pausing only once to down an energy drink in front of the open refrigerator, before grabbing his helmet and new Go-Pro camera.

The bike was still making noise as it cooled in the shade of the garage, but he wasn't going to let that continue. Since he had gotten the camera for Christmas, he'd been making more trips into the mountains. Filming himself riding through the curving terrain at higher and higher speeds. After a week, he'd finally mastered the angles and speed enough to brave an upload. Over a thousand likes in only a few days! He'd made two more since then with the number of likes and followers increasing both times. He was now practicing for a night version. So far it had gotten him one date.

But the road was too busy most of the time. Today might be different, though. A weekday and between rush hours, maybe he could get some good footage if the traffic was light enough. There was only one way to find out.

After crushing the empty can, he tossed it in the trash and hopped back on the bike. He remembered to keep the speed down until he turned the corner, as any fun too close to home would be reported back to his mother by their nosy neighbors. He couldn't stand another lecture. It was bad enough that he had to use a fake name for the YouTube account. But like most parents, his were clueless when it came to the Internet—at least he hoped so.

The sun was hot on his back, as he made his way to the highway. Threading his way around a couple of campers heading west, he finally found an open stretch and goosed the throttle. His grin was hidden by the full helmet, and only got bigger as he leaned into the first sweeping curve.

CHARLIE ARRIVED at the double doors, just as the General's Doctor keyed himself through.

"What is it?"

"I don't know; I just got here myself." The doctor moved through the doors as soon as the crack was wide enough and put out an arm to keep Charlie from rushing past him.

A group of people surrounded the General and the alarms were ringing in three different tones. The doctor nudged the nearest nurse, who ignored him while she did something Charlie couldn't see.

"Need a non-rebreather!"

"Get him portable!"

"Let me in!"

The ICU team parted on hearing the doctors command voice and Charlie caught a look of the General before the group closed around him. The General was bolt upright in the bed, clutching his chest and gasping for air. A mask was placed around his nose and mouth, and he immediately fogged the plastic. His eyes found Charlie's and the look burned into Charlie's brain.

"Pulse-ox is dropping," the doctor barked. "How long?"

"Less than five," his nurse replied. "He spiked quickly." She pulled a long strip of paper from her pocket and stuffed it in his hand. The doctor rolled it out and held it up to the light.

"Damn, where's the twelve-lead?"

"Right here."

"He's ... up, up and down. Okay, repeat that twelve-lead. One dose of nitro sublingual and then we move. You call the cath lab yet? Never mind; I'll do it."

The doctor extracted himself from the group and searched his pockets for his phone. Charlie opened his mouth, but the man stuck up a finger for silence.

"Dianne? It's Dr. Shoemaker. Prep the lab for

an incoming MI from the ICU. I'll be down there in a few minutes ... Yes ... And get Joey; I'm going to need him." He hung up without waiting for a reply and grabbed Charlie's arm. Charlie let the man lead him out of the aisle before speaking.

"He's having an MI; we're—"

"A what?"

"A heart attack. It's in a bad spot, but I'll have him in the cath lab in a few minutes, and they'll go in after it. You can come but stay out of the way."

"Okay, uh ..."

"Questions later, Charlie; we need to take some action. Just hold on."

"Coming through!"

They both pushed themselves against the countertop of the nurse's station as the team pushed the bed out of its room and into the hall. The General's color was now gray, and his head rolled from side to side as the bed moved. The doctor snagged the chart off the desk as he passed and followed them out. Captivated by the turn of the events, Charlie examined the mess of debris on the floor, where the General had been just a moment before, until the doctor called after him.

"Charlie!"

He looked down to see coffee running over his hand. It had slowly clenched into a fist without him realizing it. He didn't even feel the burn. Dropping it, he rubbed the excess on his pants before running to catch up.

---

INSIDE THE VAN, Carter slowly woke. The impact had thrown his head against the side of the wall, and he had momentarily blacked out. Now the sound of someone walking on the roof had brought him around. He followed their travel and heard three stomps before a muffled shout whose words he couldn't make out. This was followed by the sound of a tool coming to life. Its screech canceled everything else out. The grinding intensified, and Carter winced against the noise: it was like being inside a snare drum.

His foggy mind cleared when the blade broke through and showered him with hot sparks. He quickly moved as far away as he could and tried to cover his head as they rained down on him, but there was nowhere to hide. He roared against the sparks as they burned into his arms and clothing, but there was nothing he could do but protect his face.

And then they stopped.

ANNA PLANTED another round into the cliff before it disappeared behind the heavy smoke. The wind had shifted and was now blowing the cloud back toward the car. She pulled her head from the scope and measured the distance.

Not good.

She pushed the throat mic tighter before speaking into it, remembering not to whisper—it was a little late for that.

"The wind changed: it's coming back at you. You have about a minute. I can't see the car anymore."

Nothing.

"Dayton!"

DAYTON STOPPED GRINDING LONG ENOUGH to hear Anna screaming his name. He keyed the mic while he got to his feet.

"Repeat!"

"The wind changed! You've got less than a minute before it reaches you! I can't see the car any longer!"

"Get to the extraction car and keep them off

me as long as you can! Watch the road to the east, too! Go!"

Without waiting for her reply, he began stomping on the roof.

---

THE NEW NOISE caused Carter to chance a look up at the roof, and he saw that whoever was cutting it had made two sides of a square. A foot now stomped the opening bigger. Before he could say anything, a pair of heavy bolt cutters fell through the opening to land right next to him. Carter gapped at them for a full second, before the cutter started up again and then dove through the sparks to retrieve them. Ignoring the shower of hot metal, he applied the jaws to the ankle restraints and heaved.

---

SYDNEY COUGHED against the smoke and Jack soon followed.

"It's CS!" she croaked before stripping off her jacket. She tore the sleeve but ignored it and covered her nose and mouth with it as best she could. Her eyes immediately burned from the irritant.

Jack took a breath, dropped the shotgun, and stripped off his shirt. After tearing it in two, he tossed one-half to her before tying the other around his face. She tried to follow his actions but fell into a coughing fit. She squeezed her eyes shut and held her breath, until she had the fabric secured, then planted herself prone on the hot asphalt in an effort to escape the gas, but it did little to help.

Wind. Let the wind take it away. It'll be over soon. She sipped the air through the layers of fabric and kept her eyes shut, sticking an arm out to locate Jack next to her.

Nothing.

She cracked an eyelid and scanned the area between herself and the wall.

Nothing.

Jack was gone.

The deep boom of the shotgun firing reached her ears.

---

ANNA RAN. Her heart pounding in her chest as she descended the mountain as fast as she could. She had activated the device, gave it one check, and then left it. She now fought the urge to look in the direction of the car with every step, waiting for the sound of a passing bullet or the crack of a rifle to tell her she had been seen. But at the speed she was traveling, any distraction from the rocky path could spell doom in the form of a fall and injury.

She had to focus hard to get to the car, but after what seemed like forever she finally did. She impacted its side hard, using it to stop herself and struggled hard to regain her breath while she pulled the camouflage netting covering away. Her body had gone from hours of being stationary, to rapid physical action in less than a few seconds, and her blood pressure now struggled to keep up with the change in demand.

The netting caught on the mirror, and she wasted precious seconds pulling it away, cursing it in flowery language before it finally fell at her feet. She ignored it once it was free and leaped behind the wheel. The keys were waiting in the ignition, and she caressed her sidearm stuck between the seats for reassurance before starting it up. She gave the engine two seconds to build some RPMs before dropping it in gear and racing down the mountain road.

She had just caught sight of Dayton on the van's roof when the sound of a shotgun reached her ears. Reaching the pavement, she threw the car into a controlled slide across the road before him and then tumbled out the door.

---

CARTER REPOSITIONED the tool for the third time before finding the right combination of slack and leverage. The chain fell away from his ankles, and he turned the cutters blades on the chain joining his hands. It was a bit more difficult, but he soon had the angle. The chain rattled on the floor as the metal grinder over his head stopped. Another sledgehammer kick sounded and was followed by a large section of the vans roof hitting the floor next to him. He looked up to see a helmeted figure dressed in coveralls and heavy gloves peering down at him.

"Let's go!"

"Dayton?"

The man made no reply, his head now back out of the opening and focused now somewhere to the west as he squatted on the roof. Carter stepped up on the bench that had caused him so much pain and grabbed the offered hand. The man yanked hard, and he had no choice but to follow and ended up cutting his hand and leg on the jagged metal opening. Before he could get his wits

about him, the man was scrambling off the roof of
the van and onto the hood of a large truck. He
leaped down and dropped the heavy tool belt before reaching into his remaining belt and pulling
two handguns. He spun in Carter's direction.

Carter braced himself for the shot, but the gun
was instead turned, and with a fluid motion, propelled through the air at his head. He barely got
his hands up in time to catch it. He held the
weapon tight and negotiated the climb down, only
to see a car racing toward them. He leveled the
gun in its direction, only to have it batted down by
the helmeted man.

"No! She's with us!"

She? Who the hell ...?

The sound of the shotgun erased any question,
and they both dove for cover as the car stopped in
front of them. Carter ran behind the truck to take
cover, as the woman behind the wheel tumbled
out and aimed her gun to the west.

What the hell was going on? Carter looked for
an escape, but there was nothing but the van, the
truck, the man in the helmet, this strange woman,
and a thick cloud of smoke behind him.

KYLE PASSED the slower car on the right, before opening the throttle wider. Route 14 was one of his favorites, but his hope of taking it at record speed today, in order to have a good video to upload, was being defeated by traffic. The heavy metal beat was pumping in his ears, and he could barely hear the revving of the motorcycle's engine over the sound of it and his own heartbeat. He settled down over the tank and leaned hard into the next turn, the adrenaline pumping as he increased speed through it.

The cars stopped on the next straightaway, which nearly caused him to lay the bike down— but what Kyle lacked in common sense, he made up for with quick reflexes. He stood the bike up and braked sharply, rapidly slowing to the point that he could steer the bike between them. A man standing outside his car with the door opened, staring ahead, prompted Kyle to finally look up. The massive cloud of thick white smoke up ahead blocked the entire canyon. Kyle weaved through the cars until he was at the front. He stopped next to another biker, this one on a Harley, and thumbed the music off. He slid the face shield up and examined the smoke again. It looked odd.

"Is it a fire?"

"Not sure. It's not dark like a fire, and I don't smell it. Its staying close to the ground. Weird."

Kyle sniffed the air but didn't smell wood-smoke, neither. He examined the road ahead and saw the smoke dissipating. Gaps could be seen where the wind was breaking it up. It looked cool. Good video.

He snapped his visor down and revved his engine.

"Hey, man, that's not a good idea," the biker warned him.

Kyle pretended not to hear him. The music was back on, and he was already moving. He punched it enough to bring the front wheel up, and the Go-Pro had a shot of the smoke against the sky before it came back down and plunged into the cloud. Kyle weaved around and kept his speed up as best he could, moving from clear areas to small pockets of smoke and back, until it hit him.

His eyes began to burn, then his throat. He blinked away the tears and coughed but it only got worse. The smoke blocked out the sun and then lightened so he pressed on, hoping to come out on the other side. His nose soon ran like a faucet, and he began to drool inside the helmet. Unable to do anything else, he pushed the bike on.

Punching through the other side, his watering eyes were first blinded by the sun and then filled with the giant truck blocking the road. Before he could react, a giant stepped out in front of him and raised his arm.

There was no time.

———

**WANT to know what happens next?**

Get your copy of *RUBICON* direct from the author at https://randallwoodauthor.com/product/ rubicon-a-jack-randall-thriller/!

*RUBICON* is also available on all major online retailers; you'll find links at http://randallwoodau thor.com/universal-links.

(Did I mention the books are discounted if you buy directly from me?)

# ABOUT THE AUTHOR

Randall Wood is the author of the bestselling Jack Randall series of thrillers and the Half a World Post-Apocalyptic series. He is also the founder and CEO of ScribeCount, a data aggregation company that provides sales dashboards, marketing analytics, and a variety of other services to the author community.

When he's not penning stories or crunching numbers, he and his wife divide their time between the beaches of south Florida and the mountains of western North Carolina. Whether they are hiking or swimming they are usually accompanied by Henry their giant of a Great Dane.

Randall welcomes readers to his website at www.randallwoodauthor.com and his fellow writers to ScribeCount at www.scribecount.com, where he tries hard to not refer to himself in the third person.

www.ingramcontent.com/pod-product-compliance
Lightning Source LLC
Chambersburg PA
CBHW031728180726
48283CB00005B/1416